WISTWOOD

OTHER BOOKS BY JONATHAN KIERAN

Rowan Blaize
The Hand of Djin Rummy
The Starbane Exile
Confessions from the Comments Section

WISTWOOD

JONATHAN KIERAN
BRIGHTBOURNE MEDIA

Published by Brightbourne Media, USA
www.JonathanKieran.com
ISBN-13: 978-0-9885681-1-2 (Kindle)
ISBN-13: 978-0-9885681-0-5 (Paperback)

Printed in the United States of America
First Edition

For Ken, for the Andrea Empress, for Procyon starlight.

TABLE OF CONTENTS

NEEDLESS THE VEIL

Candidate Daltry:
You asked many questions in your prior email correspondence. Excellent questions, it must be said. Curiosity is a desirable quality in one seeking the available position. Let us endeavor to satisfy your curiosity.

First, it is not difficult to find Them. You expressed concern about this. Allow me to be your guide and unmistakable signpost.

The Hunt has never been difficult. Not ten years ago. Not one hundred years ago. Not one thousand years ago.

I do not speak primarily of the manner in which years are counted by those I prefer to hunt. That is an unrelated matter.

Such a thing being acknowledged, however, I must emphasize that it was no great task to find Them one hundred *thousand* years ago, when they first showed signs that they were capable of being hunted in the fashion that has been my specialty.

But what can be gained by discussing Time? Little. Preoccupation with peripheral details has rarely proved useful, in my experience. And if I possess anything, it is experience.

Even I have forgotten how long I have been appointed to this duty and gifted with this set of skills. That is because I have been hunting before Time itself came to be. Before time's first meager and illusory measurements were established by those earnest, pitiful beings that rose from the muck and the mud of this dreary outpost, which is but one of countless other outposts.

Yet, here is where I have been assigned to carry out My mission, for the limitless Now, though I am allowed to pursue certain extracurricular endeavors by sneaking through windows and doorways that open onto vistas beyond Time. I do this as necessity dictates. Indeed, I am often able to cast a rather wide net.

I mention this only to illustrate the scope of my commitment to your possible employment and to the magnitude of my devotion to those objects of prey who have pleaded with me to help them better understand the nature of my business. At whiles, some of them truly wish to know about it, though knowing avails nothing in the end, and the very extent to which they are capable of comprehending matters of such gravity is dubious to begin with. Yet, I am not unmoved. As mentioned, curiosity can be a desirable trait and it is a privilege in which the hunted are permitted to indulge, by destiny or by accident.

Perhaps it is unwise to speak of accidents. Who knows what those really are? Even I am uncertain, though I and others like me have long entertained many and various ideas. We have heard things, here and there.

Oh, we have heard rumors.

Ours is an existence spent perpetually at the behest of rumor. But that, too, is another story. For the moment, I wish only to underscore my assertion that the hunted are easy to find.

Know this, as well: The hunted are everywhere, especially on this ball of spinning, cooling fire. One who hunts as I hunt is never put to inconvenience in the search for suitable prey. Food sources are abundant. They are as numerous as are my methods of detection and discernment.

Even so, the hunt is nothing compared to the Acquisition.

Are you paying attention? Good.

Acquisition is somewhat tricky. Acquisition is fraught with the need for meticulous attention to detail and an intense scrutiny of the Chosen. Rarely, Acquisition can even be perilous for the likes of myself and those summoned to assist. I realize that this seems difficult for your reprobate and deficient brain to grasp, but that is not your fault. Things are as they are.

Some with less experience in these matters than I suggest that Acquisition is arduous because blood is involved. There may be a grain of accuracy to this theory, but it is a grain only, friend. For the most part such notions are incidental in the purview of those hunters who are truly masterful.

One with my experience realizes that blood is common. Despicably common. In and of itself, blood is almost irrelevant to the success of a completed hunt. Almost.

You see, my potential gamesman, the masterful know that it is a distinct scent of blood, the spiritual scent, and the Resplendent Hour of its shedding, that counts the most. We look for the exact ache, terror, rage or lust that tends to hang over the bloodletting. There such things dangle, like the searing, sweet silence of a universe before the moment of its birth. These elements are not at all common or vulgar, I assure you. And I am what the prey would consider a connoisseur of such qualities.

I say this: give the blood too much credit and one will spend far more time wandering, aimless and parched, in the desolate places, adrift in wastelands of the Abyss, instead of rooted amid opportunity. With care, wisdom, and precision, such opportunity offers the hunter every likelihood of attaining the prize.

That prize might be a kingdom. It might be an empire.

Even a universe of one's very own is possible.

I have seen it happen, over and over, with Others.

But let us not dwell upon Others. They have little or nothing to do with my present work. Our appointed boundaries cross infrequently. Believe me, this is a fortunate thing.

Know above all else that my gift for Acquisition has lost none of its potency. In fact, I seem stronger, especially when considering that the hunted have grown more complex since last I browsed this world and its otherwise doomed environs. It would not be inaccurate to say that I am more optimistic about my exploits than ever before.

No expense was spared in the construction of my latest workroom. Though the foundations required the utmost of my talents to establish—and more than that to maintain!—I am pleased to report that the structure is nigh flawless.

What fun it shall provide. What nourishment. I do hope that you prove amenable to the job at hand.

I am watching, Candidate Daltry. I am deciding. I am judging this and calculating that. And I am waiting.

There is so much more to be won, in this hour of all hours, when great and secret plans lurk, agonized and impatient to unfold at the edge, at the very End of All Things. There is more spirit in the hunted than ever before, and more of the sort that merits attention like mine.

Make no mistake, my little abyss of ignorance—there is no lack of those who are ready to be hunted, as in the ages of old, as far back as Time, Times, and half a Time. And the hunted are coming as commanded. Do you comprehend?

The hunted are coming and I am Acquiring. Even now my realm waxes fragrant with swift, bright rivers of blood and spirit well-chosen.

Attend me as you have been instructed and watch with keen eyes for every remaining correspondence. We shall meet soon, whether you qualify for the position or not.

Pray that you qualify.

More than anything, do not fail to forget the encouraging words that form the very bedrock of your challenge, given when first you answered my summons. Given when all realms of eternal possibility and reward were first opened to the ravening hunger of your understanding:

> *Four for the killing,*
> *each soul provided.*
> *When all have been taken*
> *your fate is decided.*

I await your further and final successes, Candidate Daltry. Do not disappoint Me.

PROXIMITY

Though no one in worlds born or waiting to be born might understand, the stars of her own creation spoke that secret language, and to such words they listened attentively.

"There is a foul scent upon the air, Larkspur. A reek of rot and sorrow. Strong. Rank with larceny."

"I smell nothing, Lady. Whence does this reek assail us?"

She gazed at the encircling horizon and into the heavens, her eyes mirroring a crimson crescent of moon as it smiled upon her island in all its sanctity, all its safety.

"Difficult to be certain, yet, of the source, my friend. But look to the stars, there in the West. The portents gather and then disperse, so many fish fleeing a pebble cast into a pool. It is our enemy. Or else I know nothing of such things."

"Him? Already? I thought he was too far removed to trouble again us so soon."

"Perhaps this new treachery comes not from his native clime but from one of his outlying snares. Whither it comes, I am convinced, Larkspur—he has caught something new!"

"He's always catching something new, Mistress. What concern is that of ours?"

"Be silent a moment! My vision is clouded. No. He has not captured one of the Deserving," she whispered, turning her iridescent face this way and that to scan the vast and glittering aurora of sky above her orchard. "I do not speak of his usual traffic. That, of course, does *not* concern us. Rather, this shift in the constellation …" she added, pointing outward to a mutating storm of light eating darkness eating emptiness. "Do you see that odd shimmer, up above the Five Fell Brothers and to the north, near the curve of Elethria's Heel? Do you see it?"

"Maybe I do, my Delight. Maybe not."

Larkspur shrugged and stooped to grumble, pondering a reflection of faint starlight dancing across the obsidian surface of his talons. He did not wish to see anything, if there was anything to be seen or not. Least of all from *Him*.

"Oh, I see it," she said. "The vision fills my being, now, along with a fragrance of black-burning ruin. Such a display signifies some change in hierarchy, Larkspur. A threat. Unmistakable and imminent. But also a splendid chance. At last!"

Larkspur sniffed a little at the breeze coursing beneath the ripe, drooping fruit that hung forever in pregnant rows, agleam in the surrounding groves. His three twisting horns glistened aquamarine in a sudden burst of scarlet lightning. He considered a distant rumble of thunder. But thunder and lightning were not special signs. Not in this place.

"I smell only the orchard, my Lady, and the sweetening of its bounty. Behold, the very soil beneath us pleads for the harvest. Branches whisper and limbs groan and leaves hiss to be relieved of their burdens. The time to be rewarded for work well-accomplished is nigh. All is exhausted around us. Look! Is it not easy to be misled by the stars when the forest stoops with the weight of such desire?"

She shook her head. "This is not the mere change of our season. Do you take me for a fool? In my own sanctuary, no less?"

"No, Lady, never! I merely suggest—"

"There is nothing to suggest. He has been away on a hunt and is but recently returned. Ah. Yes, I see it now. The fog that even he cannot maintain as an illusion across the stars has lifted. This is a filthy plan he conjured some twelve seasons ago, that hole he dug. What a burrow writhing with vipers! He has gone back to it. He has gone back to work and to rest, and something ... something is following him there. This means we have a splendid new opportunity!"

"Something is always following the likes of That One," muttered Larkspur. "Forgive my boldness, Lady, but I say it again: Look away and do not condescend to soil your vision with his schemes. Avert your gaze from uncertain signs. They clamor, but they are thankless children, whining for attention only to unload their anxieties upon you. Leave them to their endless chattering, for that is all they care to do through Time, Times and half a Time. You are weary from exertion and what strength you possess for the rest of the season must be saved for reaping."

She regarded Her charge with the withering punishment of her eyes, as terrible and beyond penetration as the Void itself in their depth. Struck by the power of that glance, Larkspur cowered in the soil at her feet, scratching feebly amid the sparkle of fallen leaves with his claws.

"Don't grovel, my pet. And don't be a fool on your feet, either. I do not scrutinize the firmament for mere amusement, nor to indulge some vanity of my darkening will. I do not pursue intrigues that will avail nothing in our present seclusion. You of all sojourners know that I can ill-afford to miss the slightest sign. I will not risk the tiniest tear in the fabric of our enshrouding barrier. But do not doubt that I can survey the weft and warp of my own creation! It is mine also to tend, and ever for our benefit do I keep vigil."

"I have never doubted you, Lady," groaned Larkspur.

"Perhaps not. Yet, for all efforts to preserve this sanctum, I fear you have come to adore loneliness for its own sake. Yes, even you, old companion. Ages uncounted will grind the mightiest spirit into dust or make of each defeated heart a grain fit only to craft the bread of regret. Some scrap to gnaw in the shadow. And those who allow the ruin must feast upon the wreckage. I do not need you to complete this work, Larkspur. You know this, do you not? I do not need you to question me and to be satisfied with your place between worlds."

"I cannot help it, Mistress. I am sometimes weary of this oasis, even unto annihilation, which would be a mercy. But only sometimes."

"Yours is a fair-weather heart, Larkspur, even at the cost of preserving your own skin. That, however, is my doing." She laughed a little in the humid darkness.

Mists came at the sound and began to drift onto the shores of the island, just beyond the orchard. Fingers of fog were sent forth like emissaries to scout winding paths among trees that brooded and wept. "I suppose I should not be so surprised and swift to anger in your regard. But in times like this I find that I cannot help myself, either. Come. Get up and be at peace, if only for the evening."

"You must forgive me, Lady," whimpered Larkspur, not daring to touch her skin. Instead he made furtive little advances toward her translucent feet, his talons plowing through the oily black richness of soil. "I speak too often of things I do not fully understand, but I do it only out of concern for your comfort."

"Then the spell I placed upon you is as strong as ever," she replied, not a little proud. "What of it? You grow weak in the face of grave matters at the height of every season, Larkspur. That is to be expected. You are not native to this place, after all. I believe you forget, sometimes, that you came upon me quite by accident. But *I* never forget it. That is why I have power over you."

"Oh, happy accident, that I should have been found by thee," said Larkspur, bowing until his horns touched the furrows he had made. "Yet … you, too, are a prisoner here."

"Perhaps not for long," she said, resuming her scrutiny of a universe that now sweltered with foreboding signs. "My place may not be of this world, but this world is *my* place. By Law and by reward was I allowed to create it, and I know its ways and its warnings. He is engaged in a work of transition, which means he is vulnerable to error. To a mistake that might secure my freedom, if I am clever enough to take advantage. He is also preparing to move against me. Soon. I can feel His intention upon the air, like blood on the tongue."

"How can he attack us? The barrier forbids it. You have said so yourself!"

"There are ways around it from without, dear one, and you know by now that his greatest chance of finding a way comes when there is a fracture between our worlds. When he summons a new slave unto himself."

"But your strength outweighs his, on this ground," declared Larkspur, lifting his face into the cooling shadows.

"I am strong only as far as I am able to foresee what he is planning to try. And even then I must find some way to prevent his coming. That is all I can do, Larkspur. That is all I have ever been able to do, since the first seeds of this orchard were planted."

"Then what is our plan?"

"Our plan is to watch and wait. Hope for a blunder on his part that gives us a chance to set matters aright. Let him claim and eat what is rightfully his, for the wretched mean nothing to us. But his chosen underlings make artful assassins, and each new creation brings hidden skills of its own. We are not the only ones who gain strength and boldness with the harvest, Larkspur. We shall watch and wait," she murmured, her eyes narrowing to follow a pinpoint comet that blazed sparks of incandescent purple above the moon gracing her Heaven. "Remember that a transition taxes him! He may let down his guard even as he coils to strike. Yes, we will wait."

"And what else, Lady?"

"What else do you think? We search the skies for murder."

NEBRASKA

Brask Adams met his sister, Emily, for dinner at a steakhouse in Palo Alto the night before he drove down the coast to Big Sur, and to Wistwood. He knew it was going to be a futile meeting. He figured he would walk away and never speak to Emily again, after all the bombs that had been dropped, over and over, across the scarred landscape of their toxic and occasional relationship. In fact, Brask had already decided to do just that. Leave for good. Forever. He loved his sister, somewhere in a seldom traveled corridor of his mind or in a secluded hollow of his soul. But he couldn't abide her.

Dinner was about saying a dignified farewell. *I love you. Wish you every good thing. Goodbye.* Dinner might also afford the chance to make Emily squirm. Brask would not rule out either purpose, though he would despise himself, at least temporarily, for the latter.

Besides, it was time to sew things up. Do some damage control, even if it would be a parting gift to himself more than anything else. He had a sickening hunch that Emily was beginning to figure out how bad things had gotten for her little brother, how low the dry Autumn leaf of his life had been blown before his book deal—the moment of all redemption and I-Told-You-So triumph—had been signed. He had heard a couple of things through the grapevine and intercepted a few cryptic remarks on Facebook when making his daily rounds at an Internet café near one of the homeless shelters. She knew something.

Damn her nosy, born-again Christian attitude!

Brask could deal with almost anybody in the world knowing about his stint as one of the nation's Great Unwashed except for Em. He had worked so hard at keeping everyone in the dark about his smothering slide into the abyss that it had become the full-time job he never managed to snag in the real world of recession and irreversible judgment. But the bad times were over, now, Baby. Long gone and never to darken another door in his future. And there was no way he'd leave town allowing Little Miss Priss to enjoy one of her infamous and sanctimonious last laughs. Still, beads of sweat swamped his forehead when he said a silent prayer to a God he didn't believe in, a prayer that she knew nothing about what had happened to him over the last eight months.

He took care to park the white, windowless Pontiac van a couple of blocks away from the restaurant, down a chic side street. The creepy-ass old hunk of junk he had bought and lived in after being forced to sell his truck. He donned a somewhat wrinkled sport coat fished from one of the jammed garment bags in the back. His hair, tousled and abundant, dusky blonde, had been cut and styled expensively that morning. First proper haircut in over a year. First decent one he could afford in all that time. Now it looked friendly instead of frazzled, neat and just above the collar of his jacket. Ready to catch the light again. His gray eyes, dead and suspicious only a month ago, were clear and sharp. The glow was back. He no longer had to cover his head in shame beneath the hood of a sweatshirt, terrified that someone would recognize him as he drove the van to camping spots between San Jose and Palo Alto for months on end. He didn't need to erase himself, eluding all eyes and whispers, ever aware of the most searing pain of all: no one really noticed him.

No one noticed any of those like him, not the way people ought to notice others, because of what he and they had become.

It had been a supreme desolation. He moved and hungered and slept and drove as always, but outside the window of Creepy Van the world had changed. What he saw with his own eyes had transformed. For all its noise and frenzy, his environment had become an impostor, a deadened and windblown landscape. There was no God, no life, not even the pale shadow of a dream across the deafening silence. Simply Void. For all of that eviscerating period, Brask had even come to doubt his own humanity. He was a mere collection of atoms having no more consequence than the infinite others around him, all suffused with equal meaninglessness. A passing cosmic shadow, born to suffer and be nothing until Nothing finally came during its random, unstoppable invasion to claim him.

Where had this icy vision, this strange planetary wasteland come from? How had it imprisoned him so completely? It was doom; foreign and light years removed from his being, yet close and swift as a memory. Pieces among pieces, spinning blind and alone beneath the smothering sky while indifferent little breezes whistled and howled their litany of ruin

Nothing exists, all is illusion, nothing remains, you are alone, alone amid this Nothing and from this Nothing you are made ...

He steadied himself against the driver's door of the van for a minute. The reflection in the window was his own. Yes. Finally there. Relief swept over him. He looked like his old self, the Brask people admired and invited to parties and took to bed, long before the inexorable spiral. Yes, his jeans were filthy, but they had been four times as expensive as the new haircut, in their heyday, and he wasn't going to get close enough to let his sister sniff-out a ruse with her born-again snout. That snout was always out of joint, anyhow, when it wasn't stuck in the crack of a Bible opened to some archaic passage delineating the punishments of Deuteronomy or Leviticus. Punishments for the worst and the best of sinners. Retributions for the clever and the merely savage.

Brask laughed and locked the van. He could set the scene already. Em would look at him with that strange mix of forced concern for his immortal soul and her usual "Don't-get-close-enough-to-taint-my-righteousness" arrogance. Then he'd smile and talk rings around her deformed worldview, scrambling her brain six ways to her own hymn-singing Sundays, wondering all the while just how fast their mother might spin in her grave to know her eldest daughter had become a braying donkey of a Baptist.

Myriad was the name of the restaurant. Monday night. He took a deep breath, went inside, secured a booth in the rear of the mostly deserted place, and ordered a Scotch and water from the busboy. *That* couldn't come fast enough. Things looked promising when Emily showed up ten minutes later, alone. Brask had expected to suffer through the indignity of conversation with her troglodyte husband, Blue, a prematurely bald insurance-company executive who had sold his sister on Biblical inerrancy as smoothly as he had sold her on marriage ten years earlier.

"Who the hell marries a thirty-two year old guy with a little King James Bible in his pocket, a toupee like a trampled possum on his head, and a name like 'Blue,' Emily?"

That had been Brask's only taunt after meeting her betrothed for the first time those years ago, but Em had been quick with a retort and it was one he never forgot:

"A girl who doesn't stand a chance in hell of making it *to* college, much less through college, Nebraska. That's who. You got a scholarship because you're so good with words, smart-ass, and you'll be out of this house soon and on your own. Blue's the only guy that our drunken excuse for a father hasn't managed to run off since I was fifteen. I don't have any other prospects. None. Zero. Blue may not be the brightest bulb on the tree—I grant you that—but he's sober, he's got some values, and he's going to inherit his dad's company one day. I'm running out of options, stuck here in this death-trap, and I could do a helluva lot worse than him, if I weren't already doing a lot worse. You understand me, little brother?"

"Yeah."

"Good. Then don't *ever* fucking judge me again!"

Her command had been ironic, because after the quickie marriage and as soon as their first bouncing baby Baptist was born, Emily never used the word "fucking" again (at least that he knew about) and it seemed that all she did with her life thereafter was judge Judge JUDGE the living hell out of all people and things around her. Clothing, cars, television programs, books, music, hairstyles, habits, and even baking soda fell under the scrutiny of her sacred purview and could be neatly and sometimes viciously relegated to her "Of the Devil" waste-basket. Approved behaviors and specimens of humanity were duly preserved in her "Blessed and Highly Favored" treasure-chest.

There was no In Between receptacle when it came to Em's methods of spiritual organization and holy disposal. Five years into the marriage, she had a quiver full of scriptural verses fit to punctuate any comment, deflect any question, and neutralize all dissent along her churchy, potluck supper-path to salvation. Worse, in Brask's estimation, his sister appeared to relish her role as God's appointed dispensatrix of disapproval. She rose to her task as the strangler of analytical thought as if she were a famished grizzly guarding a shredded carcass at the mouth of a cave. Her "salvation" had been the most disturbingly feral thing Brask had ever the displeasure to encounter in nature, which was one of the reasons he had only ever visited her twice a year, at most, and never on Easter or Christmas, for the sake of everyone's sanity.

Tonight, as Em followed the hostess to the booth, he got a lump in his throat as he watched her mince between tables in her conservative black pumps. She looked older. A lot older. But damn if she didn't look more sanctified than ever, too.

This is not going to go well. Fuck.

Emily waved him away with a weary but condescending flutter of her hand when he stood politely to greet her. She had never been a hugger. As they settled in against the plush red leather, he could only gather that she was ready to draw daggers at any moment, sitting there in her drab, knee-length coat of beige wool, staring at him beneath a helmet of high-rise evangelical hair. He had to marvel at that coif; it was fortified with enough shellac to gird a Tower of Babel piercing straight to Heaven.

Eleven months had passed since they had set eyes upon each other and hers now scanned him greedily across the table, searching for signs of sin as she shoved her purse into a corner of the booth. Brask had to suppress a sneer as she snatched a dinner napkin and folded it over her knees, prim as prim could be. He could imagine it down there, placed like a shroud concealing two corpses jutting obscenely from the desecrated mausoleum of her sexless brown skirt.

"Blue couldn't make it tonight," she began, frowning at the curiously phallic salt and pepper shakers between them. "There's been a lot going on down at the office lately and he's backed up. Sends his regrets, though."

No "hello"? No "How have you been?" No normal? No. No normal. Not ever.

"Well, it's too bad he couldn't make it, Sis. Would've been nice to see him again," Brask lied, breaking off a piece of breadstick and swirling it around the little puddle of olive oil and balsamic vinegar on his plate. "How're the kids, Emily?"

"Busy with the start of the school semester, at least for a few weeks, until the next ridiculous break begins. I can't stand how they've chopped-up the entire year into pieces for children these days. Things used to be so much more well-defined. Now the liberal machine's got everyone moving along in this mindless goose-step, or that's what they're hoping for, anyway. But Blue says we can maybe afford to send all the kids back to a private Christian academy next year. Looks like the insurance company's bouncing back from that whole recession horror."

She eyed her brother, accusing him of unspoken deficiencies over the rim of her water glass as she sipped. Her perfectly manicured nails were bright red, the only colorful thing about her. Incongruous. Brask could think only of a vulture's talons, sunk into a fresh heap of carrion.

"Blue Jr. is growing like a weed and Kadelynn is going to be baptized at the end of the month," continued Emily, bursting into a sudden, beatific smile and glancing with casual approval at a few other families seated here and there about the place. "She accepted the Lord this year during Vacation Bible School. We were all so thankful. So blessed."

"That's great, Em. How old is she now?" Brask felt a razor slice the lining of his stomach. The room seemed to spin for an instant.

"Seven, but smart for her age. Pastor Whitman says she was more than capable of making a valid spiritual decision."

"Ah. The old Age of Reason benchmark."

"Whatever you want to call it," said Emily with a little shrug. She wrinkled her nose. A tendril of brimstone fumes might have wafted up beneath the table from Perdition itself. Brask needed another Scotch. His stomach growled in harmony with the static sounds that zigged and zagged through his brain.

Where the hell is the server, any server? I need a fucking drink yesterday!

Another deep breath would have to suffice.

"Everyone's talking about how fast kids are growing up these days, Em. How it's maybe too fast, you know? I suppose yours are confronted with a lot of decisions and ideas that kids like us never had to contend with, huh?"

"Our kids aren't growing up too fast," countered Emily, flipping through the menu without reading any of it. "We've seen to that. They don't march to the beat of the progressive drum, even though we can't do anything about the school situation, just yet."

"Still, it sounds like they're getting a good moral grounding."

Brask began to twist and wring the napkin in his own lap, wanting things to go at least reasonably well. Maybe he had over-calculated. Maybe he wasn't a match for her tonight, after so long apart. Damn it! He shifted a few mental gears, determined to make whatever concessions were necessary, though he was not about to grovel. Groveling would make Emily's decade. That would never do.

"Moral standards are important for kids, especially now," he offered. "This present chaos doesn't seem to be the answer."

"Instilled values are important, of course," said Emily. "But let's face it. It's not as if you'd know anything about that, Nebraska. The raising children part of it, I mean. Oh, I guess this pasta Alfredo with shrimp sounds halfway decent. I've never eaten here before. Who knows? What're you going to have? Any ideas?"

Brask felt his face flush in spite of his determination to stay immune to calumny. She hadn't meant to exclude him from decent humanity *merely* in the sphere of child-rearing. Oh no. Even Emily's half-insults were leaden with extra implications. The only surprising thing was that it took her just a few minutes to register such blanket disapproval of his life. That level of condemnation usually came after they had spent an hour with each other, at least. He had to stop himself from grinding his teeth. What was the point of even attempting diplomacy with this bitter, uptight stranger across the table? She hadn't even asked him how *he* was, how his life was going, how *he* felt. Still, Brask was enough of a competitor to keep trying, and had resolved to take the high road by changing the subject when she blithely did it for him.

"So, I heard you finally sold a book to somebody," she said, now peering at him over the top of the menu. "Congratulations. I know you've always wanted that," she added, patronizing him, as if he were a self-absorbed child awaiting a new bicycle under the Christmas tree, as if publishing a book were some consolation prize he had been lucky to snag because the truly important successes of life—marriage, church, children—had all passed him by, through every fault of his own. "That's a fine accomplishment, Nebraska. Unless it's full of smut like everything else they're publishing these days. It's not pornographic, is it?"

"My God, Em, of course it's not porn!" He wrung the dinner napkin beneath the table until all his knuckles were white and bulging. "What kind of person do you take me for, anyhow? And how did you even know about the deal to begin with? It was supposed to be a surprise. That's part of the reason I invited you out to dinner tonight."

Emily smirked.

"I ran into one of your old girlfriends in Safeway a week ago. I can't remember her name." Em's wide eyes searched the ceiling for clues. "It was the one you started going with after Jess left you, I'm pretty sure. The hippie-chick. The one that taught yoga or channeling or whatever pagan nonsense it was. Didn't shave her armpits. You know—you brought her to a barbecue that one year and we all couldn't believe our eyes. Anyhow, she ran into *me*, actually, because I sure as sunshine wasn't looking to run into her."

"Ariel. Her name is Ariel."

"Yeah, that's the one. Ariel." Emily stabbed the tablecloth with a crimson fingertip and rolled her eyes. "No wonder I couldn't remember, with a handle like that. I suppose that's her transcendental name."

"It's no more stupid than a name like 'Blue,' for God's sake."

Emily's expression darkened. She flipped another page of the menu. Petulance well-practiced. "There's no need for you to make fun of my husband, much less take the Lord's name in vain, Nebraska Adams."

"Speaking of names, Em, don't call me that. You know I hate it."

"Well, don't blame me. Blame Dad. He's the one who insisted on naming you after the state in which you were conceived. Of course, he was drunk when he made that decision, like so many others." She wheeled to scan the restaurant. "My goodness, is there anyone who actually serves customers, here? Or do we have to wave a flag?"

"Someone'll be along in a minute. This is reunion time, right? Chance to enjoy each other's company. Just forget about the waiters for a second and tell me about this little encounter you had at the grocery store. With Ariel."

Emily began to toy with the string of faux pearls at her collar, a look of exaggerated innocence crossing her face. "Oh, that. Now, I'm not saying your old girlfriend wasn't nice, if you like that type of person. She's a friendly little thing, floating around the aisles at Safeway like she'd just been blown off the top of a dandelion. She recognized *me*—I was a bit shocked, I mean, that was four years ago when you brought her to our barbecue—and then she said, 'Hello,' and we engaged in some other chit-chat I can't recall, and then she asked me if I was excited about you getting your first novel published."

"And I can just imagine how you replied to that," muttered Brask.

"Well, I won't lie and say I wasn't a bit peeved, honey. I told her it was all news to me, because it certainly *was*. Then I said Blue and the kids and I hadn't seen you in almost a year. She said the same thing about you, by the way."

"Oh yeah?"

"Uh huh. Told me she only found out about your book from some text or email you sent her, but made sure to mention she hadn't seen you in a long time, either. Said she was a little worried about you, in fact. That she'd heard a few things to make her worry."

"What things?" Brask's scalp broke into a cold sweat.

Emily shrugged a petite shoulder, a simpering gesture too lady-like even within the framework of her prissy Baptist affectations. "Wouldn't say. Didn't want to speak out of turn, I guess. And at any rate, she didn't seem very sure of things, herself. Of course, I wasn't about to engage in gossip. She didn't use the word 'gossip' but I could tell that's what she meant. So I let it go and she said goodbye and kinda drifted on her way, like those people do. Aimless. Airy fairy. Sweaty."

"That's it?"

"What else did you expect? You really think I was about to stand in the middle of the frozen foods aisle and just carry on some prolonged conversation with a girl like Azriel?"

"Ariel, Em. Ariel. And she's hardly a girl."

"Whatever, little brother. I'm not one to pry, so pardon me for not giving her the third degree then and there. I had shopping to do. Besides, I figured if there was something you wanted to let the family know you would've told us yourself. Right? Imagine that. Well, it was just a funny way to learn about your big news, that's all. Very happenstance."

"I suppose it was. Ariel stole a bit of the thunder I was planning for tonight. Not her fault, though. I guess she assumed we were a lot closer than we actually are."

"I guess she did."

A server finally ambled over to the table, not a moment too soon for Brask's sanity.

"Good evening, I'm Lilah, and I'll be looking after you tonight. Sorry it took me a minute to get here. I just came on shift and there was a mix-up about whose station was whose and then—"

"You know, it's okay, Lilah," said Brask. "We're actually ready to order."

"Great. That's perfect!"

"Yeah." He tapped a fingernail against his empty glass. "I'll have another Dewar's, neat. The busboy got me the first one. I guess he probably told you. And ... my sister here is going to order first. Where are my manners? Em, what'll you have?"

"Iced tea for me. And that Alfredo with shrimp thing."

"Oh, that's so good" said Lilah. "That's all? No salad?"

"That's all."

"I'll have the porterhouse, medium rare," said Brask, fumbling with the pages of the menu. "Mashed potatoes. Spinach. Just the way it is on the menu."

"Well, that was easy," said Lilah.

"Yep. Dewar's first, though. Right away. Thanks."

When they were alone, Emily folded her arms and stared. She might have already eaten a full meal, so satisfied was her half-smile. Brask felt like a fly, wrapped and immovable amid his own frantic buzzing, every thread of the web alive with vibration as the spider made its approach.

"So, Brask. How *have* you been doing for the past year? Is there anything we need to know, I mean aside from this book that's supposedly coming out?"

"I'm fine, as you can see with your own eyes, Em. And my book is not 'supposedly' coming out. It's being published next year in the Fall. I've even signed a follow-up deal. Already got an advance and everything. Dinner's on me tonight, by the way."

"Thanks, and believe me, I get it," said Emily. "One story is still the same, and that's the story of good old evasive Brask. Fine. We'll just keep up the pretense. Dysfunctional families shouldn't stray from familiar turf, right?"

"What are you talking about?"

"Nevermind. I didn't mean anything. So what's your amazing book about? Is it the same one you were writing five years ago, about the nuclear submarine explosion or whatever it was?"

"No, this is a whole new story. It's about a family falling apart, one by one, as their entire belief-system crashes around them."

"Oh. So it'd be perfect as a Broadway musical adaptation, huh?"

"Right. It's complicated, Em. I did want to surprise you tonight with the news. I really did. Sorry you got wind of it from someone else."

"Hey, I can do 'complicated,' when I try real hard. My head's not always stuck in Ezekiel, contrary to what you might believe."

"That's a relief."

"I'll bet. What's the title?"

"Of what?"

"Your book, stupid. What do you think?"

"Oh. The publisher hasn't settled on one, yet, and neither have I."

"That doesn't sound too promising. Who's publishing this masterpiece, anyhow?"

"Fischer & Slade, out of New York, by way of San Francisco."

"Never heard of them. What else have they done?"

"It's an old, reputable house, Em. Not the biggest house in the world, but good. I doubt you have any of their past or current titles in the bookcase at home next to the 'Footprints' shadowbox or the Thomas Kinkade paintings."

"Well, well. Now look at who's being a tad holier-than-thou," needled Emily. "Don't worry. You've accused me of pulling the same thing often enough. I suppose I'd better be able to take it as good as I give it, right?"

"Look …"

"It's okay, Brask." She reached a manicured hand across the table and patted his hard, sun-browned fist. "But you need to know that you've always been that way, too, whether you realize it or not. Holier-than-thou, according to whatever creed it is that you espouse, if any. Doesn't bother me or Blue or the kids. Sounds trite to you, I'm sure, but we know in our hearts that God is *not* mocked. Besides, you know I'm not gonna be reading your book whenever it comes out. At least we can be honest with each other about that."

"I figured as much, and that's fine with me, Em. It's not as if I'd come to you for critiques about my stuff. Never did. But can you at least be happy that it's even happening to me? That my dream is finally coming true?"

"Sure, hon. Of course. And I am happy. I mean that. I think it's a wonderful thing when God hands an important blessing like that to someone. I rejoice in His goodness. What you do with that blessing, though, and how you share it with the world, for good or for evil, is entirely up to you."

The server, Lilah, was loitering at the bar, chatting with another employee while the Dewars sat ignored at the service station. Brask wished his eyes were laser beams in her back.

"I see they've been emphasizing the particularly passive-aggressive and backhanded tidbits of Scripture during Sunday School classes, Emily. Well done. I bet your refrigerator at home is lined with gold stars."

"Don't be wicked. You know what I mean when I say the things I say."

"Every word."

"As long as you're getting paid a living wage for this stuff you fabricate in your head and expect people to buy and read, I'm not about to look down on a man's chosen work. You *are* getting paid enough to live on, right?"

"I told you, Sis. I basically signed a two-book deal. Do you know how rarely that happens for first-time authors these days, in this glutted, back-asswards market?"

"Watch your language," Emily admonished under her breath, glancing fearfully around lest one of the bus-persons swabbing idly across the nearby tables would discover that she was dining with a heathen.

"I got an advance, too. Like I told you. I won't have to work a straight gig for a year, at least."

"A straight … what?"

"A *real* job, Emily Einstein."

"Don't make fun of me. I don't know your writer's lingo. But that does lead to my next question. What *have* you been doing in the year we haven't seen so much as a hair on your head or heard a word from you? The flower child in Safeway had no clue where you might be working. Your old phone number at the apartment on Whitney Street was disconnected. You never returned my calls to your cell. I stopped bothering to leave voice mails."

The waitress returned. Brask had to keep himself from taking the drink directly out of her hand. Emily pursed her lips in disapproval as her iced tea was deposited and they were alone once more.

"So what's the story?"

"I've been working construction." Brask took a healthy belt of the Dewar's. "What else? It's what I've done to survive for the last ten years. No big revelation, there."

"Your little contractor's company is still running?" Emily leaned back against the booth, skepticism covering her face like an Aztec mask of predation. "Through the recession and everything?"

"Yep. Want a breadstick? They're good."

"No. I don't want one." She shook her head, rueful, closing in for the kill. "Color me a bit surprised, Brask. Blue knows guys—we're talking heavy-duty, established contractors—who lost their shirts and had to leave town because of the downturn. And your company hasn't been listed in the Yellow Pages or with 411 information since … well, since I last saw you. I called a couple of times to check, just so you know."

A drop of perspiration ran down the back of Brask's neck. More threatened to fall from the top of his forehead.

"I had to do a lot of adjusting like any of the contractors around Palo and San Jose. Or anywhere in the country, for that matter. It didn't pay to keep the whole outfit operational, so I just did independent jobs."

"And all those guys that used to work for you?"

Brask waved his hands, vaguely, over the Dewar's glass. "Scattered to the four winds. Every man for himself. And Michelle, the woman that was on the crew. They had to take freelance jobs, too, when and where they could get them. But

I couldn't worry too much about everybody else in times like that. They sure as hell didn't worry about me. I managed fine."

"But you never 'managed' to let us know how you were getting along," accused Emily.

The spider drew near. Brask could smell the venom. Chemical. Deadly.

"What do you want, Em? We've never been very close, even when we were kids, in case that fact has somehow, amazingly, slipped your mind. To tell you the truth, I'm surprised you agreed to even meet me here tonight. Shit. I guess this is pretty much the way we've been doing things, when we've been together at all, since Dad died."

"I know." Emily turned her iced tea glass this way and that, contemplating the cubes. "It's a scandal, for a family to be that way."

"It's the family that was the scandal." Brask regretted the sudden harshness in his voice, but truth was truth. "If that's what you mean, then you've got it exactly right."

"That isn't what I meant, but I know what *you* mean. You need to know that *our* family—me and Blue and the kids—are past all of that stuff because we walk in the light of His word and we have chosen Him to be our one mediator between God and man—"

"Give it a rest, will ya? Damn, you'll never catch me going around quoting my own book to people who haven't the slightest interest in hearing various passages. Jesus himself didn't walk around spewing verses. He made up his own material on the spot, as far as I know. He was an original."

Emily's next words hit Brask like a steel spike, forged in unfathomable earthly fires and then hurled into the iciest seclusion of space, made lethal by exposure to the endless dark.

"I went by your apartment a few months ago." Her tone was deliberate and victorious, her head weaving just barely from side-to-side atop her neck, serpentine, the way she used to do when they were kids, when she was gloating over some treat or favor that had been given only to her.

"So?"

"The guy who runs those condos wasn't about to tell me much of anything when I asked him, but Betty, the old lady in the office, was a lot more forthcoming."

"I had to move," Brask said, calm as the eye of a cyclone. He had bitten the inside of his mouth and tasted blood between his teeth. "What's the big deal?"

"After not being able to pay your rent for three months, you had to move. Last year. Where did you move, Brask?"

He stared at his sister. How many times had he wanted to strangle her during their childhood, in the flashing, impulsive way any kid without reason's temperance desires to strangle an irksome sibling. Now, sitting in a sleepy Monday night restaurant across from her as an adult, he had never felt a more swift or disturbing urge than the one that flashed a vision of him reaching across the table to snap her neck. He was horrified, reeling toward some evasive light that pulsed amid the shreds of his soul, ousting the scene from his brain. The restaurant seemed full of a sudden and irrevocable chill. He hid his trembling hands in his lap. In a harrowing instant of agony, Brask knew this was a sensation he would never forget, a secret he would never tell. An opportunity he would recall again and again, for as long as he lived.

"Don't look at me like that, Brask." Emily's cheeks turned pink and then scarlet beneath her unblinking eyes. She knew she had gone too far. She tried to swallow a sudden, tickling worm of fear, but it wasn't going down.

"I'm a concerned sister," she sputtered, now desperate for defense. "I have a right to find out what's going on with my little brother, a right born out of love." She made a move to touch her heart, but her own clutched hands landed, tellingly, on the wrong side of her bosom. "Besides, that old lady in the rental office didn't say anything in a spiteful, gossipy way. She was concerned, too. They really liked you as a tenant. They cared about you."

"I had to regroup, that's all." Brask's voice might as well have been a tumbleweed scratching its way across the cracked earth of some desert expanse. It took every ounce of his will to keep the glass in his hand from shaking when he lifted it to his lips, never taking his eyes from Emily. "A lot of people had to shift gears mighty quick during the crash, or I guess you and Blue were spared any and all hardship. Is that it?"

Emily's eyes grew wide and she made a little gulping noise, toying again with the pearls around her neck as if suddenly aware she had crossed a line from which there could be no retreat. But she had never cared about crossing lines into places she never planned to revisit. Something very small and sickly, something weak and abandoned and clinging to life, died suddenly in the space between them. It passed away with a brief but defiant trembling of the air, maybe of the universe, and Emily felt for one disturbing moment the magnitude of what had been lost.

Then her own brush with uncertain compassion slipped away just as swiftly, and she remembered what was most important, after all.

"Blue and I *dealt* with our share of little struggles," she boasted, smoothing the napkin-shroud upon her lap. "We told you that. We told you the last time we saw you, at the height of it, or at the low point of it. But people of faith do not worry about what to eat or what to wear, for does not the Lord clothe the lilies of the field with such splendor that a king's robes could not compare? We prayed our way through the storm."

Brask could only close his eyes, shutting-out a tempest of his own. He was far from prayer.

"I'm sorry if I overstepped my bounds by snooping, little brother. There. Is that enough to soothe your pride? Good heavens, are we going to get any food in this place?" she looked about the now half-filled dining room, her Helpful Housewife mountain of holy-hair pivoting this way and that.

"My pride has nothing to do with your little detective work and its results, Emily. There's nothing to tell. I had to downsize, like a lot of people did. It wasn't pleasant, but I found another place more suited to my circumstances at the time. It's not the drama you're imagining it to be. You shouldn't have gone poking your nose into my business."

"Then I wouldn't have known anything!"

"That's the point. And you still don't know anything. For Christ's sake, I'd lived in that apartment on Whitney Street for a whole year before you even knew I was there, after the divorce from Jess. Why does it matter to you what happened two years later? When I want you or fucking Blue or the kids to know something, I'll let you know. We're never, ever going to be a regular family, Em, not ever. Not in the same city. Hell, we weren't even a family in the same house growing up."

"Then you've been okay all this time? Roof over your head. Plenty to eat. The whole deal?"

"Yeah, as a matter of fact. I've been okay. End of story."

Brask could tell she wasn't buying the tale about his general wellbeing. She believed her brother to be the most infuriating person with whom she had ever attempted to share her spiritual "witness." Giving up was not an option. Brask was the sort of challenge she believed God placed directly in the pathway of the righteous, specifically to test a believer's mettle.

A single tear made its winding way down her cheek.

"You know, Brask. I think I'm finished trying to lead you to the Lord the easy way. Your divorce from Jess was failure enough, but you just keep running from redemption. This latest deception proves it. Believe it or not, a decent, Bible-believing Christian woman in your life would hardly be some kind of automatic nightmare. No matter what you believe, a little stability and a sense of personal responsibility in this world go a long way."

"Thank you, Em, for Today's Calvinistic Word of Encouragement. And you leave Jess and the divorce out of this. I mean it."

Emily began to hiss words under her breath like a sorceress about to level a hex. "That's your problem, Brask. You're a disrespectful, sacrilegious smart-aleck. It's why your life's been so fractured for the past ten years, forget about the recession. It's why you don't have any kind of rational connection to the people who really love you and have your best interests at heart."

"Best interests? And those are supposed to come from you, Blue, the kids, and whatever prayer-circle you're running my name through at that harebrained church of yours?"

"I didn't agree to share dinner with you tonight so we could bicker and fight the whole time. Whether you want to believe it or not, I try real hard to button my lip and keep my witnessing to a minimum whenever I've seen you."

"Oh, my God! I don't believe what I'm hearing." Brask downed the last of the Dewar's and let out a roar of a laugh.

"No, wait. You listen to me. It's true," said Emily, her black, porcine eyes wild with zeal. "I try to put your comfort before the Lord's will because I know I don't get a chance to see you often. And if that means toning-down the truth, well, then the sin falls on me, Brask." She finally found the proper side concealing her heart and proceeded to clutch it. "That's right. You heard me. I'm willing to endure committing personal sin so that we might have some kind of relationship.

So that you might have someone in your life that you can call 'family,' when everyone else has left you high and dry."

Brask turned his head away in disgust. "You really are a piece of work, Em. 'High and dry?' That's the way you see me? As someone disenfranchised? Someone who's been abandoned by everything worthwhile in the world?"

"It seems to me you've gotten worse since Jess left you. The whole distancing thing you do. Shutting us out."

"Shutting you out? When are you going to wake the hell up? You were never *in* to begin with. You in my world. Me in yours. This is insane. Our pattern has been that we get together once every year, maybe, or every couple of years and just fucking tolerate each other, for God knows what reason. But we do it. I don't even know why we aren't completely estranged. We ought to be, for as much as we've gone through. What we've seen go down since we were kids. For as much as we have in common these days, beyond blood. And let me tell you something, Sis—blood doesn't mean a goddamned thing."

"Blood *always* means something," said Emily, sniffling as she dabbed at her now tearless eyes with the dinner napkin. "In fact, it means everything in Christ. Blood brings salvation and eternal life."

"Yeah, that's how Dracula sees it, too, you idiot. Spare me, Em. And as far as Jess is concerned, you don't know what you're talking about in the most colossal way yet. She didn't abandon me. I'm not a baby. We split up because we grew apart, which is something that happens in the real world. Do you get it? We tried to make it work, but we both wanted different lives and we were compassionate enough—*human* enough—to let each other go while we were still young. We did the right thing. It wasn't easy, but we did it."

Emily glared at him, nearing her breaking point, rocking on the edge of the final plunge into the chasm.

"It's one thing if you two felt you could throw away a marriage, just mock the sanctity of the union between a man and a woman, like it was a ... like it was ... some ... expired lease on a car! But you were practically out of your mind when she left! And it was all due to this writing pipe-dream."

"Shut up about Jess, you hear me?"

"See? Mentioning the collapse of a perfectly decent marriage is like asking you to pass the salt, but I say one thing about how crazy you went with your stupid writing and you sneer at me like I'm some kind of monster. That's the way it is with you godless liberals, though, isn't it? Arrogance means more in your twisted worldview than people do. More than family and sacred institutions. Environment rates higher in your esteem, even after we have *all* been given dominion over the beasts of the earth by God Himself and—"

"You don't even have dominion over your own ass, Emily."

Brask threw his napkin down on the table and pushed his way out of the booth.

"How dare you talk to me like that, Nebraska Adams? You listen here—"

"No. No more listening," said Brask, putting one palm between himself and his furious sister and another in his coat pocket to find the roll of bills he had stashed there. "I should've known this would be another big mistake. But I'll tell you this much—it's gonna be the last one, as far as the two of us are concerned. I'm far from perfect, but at least I'm not clinging to the delusion that all we have to do to solve life's problems is say a Magic Prayer, ignore reality, and then wait for some guy in sandals to come along and snatch us all up into the goddamned clouds." He peeled two fifty-dollar bills from the roll and tossed them on the table. "That ought to cover dinner and what little sanity I've got left tonight."

"You're just going to run away again?" Emily taunted, her nails digging into the tablecloth, clinging to the cliff over which she had stumbled. "From God and family and good sense?"

"I am," said Brask. "And permanently. I'm moving south in a few days and I don't expect I'll ever be coming back, not to you. That was the other part of the 'surprise' I wanted to share with you tonight."

"Moving again? South, this time? Living in your *van,* maybe?" Her voice approached the level of a shriek. Everyone in the dining room turned to look at them. "Well, I am *not* surprised. Yeah, I know all about it, Brask. On the streets. We've seen you, you know."

Brask began to pry himself out of the booth.

"Take care of yourself, Emily. Have a great life, however you want to live it. Be happy, if you can. I honestly wish that much for you, at least. And I forgive you for all of the asinine things you've said to me over the years, even since we were small. I really do. Goodbye."

"You dare to say you forgive *me?*"

"Don't you throw your Bible cult at me anymore, Em. none of this happened because of anything I did right or wrong or half-assed. It happened beyond my control. Do you even get that? Do you even want to? No. You wouldn't. You think everything is preordained by your fucking moody, scatterbrained god. Your god who's such a baby about running the universe he might as well be playing in his own shit."

Emily was transfixed with anger. The skin on her face pulled taut toward the back of her skull until thin lips stretched to reveal the mere edges of fang-like incisors. It was a reptilian rictus, worthy of a cobra preparing to spit, and Brask felt a withering chill bristle across his back. He had gone too far in his own fury. Now he would capitulate. Now he would become the chastened, the little brother of former days, deserving of retribution and exile to an outpost reeking of his own shame. He would be dismissed properly to emptiness, there to travel without complaint, where abandoned rooms and other places to hide were forever thick with shadow and regret.

"You have always had a mouth on you, Nebraska Adams." Emily's words sliced into him. A fingernail split down the middle and began to bleed as she tried to dig into the tabletop. Only Brask noticed. "Always thought you were smarter and better than everyone else. Always spoiled and selfish. Well, it's one thing to insult me, but you just committed sacrilege against your Master, your Maker!"

Her spell, her power to cow and immobilize the unbeliever, was brief. It vanished as if the air between them had been set afire and burned out of the room.

"You know, Sis. When I was growing up, around you and mom and dad, I thought the kind of shit you spew was normal. I didn't believe it, but I thought it was what I should've believed. I thought there was something wrong with me. That I was the one who was wrong. The only one who didn't know it. Then I left and learned that you're sick and twisted, but you know what the amazing thing is? You're the only ones who *don't* know it."

"You can stand the fact that people like me are possible," accused Emily.

"I don't think I can live in a world where people like you are possible."

Emily stood trembling and unsteady in the booth. Brask rose, turned his back to her and walked away. She knocked her glass over and splashed ice and lemon in a spray across the table.

"You listen to me, Brask!" Her words emerged in a shuddering squawk. Diners and servers were agog, staring at the big-haired woman in beige as she balled her fists and ground them together at her breasts. "I rebuke you in the Name of the Lord Jesus Christ! Your eternal salvation is in peril! Do you hear? Hell is real, little brother, and you are going to find out *all* about it one day, you understand me?"

"I don't think she liked the breadsticks." Brask paused, ashen-faced and sad, as he passed the stupefied hostess on his way out the door. "You might want to see if the chef can whip-up some manna. That's more her speed. Sorry about the scene. Goodnight."

IF NOT FOR SLEEP

The detectives spoke, hushed and heartbroken themselves, to the woman weeping in the hospital room. Her nine year-old son was dead.

Doctors and nurses had slipped out, sleek and quiet. Vibrations of pale green through tears. The woman's world became an empty channel, sucking sand and fading water, forged to grasp then speed away down steep shoreline, down for once and down forever, back into the sea after the crash of a rogue wave. Soon she would be lost in the riptide, united with all things that drift without power or purpose. This much she knew.

The IV and the ventilator had been disconnected from her boy, along with every other tangled wire and device, discarded or taken to float, perhaps, amid new and incoming swells, surging toward more hopeful sources of life in other rooms clustered around the Intensive Care Unit. These places, too, streamed away in the shallows of her sudden undersea world, suspended between blinding sky and sightless depth, where coral made scarlet with blood shimmered, each sound slow and loud. A knock. A hollow roar of thunder stifled. A tempest of sand disturbed in the wake of some leviathan. And everything drifted ... drifted. Stolen from the moment of First Breath and suspended, only for an instant, above the crumbling precipice before the abyss.

Goodbye.

She had fought and prayed to save her boy through these waters, safe and teeming with curious fish, his hand tiny in her own, borne on that current until they could no longer feel the bottom beneath their feet. Treading, side by side, even as his fingers spilled through her own as sand and he descended beyond sight, above knowledge. Some indifferent tide pushed her back, back where a razor-line of rocks grazed her soul and she emerged, dreadful and poised for ruin, upon the shore.

The flat line on the machine near the bed shot a soundless arrow through space and an eternity of her own Time. Someone touched a switch. Was it one of the detectives? Her life surrendered to the silence on the screen.

"We know this is an impossible time for you, Mrs. Bradshaw. You have our deepest sympathies. But this is a serious charge you've made. The longer we wait, the more difficult things will become. Do you think you might be able to answer some of our questions, for just a few minutes?"

"Brain death," she replied from behind a piece of crumpled, lipstick-smeared Kleenex. "Or just death."

"Yes, Ma'am, we know that. We're so sorry about your son."

"The doctors said his brain was dead. Said my Shawn was gone. Too much blood lost. Said it'd be better if we turn the life support off. I said 'Let the Lord take him.' I said it."

Patrice Bradshaw stared at the suits and ties worn by the man and the woman before her. She could not really see their faces. She did not want to see them.

"Course, they didn't say anything about the Lord, those doctors, but I knew what they meant. I knew. I did. They said it was my choice and I prayed about it, right here where we are, so I guess I'm the one who killed him in the end."

The detectives looked at each other, confused. They were exhausted, but not from grief.

"Ma'am, we can't emphasize enough how important it is to get every detail possible when a crime of this kind has occurred, while details are fresh in the witness's mind and memory. Can you go through this just one more time with us? Then we'll leave you to be with your son."

"I told everything to that first officer when the ambulance came, and I told the ambulance workers, too. Then I saw you two again when they brought Shawn in, and I told you, quick as I could. Can't you ask that first officer? She was a nice lady. Very kind to me. Good person."

"You weren't able to tell Officer Cortland much at the time of the … incident," said the male detective, his voice velvet, eager to soothe. He was not an unkind man. He was only a suspicious man. "You were in hysterics when it happened this morning, Ma'am, and now you're in shock. Understandably so. Every minute counts, though, when it comes to finding out who did this to your boy. Do you understand what I'm saying to you?"

Patrice Bradshaw sniffled and nodded, clinging to the steel rail of her son's hospital bed.

"We need more information," said the other detective, the woman. "Especially if this tragedy occurred the way you described it."

"If?"

A rivulet of snot had worked its way down to the bottom of Patrice's chin and was starting to dry there. She dabbed aimlessly at it with the Kleenex and missed.

"Excuse us, Ma'am, but you told Officer Cortland and you told us that you saw a policeman swerve off the road onto the shoulder and, these are your words," the detective glanced down at a notepad cupped in her palm, "… you said 'a cop hit the gas and hit my boy deliberately. I saw him turn the wheel and I saw the smile on his face when he did it and then he drove away. He drove away and I'm screaming over my baby because I think he's dead.' These are your words to Officer Cortland, is that correct?"

"Uh huh. Cause that's what happened. I saw. I saw."

"And you told us the same thing, basically, when we arrived, before … before your son passed away."

"Yeah. And now he is dead. Right here. In front of you. In front of me. Everybody."

"Yes, we understand, Ma'am. But we need to get a more fulsome account of this occurrence if we are to launch a proper investigation. There were no other witnesses to this incident, Ma'am. There aren't very many houses on that back road and nobody was outside at the time your boy was struck. Now, we have the bike and it's mangled, for sure. Forensics is taking a hard look at that bike right now. Somebody hit him hard and took off, but we need more from you."

"And the helmet," whispered Patrice. "His little helmet. It was blood all in it. My baby's blood. So much blood."

"Forensics has the helmet, too, Ma'am, and we spoke with the doctors. They confirm that all of the injuries suffered by Shawn are consistent with a high-speed impact, a hit-and-run. But a policeman? In a patrol car? This is a very serious allegation, Mrs. Bradshaw. We need to know everything about what you saw. Again."

"Can't you come back tomorrow? Or after the funeral?"

Patrice's eyes fluttered, as if they were curtains being pulled down by someone eager to prepare for the onset of night. It was getting hard to keep them open. "The Reverend from church is coming, the nurses told me. My family, they'll be coming soon as they get word."

"We understand this is the worst possible time, but we have to know what happened this morning. We need a description. We need—"

"I was walking my boy over to see his Gramma, who's sick to bed with cancer," interrupted Patrice. She didn't recognize her own voice; it was barely strong enough to get beyond her own lips. "I was gonna take him down to the ocean, later. We were gonna stick our feet in the water. Look for seashells. That's his favorite thing to do in the world. That and riding his bike." The detectives leaned closer. "He said this morning he wanted to ride his new bike over to see Gramma. He just learnt to ride it. Some nice boys from the church taught him to ride. Then we were walking. Real careful. Laughing. And then that cop came out from nowhere in his car and ran my boy down. I was the other side of the road. I saw it all then I run over to my baby and that man ... that man drove off laughin. I could hear him laughin cause his windows were all open. Rolled down. He laughed at me, and he took off, and now my boy is dead."

"Where is Shawn's father, Mrs. Bradshaw?"

"Dead, too. Three years now. I see that look in your eyes. You can't pin this on a dead man. And I know a police car when I see one. You think I don't? You think I lie?"

"No, Ma'am, not at all. We're just doing our jobs. We're looking to get the facts while they're fresh. Every single detail means—"

"Hey! You two." A doctor had popped her head in the door, professional wrath across her brow like a bandana. She came and grabbed both detectives by the elbows, dragging them away from Patrice. "I thought I told you both to give it a rest," she seethed. "Her son has just died and she is sedated. And it took a lot to sedate her, believe me. She's in shock. Now go on and get out of here. Someone will call you as soon as she's fit to answer your questions." The doctor spoke through clenched teeth but her voice was girded with steel. "I do not want another scene in ICU. Go on, now. We'll call you when she's come to her senses. Then you can pester her all you want. Out."

The detectives frowned, but sauntered off, vanishing from the room the way all the others had. To Patrice's eyes, they were an illusion of sandcastles melting into the surf against a reverse tide. The doctor turned to put a comforting arm across her floral-print blouse. The blouse boasted great blossoms of blood amid otherwise whimsical patterns upon the fabric.

"Mrs. Bradshaw? I'm sorry those detectives troubled you. Now, if you want to stay here and spend a little more time with Shawn before your minister and your family arrive, just the two of you, I want you to do that. Okay? Some other nice people are going to come and look after him in a little bit. A grief counselor is coming to see you. Some orderlies, too. They won't take Shawn away just yet. They'll treat him very carefully. But you need to stay seated, Ma'am. Or we can find a bed for you. Whatever you want. Whatever you can manage to do."

"I can sit here with him. I want to sit with my boy a spell."

The doctor nodded and left.

Patrice wept in her chair next to the bed, where she had held his hand before, during, and after his departure. She had held his perfect little hand throughout that soft escape, the farewell made while appearing only to be asleep, so brilliant and so perfect a change from There to Elsewhere that none but the machine with its telltale green line dividing horizon from black eternity might know of the passing. But she knew. A mother knows.

She had sensed her son slip into Heaven even before the machine had dared to render its verdict in front of the nurse and the doctor at bedside with her. They had been two standing-stones, in that moment, with thoughtless, unknowable faces, and hearts petrified when the green line finally sang its siren song—the green line that hummed, not for the beguiled to approach forbidden shores, but for the dead to sail away and return not again.

Patrice took her boy's hand in her own once more, in the thick, cottony quiet of the antiseptic room. She could smell the blood upon his broken body, pools they had failed to wipe away. She perceived a stain upon this shell her son had left behind, the precious robin's egg blown from a bough and smashed, signifying only what might have grown and flourished but for the shabby nest of the world in its wretched flight. Beneath the blood, she could smell his skin, even the light, sweet scent of sweat that had covered him as he showed her, grinning and near-mad with joy, how proud he was to ride his bike on the way to see Gramma.

The drug—the shot or whatever it was they had given her; she couldn't begin to remember—was a thief of the energy needed to wail and throw herself against the wall in despair, or snatch her baby from the bland white death-bier and run off with him to some place where no stranger could touch his beloved flesh. But no medicine could subdue the agony cleaving her heart. Frail in spirit, she knew they would come to take him away. In a short while they would come. Her family would come. They would raise the roof. The police would come back again, too, and the hollow remainder of her life would resume a path at last. She knew it all, as one looking through a window at someone else might know it, looking not at herself but at the different woman she had become: no longer a wife; now no longer a mother. It was not the same person she had seen in the mirror, that more reliable window, in the morning, but she stared through the portal of her grief all the same, whispering at the supine figure, dead as dreams, beyond the steel bedside bars.

"Hold the little egg in your hand. Hold the shell. The wind's gonna come and blow all the pieces away, soon. Hold on for this last time," she whispered.

And then Shawn's dead hand closed around her own. Gripped it hard.

In a fountain bursting upward from the cragged depths of shock, Patrice's senses exploded into daylight, tearing forth in an excruciating pang of joy and wonder. She gasped, still not strong enough, yet, to scream amid such sudden exaltation. Electrified, she lifted her eyes to Shawn's face, which was now turned to the right and toward her own, transfixed upon his mother's astonishment.

But what she recognized in the lifeless eyes staring back at her, unblinking and cold, she knew at once and without hesitation. She knew, from what she had heard and read and learned since girlhood of the Deepest Evil, of that Thing which walked to and fro about the world, seeking whom It may devour.

It was not Shawn.

Her son was gone and nothing could convince her otherwise, not in heaven or on earth, but what gazed back at her was not seeking to convince her. It was not of earth, nor of heaven—at least not of heaven as heaven had become after its own trials, beyond Time, Times and half a Time.

"What do you dare to do, inside my boy like this?" Her voice was a vanishing whisper. She could not pull her hand away.

Yours? The flesh is yours, Woman. It had life when it was pulled from the bloody pit between your legs. But now it is meat and nothing more. What would you do? Take it back into yourself?

"What do you dare say to me with my boy's breath?"

There is no breath here.

"You … you let go of my hand. I know you! I know who you are!"

The grip grew tighter. Patrice's fingers turned purple.

Who am I, then?

"Satan!" she tried to shriek, but the word fell to the tile floor, a cracked and hollow rasp.

You think you know me, but you are mistaken, Woman. I am not That One. You, this room, this place, this rotting meat—all would turn to cinder if That One were to grace us with Its presence.

"Get out of my boy!" croaked Patrice. "You got no right."

I have every right. Not to take the meat for my own enjoyment, true, but I can feed in other ways, while I am able.

"My boy … my boy is a child of God!"

So am I. More so than many others. But your God is powerless, here, except to sustain what certain Ones have been appointed to supervise and to play-with at leisure. Your god sleeps, Woman, and holds you in existence only by virtue of a faded memory.

"I can wake the Lord!"

No. Your god slumbers beyond all hope. You would not be heard. But you can hear my words and hear them well!

"Let go of me, devil! Filth! Unclean thing! My Lord Jesus help me."

Spare Us your muttering incantations.

The bones in Patrice's fingers began to crack. Her mind collapsed beneath an avalanche of pain and terror but she could extract neither hand nor thought from such a grip.

Behold, Woman. The crows will come, seeking to feed upon this dead flesh, but not to delight the tongue. They hunger for answers. You would give them answers, Woman, because you saw it all.

"I've seen it all," nodded Patrice, struggling for breath and weeping as she slid off the chair into a heap near the bed, still in the clutch of that hateful hand. "I saw the face on that cop who drove off the road and killed my boy on purpose. He had the same eyes, the same ones you dare to put in my boy's face right now!"

Wrong again. The eyes you saw were the eyes of a mere slave. A good slave, who only has eyes for his Master's desire.

"God help me, Lord!"

Bones crunched in her hand.

He isn't helping. He isn't here. He isn't anywhere.

"You lie!"

I do not. Lying is the folly of animals. Of meat that has been given the privilege of walking and talking and fucking, for a Time, Times, and half a Time. Lying is the domain of meat arrogant enough to believe it has the right to believe in anything at all.

"Please, let me and my baby go! I'll do anything you want. Anything you ask."

Do not beg this of Me. It is not necessary. My will is not to be thwarted. You must not tell the famished crows what you saw, for to do so would interrupt my designs. I will brook no interruption.

"I swear, you let me go and get out of my baby and I won't say anything. I swear it to Jesus."

No, you will not speak of what you have seen. You will speak no more of the policeman. You need not swear an oath, for you will die and become meat to match this delicacy, this tidbit that sprang from your loins.

"No!"

I have not the strength to do more than animate your little deadling for a few moments, and crush the hand you placed in its grip. I have used too much power already. There are Laws, after all. Even for Me. I can take within limits, but I have much latitude concerning punishment. Even where and when I am restricted, I find the means to sneak around obstacles. The consequences of doing that, however, are not your concern. They are Mine. Comfort yourself with that final thought.

"Please! Somebody help me …"

I will help you, Woman, but I can do no more at this time than tell you that your heart is weak from grief and from too much unhealthy eating. If enough pain is applied, you will kill yourself. I remain blameless. My thanks are yours. Give my regards to your God, if ever you are able to rouse Him.

"No!"

In a wrenching blast, Patrice's fingers were pulverized in her hand. The agony, white-hot, then red, then fierce as a star swift exploding, waxed until her heart was wracked with spasms. She gasped twice and then sprawled on the floor, breathless, alongside the body of her boy in the bed.

In the boy's grasp, a sad gift of the sea remained, an offering from that bitter heart of an ocean that always and ever lifts foul things to the surface on currents unable to forget, to forgive. Like the stems of scythe-shorn flowers, the corpse now clutched the pale and bloody bouquet of its mother's fingers.

WAYWARD, STILL FLEEING

Brask left for Big Sur at dawn. He hadn't been able to sleep much after the disastrous encounter with Emily. What little slumber he managed in the extended-stay hotel room was fraught with despairing dreams of Jess. His sister knew about the divorce, but nothing about the death of his ex-wife, about the ravenous cancer that had taken her by surprise only months after the papers were signed. Jess had left Brask, left town, and left no affection for his holy-rolling sister in her wake.

Now, Emily would never know what they had gone through. She'd never know how Brask had rushed to Jess's side to care for her, even after the hell of the divorce, in the final two weeks of her life. She had been alone in the world, poor Jess; no surviving family, a few preoccupied, diffident friends kept in the dark about her plight. And Brask, the amicably removed. Private, independent, stubborn Jess. But she had told him. Had reached out. Love remained, some shredded red ribbon of it. Hospice bedside tears and a doomed reunion awash with forgiveness had been Jess's last gift, but it had not been a gift powerful enough to prevent Brask's subsequent plunge into oblivion.

The crash of the housing and financial markets did not pause to mourn the loss of a vibrant, freckled angel whose summer-spun hair surrendered to the poison of chemo, whose supple body, sweet-skinned and without blemish, withered into that of a wraith, harrowed by insatiable forces of agony.

The implosion of an economy did not hesitate to consider the plight of a man wracked by loss of both love and livelihood, scarred beyond recognition to the last radiant sanctuary of spirit, where the lamps of all hope snuffed-out, one by one, until every joy was extinguished, too, and terror—fanged and bone-crushing—arrived to hold sway. Earth dimmed, every corner, every moment. Faith and features made shameful retreat, withdrawing into clouds of iron, boiling black. How had he remained upright, alone in the center of circles expanding as life took leave of him, emptying the spaces between exile and welcome? Dissolving, laying bare the pitfalls, each deeper than the one before, and all famished, desperate as nightmares refusing to relinquish a captive.

Yes, Jess had loved him, always loved him. Before she had even met him. Her last words revealed that much, the only frail blossom he could carry onward in the surrounding realm of arid destruction, amid sands so endless and at war with the hidden foundations of the world, each grain spinning away in little gusts that eroded his will to exist, clearing a path, beckoning him to Seek Death.

She loves you. She has loved you for Time, Times, and Half a Time. But she is lost and can love no longer.

By 8:30, the sun feigned wan interest in the world and Brask pulled off Highway 101 South to grab some coffee and a sandwich. There had been no desire to eat after missing last night's meal in favor of Emily's ambush. His stomach yowled, an agitated cat trapped beneath his flannel shirt. He had to get his bearings, mentally. He had been told to call Horace, the property manager for the village of Wistwood, to confirm last-minute directions. Shore things up for their appointment. 9AM sharp.

As he fumbled for the phone in the pocket of his hoodie, fingers covered with egg and sausage grease, Brask glanced at the copy of the online ad he had printed out, atop a jumble of papers spread across the passenger seat.

**FOR LEASE: 1 BDRM, 1B, recently renovated cabin
on 4 wooded acres near Big Sur.
Unincorporated hamlet of WISTWOOD.
Fully furnished. Washer/Dryer.
No couples. No pets.**

Cable/Internet & Satellite hook-up.
All utilities included. Small mountain community.
$1000.00 per month. First and last.
Very private.
Call Horace Slater at 899.778.9998
References not required.

Brask had to laugh, rereading the bit about references not being required, but it was an ironic laugh. If only such a thing were true, in his case, and not an obvious fuck-up on the part of this Horace Slater person or whoever had transcribed the ad onto the online classifieds site while idly picking his ass-crack. Yeah, funny. *Real* funny.

Nobody in his or her right mind, particularly a landlord in the godforsaken age of chaotic cultural entitlement and moribund personal responsibility, would intentionally put "References not required" within the body of a classified rental ad. Every freak, loser, perv, criminal and garden-variety cretin from Eureka to San Diego would be inquiring—and were probably already lined-up for show-ings—based upon a dangling carrot like "References not required." Brask hoped more candidates had actually remembered to ask about that part of the ad during initial inquiry calls, because he sure as shit failed to bring it up when he spoke with Horace Slater to set up the appointment a week before. It would nice if the potential herd of ne'erdowells was thinned a little by the time he got a gander at the cabin. Wistwood. Where the hell was that, anyhow? Didn't even show up on Google Maps or any search.

And what were his chances, honestly? Slim to fucking none.

Brask was stunned to even score a look at the cabin, much less the sched-uled tour offered by this Horace. Then again, maybe the opportunity wasn't so far-fetched. As things turned out, a careful cross-search of classified ads on Google, in the regional Craigslist, and throughout the online Monterey County Herald yielded zilch. Even the Big Sur Bulletin turned up no additional sign of the Wistwood ad. Brask couldn't imagine that the thing had been published exclusively in the Palo Alto Craigslist classifieds, where he had found it, for a readership living four hours to the north. Not unless the property had been listed by someone who lived in Palo Alto and happened to own a rental all the way down in Big Sur. That was always possible. He knew quite a few people inland who kept places down the coast. But why not trawl around for bites in local waters?

Still, he had a firm appointment and was not about to let a chance like this, however remote, slip away. A thousand bucks a month for anything in California was insane. Probably a complete joke, but since Horace had sounded sane on the phone and Brask was going to move south no matter what, the drive would give him something to do, a chance to look around at other possible spots. Besides, he had loved the Big Sur region since boyhood.

Like most Californians, Brask was aware that folks tended to do things a bit differently in Big Sur. Life was lived with an almost gilded edge of eccentricity in the remote little communities that dotted the panoramic Pacific Coast Highway. *But a thousand dollars a month and no references required?* Who the hell knew why people came up with any of the improbable shit they came up with anymore? That was another of his existential pet peeves. Humans and their flailing inconsistencies. The cabin rental was probably a run-down, raccoon-infested dump that would be offered to some fool ten times more qualified than he, and he would turn around in a fit and drive the wasted hours back to Palo, a grease-stained ad crumpled in his shirt pocket and desperation oozing from his pores like a poisonous sweat.

Damn, but he needed the place, even if it *was* a rundown, raccoon-infested dump! He needed it more than anyone else on earth. He deserved it.

Whether the part about the references was a typo or whether it reflected some Big Sur denizen's rejection of the need for personal references the same way so many other trappings of conventional life were jettisoned in the search for quirky individualism, the ad had screamed out to him. This cabin would be more than an ideal environment for writing the next book; it would save his ass.

Taking a small bite of the convenience store breakfast sandwich with one hand, he entered the number on his cell with the other. The call was answered even before it had a chance to ring.

"Good morning."

"Hey, er … is this Mr. Horace Slater?" Brask nearly choked on his mouthful, chewing fast and swallowing with a gulp.

"It is."

"Oh, hello. Brask Adams, here, Mr. Slater. We spoke on the phone late last week. About the cabin in Wistwood, and my appointment? You asked me to call you today to confirm? Double-check directions? I'm already on the road. About an hour outside of Palo Alto. The place is still available, I hope?"

The man on the other end, Horace, had not the slightest interest in Brask's background the first time they had talked; there had been none of the usual "What do you do?" and "Where do you live now?" chit-chat typical when making an appointment to show property to a prospective tenant. Now he seemed much more business-like.

"Ah, Mr. Adams. I'm glad you called so punctually. Yes, the cabin is still available and your appointment stands. No decisions have yet been made, of course. First and last month's rent are requested," he added. "Was that in the original advertisement? I don't believe I recall. At all events, two thousand dollars in total."

Brask thought he might shit his pants.

The thousand-dollar rent was unbelievable enough, but a mere two thousand dollar deposit in total was akin to highway robbery for almost any area in California, much less Big Sur, even if the place was made out of cardboard, held together by duct tape, and propped against a rusty pole in a field strewn with glass.

Brask's scalp began to sweat again, in a good way. He made a conscious effort to camouflage the excitement and eagerness creeping into his voice. In his experience, over-exuberance rang every alarm bell in an elderly person's brain, and he could tell over the phone that Horace was possibly very old. Only yapping lap-dogs could get away with barking neediness in the eyes of the elderly. Never humans. It was one of God's countless botched attempts at wry humor, he always figured.

"The full deposit will be no problem, Mr. Slater. I gotta say, though, I still find it hard to believe that the rent is so low to begin with. Makes we wonder if there's some liability with the place. Something that might not be worth my time and an eight-hour round-trip drive to explore. No offense intended."

"None taken, Mr. Adams. And call me Horace. Everyone around here does. You know, the rent really is a steal, given how exceptional the place is. Especially when it comes to rentals in these parts. I'm well aware of that. Of course, if you didn't have two thousand cash for first and last," he continued, sounding almost shy, "well, I suppose other arrangements could be made according to individual circumstances. It's not like we haven't worked with people before when it comes to that. As soon as you find your way down here today, we'll have ourselves a good look and a nice talk."

Brask was dumbfounded. "Cash is no problem. I've got it. Aren't you even going to ask me what I do for a living and why I want to move all the way down to that neck of the woods? Anything?"

Stop talking, idiot! Don't fuck this up!

"Sure. Sure, we want to know all of that." The sudden chuckle in Horace's throat was raspy but pleasant; comforting in the way that butter is when being spread across slightly burnt toast. "But that sort of thing's best left for face-to-face meetings. Don't you think?"

"Yeah, I agree, but it's quite a drive for me and I don't know what sort of inconvenience I might be putting you to, or possibly putting myself to, so I don't want to waste anybody's time, here, if you catch my meaning."

"But you're already on the road, Mr. Adams. You said so yourself. Besides, do you think you're such an unsuitable prospect that any meeting between the two of us would amount to a waste of time?"

There was something so round and cheerful beneath the bluntness, some languid tone of nonchalance. Maybe even imperturbability ...

"No! I mean—Yes! Er ... No. What I mean to say, for crying out loud, is that I'd make an outstanding tenant, and from the ad and from what you've told me already, the place sounds pretty cut and dry. Absolutely perfect for me right now. See, I've always had a soft spot for Big Sur, and these days my work allows me to live anywhere I wish because I've just been—"

"Well, good. Good, Mr. Adams. We can meet here in Wistwood and you can tell me all about your side of things this afternoon. Around three, like we planned before, if that's still going to work for you?"

Brask looked at the clock on the dashboard. His mind spun. "Yeah. I can totally make it there by three."

"Superb."

"So, Horace, if you don't mind my asking, could you tell me a little bit more about yourself? How long you've owned the property. Why you're renting. That sort of thing."

"Oh, I don't own the cabin, Mr. Adams, or the property on which it sits. I'm just an overseer. A hired hand, if you like. But I've been with my present employer for a real long time, I can tell you that much. And I'll be more than happy to answer any of your questions about the landlord once you get down here to see us. You have a pen handy?"

"What?"

"A pen, Mr. Adams. I want to give you those directions I mentioned. I don't guess you'd find our little community easily if you didn't have directions. Specific ones. Some folks—tourists, mostly—have been known to complain about those whatcha-muh-callems. GPS systems or whatever. You know what I mean? Those contraptions go in and out on drivers from time to time. But that's the nature of nature, around here. A coast like this one, with these cliffs and valleys and canyons? Heh. Place like this doesn't like a lot of man-made gadgets and gizmos thinking they can pry too deep into the heart of such mighty old country. Especially from some hunk of junk with an eyeball floating up there in space. That's part of what makes Big Sur and scrappy little towns like Wistwood special to the folks in these parts. It's got a sense of its own privacy, but I expect you know that. Big Sur is still big enough to make mankind and all his nifty inventions feel small. And I don't know as that's such a bad thing, these days."

"I'm with you on that one, Horace," said Brask, elated. They were hitting it off, he felt. He hoped. "It's one of the reasons I've loved Big Sur since I was a kid, as I said. One of the reasons I want to live around there now." He rummaged for a pen amid the mess on the passenger seat. "And for God's sake, call me Brask. Please. Okay, got the pen. Go ahead and fire-off those directions."

He wrote them down in a frantic scrawl across a scrap of paper held against the dashboard. He paused only when Horace mentioned a marbled stone archway and towering bronze lantern by the side of the mountain road that led into Wistwood.

"Would you repeat that, Horace?"

"It's really only half an archway, Brask. Ruined. Covered in moss and ivy, mostly. The lantern will be shining bright, though, especially if the day turns out foggy, as expected."

"Okay. Got it."

"You sure?"

"You bet. All set. I'll be back on the highway in a few minutes and down there by three."

"Sounds fine. Now keep those directions handy once you head into Big Sur itself. The little roads and shortcuts I mentioned will get you to us, but don't be impatient. Wistwood tends to hide on folks who don't know the lay of the land firsthand. Hell, it sometimes even hides on the folks who claim to know the roads like the backs of their own hands. See you at three."

Brask was thrilled. The interview, as brief as it was, had been far more encouraging than expected, given his general distaste for phone conversation and the reeling helplessness he experienced when discussing even trivial matters with someone he could neither see nor influence with any of his usual manipulative personal skills. Before the crash, he had become adept over the years at bending various arms of social media towards his purposes. But never had he been able or even interested in conquering the chasm of detachment needed to be truly effective over the phone.

It has to be a guy thing, he muttered in his mind, reassuring an irritated ego. *Guys aren't genetically disposed to get anything worthwhile accomplished over the goddamn phone. You can't argue with genetics.*

In truth, it bothered Brask to be reminded that he didn't shine at everything. Made him worry. Made him ruminate about not being perfect, sometimes for hours, on a particularly bad day. Sometimes he thought worrying about inconsequential things would drive him mad. Then again, a total surrender to madness—willful or not—might feel like a form of abject liberation. A complete divorce from the ceaseless work required to maintain a rational mind. It was tough, the daily grind of staying sane and wondering where the energy might possibly come to do it again the next day, and the day after. The burden felt heavier with each passing year, pressing his shoulders to the indifferent earth, surrounded by a society that seemed to revel in shedding its rational responsibilities at every turn. So many seemed eager to abandon the battle. The glacial maddening of society horrified and attracted him in almost equal measure. It loomed as a wall of shadow and oncoming certainty, high as the heavens, smothering all light.

Why not rush toward the advancing monolith and embrace such a promise? He had been tempted. Perhaps mercy could be found therein. More than what the world and its vulgar religious fantasies of Paradise ever dreamed of offering. Streets of gold. Many mansions. Walled estates.

Big fucking deal. We already have that shit in Silicon Valley. Or Malibu. Or Disneyland.

But, no. No madness. Not ever. There was always the chance that madness might be the most tortuous and inescapable Hell of all, beyond any wretched mental agony he had imagined thus far in his life, and to imagine it is to feel it. Luckily, he had more consequential worries than being a stilted phone conversationalist to keep him sane, these days. But it was there, in the back of his mind, the quicksilver ring waiting to open the escape hatch. What a strange and seductive comfort the whole weird possibility had come to be.

Brask started the van and wound his way carefully out of the convenience store's parking lot and back toward the 101 South exit. He was relieved to discover a palpable feeling in his gut, a thickening oval warmth of confidence about his prospects. For good and nervous measure he reread and mumbled the set of directions captured in his near-hieroglyphic scrawl. They would meet at three on Main Street, which was the only actual street, said Horace, that existed in downtown Wistwood.

Main Street. At three.

A major book being published? A town of his own? A new start after everything that had nearly jackhammered him into annihilation?

He merged onto the highway and felt three years of disappointment melt away through the floorboards and onto the asphalt beneath. It mattered little that he had no cabin keys in his hand, yet.

This was a chance. A big one. Brask was going to get what he wanted. There could be no other outcome.

LET THE BRANCHES BEHOLD

The security guard had been taken in the dark by force behind the shopping center. But he had not been not killed. That would come later. Fear slid an icy razor across spine and spirit as his abductor, the initially friendly cop with the flat-top haircut, spoke to him from the front seat of the speeding patrol car.

"I know who you are, filth. I know your name and everything about you, cause I've been watching. Watching in the dark when you slept and in the light when you walked. I've studied your face and your mouth and the sound of your voice and, one day soon, I'm gonna study what's inside you, deep in the warm. Deep in the hidden places. I'm gonna put my hands into the wet, see? Move my fingers around until steam curls up on the cold air when you're wide open. But don't be afraid. We gonna become good friends, first, you and me. During the ride. Maybe even after. Cause I been watching you, and you're gonna watch me, and you're even gonna love me. Yeah, even until the day I open you up to see what might be seen."

The guard's hands were bound with duct tape, behind his back, with a slashed square of the same tape across his mouth, tasting of tears and snot and of the gummy chemicals designed to seal things, to silence what might otherwise scream. His lips were pinched and stung, perhaps from blood that still oozed from the first punch his abductor landed once capture was complete. Now, wedged and hidden from sight on the floor between the front and back seats of the car, the doomed man felt the urge to vomit but dared not. He fought it because it was the only thing he could truly fight at the moment, a preternatural instinct hissing within his skull. All the more terrifying, words of caution floated suddenly to him over the front seat.

"You'd best breathe easy and calm yourself down back there, trash. If not, you're gonna drown in your own puke. That's the truth, now. You're gonna die, stuffed down there in the back seat, and if anybody is ever unlucky enough to find you, they're gonna find your lungs filled with your own puke. Overflowing with it. And you're gonna smell. You're gonna smell of puke and of pain. But if you hold on just a little while more—if you exercise *patience*—when I get done with you, you're gonna smell of the earth."

The sound of the patrol car's growling engine reverberated in the guard's ears as they suddenly sped—how was it possible?—through something like the thick of a forest. Amid waves of his own acrid sweat he could see the creeping fingers of tree limbs, green with moss, and hear leaves squeak and scratch and bash the windshield, a grasping, waving mob. If only. A mob would be helpful.

Let him go! Stop, Wicked One! Stop where you are and release him! Beware the forest, BEWARE THE FOREST, for we are the trees and we can stop you!

But all was chaos, all was ruin; the snapping and screeching of the trees played a fanfare to mark the beginning of an End, the demolition of a galaxy.

The patrol car bucked and rocked. It groaned, half flying above some unseen woodland path, half plowing into terrain that would not yield with ease. Stones spun upward like bullets into the metal frame. Dirt sizzled and sprayed away from the tires. The engine roared loud enough to deafen the world. Yet, for all of that, the final jolting stop of the car remained the most violent ghost of the guard's nightmare, resonating as it did upon the brink of unquestionable death beneath an electric hum of panic.

He would not look again into the eyes of his captor. Never again, though his very heart might be culled, still beating, from his chest. He did not need to see those eyes, for they were emblazoned upon his soul. How frozen were those two ashen marbles in yellowing, runny pools, staring down at him during that first moment of attack, holding sway above him during the cruel beating, eager to gloat in rheumy triumph at their prize, the captive.

When his captor exited the front seat and slammed the door, the guard began to cry, jammed as he was against the floor, tears mingling with sweat to form an ocean of despair that surged across his face, soothing waves coursing, white-capped and gentle, to destinations of unknowable night. But he made sure to weep in silence. Outside, limbs and leaves continued to whip and snap and protest. A great wind was at work. He could hear the trees trying, could sense their indignation, and took some insane comfort in the realization that they wanted so much to help.

The door near his head swung open. The officer who had taken him was huge, barrel-like below the shoulders and now hunched forward. It was early morning, maybe an hour past dawn. The guard caught a glimpse of the shiny badge and the uniform of navy blue, fuzzy arms protruding from the sleeves, knobbed and calloused at the elbows. The hands were coming for him, red with eczema and swollen from unwholesome work.

The cop smelled of dried sweat and sin, and the scent of this stink in the guard's nostrils threatened another upheaval from his gut. Perhaps that would be the better death. But how? How could it be while there was the smallest chance to fight back if the moment presented itself? He went rigid with terror, pinned in the narrow stretch of back-seat floor space, body aching and partially covered with a stained blanket, his mind thinking, thinking, thinking of the grey eyes, the eyes that first beheld him with such kindness before blazing with the gleam of murder. The grotesque, turnip-like fists began to drag him from the car. He could not bear the thought of being touched by such hands, but this was only the beginning. The end, utterly. He unleashed a great wail, muffled by the tape. It sounded so pathetic, so infinitesimal.

"You'll feel better, filth, when we've made it to slaughter and I can treat you as a good friend ought to."

The words, the voice, a rasp as harsh as the collision of worlds, made the flesh on the guard's backward-twisted arms erupt in thousands of stinging pinpoints. In a moment he was out and on the ground, eyes still squeezed shut, the ocean of sweat on his face dripping onto the earth, into its depths, where everything returned, eventually. Always and forever.

"By now you're probably wondering why it was so easy for me to take you," said the cop. "Anyone else would've had trouble. You're usually quick and wary. Always looking about, always interested in what happens at the edges of things, in the shadows of the world, off to the side, where no one else bothers to look. That's your job, ain't it, security guard? You're supposed to imagine things that are gonna happen before they even happen. But you didn't imagine me, trash. No you did not."

The guard began to whimper. The trees all around them thrashed in a swift gust.

"You didn't look with your stupid eyes to the outskirts of the East and see me there, waiting and watching. Something's been on your mind these last few months, and I know what it is. But we'll talk about it, you and I, when we get to the slaughter and I can take my time. Time to take care of your worries as a loving friend should. And you'll tell me how pleased you are to become *mine.* They all tell me that, eventually. The ones I keep long enough. But I understand you can't speak at the moment. And this forest is trouble. Even I can sense that. It's uncooperative. On *your* side, this forest. I'd burn the whole fucking thing down, if I could, but that'd be more problem than I need right now. And I have other ways to handle these woods."

The guard was hauled across the rough ground by his soaked shirt collar. The sudden stillness in the air was a guttural shock. The guard turned his head and opened his eyes at last, seeing the heels of the cop's shiny leather boots as they dug into the dirt and dragged him toward what looked like the steps of a cabin. One. Two. One. Two. The cop was grunting with effort. The guard was a big man, too. Hard work. The forest waited. The guard took in as much as he could and felt faint. His head lolled. Before he slipped into unconsciousness, he heard a thought--a thought that seemed to be thought by someone else, someone far away. A shimmering, indistinct figure, waving and calling out, barely audible, across a vast plain of scorched wasteland.

We are the trees of the orchard and we have seen this before! We have seen it! We would help if we could get near. But we cannot. Behold and see that all the world is afire. We are all afraid.

We are all afraid.

The cop dropped his prey and stomped in his leather boots onto a creaking porch. An unlocked door was thrown open. He began to whistle a tune. The guard at the bottom of the rickety steps descended into Disappearance. It was like sliding into the warmest caress of bathwater, until suddenly it was just like nothing, like nothing at all.

ONE SPARK OF FLESH
AND FANCY

I t was just after two o'clock when Brask crossed the Bixby Bridge into Big Sur, piercing through thick, drifting columns of afternoon fog. For the next six miles, the entire world was alternately blind or breathtaking, disoriented by excluding cloud or explosive with sudden, overwhelming radiance and color. The van emerged from these intermittent panels, a ghostly and rotund great white shark, gliding with absent but deceptive interest out of murky shallows and then sweeping into sunlit vistas, aiming for a kill in open water.

He kept looking from the weave of road to the hen-scratch on his sheet of paper. The Almighty Directions to Wistwood. The loose-leaf page was still atop the dashboard, stained along its edges, words smeared into illegibility by the morning's breakfast grease. He had been touching the directions over and over, as if obsessive physical contact would help him discern whether or not he was really going the right way. Whether or not he was still on the same planet. He hadn't driven this far in a long time. Hadn't been able to afford it. The whole endeavor was akin to a rebirth, but one that made the pit of his stomach feel hollow and exposed to icy, unfamiliar air. There was no GPS system. That had been sold along with his pick-up truck and precious cache of tools, his lifeblood, a year ago, when he first switched to the beat-up Pontiac that would become his temporary home.

You're almost there, man. Stop with the OCD bullshit. No stress. You promised yourself. You're back in the game!

Nine miles onward, the bars on his cellphone disappeared entirely in the vacuum of Big Sur's majestic isolation. Like everything else he had managed to hold onto, the phone was old and worse for wear. Childhood memories of Big Sur and its grandeur were not helping in the least, not with the pressure of an appointment to keep. More anxious than ever due to the time, Brask pulled into the parking lot of Splendor Gas & Cabins, a ramshackle concern nestled among a stand of redwoods that appeared to be exhaling wisps of mist from their towering treetops, an audience of casual but stately smokers paused to gaze outward at the beauty of the Pacific. There was a dilapidated sign in front of the place.

45 Miles Until The Next Gas Station

Brask wasn't going that far south, but decided to fill his tank and ask for some extra, locally colored directions. He had no desire to go in circles for an hour along the soaring highlands, looking for Wistwood while someone more punctual slipped in to take the cabin. Once out of the van, he grunted in disgust at the price of gas pasted above the three forlorn-looking pumps. He wasn't alone in umbrage; a rental RV parked in front of him spilled French tourists like clowns from a circus car and these travelers were busy puzzling over exchange rates and mumbling various curses of their own. There were a few other cars in the pull-off lot. Brask noticed license plates from Tennessee and Oregon among a handful of California plates.

He was going to have to get used to paying steep gas prices if he wanted to live here. That was the inconvenient cost—one of them—of dwelling in a genuine paradise, of becoming a citizen of the hip, unhurried outskirts and joining the tribe of those sequestered in a rustic but artful world just slightly off the grid.

Big Sur people. Brask had known several over the years. They were humble types, generally, but to the last he found them also smugly disdainful of the pampered populations reveling in the luxuries of Carmel to the north or San Luis Obispo to the south. Still, Brask found room to admire this postmodern breed of pioneer; many were people who would live in tree-houses, if they could—and some actually did—but they also wouldn't dream of being parted from their iPads, iPhones, and gourmet organic gastronomic supplies.

Now that he had the hefty book advance and another lined-up for next year, Brask could picture himself becoming one of those occasional hermit types, with racks full of exceptional wines, ready to entertain gatherings of people who felt as superior living in a state of chic self-exile as everyone else. For some, he knew, living in or around Big Sur meant having a sturdy sense of privilege and vision, a more refined taste for the elite trappings of cultured existence without having to admit to any overt, observable attachment to the world. It was a neat trick, and something of a wily ruse, for those inclined to be in obsessive control of defining themselves, planted with pride on the periphery of society. In California, that particular image, born of affectation or forever giving birth to it, commanded an aura of respect and romantic heroism not easily conjured in other, less effortlessly bohemian regions.

On the edge. Seen yet unseen. Misunderstood by the determined and stampeding herds. Were a mirror held up to such a life, any twist of light or shade might cast forth a reflection of homelessness in all its horror, a swift but searing vision tendered by agents of mischief and deceit. Brask knew too well the truth that dwelled unchanging beneath shifting reflections, one reality but a breath removed from another illusion, each disposed to exchange places in the pass of a shadow. He wanted no part of any looking-glass. Not now. Not ever. One's own eyes upon the world were enough.

He filled his lungs with the clean, bracing ocean air and stretched toward the sky until his back made a satisfying crack. Before filling the tank he slipped inside the adjacent store to pay cash in advance. Credit cards were long gone, too.

Not for long. Not for long. You're back in the game, man!

The shop was tiny, smelled of dust and burned coffee, and staffed by a woman of perhaps nineteen or twenty. Maybe twenty-one. She was shivering a little behind a countertop register, the tips of her fingers stuck in the depths of a wool sweater as thick and as gray as the fog lurking in forest depths outside.

"You wouldn't know it was early September, the way this stuff rolls in off the coast. At least not in this part of California," Brask remarked, extracting a Diet Coke from the beverage cooler and offering a polite smile.

"I'll say." The young woman behind the counter returned the smile, fleeting, perfunctory, and pretended to look for something in the chaos of shelves below.

Brask scrutinized a display stand filled with various road maps and one huge, moldering Rand McNally Atlas that looked as if it would never find a home beyond the dreary confines of the little station and cabin rental office.

"I suppose you don't sell a lot of these printed maps, anymore, what with everybody using GPS. Surprised you have any at all. Kind of nice to see, actually."

"I dunno. Sold two or three California maps to a couple of elderly people," said the young woman, still fiddling with shelves and unseen papers. Then she paused to think for a moment and made a strange little grimace with one side of her mouth. "And when I say 'elderly people,' I'm talking people who're really old, you know? The kind old enough to be completely terrified of using anything in their vehicles except maybe the radios and the air conditioners."

"You forgot windshield wipers and turn signals," said Brask, leaning his head slightly to the side and giving her a good look at the stubble sprouting beneath his smile and across the deep cleft of his chin. Employed artfully, at just the right moment and with the proper, half-lidded glimmer of his gray eyes, the move had always served him well. But the young woman wasn't impressed.

"Windshield wipers, maybe," she shrugged. "But I'm not so sure about turn signals. Nobody ever seems to use those, at least around here. Turn signals are the things that local people and tourists fear most in the whole universe."

Brask chuckled. Even a little laugh felt salvific, as if oppressive but hitherto unseen mountains were suddenly hurrying to get out of his way before arrival. But he still didn't quite know where he was going. Not yet. He placed his drink on the counter, along with a small map of Big Sur, and opened his wallet to fish for some bills.

"You speak the truth about turn signals," he admitted. "And I shouldn't make fun of anybody because I don't use 'em all the time, either."

"I always use them, just to be counter-culture. You know?" She smiled sincerely this time, cheeks lightly freckled but creamy beneath doe eyes that flashed winsome shyness and good humor. "I take it that's your van out there by the pump?"

Brask tried not to flush with embarrassment, but was only half-successful.

"I belong to the van, is more like it. It's a long, tragic tale of codependency. Gruesome stuff. Appropriate for a windowless white van. By the way, I'll need forty bucks worth of gas, too, please."

He unleashed the full radiance of his charm, now. This young lady wasn't necessarily too young; he could already tell she liked him, at least at first glance, and fresh-faced woodsy types—especially ones with cascades of naturally wavy hair, aglow with health and little fuss—had always been his weakness, more or less. He was nevertheless surprised to suddenly picture himself, while paying for gas, drink, and map, going on a date with this girl. Was it beyond the realm of possibility? Not if he was going to become a local fixture. In one frenetic vision he saw the two of them flirting over a couple of beers at a picnic table by the River Inn he had passed a few miles back. He next imagined, more briefly and in grasping shadows, a breathless fumble as clothes fell to the floor of the cabin he had not yet seen, much less secured, as his new home.

Definitely. Divorced at twenty-four. Homeless at twenty-seven. Maybe possibly hopefully moving into a one-bedroom cabin at twenty-eight. She'll love to hear about all of that over beer. Think of the laughs. But, you really are *back in the game …*

"You passing through?" Her words seemed more a statement of fact than a question.

"Well, yes and no. And thanks, but I don't need a bag. I can carry this stuff. I'm in town to …" He looked around doubtfully; there was no town in Big Sur, not in the traditional sense. "I'm here to see about renting a place up past Crystal Creek Road."

"No kidding." The young woman had produced a brown paper bag, anyway, from one of the decrepit shelves. She reached for the map and the Diet Coke. "Wait. Sorry. You said you don't want a bag."

"That's right."

"I'm so conditioned. A total automaton. Can things get any worse?"

"Wow," said Brask. "You sound jaded. I like jaded."

"Full disclosure—I haven't even been working here a week. Still getting the hang of it, I guess. Not that there's much 'hang' that needs to be gotten. Unless it's hanging around bored out of my mind. Most people pay outside at the pump with credit cards and don't even bother to come in, especially when they read the sign in the window that says we don't sell cigarettes. It gets lonely."

"Is that so?"

"Yep. But that's the fate of someone brand new on the job. Can't you tell? I'm not even experienced enough to properly handle a paper bag refusal! I'm hoping and praying every night that the necessary skills will come to me with intense practice, though."

"I don't know if prayer will work for you," said Brask with his first full laugh in many days. "I have a sister who considers that to be her area of expertise, and you wouldn't want her around telling you how to run your show. Trust me. Anyhow, I have no doubt you'll not only acquire but master the art of accurately discerning the packaging needs of every conceivable type of client."

Brask drawled in his most humble, dashing cadence, low and soft around the edges, but with just enough sex in the middle to keep even the most glib comment on the praiseworthy side.

"And while it's true that I do not require a bag today," he continued, "I could definitely use some directions, if it isn't much trouble. My memory of Big Sur is pretty faint and the directions I wrote this morning when I left Palo Alto are covered in sausage-muffin grease. I can't have this fine new map of Big Sur—accurate and up-to-the-minute as I'm sure it is—spread across my dashboard as I maneuver the switchbacks and hairpin turns around here. I'll go over a cliff."

"I wouldn't advise taking your eyes off the road," agreed the cashier. She blinked languidly at him. "Enough locals have plunged hundreds of feet over the cliffs, or so I hear. Big Sur has a reputation for it and we wouldn't want you to add to that rep. You seem way too good with words to end-up as a gruesome Pacific Coast Highway stat. Let's leave that to the tourists. Especially the ones from France."

"Whoah! Here only a week and trouble with the French already?" Brask nodded toward the gathering of tourists, still squabbling around their RV outside.

"Let's just say that the ones who met me probably won't be going home with a deeper appreciation for American hospitality."

She punched a series of buttons that made deep plunking sounds on a register that looked as if it had been squatting, grimy and belligerent, atop the counter when Brask's parents were children. A series of white-flagged numbers snapped to attention at the top of the cumbersome thing.

"That'll be fifty-seven seventy-five for gas, the Diet Coke, and the map. Directions are free, if I'm able to give you any at all."

"Much obliged, Miss …?"

Brask willed into existence his bedroomiest eyes, strongest brow, and squarest jaw as he handed her a Ben Franklin. She still wasn't biting.

"Where is it, exactly, that you want to go?"

She handed him his change and proffered her own lidded look, rife with a coy unwillingness to dance in the exchange-of-names direction, if any directions were to be given or taken. She wouldn't rule anything out; Brask could sense that much. But not yet. "You said something about Crystal Creek Road?"

Brask shoved the bills and a quarter into a back pocket of his jeans. "Yeah. But the town I'm looking for is actually off of Crystal Creek Road. It's Wistwood. I've gotta meet a property manager at three."

He glanced at the plain little office clock ticking rigid aluminum hands on the wall in front of him. He still had forty minutes. That was lucky. "The guy himself gave me directions but every little side road I've seen looks like a bike path. And most of the signs are too small to see. Plus I'm hopeless."

The cashier frowned, confused.

"A town off of Crystal Creek Road?"

"Yeah, Wistwood. I'm supposed to take Crystal Creek Road and then go all the way up the hill until I see some kinda big brick archway at the edge of the redwoods. And a lantern post. This fella, Horace somebody, said it was about a mile and a half up Crystal Creek."

Brask searched the girl's eyes for understanding and couldn't help but feel a stir beneath his belt when she ran a hand, casual and full, through her luxurious tangle of hair.

"Westwood?"

"*Wist*wood."

"Off Crystal Creek Road. A town."

"Yeah. Haven't you heard of it?"

"Sorry. No bells ringing for me on that one. A huge brick archway near the redwoods?"

"Hey, I thought that sounded like a strange entry for some little podunk in Big Sur, but this old guy—Horace—said I just had to follow that road to reach Wistwood. He said the town itself is a half-mile inland, among the hills. Have I been hoodwinked or something? The rental ad did strike me from the start as almost too good to be true. Damn it all, if this has been a goose-chase."

"I don't know about any of that. And I think the most important point is that I'm probably not the best person to ask in the first place. I just moved here from Santa Rosa a few months ago. Seems I would've heard about this Wistwood. A town off Crystal Creek? I mean, I know my way around the coast, around the highway, but nobody's ever mentioned the place, at least not south of Bixby Bridge."

"Then I could've just missed seeing it or written the directions down incorrectly," Brask fretted.

The cashier shrugged and gave him a little smirk while coiling and uncoiling a lock of shiny hair around an index finger.

"Maybe. Or maybe not. I mean, there's lots of little neighborhoods and ridges and canyons and clumped communities along the coastline, but I haven't heard of that one, until now."

"You know, I Googled Wistwood before I left Palo and got nothing," lamented Brask. "But my guy Horace did say it's a real small, unincorporated hamlet, or some such."

"Don't know what to tell you, man. Sorry. I can point you to Crystal Creek Road easy enough. It's only a couple of miles south."

"Well, that's perfect, then. I mean, I know Big Sur isn't the most conventional place on earth. I guess that applies to the way the communities around here are laid out, too. Sorry if I seem like I'm freaking out over being lost. Just had a rough day. Rough week. Rough month. Rough year, to be honest. I don't feel like being late for this appointment."

Brask's embarrassed smile, the frank innocence and freely surrendered helplessness of it, drew an understanding glance in return.

"Don't worry about it. I know all about guys and their phobia when it comes to asking for directions. Like I said, I've only been working here a week, but it's the wives that come in every day asking the easiest way to Hearst Castle, or where to catch 101, or where, exactly, to find 'Neppenty' restaurant, or 'Michelle Pfieffer State Beach.' Pretty funny, sometimes."

"Well, I don't have a wife, so I guess you're my only hope of not blowing this rental interview by showing up late or not at all."

Brask's new friend shook her head and brushed another rebellious tuft of bright curling hair behind an ear as pale and dainty as the handle of a china teacup.

"About two miles south on the left. Crystal Creek Road. Goes straight up-hill. You can't miss it. Sign's clear as day, too. If there's no fog."

Brask bowed his tousled, sandy-haired head with as much chivalrous gratitude as he could summon and lifted his Diet Coke can to toast the pleasant interlude.

"Thanks a million. My name's Brask, by the way. We might end up being neighbors. Or I could end up being a regular here, or something."

"That's good. I'm Kara. Here Monday through Friday until seven every night. Good luck with your rental."

"Thanks, Kara. See you soon, maybe. And don't hold that white creeper van against me. It's only a temporary ride."

"For temporary body disposal?"

They both laughed.

"That's ... pretty smart-assed, Kara. I like it."

"Have a good one, Brask. And welcome to town, if you can find your town."

Brask strolled outside to fill the gas tank, smiling through a new and dense curtain of chilly mist, map under his arm, Diet Coke in hand. He had another swift vision, then. One vivid with imagery fueled by a sudden, snaking heaviness between his legs as he walked. It might be well worthwhile getting to know Kara with the doe eyes and gleaming mane. Well worthwhile, indeed.

But Wistwood came first, and time was running out.

ACQUIRING

The priest stood before the manor house in all of its grandeur, but it was too late to go back. The agreement had been sealed in blood. He was not ready to be Acquired, no matter how redeeming and liberating the transaction might be.

"A moment of fulfillment," the others had said. "An awakening to life beyond the capability of this world."

Something told the priest that the others were liars. Yes, all liars. That's what they were.

So was he.

Little wonder he had always possessed such a gift for discerning and perpetuating falsehood. Oh, he could smell a lie. He could smell it like the thick, sweetsick scent of cancer eating in the dark of a body, gnawing a black and insatiable path toward the light, vomiting rot in the wake of gluttony. He hungered like this, as well. He was famished for emancipation, starving for release from other, lesser contracts long ago established. He could bring entire worlds crumbling down upon themselves with the force of his own lies, if those lies promised to feed his need.

Had they not done so?

The manor house stood silent in the twilight. Waiting. Understanding each thought.

The priest was such an expert in these matters that, despite the fear now clawing a row of fiery lacerations in his spirit, curiosity was about to prove the stronger. He would not lie to himself, not as he had done to so many others. He longed to obey this summons. To know what wonders had been kept from him. What secrets lurked here for the revealing. Does not excellence reap its appropriate reward, eventually? Do not the most gifted illusionists ache secretly to share their techniques with the awestruck seated in the shadows, even if it means the death of magic? Far from help and farther still from heaven, he was a priest, after all. Magic and secrecy were his dominion.

A godly sort is needed around here. I don't know why, because I don't make the rules. All I know is that there's always got to be one of your kind, and the last one came to the end of his tour of duty. You're the one that showed up when Time came to look for another, so we're going to give you a spin and see how it works.

Yes, the one with the call had received yet another call. The priest was needed. Equal portions of fear, fear of the unknown and terror in the face of mystery, had forever drawn him to the seductions of what could not be seen and what *would* not be seen. Why should anything be different, here? Here at the crossroads everyone was destined to pass in the speeding midnight of the soul. Here where a life plummeted toward reckoning, heavy with unsettled transgression.

They were going to give him a spin and see how it would work.

Had he not dreamt of something like this all his life?

Looking around he admired the diadem of sky that flashed purple and malignant, though all the remaining world at its horizon was ablaze in a storm of daylight. He had never imagined such glory. What temptation lingered about this place! What sanctity! A strangled and raging halo of cloud hovered protectively above the crumbling peaks and gables of the old mansion on the hill. But why was it falling apart? Why had the owner of such a wonder failed to repair this derelict treasure?

No, I am more afraid than curious. It is no lie. I want to go back. I was tricked. This is not the job I was led to believe I'd be taking! No one's fooling me anymore. I know what this is. This is a nightmare and I don't belong inside it. I don't deserve this kind of treatment, Whoever You are. I am a priest of Jesus Christ in the Holy Church of Rome. I demand you release me. In His name!

No answer came in the silence. The circlet of cloud roiled for an instant overhead, as if stirred by his prayer, but that was all.

He walked toward the grand yet ruinous house, but his feet obeyed no command of his own. He marveled at the façade, framed in worm-eaten wood, as he crossed great flagstones of polished marble. Here was a thrilling and noble shrine of putrefaction, stalwart and as authoritative as St. Peter's in all its majesty. The mammoth edifice boasted stained and weathered white columns along its porch, with frieze reliefs decorating the capitals—scenes of despair and perversion that the priest could only compare to the efforts of Blake and Doré to illuminate Dante's most infernal visions.

His erection throbbed with agonizing ecstasy. This sprawling and abandoned haunt inspired as much awe as had any structure ever encountered in the labyrinthine quadrants of Vatican City and its Roman environs. But this was a palace of decidedly unhallowed antiquity. The priest could smell that, too. Holiness was banished from this spot, exiled as if flung amid the mighty howl of a thunderstorm, hurled across time and space in one furious expulsion, spit forth by unremitting darkness.

Here stood a vast and most wretched dwelling, one home of degenerate splendor atop a hill of incomparable grandeur. The porch was preceded by a fence of iron arrowhead-spikes, black and jutting toward the bruised sky atop an army of spears. Squinting up into the boiling malevolence of cloud, the priest moved his tongue across cracked lips. The breath hissed from his lungs, a weary wind passing over leaves burnt by the now occluded sun. He trembled from the core of his being to see that each arrowhead spike atop the loathsome fence pierced the body of a dove. Each immaculate victim in the endless expanse was yet alive, bleeding and shivering against the metal that erupted from its breast, desperate to escape even as life was drawn from the tips of feathers marred by crimson.

The doves were looking at him, seeking to twist their delicate heads down and around to catch a glimpse of The Priest as he moved beneath, begging to catch his glance one last time. But it was no use. He beheld them once, and then looked away.

Drops of blood spattered and fell from wings weakly aflutter, staining his eyelids and the plump part of his hand between thumb and index finger. He looked down in wonder. They were so scarlet and perfect, these drops, so delicate, even in the lustrous dark. He wanted to weep in their honor, to weep also for himself, for the inevitability of pain, for the whispering terror that there would be no meaning to any of this summons, inevitable or not.

Standing in the face of a burgeoning tempest above the house, speckled with blood, he knew then that true agony was none other than a black dog that prowled in the murk behind the great topiary trees, all festooned in velvet bows and lined like grim soldiers around the sprawling property. Leaves chattered with accusation in a sudden breeze as bitter and empty as a tomb plundered and left open to the desecration of the elements. Yes, there was a beast there, merging with the thickest shadows, watching him, wondering, waiting for him to weep, as he wanted, for the doves, each a pure snowfall atop an unconquered mountain, each struggling to leave this doom.

Another spurt of blood fell and streaked the priest's hand as the nearest dove convulsed and unfurled a grasping wing. He did weep, then, staring at the beads of red so radiant upon his skin. So damning. The voice came then to his ears. It was the mansion. The gate. The iron-crown sky. The trees. The black dog in hiding.

Behold! It is your hands that have damned you more than any other thing in the heavens or upon the earth or under the earth.

A stand of spruce trees swayed, a sisterhood of widows overlooking some grave in the icy gusts of a winter that had claimed many husbands. But the voice came from everywhere and everything else, too: from the tinkling leaves all around; from the wrecked and gaping maw of the doorway beyond the porch of columns; from the shadow-dog panting in the echo of an emptiness deeper than some stray universe, spinning blind and alone away from the moment of its creation.

Your own hands condemn you. I know all about it.

"As do I," said the priest. "I have never denied my guilt."

Precisely. And that is why you have come to me freely, for I can redeem you in ways that Others cannot. I can work around the Laws of Abomination appointed to my oversight—mine and mine alone. Your hands are your undoing, but would you not find it sweet to strangle those who have lied to you concerning your ultimate fate? Would it not be satisfying to crush the life and the breath from their bodies? They would abandon you to eternal torment without first speaking of more merciful alternatives.

"Yes. I would like to … to …"

To what? You have only to say it!

"To choke the life from them all! To rip the *lies* from them all."

The priest fell sobbing to his knees upon the marble flagstone nearest the entry gate. In the instant he fell, the fuming circlet of plum-colored cloud above the manor let pass a ray of ivory light that pierced across the columns of the house. A full moon rose in painful hours over the peaked roof of the dwelling, and after a time, soft songs of owls and other night-birds were heard in the deep fields beyond the enclosure of undulating trees. The priest drew an astonished breath. How long had he been kneeling next to the gruesome gate with his head in his hands? Hours?

Not even an instant, fool.

Behind the topiaries and the spruce trees, something much larger than the black dog began to move. Something old and vile and ponderous, like a shift in time itself. It turned to face the priest, though he could see nothing in the cold comfort of endless moonlight shimmering like milk spilled across the vast table-top of night. He stared at the columns of the mansion and then at his hands. All were white, dreadful as exposed bone, but the drops of blood still shined red upon his skin, taunting and accusing, and each drop was as precious as a little jewel that had been given to him as a reward for his work.

Scream, Father. We could do with a bit of music around here.

He screamed, loud and long until the muscles of his throat bulged and his cries were reduced to little more than pitched and pitiful whistles. He shoved a fist into his mouth, then, and sucked hungrily at the blood, licking the drops and tasting the rancid flavor of his own despair. It was as familiar to him as the taste of wine he had once consecrated and held aloft to the faithful and then to his own lips, parched with hypocrisy and every manner of deceit.

Hic est enim calix sanguines mei novi et aeterni testamenti …

His teeth pierced and tore into the flesh of his hand, drooling rivulets of his own blood, sobbing anew. The harrowing voice sounded again, a pernicious serpent weaving out of desolate corners of the domain.

Do not partake of your own sad flesh, priest. Such a feast is not for you to savor. But you have done well to make it this far and shall be rewarded. The door of the Manor is open beyond the Columns of Regret. Enter of your own will and dare to treat with me.

He dropped to his hands and knees and crawled toward the moonwashed stone stairway at the colossal entry; but he had not the strength to do more than that. The vast thing that groaned beyond the line of spruce shifted. The trees tore their boughs like mourning gowns and scratched the surreal firmament with their peaks. All things turned to watch the priest's progress. He could sense Its eyes upon him, Its mind within his own, boring into his soul with a plunging grasp as icy as the surface of the watchful moon in the sky.

"So this is a church, after all. And you are the god who dwells within," he said as he crawled. His hands dragged through what seemed like a patch of grass, but whatever earth might have been beneath was strangely warm and pliable, like the hide of some sleeping animal, the growth wiry and thick as tufts of hair.

A most venerable place. But think again before uttering a prayer in this sanctum, priest. To say a prayer in here is a dangerous undertaking. You may try, if you wish, but it has been so long since you truly prayed that I fear you are incapable of providing us with so meager an amusement.

"I cannot pray, it is true," he choked, collapsing face-down into a heaving breath of the ground that was now very much alive and undulating beneath him. "I will not pray."

Then we shall satisfy ourselves with the settling of accounts, instead.

Struggling to attain the first step of the brooding, columned porch, the priest's body was wracked by a flash of agony that overtook every last joint, each limb. Every pore on the surface of his skin began to wax hot and then freeze, fire upon frost, until the stinging was too fast and too furious to endure. He went rigid in the throes of his agony, a sparrow trapped in a cyclone of flame yet not consumed. When the torment threatened to smash what was little was left of his mind in a burst of incandescent annihilation, he saw his moment of escape. There it was, the edge of a curtain fluttering beneath an open window. He longed to reach out and pull himself through that crevice, amid the depths and heights of transfixion.

But it was not to be, for he was lifted and then dashed, suddenly, as limp as a rag doll, against one of the immense columns. As soon as his face struck and was fractured against the surface, he howled to the unconcerned heavens and clung to the stone pillar with what pitiful remnant of his life remained. The pain subsided, then, and left him a withered and rejected thing, curled in a panel of moonlight. The voice took up its insistent whisper once again.

Ah! A near escape. Is that what you saw, priest? A window of death through which you might have slipped from us, cunning as a fox? Is this how you would repay us for rescuing you from harsher climes? Alas, you were not swift enough to enter the portal and betray the term of our arrangement. Death is not an option, here, priest. Not anymore.

He was gasping, near death, he was sure of it. How could a body and soul not be near the end under the weight of such pain? His strength evaporated as he slipped down the cool surface of the column, his battered face drooping against the stone.

Death is not an option!

The unseen hulking monster hissed beyond the trees, which were now churning angrily, the layered skirts of their boughs seized by a whipping gale that sought to denude them with violence, to shake them from their roots in a tantrum.

"This tempest is *your* doing!" the bothered boughs shrieked at him, appalled at their treatment.

"Let me rest," he mumbled. "I beg you. Let me sleep and I will come before you all and give you the worship you deserve."

You think I am so vain as to require worship?

The voice pounded like rocks battering the interior of his skull.

You mistake me for your former god. He is the one who demands coddling and constant reassurance of greatness. Not I. As for rest, you shall not have it. Rest was not mentioned in our agreement.

"I beg you … a moment only, here against the stone."

I must tell you, Priest of Rot and Priest of Worms, the pillar of your consolation is not fashioned from stone. It is enamel! Polished and perfect. It is made from the teeth of the dead, from the jewels plucked or left to fall like trinkets in the dust, from the mouths of those who were raped like squealing little cherubs by you and your brethren, unto the ages of ages unremembered. Behold!

He pushed himself away from the grisly column and fell on his back, down and breathless upon the pulsating earth.

"You lie," he managed to croak, drifting in and out of consciousness. "Why do you torture me so? Your covenant promised there would be no shame. No shame! I would endure your pain—you said that it would pass—but you swore there would be no shame. This is why I agreed to come to you."

How rich that you insinuate some violation of our fine agreement on my part! I assure you—nothing of the sort has occurred. Any shame you bring here is your own, and I am not responsible for it. Perhaps you should have prepared yourself for the rigors of my gauntlet with greater forethought. Moreover, what shame can one such as you feel when looking upon the fruits of your glorious handiwork?

"Liar! These were never my works! Not all of them! This is not what you claim."

But I do not lie. Behold the craftsmanship, priest. Out of the mouths of babes, indeed. Enough gems to embellish masterful structures. All of My columns are made from such dainties. Touch them again and deny that your wicked backbone shudders with knowledge of your complicity. Oh, I shall confess, priest, that it required much work. I engaged in labor beyond imagining to collect these precious materials. You would be surprised to see the mountains of graveyard dirt that I sifted, centuries and centuries of it! Layers of buried secrecy and destruction. Most exhausting, even for one as powerful as I, but—

"No, no more! Tell me no more. I will come in and complete the Acquisition as agreed. Just … just make these things go away. You who can turn the day into night and scour the earth and the depths of the sea for tokens of damnation have the power to spare me this."

You give me too much credit, Father, and that is one thing I do not require. Remember, I am not your god. Enter, then, and bring your work to fulfillment so that mine may be henceforth embraced.

With a quavering scream and one, bone-cracking heave the priest brought himself to his feet and staggered up the steps, spewing blood from his mouth as he wavered, the hem of his cassock brushing against the first horrid column. Before the midnight portal that opened to receive him, he heard laughter, the happy trill of thousands of innocent voices echoing between the columns that glittered and shined. He was lost within the sorrowful house by the time the laughter turned into unending wails of pain and pleas for help that would never, ever arrive. Not in this world, where the waves of the ocean practiced silence, and the stones of the ground refused to tell the tale of all they had witnessed.

The grievous echoes faded. The moon and the circlet-crown of inky cloud were absorbed, vanishing into the light of a soft golden sunrise. The mansion— its trees; its vast stepping stones; its fence of bloodstained spears; the cumbersome Shadow Thing that prowled as an unwelcome memory on the outskirts of sleep—all of these disappeared like dust in the rise of a quickening fire, never to be seen again.

The green hilltop was all that remained. Soon, birds began to sing, playful and eager in the tranquility of swelling daybreak.

SCHUYLER

When the call finally came to Schuyler Brody, she answered her cell phone on the third pulse, as always. She made it a point to wait for three, if she ever wanted to answer the thing at all, these days, just before voice-mail would take care of the decision for her. Three was her lucky number.

Caller identification revealed nothing. No name. No number. Only blank screen.

The phone buzzed on her desk like the frantic wasp she had trapped in an upended Pyrex bowl the week before.

It can't sting you if it can't get out. I'll leave the bowl over it until it dies. How long could that take? A week?

"Hello."

"Good afternoon. May I speak with Miss Schuyler Brody?"

"Speaking. Who's calling, please?"

"Ah, Miss Brody. Glad to catch you. Is this a good time to talk?" The aged and raspy voice was polite, but left no time for the question to be answered. "This is Horace. Horace Slater. We spoke on the phone Saturday, briefly, concerning the newspaper advertisement. Are you still interested in leasing the antique shop in Wistwood?"

"Yes, hello, Mr. Slater. I'm glad you caught me. I was hoping to hear back from you."

"Well, you'll have to excuse me for not getting back to you sooner, but a number of other matters have demanded my attention the past day or two. This is the first opportunity I've had to offer you a definite time to come by and peruse the shop."

"That sounds wonderful. When can I have a peek?"

"If Wednesday afternoon at four is convenient for you, you can come then."

Any time, any day was convenient for Schuyler, but she wasn't about to tell the old man about that circumstance. Plus, she didn't want to sound too eager. Her grandmother had ever warned her about the frightful ways in which a young woman who sounded too eager might be misinterpreted, misled, mistaken, and sometimes even missed altogether in this untrustworthy and judgmental world.

"Thursday around the same time would actually be more convenient. Is that okay?" she offered in her best gee-whiz, half-interested, half-indifferent, I'm-going-to-have-to-rearrange-my-busy-schedule-for-this bargainer's tone. But there was not, apparently, a bargain to be had. Nor was there the slightest hesitation in the reply she received.

"I'm very sorry, Miss Brody, but the shop can't be seen on Thursday at any time due to prearranged appointments with other interested parties. Wednesday at four in the afternoon, promptly, is the only widow of opportunity through which a truly interested bird might fly to have a serious look at the place. Interest in the shop has been considerable. I am at liberty to report that, Ms. Brody. I assure you I am at liberty to report that."

"Yeah. Okay. I imagine interest must be considerable, if you've got such limited window openings for all of these eager 'birds' attempting to fly in," murmured Schuyler into the receiver. And she had noticed the snotty little shift from 'Miss' to 'Ms.' as well. This guy sounded like he had quite the stick up his ass, but she couldn't help revealing at least a trace of her desperation to see the shop, which represented the opportunity of her dreams.

"Look. Horace …"

"Yes, Ms. Brody?"

"Please, it's 'Miss,' or you can call me 'Schuyler.' Not a lot of folks go in for the whole Ms. Business around here, as I'm sure you must know. You're fairly local. And I'm an informal gal. Very easy to get along with."

"As you wish, *Miss* Brody. Can you attend the four o'clock appointment on Wednesday or not?"

She felt like saying, "Just keep your damned pants on, pal!" but this was something her mother—or worse, her grandmother—would say. And even if this property manager sounded sullen and more arrogant than half of the insufferable students to whom she taught English literature, she would bite her tongue. Even if this crank annoyed her like tenth-graders more concerned with how to *become* future adulterers than in reading Hawthorne's description of a repentant one, she was not about to let her chance for happiness slip away.

"I'll be there Wednesday at four. It's not a problem. I'll just reschedule my own day."

"Excellent. Then we're all set and I'll see you at the agreed hour. Do you have a writing utensil handy? You would be wise to take down a few directions. You'll *need* directions."

Schuyler fished around in a kitchen drawer for a pen, hoping to God she never came across to her students as condescendingly as this jackass was coming across to her. Kids at school ate even the most authoritative teachers for lunch, these days. It was little wonder that trying to reach them with a modicum of palpable confidence had been like trying to navigate a tightrope stretched across an abyss in the midst of a hurricane. On stilts.

"Got the pen. Go ahead, Mr. Slater. I'm in Watkinsville, as I mentioned when we talked Saturday."

After the man had recited an uncomplicated list of directions, Schuyler looked them over again, puzzled. Her lips pursed.

"This sounds easy enough to find, at least on paper. I guess I can just zip right along the interstate and take the shortcut through Perry. You say it'll only take me half an hour to get there?"

"That depends, Miss, upon the extent of your skills when it comes to 'zipping right along,' I suppose."

Wow. She truly wanted to tell this shit-heel exactly where he could do some zipping of his own. Schuyler knew the type too well: full of resentment and suspicion when it came to women. The hills were alive with men like that. One grumpy, withered old dick. The combination of bad male attitudes and underwhelming physical attributes often came as a deluxe set; she was sorry to have learned this from past experience. It would feel so good to rip him a new one.

Damn. Not worth the risk. She wanted the antique shop, if it was up to snuff, as her Gran would have said. Moreover, sheer desperation might rob her of the wicked wit she needed to deliver a stinging putdown out loud, outside her brain. Like many people, Schuyler was usually gifted with the ability to produce withering insults many days *after* she had been insulted. It was an annoying burden to bear, but she tried not to hold it against herself. Her mother had tried to extinguish any sign of sassiness in her spirit from the time she had been old enough to speak. Subsequently, her education in rapid-fire wisecracking had been sorely neglected.

"Look, I know you're only in the next county and I'm right here in Chesterville, near the border of both, but I've never heard of Wistwood before, Mr. Slater. Most towns—at least all the ones I know about—have got road signs to indicate that a person's getting close. But a big stone archway with a lantern on top of a column? On the edge of the woods? I mean, I'm sure I'll have no problem seeing that, but I'm a little concerned. We don't have any woods around here. At least that I know of."

"Wistwood is an older township currently being revitalized, Miss Brody. Oh, it's not a very big forest, I grant you. It's a humble and unassuming kind of place. This vacant antiques shop represents a rare opportunity, let me tell you. The right person will have the chance not only to lease the business and property, but will have the option to buy it at some stage, as I'm sure you noted in our original advertisement. I explained this to you during our quick chat Saturday, too. And I must be frank when I tell you, Miss, that we will only consider the right person, a truly deserving person. I'm sure you understand, being a teacher, a person in the process of educating young and impressionable minds. It all comes down to the indispensable quality of matching the right tenant with the right property. That's something in the best interests of all parties concerned."

"I agree and my interest *is* enthusiastic, Mr. Slater."

"Then you'll come freely and we'll see you Wednesday."

"Yes, I'll find it. And you're sure this is the same property advertised, the one with the bedroom, full bath, and living quarters above the shop itself?"

"None other, Miss. I'll see you at the appointed time. Take care to follow the directions to the letter and have yourself a very good day."

The connection went silent. Schuyler stared at the cellphone for a moment, as if it had somehow failed her as a communication device and must be punished for such a deficiency. But, no, it wasn't the phone's fault. This Horace—whoever he was—was just a prick, an ass. A misogynistic old fart. But there had been something haughty and hollow in the voice, too, something that gave his snide words an automatic gilding of superiority. In any case, she was as uninterested in the prospect of meeting such an unpleasant person as she was painfully excited about seeing the shop itself. Imagine her luck if she could score it! A full inventory of quality antiques ready to be taken-over and a "quaint, clean upstairs living-space fully furnished and ideal for a single lady or discreet gentleman."

The ad in the local newspaper had practically grabbed her by the throat.

She took the newspaper clipping from her purse to read the listing again, just for fun. Yes, it specifically used the word "quaint." Her heart was captured.

What a relief it would be if everything measured-up and this irritating Horace turned out to be more malleable in person than he seemed on the phone. Some people simply couldn't convey their more favorable characteristics over the phone, in her experience. Especially men. Maybe Horace was one of those. Whatever his story might be, she was going to have to be ready to negotiate with him and move fast, with prudence, if the place proved as ideal as she dreamed it would be.

As she was pleading and begging her lucky stars it would be.

Thank God she didn't have to worry about classes anymore, or stepping-up in front of a room overcrowded with suspicious, hostile faces that didn't even attempt to conceal their collective resentment. She could still see the inner wheels and cogs behind those baleful stares, plotting ways to humiliate, undermine and relativize her very personhood in the midst of their disenchanted lives. The three or four of her students who had actually given a damn, and who had worked five times as hard as the rest to excel and curry her favor to the point of obsequiousness ... even they had stopped making the whole illusion worthwhile months ago.

Those kids might do for some of the Pollyanna teachers who didn't know any better, yet. The Suck-Up Brigade might suffice for those wrecked, soul-drained veterans who needed a stiff drink every morning before school and who kept the finish-line of imminent retirement in their wavering crosshairs, visions of pension plans dancing like sugarplums in their heads.

Maybe that was what the old-timers needed to make it through the day without strangling or stabbing one of the little bastards, but it wasn't an option for Schuyler. She'd be damned if she woke up thirty years in the future to have some doctor late for a golf game tell her that her liver wasn't going to make it to retirement with the rest of her. She wasn't about to "buck-up" and survive decades of necessary alcoholism, chronic stultification and excessive psychoanalysis just to collect a monthly check. She knew too many teachers doing just that, desperate fools who didn't even realize that their brains had already been reduced to a pudding-like consistency.

Schuyler put a fingertip to her lips and half-laughed, half-sobbed. It was a frightening, feral sound. Opening the fridge, she grabbed what was left of last night's Pinot Grigio. There wasn't much in the bottle, but she poured it into a tumbler over the kitchen sink and downed it in two emphatic gulps.

There was no getting away from destiny. She believed that. But she was already drinking too much, like the others, and it was time to make alternative arrangements for her life. People who loved and respected themselves did that sort of thing. People who wished to remain sane exercised good judgment at critical junctures in their lives because they were smart enough to recognize that change was coming, that it was going to hit them hard whether they liked it or not. Therefore, it was best to anticipate and welcome that change when it arrived, even if drastic measures needed to be taken to accommodate an agonizing transition. For people who were wise enough to act, and to do so in a timely fashion, good things were waiting on the other side of every turbulent river. Wonderful things that demanded a surefooted and successful crossing.

Schuyler put the cool edge of the empty tumbler against her forehead, which still felt like it was burning up due to the September humidity and her own gnashing anxiety. Why wouldn't it stop? It all felt like knives scraping and whirling at the forefront of her skull from the inside. She glanced at the Pyrex bowl on the dining room table. The wasp within, curled and silent, had still been circling its trap a few moments ago. Surely it had been able to see the world it wanted through the clear glass, wandering and whining in frustration, circling until the little spark of life inside the crisp, shiny husk was spent.

So it had taken a week for the thing to die, after all.

She would leave the wasp there for a while, just to be sure. There under the bowl. And she would do whatever she had to do to secure the lease on this dream shop in the unheard-of town of Wistwood, not far across the county line, near some forest with a crumbling archway and a tall lantern post.

Just to be sure.

Schuyler put the glass in the sink and decided to run to the bank and get a cashier's check for the deposit. Best to be ready for Wednesday. Flash the money. All of it. The thought that she might not end-up liking the place did not occur to her. Nor did she wish to drive out to the place secretly and preview the property ahead of time. No. That would give her too much time to talk herself out of it. After the bank there was going to be a run to the grocery store for another liter of Pinot Grigio. Two, in fact. That was for damned sure. She didn't have plans to be hungover on Wednesday afternoon, but a couple of quick glasses before driving out to find this place would be advisable. This was her future, after all.

Maybe three bottles would be best. She always felt that interviews and dates and speeches and classroom lessons went more smoothly if she was just tipsy enough without being obvious. Sometimes she worried she was far too young, at age twenty-six, to feel so certain about such a thing, but then she remembered she had the luxury of youth, above all else. Besides, ambiguity had its advantages, even for daily connoisseurs of Pinot Grigio. *Especially* for them.

She grabbed the house keys, her phone, her purse, and headed for the door, heels clicking on the polished wood floor.

"I'm going to get that goddamned shop and then get the hell into life," she declared to the endlessly flat, stifling world outside. Even crotchety old Horace had intimated that she, above all, could appreciate the significance of such aspirations, of the inestimable value of matching things properly in existence.

Since you are a person in the business of educating young and impressionable minds.

As she backed out of the parking lot in front of her apartment building and wheeled off toward the downtown bank, however, Schuyler didn't think a thing about the fact that not once during the course of her conversations with Horace had she mentioned that she taught school.

OF MIST AND
VANISHED EARTH

Sunlight streamed in panels of frosted radiance through the fog, each one a weary beam descending to probe little edges of overgrown woodland as Brask made his way up Crystal Creek Road. The van wheezed and groaned to the top of the high hill, flanked on each side with soaring redwoods, tilting sycamores, and patches of thick highland scrub. The immediate world was lost in the slow revels of ghosts, low and blind, clutching outward from the forest floor or aloft in nebulous clusters amid the treetops. Phantoms came and went, came and went, draining here and fading there, swaying from bodily forms into sudden swirls of iridescent droplets, disintegrating. In other spots—by a ridge of scattered boulders, near a slope that flashed glimpses of golden grass—spectral travelers spiraled into this misty kingdom, emerging from secret voids, eager in their freedom to cover everything in sight and extinguish all remnants of human interference.

Brask was thrilled by the strange beauty of it all, but worried. California fog was one thing. He was used to it and had encountered plenty of it on the drive from Palo Alto. But this clotted miasma was impossible to navigate. At the top of the hill he put the van in park, adjusted the high-beams, and yanked the emergency brake, hoping that no other motorist would come hurtling out of the roil of cloud to smash him head-on or crush him from behind. After a few minutes in the impenetrable gloom he felt a rush from his gut to his brain, some queasy waltz into vertigo, as if he were perched at the brink of a hungry and bottomless chasm waiting, forever patient, beneath the mist.

The fog thickened.

Brask had no point of reference. There was nothing but the disturbing sense that firm ground was no longer beneath his feet, his wheels. The interior of the van remained real enough; the sound of the stressed and stuttering engine reassured him in its sad, familiar way. But the silence dominating the swath of turbulent gray outside was insolent, a whispered threat from some enemy unheralded. He drained a plastic bottle of spring water that had been rolling around on the passenger-side floorboard and then rolled down the window, looking this way and that into the murk. Which way was up? Was he on a hill or floating in the middle of the ocean? When he opened his mouth to breathe the cottony air, there was a hint of metal on his tongue, like pennies his mother had warned him not to taste as a child.

I'm flying blind, he thought. But there was nothing to be done. He had to sit at the top of this hill and wait until a breeze from the ocean or some warmer gust from the dry mountains inland breathed strong enough to dispel the soup. He dared not turn off the engine to spare it from overheating. It idled in something approaching agony. Other drivers needed to know he was there, or here, or wherever he was. Where was he? Where was the archway and the damned lantern post? He thought about stepping out of the vehicle if only to put his feet on the rugged road and reaffirm its existence. But stretching his arm all the way out the window, he was astonished to see his hand disappear at the wrist. No, there would be no exiting the van, not even to relieve the creeping nausea or the nebulous feeling of claustrophobia that seemed to rise up from his seat.

He snatched the map of Big Sur from the dashboard and tore it open to distract himself from the sense of disorientation. The extreme climactic differences between living in hot Palo Alto and possibly living in the Big Sur area were going to take some getting used to, if he got the cabin, but Brask knew that beyond the fog there was brilliance to be savored, so much more scope for the imagination, born daily anew of the topographical glory. If he came to live here, occasional bouts of milky disorientation would be worth the rewards. Besides, fog like this could keep him hunkered over a desk writing tragic masterpieces for weeks on end. All he needed was a few guttering candles like sentinels on either side of him. Perhaps a monk's cowl to droop low over his unshaven face as tales were spun. That would fulfill every morbid writer's fantasy he had ever entertained. Wouldn't *that* scare the shit out of his sister. It was a fun thought. But he had to get situated or else the whole dream would dissolve like the light from his high-beams into the mouth of the weather, useless and stolen by greedy wraiths for their own unfathomable purposes.

He looked at his watch and then compared it to the time on the screen of his cell phone. Damn. It was now only ten minutes until three. This whole endeavor was going to fall apart. Damn it! What a colossal waste of time it was going to be. Landlords were sometimes worse than employers when it came to gauging a prospect's worthiness by punctuality.

Great. I drove all this way, with gas as costly as gold and my sanity more valuable than that, just to piss off some cranky old bastard who'll tell me that if I can't be on time then I might as well not bother wasting his share of it, thank you very much.

Every day spent homeless had been pushing Brask toward the edge in one way or another. Now, with a solution close at hand, even if it was remote, every minute nudged him closer to an anguished landscape that promised nothing but panic, as far as the eye could see and the mind could think. That territory had been traveled before. There was no way he could lose his grip now.

Fuck, why won't this fog lift? Why now?

He had to get the cabin!

Brask Adams had always considered himself a contender for membership in the camp of human success, once the foundations of his life were reasonably restored. He believed enormous success, tempered by integrity, was attainable, for he had earned the gift of perspective, had forged it like a gleaming blade in fire—a sword capable of slicing through the filth and the bullshit and the illusions of life to separate the valuable from the ephemeral. He could discern what was honorable from the intransigent soullessness and degradation that swept like an infection across all levels of Western civilization, replacing substance with so much pedestrian affectation. Supplanting character with characteristics, and bravado with an almost wheedling vulgarity. Bleak enticements, to the last.

As for God. Who needed Him? Or it? Or what?

He thought about his sister. Something acidic and wrenching hissed in his stomach, a serpent coiling into deeper, safer places upon a trail of venom. Brask, too, had been religious, once. He had toyed with the notion of God as a youth under the guidance of his devotedly Catholic mother and a few decent priests, but manhood and travel and study and experiences—the formative and the disfiguring—had soon disabused him of the need for institutional splendor. He had no patience, any longer, for surety that was only as clear as the cracked prisms through which mystery filtered, fading to the point of murky and irrevocable distortion. Once the glorious and awe-inspiring outer architecture of religion had collapsed in ruins at the feet of his reason, the rudimentary scaffolding and bits of infrastructure that remained were examined and found wanting.

At least the breathtaking facades still had occasional power to captivate, sometimes by virtue of grandeur alone. But stripped of interior radiance, the bare bones and smoldering remnants of doctrine could not hope to maintain a grip upon his imagination, and illusions could not presume to satisfy. All of this was thus dismissed and left behind, abandoned in quiet grief. Nebraska Paul Adams had packed up and traipsed away, as one would depart the scene of a family home reduced to charred debris, nothing left but sentimental wreckage felled in a conflagration caused by its own faulty wiring. All he possessed now in place of faith was a blunt sadness, and a bit of pain at the realization of what had been lost.

Faith. What a con game.

But what could one expect from an impulse that was never built to last much longer than the hushed, candlelit aura that flickers around idealistic impressions? Even if youthful delusion concerning inviolable truth and the permanence of such matters was snuffed-out with the candlelight, emptiness was preferable. Brask knew there would always be pangs of regret, tiny flutterings of wings against stone, the wheeling of some panicked sparrow trapped indoors, lost in the shadowed corridors of longing. There would be gentle movements, too, suggestions from the outskirts of thought that, perhaps, the entire and magnificent City of Magical Thinking could one day be rebuilt, if he would reject pride and surrender to a harmless bit of myth, here, or the childish desire to pray for consolation in the dead dark of night, there.

Let other people fool themselves. To hell with them and their ways. You're back in the game, and now they can play by your rules for a change.

Just when it seemed as if the tumbling puffs of fog were intent upon keeping the van somehow circling and yet lodged in the eye of a sleepy divinity, a great curtain of the stuff was swept aside. Shuddering wind gusted from the nearby mountain peaks into the canyon, obliterating all mist in a matter of seconds.

Holy shit.

Brask drew an amazed breath. It was like being reborn instantly within the lush green safety of a world both pristine and beckoning, a realm that could never be obscured by something as insignificant as the need for directions. A vision unbothered by the shattered glass of youthful certainties. All was bright and fresh in its preening majesty, confident in its own existence beyond time and across ages.

He watched the fog bank retreat down a thin, winding slope of Canyon Creek Road, as if being drawn back by some great inward breath of the cold Pacific itself, inhaled and retaken until the time should come for it to be unleashed again among the rocks and the redwoods, banishing knowledge of the real world from the eyes of the unworthy.

Only a hundred feet ahead of him stood an archway of ancient-looking stone, green with moss and damp from the previous caress of the fog, as high as a three-story house. Its fractured Roman cornice was level with the flicker of lantern-light atop a tall metal column, like part of a stately old aqueduct that had been torn from time and planted to gaze outward from the Big Sur forest. Beside the lantern post stood an old man, stooped and leaning on a cane. He waved at the van.

It was waiting. Waiting for all the world to arrive, as if all the world had been expected to arrive. The sight of the entry, incongruous but lovely as it was, seemed a beacon, a talisman. It was a visual clarion call to Brask's heart, one that summoned him to banish poisonous and meddling anxieties from the mind forthwith, surrendering every regret to embrace good sense and the redemption of welcome.

He had reached the gateway to Wistwood at last, with five minutes to spare.

SUNFLOWERS

Damn, he was tired! If he had to touch that bag of skank again, he might shit his own pants, and the Employer might hear about it, the way he found out about most everything. However that was. This was no time to jeopardize the promotion, and Shep was frankly a bit surprised at today's bout of physical disgust and nausea, considering the activities in which he had been participating, of late.

Fuck it all, anyhow. He sure as hell wasn't shooting for any kind of pat on the back down at the station, not these days. There would be no raise, no notice in the paper or even in the monthly online goddamned newsletter concerning his "step up" in the world of law enforcement. Not that he cared, but any chance of scoring a raise in pay, rank or even better desk placement had been wiped out after last winter's embarrassing situation with the sow. He had to bash her good in order to get the beast to stop sinking her yellow teeth and her bloody gums into his forearm.

Shep had taken a lot of flak for that. The scumbag bitch had barely survived and even though she'd gone into the hospital with gobbets of his skin in her gullet, screeching and kicking and practically speaking in fucking tongues with her face split completely open down the middle, the press went after *him*. Fuckers! All they had wanted to focus upon was the fact that Shep Daltry, a far too eager and excited new white cop had pummeled a poor black mother of five from the projects.

Damn right.

He pummeled her until one of her eyes had popped open like a grape and was leaking blood and vitreous fluid all over her purple spandex outfit with the pastel sunflowers on it. The outfit that smelled like six months of unwashed pussy and cum splattered onto her from God only knew how many wasted johns.

Damn right I tuned her up.

The crybaby media didn't want to mention that precious aspect of her motherly attire. Oh, no! It was all

pastel sunflowers pastel sunflowers pastel sunflowers pastel sunflowers pastel sunflowers pastel sunflowers pastel sunflowers pastel sunflowers pastel sunflowers

Over and over on the TV, on the radio, in the papers they kept repeating that bit of incidental fuckery, like some sweet little goddamned nursery rhyme celebrating the whore's innocence. Like Shep had found her sitting on a unicorn in a sunlit field of daisies, blowing bubbles with her babies laughing and dancing all around her. He told the sheriff and press that he found her blowing some crab-ridden junkie near a dumpster behind Winn Dixie. It wasn't true, but he could produce the crab-ridden junkie and make him say anything, and it sounded a hell of a lot better than admitting he mistook the cow for some other fool reported for shoplifting at the store. He had to cover his ass, after all. Had to make it look good. What the fuck was wrong with that?

pastel sunflowers pastel sunflowers pastel sunflowers pastel sunflowers pastel sunflowers pastel sunflowers pastel sunflowers pastel sunflowers pastel sunflowers

The media sang that shit like a fucking chant, a spell. Like it was a set of code words that had to be included in every article and thirty-second installment on the six-o'clock news so that some liberal teleprompter jockey with smart tits and a hemorrhaging heart could stare at the camera in horror and act as if she was announcing that the goddamned Pope had been beheaded in broad daylight:

And reports indicate that the young mother of five small children was taken to the hospital in and out of consciousness, leaking vitreous fluid from her ruptured eyeball onto her dress, which sources tell us was covered in a cheerful pattern of pastel sunflowers.

The bastards just couldn't stop. He had been forced to think of something, after a mistake like that, a mistake that could have happened to anyone. Besides, who knew how many times she probably shoplifted, even if it wasn't *that* particular time? So he yanked her out by her hair and let her make a run for it. And then he made it look good.

The only thing that saved him was that he'd beaten the memory out of her head. Later they later found her babies crawling around some roach-filled apartment in various stages of addiction or withdrawal. Thank God for that. Even then, did the news folk care that Officer Shep Daltry had lost three ounces of his arm?

No they goddamned didn't.

"I don't know what this world is coming to," one of the skank's relatives had said to the bloodsucking press.

Shep could tell them exactly what it was coming to. The world was on its head. That's what had already arrived; there was no "coming to" about any of it. Here. Now. Front and center in every living color under the sun. The things that ought to count don't count. Lawful and respectable folks are derided in favor of chaos and vulgarity. And everybody's an artist, everybody's a painter, working on whatever goddamned picture they want to paint just so nobody will ever figure out that it's already gone to hell. Handbasket not included or necessary. People thought they were living in an unacceptable world that could be made better. Shep had news for them.

pastel sunflowers pastel sunflowers pastel sunflowers pastel sunflowers pastel sunflowers pastel sunflowers pastel sunflowers pastel sunflowers pastel sunflowers

Accusations of police brutality. Protests in the town square. Preachers thundering from the pulpits of the African Methodist Episcopal Church about a war on the defenseless. Old women swooning in the pews in fear, certain that they were sure to be the next victims beaten by dirty cops until their eyeball juice squirted all over whatever the fuck they happened to be wearing, too.

But the department had cleared him. Anyone could see the six-inch chunk of skin and muscle missing from his forearm and testify to the regimen of tetanus shots and antiviral drugs he had to endure because the cunt had been HIV positive, for the love of God. Shep's life had flashed before his eyes every day for months until they told him he was in the clear. What a clusterfuck.

Lucky for Shep, damage control—when it came to the mayor's image—was a hell of a lot more important than controlling the scum of the earth.

What was it they had told him? What had the Sheriff sent him in a letter, while he was still in his own hospital room?

"The edification of civic morale and a relationship of mutual trust is more vital to the community's wellbeing than dwelling upon the gruesome details that might be associated with the unfortunate experiences endured by an upstanding officer in the line of duty."

"Think of the department, Officer Daltry. Think of your fellow brothers in blue and how best you might be able to serve them by seeing the proverbial big picture. You have the power, Officer Daltry, the power to vouchsafe them from any overarching scandal and a complete deterioration of crucial public relations that might hinder or diminish the capacity of the department to effect change in law enforcement on a pervasive scale."

Bastards!

They had brought in some slick corporate attorney with red hair and freckles who looked like a twelve year-old kid in his daddy's suit. Brought him all the way from Atlanta to feed that festering line of shit to him.

What was the world coming to?

Yeah, Shep would tell them all, in his own time, in his own way, with the Employer behind him. He had seen the big picture and had seen it well, because it became the portrait of his own life for nearly a year of modified detail, right up until activists latched onto other astonishing cases being churned out regularly by the production-line of Hell On Earth. There was always another story. Even the vast arterial reservoir of the media's throbbing heart began to grow a little dry on Shep's account and got caught up with newer events they could twist and manipulate to fit their narratives. Miss Fonda Latray-Lord was just a flavor of the month.

Still, it was only because of an increase in crime and the loss of any need for his desk-job that they had found a way to get him back in a squad car. By then, Shep's wife, Maddy, had left him and moved all the way back to Texas to live with her chupacabra-fanged mother, Irene. Maddy blamed the split on Shep's drinking and *not*—she was quite clear on this—on his professional disgrace or demotion or whatever they wanted to call it. She did not leave him because of the scandal of it all or because of his new reputation in town, his blood-scarlet letter. No, it was the alcohol and the fact that he was mean. It was not intended to impugn his manhood. Oh, she had wanted to be so super-fucking-clear on that count. His manhood was never in question.

"I still think you're a fine man and that things are gonna get better for you," she had said with the little set of faded blue suitcases stacked neatly at her side and a taxi waiting *(SURPRISE!)* in the driveway.

It had been all Shep could do, it had taken all he had within the bank-sized vault of his manly self-control to keep from slapping her around throughout the whole ordeal. She had always been a mouthy little piece, for good or for ill, and even through all of his binges he had had enough sense not to haul off and smack her. That would have given his plunge deep into the cesspit of life a brand-new set of wings. Those wings would have let him fly straight up into the sun, where everyone would have a clear, clean shot at bringing him down with one bullet, once and for all.

Like hell he'd ever let that shit happen.

So he had kicked her suitcases straight into the road behind the taxi and she had whimpered a bit, but he had let her go. Told her, in fact, to get the fuck out of his sight for good and not to even think about seeing a dime of support, since it was her big idea to fly home to Mama. The cab had squealed its way out of the drive, whisked her out of his life, and it didn't matter to him for five minutes, not five goddamned minutes. Sure, he had gotten a few stares and timid little looks from neighbors out watering the azaleas or fetching the morning paper. That didn't matter, either. Shep had long ceased to expect any loyalty or understanding, from anybody. All of this made it easier when one night at a bar he finally admitted to a couple of drinking buddies that he had never particularly liked women much in the first place.

That was when Shep decided to start doing things his own way. Oh yeah. He played the game. He sobered up and began to act alive and interested in his special role as part of the "capacity of the department to effect change in law enforcement on a pervasive scale." With care and a healthy dose of stealth—*a healthy cop is a stealthy cop*—Shep had found a whole new lease on life, on his job, on his view of the world and God above and Hell below and how everything was working together, spinning through the fuckwad universe to some extraordinary, reconciled ending. He began to realize how he was personally helping that greater process along. The Employer was the icing on the cake. And the job was almost Shep's.

In secret. It had to be in secret.

Luckily, his patrol beat had been reduced to little more than a secret for purposes of public relations. His detail was just a few notches more dignified than writing parking tickets or working as some sort of bank security guard. Back road patrol. Country cruising. No, the job did not provide him with much scope for the imagination, anymore.

But it did supply him with material.

In fact, as Shep drove, he saw some potential material right now, up ahead, taking a piss against the concrete underpass in broad daylight, before God and all His children. It was time for a pitstop.

Four for the killing,
each soul provided.
When all have been taken
your fate is decided.

LISTEN TO THE EQUATION

B rask pulled the van to a rolling stop as he entered the strange woodland turn and stuck his head out the window. He was perplexed at the sight of the incongruous figure of the old fellow on the roadside and baffled by the presence of the gigantic, half-broken archway itself. *What the hell?*

"Are you Horace Slater by any chance?"

"I am indeed. And I'm guessing that you're Brask Adams. Right on time to the very minute."

The man astride the dirt road snaking off into forest beyond the crumbling arch was old enough. Maybe as old as the strange monument itself. Seventy-five or eighty? That was Brask's guess. Dressed in a battered hunting cap and an equally mangy blue-checkered coat above baggy gray work-trousers, Horace was an eccentric sight. The cuffs of the trousers had been stuffed into gigantic Timberland boots loosely tied and caked with mud, the tongues lolling outward like the drooping petals of some leathery carnivorous plant. Bright, black gimlet eyes stared at Brask, twinkling above purplish lips that smiled amid the tangle of a brilliant white mustache and beard that flared down beyond his collarbone.

Shopping center Santa Claus? Maybe if the poor guy had some meat on his bones.

There was an expression of knowing humor in the man's eyes and a twitch of the bow-tie moustache as he extended a gloved hand in greeting. The engine of the Pontiac puffed and chugged gratefully for the privilege of braking on a bit of flat terrain at last. All around, the forest was resplendent, hushed beneath the muted haze of some uncanny sacredness, an aura of sleepy confidence in its own beauty. Little lizards the same color as the moss skittered and scampered about the bricks of the archway. There were dozens of them. He shook Horace's hand, bewildered by it all.

"Good to meet you, Horace. Surprised to meet you."

"Likewise. And just look at us. Here we are. The surprise is my doing entirely."

Horace took a few shaky steps away from the van's window and gestured at the surrounding glory of the landscape with a pass of his crooked, waist-high cane.

"We sure are, but I'm not so sure about being on time, like you said. I was supposed to meet you in downtown Wistwood, which means I'm late. I apologize if I've inconvenienced you, Sir. I never expected to meet you out here by the road."

Horace laughed a little and waved the comment away. "Stop with the 'Sir' business. Just 'Horace,' will do. And you put me to no trouble at all. I was worrying since this morning that you might get lost on the way. Some folks do, when the fog rolls in. So I figured I'd come out and meet you."

"That's very kind. I actually had to pull over onto the shoulder just across the way, where you saw me and I saw first saw you. I pulled over at least as much as I dared, to wait it out. Never saw fog that thick before in my life. It was something."

"It still *is* something," said Horace, "wherever the wind has blown it. And you can expect to see it again, before the day is done. The fog and the wind have minds of their own in these parts. They move where they want. Folks either get lost, get out of the way, or move right along with them. But you need experience to do any of those things, at least when the fog puts its foot down."

"Even getting lost?"

"Sometimes, Brask—may I call you 'Brask'?—a person needs extra experience for *that*. Luckily, I know my way around and can get lost better than anybody. Call it a gift."

"I'm sure it is." Brask tried to smile through his perplexity. The old man had seemed so business-like on the phone. In person, he seemed ... a little fey. "Say, if you want to get in your car and lead the way I'm sure we can make up for lost time. I'll follow you to the property, now that I've found your grand entrance, at last."

"I didn't drive a car up here," said Horace. The corners of his eyes creased into oily crow's feet that sliced into his sunken temples. Curly hair grew up and outward from his ears on its way to meet the crow's feet. "I walked up from town to look for you."

Brask couldn't help but glance at the knobbed cane and the mountain boots that appeared ready to fall off with the slightest misstep.

"I'm spryer than I appear," said Horace, gimlet eyes agleam, two wet marbles fixed upon the skeptical visitor.

Brask scratched at the stubble in the cleft of his chin, a bit out of sorts. He had intended to give a much more competent first impression than this. He couldn't explain it, but now he felt like he had been caught sitting in the van without any clothes on. This wasn't the plan. Why had the old man walked through the dense forest? What was expected now? Optimism evaporated, as if he had crawled, gasping and mad with anticipation across a desert, only to find an empty pit and a bleached skeleton at the scene of a once-shimmering mirage. Horace, meanwhile, took a moment to look the humdrum van up and down, side to side. Brask could just imagine the magnitude of contempt forming in the old codger's mind. He had no chance of getting the cabin if success depended upon looking like a man with his wits about him, right here, alongside the road, driving a piece of shit even creepier than the fog.

Is he here to make a preliminary visual assessment and then wave me off without even seeing the property, sparing us both a waste of time? But if that's the case, why would he even bother to walk all this way?

Horace might have been reading his thoughts. "Fine old workhorse you got yourself here, Brask. Guess she's got a lot of miles on her, from the look of things. But she got you here safe and sound. That's half the battle. What do you say I hop in, if it's not too much trouble, and we'll go have a look at town and then the cabin. Sound good?"

"Absolutely," said Brask. "Here, let me clean off the front seat so you can get in."

He strained against his seatbelt to grab an old laptop, his mess of papers, the Big Sur map, his cellphone, and the empty can of Diet Coke he'd bought at the gas station. Fingers fumbling, he stuffed them into various nooks and crannies of the van's combination backseat and bed. Horace shuffled around and climbed inside with a huffing, puffing effort.

Spry, my ass, thought Brask as his new passenger brushed aside part of the seatbelt, his hunting cap scraping against the ceiling.

"It's a bit disorganized in here, Horace. I apologize. Been so busy working lately I haven't had time to tidy up the way I'd like. It's no reflection on how I keep a house," he added with a wormy grin, internally livid that he had failed to clean the interior at least a little. But he had not been expecting to give rides to landlords or property managers or whoever this guy was. "And … er … sorry, but most of the seatbelt on your side is kind of missing. A casualty of the years, I'm afraid."

"Not to worry about any of it," said Horace. He closed the creaking door with a hearty slam and settled into the cracked, discolored leather seat without a glance toward the happy rat's nest of the van's modified rear interior. "If I can't make it back into Wistwood without the aid of a seatbelt I don't deserve to get back, not at my age." He leaned sideways and whispered conspiratorially, "And I won't breathe a word about your vehicle's unfortunate code violation to any of the local authorities, either." He nudged Brask's arm playfully with an elbow. "Especially since the fines are as steep as the cliff-sides. We'll take our chances, you and me. The road into Wistwood looks rough, but it's smooth as silk once you get going."

Then he winked.

Brask's initial feeling of awkwardness dissipated in the little wave of home-spun good humor that Horace had allowed to curl and break upon the shore of his anxiety. The old man made himself comfortable, as if they had been fellows destined for swift friendship, or perhaps negotiating the amiable parameters of a bond already long established as creatures of the same sex. Horace liked him—that much was now apparent—and for Brask this was an invigorating omen.

"This gate or arch or whatever it is," said Brask, wheeling gently onto the dirt road that cleaved a winding way into the redwoods. "Doesn't look like anything

I've ever seen in this part of California, way up in the forest like this. Was there some kind of old industrial building here at one time? I don't know much about the history of Big Sur."

"Oh, that old archway's got historical value, I dare say." Horace ran a hand slowly along the dashboard. It was still damp from the mist. "But it ain't never been part of any factory. The owner of the town, the Landlord, imported it, actually. Picked it up in his travels. Had it put in. Same with the lantern post. He likes the look of it. You like it?"

"I have to admit, it's unique. And quite an undertaking to import and reassemble, I assume." They drove beneath the arch and entered the gloom of sylvan shadow. "So the town of Wistwood is actually owned by somebody? By one person?"

Horace smiled, exposing a neat but yellowed row of peg-like teeth. "Every town has a proper owner, Brask. Every town in the world. In a manner of speaking. But we'll get down to all of that business after you've had a look around. You've come this far, after all. Let's head on in. The drive'll give us a chance to get to know each better. Wistwood isn't seven minutes through the forest, as I said when we first spoke."

"We are off and on our way," said Brask, heartened by a sudden thickening of sunlight that streamed beneath the vault of trees. It was one of the most extraordinary things, to enter the fullness of a forest, he thought, where time seemed to compress itself into a story, or a vision to be savored, rather than a measure of existence to be endured. The shadows traded spaces back and forth with the heaviness of the light, and everything that could be seen was forever weaving together, over and under and within itself, spreading out and away in a sumptuous tapestry that knew no imperfection, no errant stitch. All was ever as it ought to be, in a forest. Brask had believed this—or something like it—for as long as he could remember.

He basked in the lush expanse as they moved deeper into the majestic glade. He could no longer smell the sharp salt-sting of the Pacific through the open window, but the rich scent of this grand metropolis of trees enlivened his senses. "Beautiful," he said. "Beats driving anywhere in Silicon Valley, I can tell you that."

"I should say it would. And don't mind the road, as I said. All the roads in and around Wistwood are unpaved and rugged at the present time. Except for Main Street, downtown, which you'll see soon enough. Best to use caution driving anywhere, even though it's a pretty lazy corner of the world. Gotta keep your eyes out for wildlife, too. If we get charged by a deer or a wild boar and I'm flung through this windshield, just drag me off into the ferns and make your escape. Nobody'll be the wiser and no one'll miss me, I expect."

"Let's hope it doesn't come to that, Horace."

Brask grinned and eased up on the gas, worried that he was going too quickly through the tight little road that darted off between the looming trunks. Sitting next to Horace made him feel as if he were out for a drive with a crazy uncle, but it was a drive into the future. He steered through the shimmering panels of residual mist mingling with sunlight, the dirt road crunching a comfortable sound of welcome beneath the wheels. Soon enough, he would find out if Horace's little personality quirks could be turned to his advantage.

It never took him long to fathom, one way or another, with most people. If his inner-manipulator was working—the one gift he ever received from his father was the gift he prized most about himself—if he could somehow resurrect that crucial device, get it really humming again, then all of the remaining pieces of his existence would fall back into place. They would return to him, these fragments, from all the godforsaken places to which the recent series of storms had banished them in bursts of sadness and violence.

He wondered idly if his father would be proud to see him work that one talent, that one and only characteristic that had ever meant anything to the dilapidated drunk who spawned him.

Forget it, thought Brask. *It's probably a good thing you'll never know the answer.*

⊷⊶

"Get over here, Brasky old boy. I got something to say and you need to listen. This is important stuff about getting through this shit-hole of life. Are you listening? Can you hear me?"

"Yeah, Pop. I hear ya. For Christ's sake, I'm only two feet away. You're yelling. Everybody in the neighborhood can hear ya."

"Yeah? Well, fuck them. Real good. Now, listen Braskers, a man has got to use his talents in this world. Not just when it counts, but when he himself can't count on having a chance to use his talents at all."

"What?"

It's happening again. Thirteen. Same speech as before.

"You got to create opportunities where none exist, Braskaroo! You hear? You got to pry into people. Look 'em over and then pry into 'em with your wits. Find out what makes 'em tick and once you do, you gotta open 'em up like you was guttin' a deer, only you can't let 'em know you're doing it, see?"

"Yeah. Gut 'em. Got it, Pop."

"Now, don't be smart with me. It's true. You got to see what's inside once you open 'em up. Gotta see what's there that you can work with. What's useful and what's meant to be thrown out."

"Do I really have to listen to this again? Emily never has to sit around for this kind of stuff."

"That's because she's a girl! She's got her own set of rules she'll have to figure out and follow, and I don't have a thing to say about that. If your poor mama hadn't died, she'd be here right now seeing to Em, but there ain't nothing I can do about it. Girls don't have the same troubles. They got different ones. All they need to do is keep their legs shut long enough to keep a man crazy hungry for it, then hook some fool by the lip, just like a fish. Then they're set for life and they don't have to worry about another thing."

"Are you serious? I mean, I'm fourteen, Dad. They taught us the word 'misogyny' in school, you know. Even I know the world doesn't work that way anymore. It never did work. You can't think of girls that way."

"Bullshit I can't. And don't give me any lip, boy. I may not be as quick as I used to be, but I can still bust your mouth wide open, if I want. You're not too big for that, Mr. Fourteen Years Old."

"You can hardly get off the couch, Dad."

"Yeah? Well, it might do you some good to show respect and listen to something that'll change your life. Maybe make a man out of you before I die and you got no one to guide you along. Where was I? What was the last thing I said?"

"You could still bust my mouth."

"No, jackass, before that! My point. What was my point?"

"Looking inside people to see what makes them whirl or tick or something. Who the hell knows? Stuff you keep and stuff you throw away."

"That's right. You've got to cut people, and cut them fast, Brasket. Mentally, I mean. That's how you do it. You got to dig for an opening and get inside their heads and once you do, they'll be putty in your hand."

"Wow. Putty. Just what I always wanted."

"I mean it. People're putty in your hands, if you play the game right. And don't forget the most important thing of all."

"What's that?"

"Oh, I know you think I'm a drunk and I know better than God exactly what kind of drunk I am, but remember this—everybody on earth can be owned, Braskatask. One way or another, if you're clever enough to find a way to get inside 'em. Even the hardest, most contrary sonofabitch you ever come across in your worst nightmare can be owned and worked, if you get real good at it."

"And you were the best at it that ever lived. I know this story, Pop. I know how it ends, too. I'm looking at how it ends. I'm gonna go play basketball over at Lloyd's for an hour. Maybe smoke some grass. You want me to make you something to eat before I go?"

"You wait up a minute and don't fuck with me about smokin' dope, little mongrel. I ain't finished having this talk with you, yet. We got any of them microwave pizzas in the freezer?"

"All flavors."

"Well, I'll have one of those before you head out and you can freshen this drink with some ice. There's another bottle of Jack behind the stereo speaker. The one with the back that comes off easy, up to the top of the bookshelf. I hid it up there so you and your sister wouldn't find it."

"Hid it from yourself, you mean. I can't believe you think we're that stupid."

"Just remember, Braskerino. Even if a man don't got a pot to piss in, at first, the clever man always wins, and let me tell you, he's the one who gets to tell other people when, where, and how they can piss. And how high he wants the stream to fly. Mark my words. Now, women, from a purely—whatcha call it?—objective standpoint, *they ain't so much a different story so much as they are a case of creatures requiring different methods of surveillance and investigation. You're sister's gonna find that out the hard way, one of these days. They all do."*

"You saying Mom found out the hard way? You showed her what life was all about the hard way, Dad?"

"Now, don't get your back up, whelp. Your mama was a different story. She was a goddamned SAINT, your mama was. That's why God took her away from us, the selfish bastard. But we'll get into that some other day."

"Nah, I don't think so. I don't think I want to hear you talk about her ever again."

"Fine. All you need to do is remember how your old man told you one day about how every sonofabitch on this planet got a secret spot that only you can find and exploit, if you look for the opportunity. You remember how I told you that, and then don't ever say your old man didn't lay some hard truth down on your empty friggin' skull when you was a kid. Don't ever say I never did you a big goddamn favor."

Never ask Dad for examples that show how he knows such things. Don't pry. Don't pin Dad down to the details.

Listen to the equation. Think about the theory. Never ask to see how the math is done. Just arrive at the answer. Don't dig. You might get a belt upside the head. One that puts you in the hospital overnight. One that gives you a mild concussion. One that leaves you too cotton-brained and dazed to remember important stuff. Learn fast. Learn well.

Learn on your own.

Survive.

Never be hurtful, even when you have to read people to get ahead. Never step on anybody. Never betray.

Keep your promise.

Keep it forever.

BIG BAD MIRACLE GOD

Now the back of Shep Daltry's patrol car smelled like puke and piss-saturated denim. The reek of it stung in his eyes, his nose, his brain. This kind of thing didn't usually bother Shep. He was getting rather accustomed to it. But today the stink was so strong he had to swallow a little harder than usual and grip the steering wheel until his knuckles were bone-white and streaked with red. His fingernails dug into the vinyl, leaving little crescent marks as he squeezed and squeezed again. Was he getting tired, physically? That would never do. He had come too far. Risked too much already. Daltry prided himself on having a tough stomach for the job, but also for his own work, which were two entirely different things. Lately, though, the two jobs had become intertwined. That was a glorious convenience. Not sleeping for three days was an inconvenience, but a minor one.

Screw it. He was on a long stretch of rural road and the shoulder looked wide and smooth. Why, it was practically a jet runway compared to some of his other discreet workstations and drop-spots. Endless rows of tobacco surged and swayed in green waves on either side. Man, the stink was bad this time. He figured at the very least he could always pull over, out here in the middle of nowhere, and barf his own guts up if it came to it. He wouldn't think less of himself for doing so; work had been especially difficult the last several days, just like the Employer had predicted. No one else was ever going to know if he lost his lunch from the stress and smell of it all, so it didn't really fucking matter.

His fellow officers were miles away, light years removed from him and from the masterpieces he was creating. Some were having lunch or coffee in crummy box-shaped restaurants. Others were busy back at the station, kissing the sheriff's rancid brown asshole in the hope of advancing from their present shit duties to less shittier duties.

Shep wanted no part of that. He was proud to remind himself of this every day he woke up and faced another challenge in the workplace. Headquarters was two hours away. It was amazing how easy it was to slip away and do his own work while employed by the county. They were so goddamned stupid and incompetent. It was a wonder anyone ever got arrested at all. Luckily the bad guys were even more idiotic than the squad.

The front windows were rolled down but somehow the smell of all that growing lung-killer, rich soil, and sun-kissed earth brought a new, sickeningly sweet layer of air that did not blend well at all with the fragrance of Shep's newest festering and putrid passenger, cuffed and dripping snot in the back seat behind the protective cage screen. Ironic, that screen, thought Shep. It wasn't protecting *him*.

It didn't need to.

He whistled idly as he drove another five miles along the remote road and tobacco fields turned to corn fields. This was a part of the route that he and a few others called the "Cornhole Corridor." Shep didn't even feel tempted to look back at the piece of human filth stinking him out of his own head, much less his own patrol car. Wait. Human? No, this sad excuse for flesh and bone didn't deserve to be designated as a human, which wasn't much of a designation to begin with, he had to admit. Still, he had encountered his fair share of dirtbags, and this thing in the back was by far one of the most unworthy of inclusion in the race of men. He felt sure if he took a look back into those hepatitis-and-baby-shit colored eyes and saw the greasy hair dangling in grimy strings over the acne and meth-scarred face … well, he would hurl all over the dashboard.

"Do you realize, you poor sonofabitch, that you smell so rancid I think your filth is forming bacteria on the air and that bacteria is floating into my nose and hooking its claws on my nose hairs? I can feel 'em crawling around in there. You are the first sorry fuck I ever met in life who's got himself a bad case of air crabs. Did you know that, Mister?"

Shep smiled wide into the rearview mirror, a gleaming rictus through the screen of steel mesh.

Benny, the junkie who had gotten himself into this spot of trouble by daring to take a piss outside the little homeless encampment north of the city, blinked weakly, his head making little jerks with every segmented crack of roadway they sped between the blurred fields of corn. Was it corn? Was there bright light or some kind of strange sunset behind it all? He couldn't tell.

pastel sunflowers pastel sunflowers pastel sunflowers pastel sunflowers pastel sunflowers pastel sunflowers pastel sunflowers pastel sunflowers pastel sunflowers

The smell of Sterno and piss and puke and Thunderbird barely filtered by a swollen, cirrhotic liver blossomed in the car like a puff of smothering nuclear fallout, a choking pyroclastic flow borne of lifelong shames and fragmented nightmares of defeat that even Shep could not begin to wrap his mind around. But Shep was sensitive; he could detect Benny's shame, could tell he was maybe just a little bit embarrassed about being Benny. And that was more than enough.

"Now don't go getting sad on me back there, brother," said Shep. He was a preacher preparing a sinner for the moment of riverside baptism, some Full Gospel watery submersion and rebirth to a spotless new existence. "There's no cause for shame in this car. Matter of fact, I was once known to take a little bit too much to drink, myself, on occasion. A man's got a hard life in this world. Am I right?"

"Y-y-yeah. You got that right."

"See, we men got to relieve the stress every once in a while. Got to enjoy ourselves with a refreshing beverage, now and again. If that's against the law, then I, patrolman Shep Daltry—formerly an officer, but that's how the cookie fucking crumbles—am as guilty as the next man. Maybe even as guilty as you, Benny, though you hardly strike me as being 'the next man,' if you'll pardon my saying so."

"No. N-n-no offense taken."

"Ha! There. See how good we can get along, the two of us men, when we admit our common faults?" Shep raised a hand of admission and solidarity, smiling wider than ever, his teeth shining grey and greasy in the mirror beyond the steel mesh. He shifted his eyes back and forth across the road, scanning the endless, shifting twin oceans of the cornfields, still swaying like a silent, watchful crowd of millions. Expectant. Waiting.

There was no one else on the road. He hadn't seen another vehicle in half an hour, but then again, he didn't expect to see another; this thin stretch of country highway had been closed-off for construction work at both outlets on this particular day. Of the many who knew about this special arrangement, Shep was one of the very few who had authority to travel this road if he wished. Apparently, he was the only one who wanted to do so on this afternoon. Thus far. His window of time was not open indefinitely. No way. That could become a problem. Shep didn't mind problems if he could see them coming, but he had issues with things unforeseen, problematic or not. Severe issues.

"Now, if you and I are to continue to get along, bro, especially since I am being polite enough not to let my body do what it wants and blow chunks all over this front seat due to your odor, it strikes me that you could at least try to engage your arresting officer in some philosophical discussion as we travel the lonesome byway. See, I'm not much for music and we can't play music, anyhow, on account of the fact that we need to have the patrol radio on at all times for purposes of monitoring potentially dangerous situations involving criminal activity. You think you could rally yourself enough to have a little chat with me?"

"Yessir."

"Excellent," said Shep. "Now think about the irony of all this, Benny, my friend. I'm guessing you got it in your heart to humor a bitter, disenfranchised bastard from the police department, like me. I can't imagine you'd be unable to find it in your soul to sympathize with a fellow member of the race of the misunderstood, right?"

"S-s-sure."

"By golly, we're practically brothers already, Benny. You and me. Brothers. Imagine that shit for a minute, I ask you. But it's brilliant. Just brilliant. Here I am, driving this car and pissing my life away as surely as the sun is on its way to setting in the no-good goddamned liberal West. Yet I have apprehended and am charged with the legal detainment of a man, a fellow member of my species. I am responsible for someone actually there, beneath the dirt and the stench and the layers of God knows what kind of dried-up swill you've been wallowing in. And I, pissing my life away as mentioned, am suddenly in the position of taking away your life, such as it is, for ... the act of *pissing!*"

Shep began to laugh so hard that he slapped the wheel until it shuddered and the car swerved on the thin grey ribbon of road, threatening to slice like the blunt blade of a scythe into the cornfield army, deflowering its repetitive perfection, its monotonous virginity, to introduce an unmistakable stain of chaos. Thin and pliable as a discolored pipe-cleaner, Benny tilted painfully against the lap seatbelt and banged his head against the molding of the door with a yowl. Shep regained his composure and brought the car squealing back onto the road. This wasn't supposed to end in some sort of accident brought on by incompetence. Far from it.

Benny tried to sit up, groaning and reeking anew with what little sweat remained to push its way through his pores and activate hitherto unrevealed odors from within his malnourished body. He failed. He had barely enough equilibrium to keep his head from bashing against the steel mesh of the cage as he sagged first one way and then swung another.

"I'm gonna ... I'm ... I'm gonna be ... thick ... I'm thick ..." he managed to croak when his back slammed against the sticky seat behind him and the car sped faster down the road. His eyes rolled up into his head, long hair splayed down his face. To Shep observing in the rearview mirror, Benny appeared under assault by some deep-sea creature unraveling its tentacles to ensnare and consume the two yellowed and unhealthy egg yolks of his eyeballs.

He snorted in derision.

"You gonna be 'thick,' huh? Yeah, that's a real laugh, pal. A knee-slapper. You gonna be 'thick' when I'm the one's been nearly about to heave a full belly of Denny's biscuits and gravy patties all over my own godforsaken self cause you stink worse than roadkill bloating in the sun. Even the fucking vultures wouldn't go near you, man. You know? I'll bet you could drop dead most anyplace, a piece of barely cogitating garbage like you, and the damn pests of the earth—the things that eat and scour away putrefaction—wouldn't touch you. The motherfucking bottle-flies wouldn't lay maggot eggs on your carcass. They'd rather fly into a spider's web than take a shit on you, boy."

Benny moaned again, as if to herald an oncoming torrent of vomit, but he did not possess the strength to produce a single heave and there was nothing in his stomach left to expel. Not even bile. His wrecked body wasn't producing that stuff anymore.

"Y-y-you s-s-sure got a ... f-f-filthy mouth, even for a cop. I may be dirty, but your mouth makes me smell sweet as a magnolia blossom, compared."

Benny surprised even himself; he had not spoken as much, or as coherently, in months. He couldn't remember the last time he had bothered to utter much of a sentence. He didn't even talk to himself, as many of his peers did. The only small, fluttering silverfish of pride he still possessed in his life was the knowledge that he wasn't crazy, at least not Talking to Himself crazy. It was a pin-feather of humanity brushing, however faint, against the cloud of self-destructive Death billowing from every horizon, the thundercloud, the supercell that had been churning to catch him for years.

The great cloud didn't even seem ominous anymore, only certain. Only capable of robbing the atmosphere of those few things his intoxicated faculties could still perceive of himself and the world, when bleak hours became days numb and full of forgotten thoughts. Those days had turned into years that mocked, each one a lazy, droning murmur. It was Time. Time lost while staring outward, sprawled on his back and seeing nothing, not even the blank canvas of sky, between bouts of drinking, shooting-up, and dreamless oblivion. It was an oblivion nowhere near as comforting as the kind found in the forest or in the bushes and trash-strewn underpasses, in the nowhere places.

"So!" gasped Shep. "It does have the power to string a few words together, after all. It can form a few sounds. Get a thought across. Or was that just a freak accident, there, Benny? A last gasp coming from something that don't even exist no more? Was that like a camera flash that happens after somebody already took the goddamned picture? And it sure as hell ain't a pretty picture, is it? Oh, Benny. You just had a leftover shoot out your mouth, boy, and you don't even know it."

"M-m—my ..."

"Nah. Don't bother trying to say any more. I know you can't. It don't matter. It's what I say that counts. In this car, on this road, on this day. Your most unlucky day out of all the unlucky days you got under your belt."

"W-w-w-what you g-g-gona do to me? Kick me across the c-c-county line? Been done to me b-b-before. I know how to get outta town good enough, when s-s-some cop drops me on the other side of they's own territory and say 'make tracks.' Even I know they ain't no room for me in a lock-up or drunk tank. Even round here."

"Woo hoo!" cried Shep. "Wonders never cease. It's like the back of my patrol car is filled with some kinda life-giving force, some unknown energy from outer space that brings dead brains back to life. I'll have to alert the sheriff about this phenomenon as soon as possible. He sure would wanna know that he's had a regular miracle car under his nose all this time and wasn't even aware of it. Yessir. I'll probably make the news all over again. This time in a good way, with a white man. Imagine that shit, Benny. Why, they'll likely even give me a promotion, now. Me—Shep Daltry—promoted for discovering the power that gives speech to the dumb and the shit-covered. There'll be book deals and movie deals. Hell, even the damned Pope over in Rome'll wanna get a look at this. Make some holy investigation. The Catholics love that sorta shit. You Catholic, Benny?"

"N-n-no."

"Hmm. Coulda fooled me. You look and smell like one. Either way, I'll be famous and rich and successful and I'll have you to thank for it. See, you ended up being the guinea pig, Benny … with emphasis on the pig part. But there's always a downside to every good thing. Even miracles. You can trust me on that. I know it. Then again, maybe God likes things good and rotten. Maybe He gets off on the smell of hobo piss. Yeah, I got a hunch this big bad miracle god my mama taught me to be so scared of with the back of her hand actually *enjoys* things being fucked up and messy. I think He appreciates the variety that comes when scum and slime shows up and pollutes this fine old world. I mean, He'd have to like it, right? There ain't no question He sure has stocked the larder pretty full of junk food. And you know what else? I think He likes hating the fuck out of this world as much as I do."

"I-I think … I think you are one crazy damn cop and I … I don't wanna hear no m-m-more of this. You … you … something ain't right with you, man. I seen a lot of folks in my time who ain't right, but you … you got something else goin' on."

"Oh, you don't know the half of it, Benny. Not even a sliver of it."

Shep's eyes burned backward through the rearview and the steel mesh.

"I don't want no trouble with you, Officer. I am what I am but I done you no wrong, man. You just take me off to the tank and lock me away or drop my ass in the n-n-next county. I won't complain none. I won't hold nothin against you for the stuff you said. I don't even r-r-remember what you said. Let's just get to where we're supposed to be going. I'm... I ... I'm gonna stop talkin. I ain't said this much to nobody in ... I dunno how long. But I ain't feelin so good, and I don't wanna cause no more trouble than what I did already. You in charge, here. I don't want no trouble. You in charge."

Shep whistled a couple bars of Turkey in the Straw, contemplating the world. Then he turned to speak again over his shoulder.

"Well, thank you for that news flash concerning my position of authority, Benny boy! But you're a bit behind on current events. Especially the ones that've been staring you in the face. See, I'm a few steps ahead of you in the world of current events. I know I'm in charge, fuckbrain. Just like I know you're in a heap of trouble, whether you want trouble or not. That's the thing about trouble. When you're in it, you're in it, and it takes the clever and the powerful to get out of it. News flash for you, Benny: you ain't neither one of those things."

"Please, man ... Oh, Jesus Christ awmighty. I'm sorry for stinkin up your car and sorry f-f-for whatever the hell I done, but I ..."

"No, you got it all wrong. But don't be too hard on yourself. Ain't as if you got a lot of brain matter to work with when it comes to making sense out of life's unexpected detours. Hell, even people who got plenty of smarts in their heads ought to just stop trying to make sense outta life. They'd spare themselves a lot of unnecessary energy and grief, in my informed opinion."

"I don't know what you mean. I swear I don't."

"What I mean, Benny, is that this 'trouble' I'm talking about hasn't got a goddamned thing to do with you, directly speaking. This trouble is all about me."

"Please, just let me out by the side of the road. I'll crawl off into the corn and you won't never see me again. I swear it."

Benny strained against the handcuffs and the seatbelt and nearly fainted from the effort, feeble as it was. Shep raised a large comforting palm from the steering wheel and grinned into the rearview. He stepped on the gas. The corn-fields became a blur on either side. The sound of the engine was a threat and a scream.

"You'll understand everything, Benny, before all is said and done." Shep's eyes searched the sky beyond the windshield, forlorn, as if he were merely disap-pointed that life was sometimes a bit difficult to comprehend. "Come to think of it, friend, none of the material I've been working with lately has really understood anything about my situation. All I get is looks. Strange ones. Looks that tell me plain as plain that they haven't got a clue."

"You damn psycho cop. Let me outta here."

"Maybe I've seen a little flicker of comprehension, here and there," continued Shep, scanning ahead with greater intensity. "You know. Like a light bulb that's on its last filament or whatever the hell it is, and it won't quite brighten up the way you want, but it won't just go out, neither. Not until you smash it. An an-noying thing, to be honest."

"In the name of God I beg you, Sir ..."

Benny began to weep, his face contorted with fear. No tears would come. He seemed to have no moisture left but his blood, which pounded painfully through his brain and sounded in his ears like the deafening rush of a great waterfall alongside the car's bullied engine.

"And by the way, I'm not psychotic, Benny. No. I ain't. I ain't that at all. See, I'm just a man who's about to change jobs. About to make a career move. I've been putting a great deal of thought into the matter and, being unhappy with my present employment for some time, I have been looking around for other exciting opportunities. I believe I have found one such opportunity and I am at long last prepared to make the transition."

"What?"

"You know, it's so amazing how one online ad can change a man's life in this day and age. They say a fella shouldn't spend too much time on the internet. It'll make his attention span deficient or some such horseshit, but there's nothing wrong with my attention. In fact, my head came right smack to stand-up attention when I saw that ad, buried like it was hiding on me among all the hundreds of ads I've looked at. But it was special, and soon I'll have an interview."

"An … interview?"

"Of course, I haven't given my notice yet at the department, but I'm pretty confident I'll get the job. I don't know why I'm so confident. I just am. Maybe it's because I've been carrying out my instructions to the letter. Maybe it's because a person just knows, sometimes. Do you ever just know something deep down in your heart, Benny?"

Shep glared, his ice gray eyes glinting, two sharp chips of stone hammered from a boulder, ricocheting off the rearview and hissing through the grille into Benny's clammy, pallid skin, razor sharp.

"Do you ever just know, in your heart?"

Benny trembled violently, drawing on some energy he couldn't possibly have possessed, save for that remaining spark of terrified life that sometimes refuses to depart even the most unlikely and uninhabitable house of decrepit flesh and bone.

"I'm gonna get that job, stinky Benny. And I'm gonna get a new office to go with it. That's part of the arrangement. The offer. And that's where you come in. You see, when men like me change offices and jobs and what not, we have to be very careful to clear our stuff out. We have to be very meticulous, so we can bring some of our things—you know, awards we may have won, some trophies—along with us and proudly display stuff when we get to new accommodations. I have been encouraged to do just this, and to accumulate even more professional honors to accentuate my impressive resume."

"I don't want no part of this. Please. I b-b-beg you. You let me go, mister, and I swear to God I will spend every last day of my life saying a prayer for your success."

"Oh! Look at that!" said Shep, glancing sharply to his right across the eternity of cornfield. "Now doesn't that look like a perfect patch of lonesome road, over there on the shoulder?" He gestured with his smooth, chiseled jaw and the shuddering stick that Benny's body had become convulsed as he lifted his gaze and tried to see where they might be going. Could this be an end at last? Was the cop going to let him out? Even to get outside in the air would be salvation.

Shep turned the wheel and slowed the car, moving onto the shoulder without a sound. Ahead was the carcass of a deer that had been hit probably a few days before, bloated and partially ripped open beneath the hungry sun, in front of the rows of corn that waved and fluttered gently, unable to move but thoroughly able, somehow, to say

Behold!

Three large crows were pecking at the fly-riddled doe and at a pile of her entrails pooling from her gut. The innards were sun-dried and stuck to the ground, a knotted and now-flattened bevy of snakes that sought to escape the beast's belly after some explosive impact, as if the deer had been dropped from the sky. Shep came to a stop and turned off the engine. Benny began to wheeze, the desperate work of his lungs whistling and shrill. Crows flew up from the carcass in front of the car, cawing, flapping, each one a mad, shiny shard of midnight in the vast illumination of the tranquil afternoon.

Stepping out with a weary sigh and stretching his body, Shep looked up and down the road. There was no one around. Not even any of the construction vehicles he had expected he might see. He checked his watch. The road would be off-limits to commuter traffic for another two hours. Plenty of time.

"Yeah, this is the spot, Benny." He pointed to the disgusting roadkill ahead. "See, I always look for signs, and this here is a great one. Not the dead deer, so much, but the crows. There was three of them. Did you see those crows? They've flown off into the corn but they're still watching us, you can bet on it. And I counted three, sure enough. You ever hear what they about three crows being in one spot? My old granny—she was one of the mountain grannies, tough as oak, nobody wanted to mess with her—she knew all sorts of important sayings and shit."

"I don't know nothing about crows," mumbled Benny, his face pressed helplessly against the window.

"No? Well, my granny had a saying about them." Shep took his hat off and placed it, almost lovingly, on the front passenger seat as he leaned back in the car and opened the glove compartment. He rummaged for something that emerged, gleaming and bright and very sharp in a ray of sunshine that bathed it with a kiss through the windshield.

Benny's throat rattled and choked on his dry tongue in the back seat.

With a shift of his muscular torso and a belch of biscuits and gravy, Shep loped around the car, whistling a bit as his steel-toed boots made sharp, clean sounds on the crumbling shoulder asphalt. His nose caught the first hair-raising scents of the dead doe as the wind shifted.

"You know, Benny, I think you actually did me a favor, stinking like a hog covered in twenty years of its own shit. Ain't such a shock to smell this deer now that I'm out in God's green and glorious world."

He opened the rear door of the patrol car. Benny was blinded by a torrent of sunshine but that wasn't why he trembled and began to squeal, coarse and cracked though his voice was.

Shep looked down at him, running a finger along the blade of a curved gutting-knife, his eyes sizing Benny up, pondering, considering, maybe even admiring, despite the repugnant and wretched form of the dreadful human being slouched against his legs.

Glancing through the white burn of the light, Shep thought he saw a faint shimmer of forms amid the corn rows, morphing from one vision to the next to the next: a child giggling in its crib, grasping playfully for a sunbeam; then a wiry young man with good skin and a full head of hair; then a man well-groomed and clad in a business suit and tie, and then, at last, the bum … Benny.

The material.

He would have thought it all a trick of the marauder sun, but Shep had witnessed this kind of entertaining glamor before, in other ways, with some of the others who had been fortunate enough to capture his eye, to dare to inform and inspire his work. To pad his resume.

The gutting knife gleamed anew, anxious on its own, and Benny did, at long last, manage to throw up, though the heave was as arid as his soul had been for years that were now beyond recall.

"You know, Benny, as repulsive as you are, when I saw you takin that piss against the underpass, I said to myself, 'Now that is one of the straightest spines

I have ever seen, especially on a man whose nutritional habits and bone density have got to be questionable, to say the least.' See, I figured you were worth it, Benny. Worth checking out. And now that I get another look at you, I'm convinced of it."

"P-p-please."

"I don't need all of you. Just the backbone, up to the base of the skull. Them crows we saw can tend to whatever's left. But the display I'm planning for my new office can use a few pieces that you, Benny, don't really need anymore and haven't needed in a while, seeing as you ain't had a life worth living for a long, long time. Don't you think?"

Benny tried to struggle in his cuffs but didn't have the strength to wring his wrists with enough force to draw blood against the metal. He could make no further sound.

"Don't you worry, Benny. What I find suitable shall be submitted for the inspection and interest of my future Employer and thereafter mounted on a wall in my new digs. It's the last and only thing I promise. You're too weak and scared to get out of the car yourself. But don't fret. I can get hold of you by the hair and yank you out the same way I shoved you in. Then, when you're outside in this beautiful day, this gorgeous fucking day that the Lord has made, you'll feel like a new person. A new strength will come into you, one you didn't even know you had. And when you see how wonderful it is, when you smell this field of living food and know that everything you ever thought, good or bad, is honest to goodness true ... well, then you and me are gonna take a little walk, yonder. Yonder into the rows."

EARTH AGAINST EARTH

"Mama, it's only something to do for a day. I'm just going to look at the place. For fun."

On the other end of the call, Schuyler's mother pretended to weep into a Kleenex. Schuyler knew it was all a ruse, had been through it before, but felt a dagger move across her gut just the same.

"You're like your Grandmother," sniffed Mrs. Brody. "No wonder she left you the money instead of me. She never did give one thought to me. That *woman!* Sun rose and set on you, though. Now look what you're up to. An antiques shop in a town I ain't even heard of. Really, Schuyler. You're less responsible today than when you were a kid. And you're pushing thirty."

"Mama, it's worth a peek, only. Jesus, I shouldn't have even told you. But look. You can come along, if you want. Criticize it. Run it to hell and back. Gee, that'll be a fun mother-daughter outing, don't you think?"

"Don't be flip, Sky. I'm just trying to keep you from doing something idiotic. You have your job to think about. And finding a husband. Babies."

"Please stop."

More sniveling. A grating rustle of tissue against the mouthpiece.

"Well, it's not something way out of left field, to want my only child to get married. It's a hard core reality of life. Starting a family. Being part of a community."

"I am part of a community, Mama."

"Yeah, and I expect you stick out like a sore thumb. Young woman as pretty as you are. Nice teaching job. Some inheritance money in the bank. And *no man*. Not so much as a tire-mark of a man's vehicle in your driveway, from what I understand."

"How the hell would you know anything about that one way or the other, Mama?"

"I hear things, honey. Mothers have eyes all over town. It's one the last skills they've let us hold onto."

"Except you live four towns away. In an assisted living facility."

"Doesn't matter. We get wind of things from all sorts of distances. You'd be surprised. But if you were a *mother* you wouldn't be. And that's part of the reason I'm worried."

"Mama, we've been through this. I'm not gonna have this conversation again."

"I didn't start it, girl, you did."

"You're the one who called me, Mama. You're the one who called and asked me what I've been up to, what I'm going to be doing, and when I casually tell you I'm going to take a look at an antique shop for rent, you go completely nuts for no reason."

"*Not* for no reason. I'm worried about you making a big mistake. You've made some harebrained ones before, need I remind you. It's already easy enough to imagine you sitting in that condo forever and becoming a spinster. But sitting in an antiques shop? Christ on a cracker, Sky, that literally paints the damn picture, and it ain't a pretty one."

"Look, Mama, I gotta go. We'll talk about this another time."

Mrs. Brody began to cry, for real this time.

"You just don't want me to be happy."

"Mama, that's not true."

"It is. I've known it for years. Your grandma was the same way. Even the little things you do, the throwaway things you say, are meant to hurt me and shut me out."

"Yes, Mama. That's right. Exactly right. You're onto me."

"At least you'll admit it. I never could get your grandmother to do that. Damn that woman."

"Yes, Mama."

"Promise me you won't go renting some stupid antiques shop. You'll lose the bra off your body, and all your grandmother's money. And there's nothing I can do, here in this no-good facility. Bored out of my wig. I can't save you from yourself anymore, Schuyler."

"I know, Mama. It's okay."

"Promise me you'll start dating again. Find some nice guy to share your life. Help you become stable."

"I promise, Mama."

"Well, then, I'll let you go until next time."

"Okay, Mama. Have a good day."

"I forgive you, Schuyler."

"For what?"

"For everything, of course."

"Goodbye, Mama."

"Bye, honey."

Schuyler put down the phone.

Here she was again. Stuck in one of the lost places, a piece of scrub on a wasteland astride some desert highway of life. No God, no enthralling beauty, no inspiration. Just a dead, abandoned planet that would one day be incapable of hosting even the smallest bit of life amid the constant quiet. She could see it all, as if passing by in a spaceship. The detachment of the universe, its randomness: a few planets with icy pools; others with endless, empty valleys, turning and turning through space, never hosting the sound of a voice, a tickle of laughter. Spinning. Spinning with no point or purpose, thrown from an explosion that had no more meaning than the elaborate swell of its aftermath.

Shit. At least she was still good with people, such as they were. Schuyler was all too aware that she had been able to walk social fence-posts with ease, single or not, comfortable with and unthreatening to humans in all sorts of spheres, real and imagined. Much of it was due to her looks, and how she calibrated those looks: never too fashionably dressed, in a competitive way, but never plain, and always generous with the earthy bewitchment that came so easily to pale green eyes above a wry smile. Quick with wit, but only when it might count. Only when there was something to be gained.

What a sham of a life. How do I get out? Mama wants me to get out more. I've got her permission.

Sometimes, Schuyler felt a twinge of the stage-magician's conceit, coupled with a free-floating sense of guilt for being so effortless in her interactions with others. But her talents could rub some the wrong way, too. Occasionally, people considered her facile nature to be uncanny. Men mostly. And there were those women on earth who enjoyed making another woman feel small and unsuccessful if she did not—or could not, in a pinch—piss-off a significant portion of the population.

A few former friends had come to resent her for not automatically alienating this faction or that faction, simply because of who they were or who they supposedly voted for. For such acquaintances, Schuyler's identity was valuable only if it was bound up with an assortment of pedestrian ideological litmus tests. Luckily, she had been expert at evasive maneuvers where such tests were concerned and, when all was said and done, guessed that this skill explained the chief reason she was generally well-liked. In more sheltered moments, however, she wondered if such elusive and finely honed qualities also explained why, at age twenty-nine, she did not have a serious lover or anyone she could truly describe as a lifelong friend. Still, up until recently, the sheer volume of good will she received from those who barely knew her always seemed to fill the occasional chasm of longing. The yawning maw. Earth against earth. Void against void.

There was nothing to be done. What was one person supposed to do, anyhow? She had already seen far too many soul-mates, kindred spirits, and married couples disappoint or outright harm each other in excruciating, irreparable ways. Screw that. She could live contentedly between worlds because the disparate realms weren't all that real to begin with, and she did not, on the whole, suffer debilitating regret in any form whatsoever.

This was how the world operated and functioned, when it functioned sensibly, which was rare, and for all its incessant babble, humanity was not exactly eager to give up its best tips and secrets for survival. Schuyler, alone on the island of her own, constant counsel, was in possession of a great secret—the secret of a mundane-yet-gentrified diplomacy. A magic that had served her faithfully when so many of life's other little talents and tricks had not proved nearly as reliable. You had to take what you could get in this life, she believed. A woman, especially, had to play-up cunning thoughts and gifts and use them to the best of her ability, even if the rest of life's canvas remained conspicuously unpainted. So what if hers was barren? Happens to the best.

Use what you've got. Don't hurt anybody, but don't let yourself get hurt or used. Not if your talent can help you avoid it.

Despite her cool, Schuyler wasn't certain about the majority of things when it came to the world, but she had heretofore managed to overcome a potentially lethal cynicism by forcing herself to attend the fading ghost of human goodness, wherever that disintegrating phantom might be found. But that act was all over.

She didn't believe in the basic decency of people anymore. It was that simple.

The once-solid bedrock that used to anchor her restless psyche to the consolation of the earth was gone. Even so, the almost bitter awareness of being a part of it all, of understanding that, despite everything, she somehow still belonged, kept her upright. The knowledge that she remained flesh and blood and capable of moving about in the midst of the screaming, viral uncertainty; all of this convinced her that she could survive.

She could survive. She could fight for more and still play some role in her destiny, even if that fortress of surety had long ago been besieged and its foundations, along with all labyrinthine dungeons, were thrown open by violence, exposed to the scrutiny of a cosmos that cared nothing for long-fortified devices. It was cold. Cold out there in space, and colder, somehow, within the mausoleum of her bourgeois, wine-savoring disbelief. Damn, but she had grown weary, and what energy she still possessed was needed for a swift escape.

It was time. Time to forget the ruins and seize the shadow of the vast, winged creature she had only glimpsed on the outskirts of her hopes and desires until now. It was time to soar with that exhilarating beast, unafraid and untroubled by faithlessness, and by the sickening temptation to look down and doubt. One look and she would lose hold to plunge, forever tumbling and lashing out at the uselessness, wailing in the silent free-fall that could only end in something far worse than death.

For Schuyler, emancipation meant owning nothing fancier than an old antique shop, one in which she could grow old and fade, eventually blending in with the merchandise. Dust to dust. Such a small answer to towering mysteries. So plain. But she knew it was going to happen. She planned to make it happen.

Look out, Wistwood, wherever the hell you are. That shop is going to be mine, even if a hundred other, better people are in line to get it.

WISTWOOD

Writer though he was, Brask could have scarcely imagined a small town more suited to leaving the rat-race than Wistwood. At first sight, it was breathtaking, if only for its abject lack of modernity. In the woods, but not of it. Repudiation of the wider world seemed to leap from the buildings along the rustic Main Street. Nestled amid the rolling, majestic hills and high chaparral, the place looked marginally more functional than one of the Wild West ghost towns his parents had dragged him through as a child during family excursions, but that was okay. From first glance at the minuscule but tidy downtown square he could sense that Wistwood was in harmony with his vision for a once and future home, an ideal place to melt into the very air, the grass, the isolation. Clean white sidewalks, a cluster of ramshackle storefronts along the strip; this was seclusion to be savored.

"Well, what do you think?" asked Horace, his arm dangling out the passenger door window, fingers moving playfully.

"First impression tells me this is exactly what I've been looking for."

Brask drove into Wistwood as if he had always been hovering somewhere too far above, an angel scanning the countryside from a separate realm, casting an envious glance into a foreign existence of unrealized dreams, an irresistible otherness. The mad, *other* world with its barking noises and instant judgments, whipping around with no destination on a carousel of relentless punishments, began to fade.

"Not much to look at," admitted Horace. "Just a spot for folks who like life served-up on the slow side. But it's home."

"Amen to that."

A rickety bar and grill. A dusty-looking mercantile. An antiques shop with cobwebbed windows. A used bookstore. A small brick church or chapel in the process of being built.

Who would have guessed that places like this still existed in California, much less that they were inhabitable?

Gazing at the strange and desirable ordinariness of the place, Brask rose, breathless and astonished, from some forced baptism by immersion against which he had been struggling; it was a physical wonderment, still and quiet and so preternaturally surprising that all he could do was gawp around in bewilderment, spirit attuned to seize upon the slightest mystical affirmation of a new, chosen life with every fiber of his will.

He caught a lump in his throat and for a few helpless moments as he glided up the lazy street, he was afraid he might dissolve into tears of relief. The edge of the world had been reached at last; here he could seize what might be redeemed, no longer in spite of the ordinariness of life but because of it. Yet, he did not weep. It took a lot for him to do so. He had been a boy and then a man wired for the steely set of a jaw and the grinding of however many teeth it took to keep from shedding a tear or allowing a lip to tremble. What was the proper response to this? His spirit had been pierced by the sweetest of poisons, smoldering on the tip of a fateful arrow. A sigh of delight served the purpose that tears relinquished. Horace peered at him out of the corner of an eye, a grin curling and uncurling beneath the wiry white mustache.

"You think you could get used to living around here, Brask Adams?"

Exultant visions evaporated and Brask was a child again. A boy trapped in the bodily prison of a faltering young man, rending skin and smashing through glass in the fury of impulse, snatching some long-coveted treasure, a mere trinket, from a store window. Clasping the talisman of desperate hope to his soul, he prepared to run for his life, into the arms of reckless escape. He would run for an eternity like this, if he could. He would run unseen and flush with the exhilaration of triumph. But someone was watching, after all. Someone always had to be watching. He knew no other existence. There was no certainty beyond the clutching reminder that, somehow, everything he ached for, everything he knew and all he believed himself to be, had already been discovered and darkened by judgment. Was there anything left to salvage from a life lived at the mercy of such forces?

"How could a place like this *not* be made for me?" he marveled. "I've been craving a real small-town experience for so many years. Never found the right time to actually go after it, for the benefit of my work and my future, you know? But *this*. This has the kind of feel I've been dreaming about. Great first impression? That's putting it mildly. Of course, first impressions only go so far. That applies to the impression I make on you, obviously. Details count. How far is the cabin from downtown?"

"Just a mile. We can come back and have a nice, longer look around downtown after you see the cabin. Sound like a plan?"

"Point the way, co-pilot."

The van meandered through the rest of Wistwood and into the adjacent creeping woodland. It might have been a plump little whale, ghost white and navigating the depths of a murky undersea canyon along twists, turns, switchbacks, and thickening curves of forest road. Deeper and deeper, rising uphill in some spots and plunging down into cavernous dells elsewhere, Brask drove on.

The great vaulted ceiling of redwood limbs high above had given way to an expanse of highlands, with little hills tucked behind bigger ones and scattered groves of oak and sycamore weaving up, around, and across a buxom landscape golden and illuminated by gentle sunshine. Sweeping acres of wild country zoomed off in one direction and were caressed by shadows of burly clouds in another. Wraith-like fingers of fog still curled with mischief, casting atmospheric brushstrokes upon the canvas of green, gold, and damp, purplish grey. Atop one hill, heaving fields filled with choirs of lavender sang welcome in the afternoon glow. California poppies the color of buttery saffron streamed in vibrant rills across hilltops and down into the valley. Hundreds of oak trees, craggy and acrobatic in their gnarled complexity, hugged the landscape as if strewing great cascades of these glowing petals amid a revel.

It was the most beautiful mile Brask had ever experienced, all sultry heat and comforting shade, side by side, merging and morphing, exchanging places and even shapes with the shifting of clouds adrift in a sea-sky of pale blue cream. The road was rough; gravel, lumpen rocks, washouts, and a moist marbling of volcanic red clay led the way. Horace gestured and they turned behind a great boulder that had come to its final roadside rest, wearied by the ages and never more to tumble from precarious heights. There, at the end of a short driveway, the cabin awaited, lonely in a glade encircled by grasping oaks, eldritch limbs joined in the throes of a protective waltz.

forever around forever around forever around

He turned off the engine and stared. Brask was home.

CHIAROSCURO

The mere sight of the latest email was a balm to the wounded and uncertain heart of Shep Daltry. Midnight death he could stand. Reek and bloodstain tendered no despair. Torture was food. Murder was drink. Even secrecy could be tolerated, though every impulse raged against his restraint, demanding that such magnificent work be unveiled for all to see, for earth, sky, and others who had wronged him to behold, aghast with envy. For all of these had wronged him, above and beneath, behind and into the unknowable distance.

There had been no word of encouragement for hours. No champion's voice to smother insecurities as he toiled.

It is not a bad thing to need guidance. Even great men—and he was among the great, for the great accomplish their wonders in blood—require surety.

But nothing had been offered unto him until noon. It was a message from the prospective Employer. There, atop his inbox, above another from his present employer. He opened the second first because he wanted to get the hate out of the way. It was short. Just like the text that had been sent to his phone.

Need to see you at office ASAP.

Fuck him. The Sheriff could wait. Until his bones were dust by fire or by pulverizing centuries, he could wait.

Only one correspondence mattered. Only one summons would be worshipped and obeyed.

Shep's face twisted, fixed in a mask of disfiguring ecstasy. Sweat flowed in oily streams from the top of his head, from under his arms, onto the carpet. His cock throbbed large and voracious against the front of his trousers, demanding release. A trembling finger clicked-open the email.

One gift remains to be given. You have done well!
Prepare to gird yourself and leave this place. Rise up to abandon your shackles and your chains.
Hunger to depart your vile masters while they sleep and then come hither to a Place I have prepared, a refuge void of slavery and judgments of the Light.
Make haste to come away and enter the shadow of the Last Needful Forest, yonder.
Here, you shall partake of eternal waters and sample the fruit of undying orchards.
Rest from worldly labors, the pestilence of earth, unseen by those who would seek to persecute you.
Be hidden from the sentinels of your prison and know the pleasure of true Power.
You will satisfy yourself with women and with men and with spirits, as you please.
You will ravage souls until they plead for mercy and are cast aside.
Come, raise for me an army in your days of freedom, offspring of mighty and fulsome spirit!
Make ready to flee into the night and toward the dawn that I have defeated.
Enter and be forgotten by those who matter little to the stars.
Do not tarry in this place, for within one day all that hesitate and choose to linger will be abandoned to weakness and its reward.
You have done well! Yet one work remains. Await my signal with patience.
Prepare.

GOODLY COMES THE OFFERED HEART

The cabin was far more than the broken-down affair Brask had been expecting.

To be certain, "cabin" was a term that could be used rather loosely in the lexicon of California real estate. This one dwelled within the finer side of that spectrum. There were four rooms. A well-lit and tidy kitchen with a polished stone floor supported a horseshoe formation of old-fashioned but serviceable appliances and a new double sink of stainless steel. Then there was an expansive living room beneath a vaulted ceiling of redwood rafters. Below were sturdy floorboards of the same composition. At the edge of this, the largest wall was dominated by a hearth of smooth, round river stones, immense and dark, stacked artfully in mortar that was cracking in many places but still imposing and sturdy. The fireplace itself narrowed and swept like an upside-down funnel to the ceiling and through the roof. The grate within was swept clean and blackened, home only to a few spiders that hung drowsily on webs stretched across the deeper corners. They didn't even move when Brask bent down and stuck his head in to inspect the flue.

Looking up, he felt a downward rush of fragrant, wood-burnt air, like the ghostly smoke of many cheerful fires of the past puffing-by to greet him. The ancient, unbreakable smell of strength emanating from the arranged river stones was just as beguiling. Nearby, Brask spied a wood-bin of generous size. Beyond this, the living area dwindled down beneath an archway—also fashioned of river-stones in mortar—and this opened onto a tiny bedroom that had the ambience of a cove or grotto, jutting outward from the main frame of the cabin. Four identi-cal windows of tall rectangular shape were grouped here and these overlooked the back yard, dense with oak trees.

Horace pointed everything out, but stood mostly silent as Brask explored. Already he imagined turning the big living room into a combination sitting room and bedroom; a wide portion of wall to the left of the fireplace seemed an ideal spot for a bed. Then he could transform the "master bedroom" under the magi-cal archway into the perfect writing study, replete with his desk and some two-hundred books kept in storage in Palo Alto. The thought of having those volumes around him again was an ecstatic heartache. The books taunted him from afar even now, captives awaiting liberation at the hands of their distracted and unreli-able warrior.

Shelves were needed, but he could build some easily enough. Indeed, he envisioned a labyrinth of books wending a perilous way to his desk. The four stately alcove windows could be jammed with guttering candles, and atop his desk would sit the bleached coyote skull he'd found six years earlier on a trip to Sajulita, Mexico, with his buddy, Aiden, in better times.

Some antique ink-wells and a few other writerly odds and ends would com-plete the tableau.

Perhaps best of all, the place came partially furnished. The original ad hadn't mentioned that.

"This stuff is really nice," said Brask, passing a palm over the smooth oak of a high-backed chair in the corner. "Looks like it was made locally."

"Good eye," rattled Horace. "And it's more than local. The Kimbertons made all of this themselves."

"Who are the Kimbertons?"

"The previous tenants."

"So they were professional carpenters. Damned good ones, too, by the look of it."

"Well, I don't know as I'd go that far," said Horace. "Neither one of them did woodworking for a living, but they were real handy with raw materials and the right kinds of tools. Husband and wife team. Carpentry was more of a hobby for them. Old folks. Not as old as I am, but old. They even made a few pieces for some of the other residents here in the Wistwood hills. Oh, and all of the structural upgrades in the cabin were done by Mr. and Mrs. Kimberton. From the front porch swing to the window frames in the kitchen. All of it. I guess they *were* pretty good at it."

"And they just left all this great work behind for the next tenant?" Brask inspected the redwood paneling for any deficiencies but couldn't find any.

"They left everything behind. Right down to the dish ware in the cupboards and the silverware in the drawer next to the stove," added Horace, as if everything about the marvelous little place was obvious enough to require no particular explanation.

"Pretty generous of them," said Brask, impressed to the point of glowering at the wealth of fine little appointments and accents all around. "What were they like, the Kimbertons? Not that I'm disappointed for my own sake, but why'd they leave such a fantastic spot they worked so hard to refurbish and decorate?"

Horace gave a little shrug.

"Nice older couple," he said, face as blank as an irretrievable memory. "Very private people. Retired. Moved a month ago all of the sudden. To greener pastures, or so they believed."

Brask sat in one of the slanted, cushioned chairs clustered around the hearth, admiring the simple comfort and sturdiness of the handiwork. He wondered if the Kimbertons had left the furnishings amid some emergency. This was a perfect place to retire, especially in the temperate climate of Big Sur. He considered, without knowing why, the possibility that one or the other of them had died, drifting out of the life and warmth of their cabin like gossamer on the dreamy upper reaches of sun-pierced thermals, carried away away away into the ultimate invisibility. The cabin, as cozy as it was, did have a petrified quality to it, as if it were fixed in the sudden, immobilizing amber of an unexpected transition. Otherwise, all was tidy and in order, with no indication of being hastily abandoned, for greener pastures or drearier ones.

No references required.

"So what's the name of the guy, your boss, who owns the town? Does he really own it or did he just found it?"

A swift but passing shadow of unwelcome surprise crossed Horace's cragged face for the first time.

"What? The who?"

"The owner you mentioned. What's his name? I'm sure anybody interested in renting around here would want to know at least that much."

Horace gathered himself, wrinkles appearing to vanish for an instant as the great white wings of his mustache spread outward like a dove about to take flight … or perhaps intimidate an unwanted pest. Sharp, bristled ears buried amid darker tufts of hair wiggled curiously with the bothered movement of his jaw.

"Mr. Palmarah. But everyone around here just calls him the Landlord. Very discreet man. Very private." He cracked an obliging smile, turning his hunting cap ever so subtly counter-clockwise in his fingertips atop a flannel-covered potbelly. "He doesn't mingle. A person of means, obviously. Some might even say eccentric. But everyone who comes to live in Wistwood, whether they buy or lease or rent, gets invited up to the big house for a friendly little chat. Very good manners, has Mr. Palmarah. By the by, whoever is selected to sign the lease for this property will see my name featured on the document, as I am town manager. I am the landlord's proxy, if you will." This last seemed to Brask an unmistakable arrow; a reminder that no one had been selected, as yet.

"And the name of the town, 'Wistwood.' There's something interesting about it. Lovely name, but I was thinking about the etymology and it escapes me. What's the story there?"

"Oh, what an interesting question, but not one to be unexpected from a wordsmith, I reckon." Horace made an approving little bow of his head. "The 'wood' part is obvious enough, I should think, but the first part, if a few past remarks from the Landlord mean anything at all, seems to be drawn from an archaic English or maybe German term. Wist spelled with an h, or maybe a y, making it whyst. Or with an added e to make it wyste. It supposedly denoted one's accrued larder for purposes of nourishment, in Ye Olde days. Something like that. Easier spelled with an i, perhaps. Don't know why it was chosen, but pleasant enough, eh?"

"Unique, without doubt. And it has a certain ring to it. Quite pleasant," said Brask, trying to look casual without appearing vulnerable or bothered as he sat in one of the Kimberton chairs. No one respected the vulnerable when business of any consequence was to be done, money was to change hands, papers were to be signed, and futures—however transient—were to be decided. His father's instructive bullying came to mind again. Or was it his own?

Christ, Brask, feel this guy out a little better. Read his moods, for God's sake and play his personality like you've been sitting with the fucking orchestra for more than half a rehearsal.

"You know, I want to take a closer look at the bathroom, Horace. That's the last place a guy wants to take a cold seat when winter comes to highlands like these."

They toured the cabin again, more aimless this time. The moment of truth was arriving. The bathroom was small and also in a room that had been added onto the central structure of the house. But it was clearly the most recently modified space in the place. A shining white porcelain toilet and Grecian pedestal vanity stood dutifully alongside each other beneath a mirrored medicine cabinet. A claw-footed, antique white tub featured a mammoth modern shower-head of burnished bronze behind a pastel draw-around curtain emblazoned with what appeared to be Zuni symmetrical symbols.

Perhaps the best part of the cabin, for Brask, was the screened porch directly off the living room. It ran the entire length of the facade, perhaps thirty-five feet, looking out onto the dancing oaks and the driveway of packed, volcanic red clay. The whole expanse was in good repair, inhabited by two hand-crafted redwood rocking chairs that looked uncomfortable in a complex, gyroscopic way until he sat down in one at Horace's encouragement. He was delighted to find the experience akin to weightlessness due to the weird curves and workings of the design. Like the other furnishings, it had been built without nails or screws, fashioned rather by a brilliant conglomeration of slats and pegs. The rocker moved the seat forward and back in almost sensual spring-like passes. It was like a living thing.

"This is great!" Brask imagined curling up daily with a journal in his hands. "And the view can't be beat."

The air in the sumptuous, secret grove was enthralling to him, full of the brooding thoughts of trees and ponderous boulders lodged sleepily here and there amid the leaves and grass. The efforts of the powerful oaks to attain majesty by constantly clutching at each other and reaching toward the sky created a contained, chamber-like atmosphere in the vicinity. The space was humid but refreshingly cool, with a hint of fog-kissed delicacy on the air. To dwell amid such cleanliness would be like lingering ever in the aftermath of a purifying rainstorm, cocooned in stillness following the chastisement of thunder; this was a realm potent enough to dispel any and all unwholesome specters. Brask found his heart breaking at the thought that this could really be his home. And that it might not be. Despite the ache, such enlivening pain was exquisite. Lately, he had begun to doubt there was a heart left to be broken at all.

But a spell could be broken. The slurring insistence of his father's voice emerged again in the back of his mind, an echo that tumbled through a suffocating mist.

If somebody hands you something on a goddamned silver platter, boy, you can drool all you like. Nothing wrong with that. But you better start asking some serious questions and find out what that silver platter is gonna cost you when all is said and done. There's a lot of silver platters handed over in this world, all shiny and heaped-up with everything you could want. But mark my words, they all come at a cost! They all got strings attached and not nobody is ever gonna hand you something for nothing. You got to decide, boy, just how hungry you are. Maybe it'll be worth it to you, maybe it won't. But it's gonna cost you something if you take it. Maybe a little. Maybe a lot. You got to get into the thick of the game being played and find out if you can afford to play along!

Brask rose from the rocker in the underlying chill of a breeze that spun its way down the driveway from the main road, caught the edge of the cabin, and then whistled mournfully in a new direction through the clustered oaks. He hated hearing his father's rants in his head at the best of times; getting a flashback when he was stressed out and on edge of a major moment elicited the urge to vomit. But was there not a ring of truth amid the drunken rambling of that ghost? Nothing is easy in life. Nothing is really free. But Brask had learned that all by himself, the hard way, and didn't need a whiskey-fueled harangue from the past to remind him.

"Horace, I'm prepared to offer you six months' rent in advance, along with first and last, not to mention any security deposit you might be asking."

"My word, you are eager, young man."

"Your ad didn't mention anything about a deposit and we didn't discuss it in our first conversation, but I'll give you whatever you want. I've got to have this place. This cabin … it's … it's exactly what I've been looking for. I have the cash with me. Right here in my pocket. I can pay you now, every dollar.

"Well now, Mr. Adams, I …"

"I'm not going to beat around the bush, Horace. Not gonna hold my cards too close. Not gonna play some game where I pretend to be only 'so' interested and try to dicker down the price. No song and dance. Whoever else you've got looking at this place—whatever their good qualities and advantages might be— I'm guessing they haven't offered this much to you up front."

Brask pulled the roll of hundred-dollar bills from the inner pocket of his jacket. The money felt heavy, a cylinder of lead in his hand. Horace stared at the cash for a moment, unimpressed. Solemn.

"This money's weighing me down, Horace. It needs to get out of my hand and into yours, or into your boss's. Mr. Palmarah's. This is the full-tilt. Will you take it?"

Horace did not reply.

"Look, even if you let me have it for six months. Paid in full. I'll sign a modified lease, if you want. Hell, I'll sign anything. I need this place. I want this place."

A low, rasping chuckle emerged from Horace's throat. He tugged thoughtfully at his sprawling Santa Claus beard.

"Listen, Brask. Hang on to your cash, there. These woods are wild and greedy. You don't want some vulture to swing down out of the blue and snatch up your savings, do you?" Horace leaned with both palms pressed forward atop his knobby cane. "There's no need to go to great lengths to convince me. Though, I must say I'm tickled by your enthusiasm for this humble abode. There's still quite a lot we need to talk about, man to man, before any decision is made."

"I understand." Brask's hand closed around the roll of bills in a clammy sheen of sweat. His knuckles were on fire. This was the moment. It had to work. A few more minutes of uncertainty might find him hyperventilating.

"We haven't yet come to any agreement," Horace continued. "And no matter what happens, nobody here would ever take more from you than what was *required* from the beginning."

For Brask, the world was suddenly a rug being pulled out from under his feet. Swollen confidence deflated as if a hole had been ripped at the bottom of his being. Onto the floorboards of the porch it spilled. *Damn it!* He had jumped the gun. He had gambled by making a big, fast impression with the show of cash, and he had lost. The old fart wasn't going to be moved by any dramatic gesture. Surely, there were other candidates he was still considering. More dignified people. Better ones.

There was always somebody better, more qualified. Always. Always. Fucking always.

I blew it.

Elation was replaced by a crushing glacier of resentment in Brask's gut, an icy, spreading hatred for the world and for everything about the way it worked. The way it lifted this one up and tossed that one aside based upon a few flimsy contrivances like padded qualifications and references. Things that nobody really gave much of a shit about or would ever bother to remember.

I blew it.

Mounting bitterness surged to his very nerve-endings, causing his skin to tingle and his mouth to go dry. God, he despised society. People—good and worthy people—could be brushed aside like dust particles, depending upon which way the goddamned wind blew on any given day. What a shit world.

"Sure. Of course, I understand, Horace. We definitely need to sit down and discuss the possibilities." As if to punctuate the sudden wave of despair, his hoarse reply was caught and then lost on another gust that whipped its way up the driveway. Even his words were being snatched away by the whim of the elements.

I blew it.

He had witnessed the arbitrary foolishness of the civilized world in action so many times he wanted to scream. Only two months earlier he had been in the office of his literary agent, Jeanine, in San Francisco. They were getting ready to head out to Chinatown for dim sum, for a chat about the plans for his brilliant new novel and the latest challenges faced by the industry, when she paused at her desk to peruse a manuscript submitted by another prospective client.

"You know, Brask," she had begun with astonishing candor. "I read a manuscript last night in bed and was totally jazzed about submitting it to an editor over at Knopf, a guy who likes that kind of thing. But I swear to God, this morning I ate an old cupcake that was in my fridge too long and now all I feel when I read this guy's work is acid reflux. Isn't that wild? I mean, I'm sure my first hunch was right and it's good, but I just can't focus on it now. It makes my stomach turn. My pal, Jared, over at Knopf, leaves on vacation today and I've got to make a few recommendations he can take along with him or wait. In a couple of weeks, my desk is gonna be piled high with new stuff. Sure, one or two things might be gold but most of it'll be garbage. The real kicker? You need a whole lot of garbage and maybe one gold nugget to keep up appearances in publishing these days. Sad. But this poor guy and his manuscript? Damn, he caught me on a day when I got indigestion. Too much of it to give him that extra look. How crazy is that?"

Then she had chucked the entire manuscript into the ready-for-shredding pile aside her desk.

The world was certifiably full of shit. As random as a raindrop on the tongue with one's mouth wide open and face tilted toward the boiling clouds of a tempest. Worst of all, humans, those beings who fashion themselves arrogant enough to impose meaningful order upon monotonous chaos, were losing the capacity to even bother going through the motions, too pressed to maintain the whole ridiculous illusion.

Fuck it all.

Horace's voice jolted him from the nose-dive into despondency.

"I'm prepared to let you have the place, Brask."

"Huh? I mean ... excuse me?"

Jesus, I must have looked catatonic for a minute! Standing here like an idiot. What am I doing?

"It's yours, if you want it. Simple as that."

Now it was Brask's turn to wonder if some gremlin in the great ironworks of chaos had perhaps tripped a lever accidentally in his favor. He couldn't believe his ears.

"Really? That's ... that's excellent."

Light reentered the realm of the living. Thunderclouds sped to far-flung hideaways.

With as much composure as he could measure, given the whiplash of emotions his mind had endured within a span of seconds, he tried to form a sentence.

"Uh ... we haven't even talked about much, yet, and you're offering me the place. That's amazing, Horace. I mean, we had a nice drive in and a fun little look at the downtown strip, a chance to chat a bit, but not about—"

"Your past?" said Horace with a slight tilt of his head. "You must've noted in the ad that we do not require references for this particular property."

"Yeah, that was one of the features that leaped out at me the most, I have to admit."

Brask's head might as well have been a helium balloon. It might have disengaged from his neck and floated up and away on the breeze, carrying every muddled thought and misfiring synapse into the stratosphere. His body would not have minded the separation. Steadying himself with a hand against a post on the porch, he tried to make things look casual, to appear masculine and assured.

I've got the place. I'm officially not homeless anymore.

"Sounds like you are about to hand me a contract, Horace."

The old man smiled faintly and reached inside the folds of his crumpled coat to produce a single white sheet of paper folded neatly in three sections to form a rectangle.

"This, Mr. Brask Adams, is the lease agreement."

Next, he took off his gloves and reached into another pocket with stubby, calloused fingers and produced an object that glinted sharply in a stray panel of sunlight beaming through the treetops, flashing a momentary blindness in

Brask's vision. He blinked with discomfort and held up a hand instinctively. Both eyes began to water. Not the tears he was expecting to shed.

What the hell? It looked like frigging Excalibur coming out of the old guy's pocket. But it was not.

"And here's a pen, Brask. With which I hope you will sign our lease."

Brask wiped his eyes with the bottom edge of his untucked shirt and squinted at Horace's fingers. It was just a plain, silver metal ballpoint.

"You've told me on the drive that you're a writer, Brask. One who writes books about people being given second chances. You told me they have paid you a fine advance or whatever it is you call it. I myself find you to be most suitable for this rental and, so long as you have the money and are prepared to sign after funds have been freely exchanged, the property is yours. I can't tell you what to do, of course, but for a hotshot author who knows a thing or two about second chances, I can offer one opinion; I believe you've hit upon a good deal, here. And so have we."

"Just like that?"

"Just like that. Will you render me the grace of signing?"

Horace held the folded piece of paper and the pen toward him at equal distances from his body, as if bearing twin torches—torches that burned a brilliant, salvific light outward into a previously murky future now agleam with redemption. It was a radiant moment, as if a cavern long undiscovered had been illuminated for the first time in the very depths of the world, its beauty and its secrets exposed, ready to be explored for a lifetime.

"You'd better believe I'll sign!" Brask let all of his relief and burgeoning elation spill forth in a quick fit of laughter. He slapped his own kneecap for emphasis.

"Hell, yes! This place is made for me, Sir, and I would be honored to prove myself the best tenant you've ever encountered in the entirety of your property managing career."

He reached forward to take the pen and the paper but when he did so Horace's face darkened; a low cloud seemed to pass overhead and block the early Autumn sun from their corner of the forest. Horace drew his hands back, not completely, but just out of reach of Brask's fingers, which remained suspended a bit awkwardly in the space between them.

"You do have to pay the first and last month's rent, before anything else is done," said Horace, with almost grim authority. "You don't have to pay a deposit. You do not have to offer me a dime more than the amount indicated in the original ad and in the lease itself. But you must pay first."

Brask shook the excitement from his mind. An observer might have surmised that he had been uncomfortably disturbed from an episode of daydreaming. He patted his pockets forgetfully, aimless and a bit dazed. When he opened his mouth to speak he began to stammer.

"I ... gosh, yeah ... I mean, of course. I'll pay. Where'd I put my money?"

He was almost in a full-blown panic again, one that had leapt out of nowhere to sink throttling fangs into the back of his neck. At last, he located the roll of bills he had returned to another pocket after the final walk-through.

His hand trembling with a mixture of excitement, relief, and the irrational, almost preternatural fear that Horace would withdraw the offer and rescind his approval at the last possible instant and declare the whole thing a colossal prank, Brask removed the rubber band from the wad of cash and counted out twenty bills. Then he counted them again, this time aloud, placing them into Horace's outstretched palm, right on top of the folded lease. Each bill was as dusky green as the oak leaves quietly chattering in a stir of breeze outside and above.

"There. That's two thousand."

Why in the hell am I so jumpy and scattered? You know why, man. This is big. This is getting out of a nightmare. Stepping off the train to nowhere. Own the fucking moment.

Horace's fingers closed in a tender clutch around the bills, his thin lips retreated to expose shiny gums, and the riven avalanche of his mustache spread wide above a smile blooming with yellowed and painfully crooked teeth. He gestured toward the cabin.

"Why don't you read and sign right here on the porch sill, Brask? Where the light is good. Then you'll be all set."

The lease was a document as simple and as straightforward as the abode. Brask had signed leases in his life that were ten pages long, not including the fine print and addenda that inevitably attached themselves to formal arrangements between landlords and new tenants. Here were only a few meager sentences, and those had been apparently pecked out on some old typewriter in dire need of a moist new ribbon, if any still existed in the digital world:

I, _____ agree to pay _____ the sum of one thousand dollars ($1,000.00) per month to occupy and dwell alone in the property agreed upon in the community of Wistwood. Rent is due exactly thirty (30) days after the first payment and move-in date and is to be tendered to Horace Slater, overseer. No alterations are to be made to the property without the express consent of Horace Slater or another duly authorized representative. By signing this lease agreement below, tenant agrees to abide by all responsibilities inherent upon residence in the property according to the strict and explicit instructions tendered for the duration of the lease agreement. This lease agreement may be terminated by either party with sufficient notice of thirty days, upon which tenant is obliged to vacate the premises no later than the thirtieth day. The owner and/or his representative reserves the right to withhold or demand payments according to the terms of the lease in the event of a violation of the lease agreement and at his sole discretion.

Lessee _____Witness _____

Date _____

Brask was amazed.

"This is the most uncomplicated lease agreement I've ever seen. Hell, I had to pore over thirty-five pages of nonsense and make a dozen signatures when I entered a contract with my cell-phone provider."

"Like I said, we prefer to keep things simple and friendly around here, Brask. A person's honest word, and the willful good faith he uses to uphold that word, are the two things that carry the most weight in our little town."

He offered the gleaming silver pen to Brask.

"Sign and date the document. Freely."

Brask took the pen and placed the pertinent part of the lease flat on the clean, whitewashed sill crafted by the long-gone Kimbertons. He tried to click the top of the pen to expose the stylus but discovered there was no such apparatus to be found.

"Oh," said Horace meekly. "It's one of those pens that turns, you see. You have to twist it right there in the middle."

"Sure," said Brask, but as he gripped the pen and gave it a clicking turn, some minuscule but sharp sliver of metal cut the pad of his thumb and a few drops of blood streaked down onto the immaculate white margin of the paper.

"Ow! Oh, shit. What'd I do?"

"Ah, drat that old pen of mine." Horace reached forward quickly to take Brask's hand in his own and inspect the wound. It was only a tiny slice. Thin as a paper cut.

"I've been meaning to replace that old pen because I've done the very same thing to myself on occasion. But I thought I'd fixed the damned thing, you know? Hey, I think the Kimbertons left some of that antibacterial ointment in the bathroom medicine chest when they left. Yes, I remember seeing a whole tube of it in there. I'll go and have a look while you finish signing and dating, whaddaya say?"

Brask sucked a bit on his thumb. It had already stopped bleeding and it didn't hurt in the least. He held the pen up to the light and inspected the shaft for some jutting tine of metal or perhaps a warped portion of the joint, but found nothing.

"What?" he asked Horace, distracted.

"Antibacterial goop. There's some in the medicine chest, I reckon. I'll go get it while you sign and date."

"No, no it's okay. I've got some antiseptic in the van. It's barely a scratch, anyhow. I'm just sorry I dripped a bit of blood onto your lease. Not exactly a clean start, eh?"

"Well, then, just go ahead and sign, Brask. That's a good man! Now, give me the pen and I'll sign my parts. There now. Will you look at that? The good people of Wistwood have themselves a brand-new neighbor—one who's a famous author, to boot!"

Brask beamed. He hadn't felt a rush of happiness and relief this stratospheric since he had taken a hang-gliding trip down some ethereal mountain in Maui on his twenty-third birthday. Given all he'd endured the past two years, this acquisition, this conquest, this place to finally plant his feet and call somewhat "his own" again meant everything. He began to choke up, but caught himself. Maybe later.

"I'm absolutely thrilled, Horace. I want to thank you for talking to me, meeting me out there by the main road like you did, spending your time and, well … going with your gut instinct. And I promise that I'll never let you down."

They shook hands.

"The best part of all, Brask, is that you could very well start moving in today. This hour, in fact. I'm not trying to stick my nose in where it don't belong, but I couldn't help noticing that you've been living in your van out there. And you have been living in it for some time, I expect."

Brask's cheeks burned a swift crimson. He was breathless with embarrassment. Had he really been so oblivious to the likelihood that someone—anyone—getting into his van would have been able to deduce his secret with even a modicum of snooping? The ache of mortification swallowed him in a strange tide, a whirlpool pulling at his prior sense of exaltation. He was speechless. All he could do was stand with his hands held slightly in front of him like a fool attempting to catch a weight that would, if he were lucky, annihilate him completely in such an awkward instant.

Horace, for his part, smiled in grandfatherly fashion and tut-tutted any discomfort on the part of the new tenant.

"You've got nothing to be ashamed about, Brask Adams. Oh, I know all about it. Times have been tough on many a young man these past few years, what with the economy in a state of collapse and so many bunglers doing nothing to help matters much. But we don't judge folks like that around here. No references required, remember? Besides, with your big book contract, the whole world has changed for you. This is a new beginning! And we support good people seeking new beginnings in our little corner of the world. Our Wistwood."

"I … I really don't know what to say," Brask croaked. "Thank you, Horace. Just … thanks."

The old man let out a sigh of pleasure. "Well, you are home now, my friend."

He carefully folded the blood-spotted lease and tucked it safely within some inner coat pocket. The flesh-slicing pen vanished along with it.

"You know, Brask, Donovan's mercantile is open until seven tonight. You can grab enough food to tide yourself over. Have another peek at our humble little strip downtown, too. Hell, you can even stop by Margie's bar. Introduce yourself to the supper-time crowd. Have a little drink or two, maybe. Oh, here are the house keys, though I daresay you won't need to lock anything up. This ain't Palo Alto."

Brask took the keys and felt a chill. A good one.

"I'll never forget what you've done for me, Horace. You're a godsend."

"I don't quite know about *that.*" Horace's mustache twitched. His veiny eyes glinted. "But I do know I need to high-tail it out of here because I've got chores to attend. I don't want to fall behind."

"You won't, Horace. Even if I have to carry you back to town on my shoulders. Let's hit the road."

STAR ORCHARD

"How many did you see entering the trap, Lady? For my part, I have been watchful of the heavens and all that these wretched stars might seek to reveal. Alas, fortune has withheld reward. Signs, visions, and portents evade my weary eyes. Blinded. Blinded. Now I despair of failing you in your hour of need."

"Do not be anxious, Larkspur. The silent sky is not of your making. All reliable stars were hidden last night, behind a veil drawn across the length and breadth of the firmament. We know exactly who pulled the curtain in front of our faces, do we not? I, too, failed to see or sense anything useful, save for the certainty that he is drawing some new and powerful tool to himself, and that the Acquisition is nearly accomplished."

With only the gleaming backs of his talons, Larkspur brushed the smooth skin of Her arm, now phosphorescent and as inviting to touch as any sweet-bursting fruit of the orchard. He was overcome with a desire to comfort, to re-assure. Her breasts, darker than the lightless heaven and yet aglow with living obsidian milk, breasts that had nourished entire armies beyond each boundary of space and Time, tempted him, too. How fiercely he had longed to suckle there, to kneel and extend his tongue for but one stray and holy drop. But such sustenance was not for his kind. In agony he would remain, until Forever was no more. To the orchard he turned, shamed by his lust, and the trees accused him.

"I thought the last menagerie would keep him satisfied for a good while, Lady, but what do I know? You perceive his ways better than any who ever have been fated to treat with him. You can peer through any shadow he might throw your way! How many has he got on the hook this time? Come! Tell your faithful Larkspur what you know."

The tresses of her hair, fiery silver as frost at the slothful outskirts of a dead universe, beyond reach of all eager and envious phantoms, began to coil and uncoil around her delicate ankles. She summoned her power and felt what she could.

"Three. Maybe four. And one of them, as we know already, is not meant to be a plaything and a meal. One is for employment. That is not good for us but possibly good for us. All of it. I care little if He plays with His food. To that he is entitled. But great danger is imminent and I cannot yet see enough to ensure that we are ready for the challenge. On top of that, I must be vigilant for his slightest mistake. This is when his errors come and my hopes wax alongside the threat."

"You will find the answers you seek soon, Lady. You have before."

She smiled down at her own obedient acolyte. A spark of incandescent blue sprang from her lips and somersaulted over and over through the air until it touched the great river around the island and burst into millions of glittering needles. These danced and hummed above the rapids, danced and hummed in gladness, for seldom did she smile.

"You assign me too much power for peering into his thoughts, Larkspur. I know I am not getting any older, but I do feel myself getting weaker at times. I suppose that has always been part of his game, as well. He aims to wear me down, one day. One moment. I daresay he may succeed. Of late, when I try to look into his affairs, half the time I can only see bluebottle flies and rot, the burnt flesh of sacrifice. Sorrow. So much sorrow, like meager diamonds of rain clinging to the leaves after a deluge. And I see other things."

"What 'other things' do you see, Lady?"

"Dust. There is a great deal of dust and He is kicking it up in my face, stirring it up with that tail he occasionally uses until my eyes feel scratched and bloodied from the fury of it all. And there is no thunder or lightning like there used to be, not a thing that might guide one out of the fog, or give one at least a sense of direction."

"This is sight, Lady, but do you not hear anything?"

"Nothing beyond the howl of his whipping dust-cloud and his laughter. Laughter that matters not to him, in terms of letting me know what is in his thoughts. That is because he knows he remains the victor, in a way. For now. Maybe he knows it for always, but I do not know that, yet, and until I do, I am going to keep my gaze fixed upon things and do what I can manage. It will not go well for us if I lose heart, Larkspur. Damned be the stars that he has strength to hide from me. They are my very own!"

"My Lady, I have only ever wanted to encourage you and assist you. I did not seek to draw attention to our disadvantages and thus diminish your spirit."

"I know that, good friend." She gave him a playful scratch under the chin and he wept at the grace of the touch. "Yes, I know that well enough. But the fact remains that there is a particular concealment at work, even as we speak. The veil remains across the stars. This could mean his power is waxing or also that he knows he is in a particularly vulnerable period and is desperate that no one else perceive the weakness, the transition. Either way, we are locked out for the moment and must be ready for any and all troubles."

Larkspur began to shiver, even in the balmy, fragrant clime of the orchard.

"Do not be alarmed unduly, my Steadfast. There *are* other places to explore besides the heavens, hidden or not. There are little corners and out of the way windows that even he doesn't know about, quite yet."

"Indeed, my Lady?"

"Oh, yes. Forgotten mirrors and keyholes through which the resourceful adventurer might glance, if she has a mind for discretion and a will as forceful as the explosion of a star sent spinning, lost and alone, to blaze and then turn cool, allowing its children to course unstoppable through the universe. If she is as mighty as Trueiron. Yes, there are other places to look—for those who know where to look and how long to look without getting caught!"

"Ah! When you do espy something worthy, Lady, tell me at once, I beg."

"I might. If I have my way, I will work around his walls. There will be little to tell of the prey; they are usually too indistinct. Even if one tries to perceive them as music, the notes that return are distant, discordant, barely an echo. Like a melody known to be fair as one's own heart in the midst of a night terror, yet snatched away in violence upon waking, save for a clipped tone here, a whisper there."

"Why should we care to know much about the prey?" Larkspur splayed claws to the sky in frustration. "We cannot assist them and they are certainly of no value to us. His possible intrigues and plots against us are the reasons for worry."

"You may change your mind about the prey before the end, Larkspur."

"Then you will have spied something truly extraordinary through one of your hidden keyholes or mirrors!"

"Perhaps, but it is too early to ascribe too much significance, if any, to what I see, or what I think I will see. Of greater concern is the new disciple, the gamesman. That one has been rather apparent in the midst of my secret browsing for some time, as you know."

"Bah!" spat Larkspur. "We had barely gotten used to the current snake!"

The cry of dejection rang in the dampness of the orchards and reverberated in the crystal caves beyond.

"A new weapon will assail us soon, Larkspur. We are witnessing both destruction and opportunity, near at hand."

"Yes, he is most dangerous when most vulnerable, Lady! And most vulnerable when most dangerous. Experience has demonstrated this to us on more than one occasion. What could be the catalyst, though? The helper he has now has not even been with him very long."

"Ha! Longer than you think."

"It cannot believe it is time to replace him already."

"But it is. His henchman has grown older and I suspect more careless in his service, which is the key. I feel it! He has made or *will make* a mistake of some sort. A mistake that is costly and of potentially supreme benefit to me."

Larkspur sniffed a bit, woeful in the night. "To *us,* my Lady?"

"Of course. Yet, you know that our enemy does not have the power to preserve his favorite puppets indefinitely. He can do whatever he likes with the prey, once they are in his clutches, but the acolytes operate under a different set of laws.

They are obtained under different spells and circumstances. Surely you have not forgotten everything I taught you, Larkspur."

Larkspur now threw all four of his arms up to the indifferent sky.

"Who can deign to remember so much when each day is as lost to us as Time itself?" he cried. "Who can retain all things when the wheel of our misfortune spins without cessation, and the memory of your former splendor fades like the last glimmer of sunset, sinking into eternity? How can we abide this existence?"

"You know how and you know why!" Her anger was stirred and Larkspur cowered against the trunk of a tree. "But all is not lost, friend, though the dying sun of which you speak should chain itself or be chained forever to the edge of ruin, taunting us at the brink of worlds or worlds-within. Our moment is still possible, Larkspur—never forget that! Though the slow decay of Damnation Hours has robbed you of the memory of your true name, of the courage that is your birthright, be assured that our moment shall come. Know that destiny is not yet determined. Not for us!"

"Your faith and wisdom remain the last and only beacons for me, Lady, and for others like me, wherever they may be lost and exiled, just as I was lost and exiled. Forgive my despair."

"It is forgiven, and it was not quite despair, Larkspur. The moment either of us truly embraces despair is the moment when all beacons are extinguished and any hope that remains for consolation is fodder for oblivion. That is what he seeks from us, our despair. Do you not sense this above all other things? You know how he prefers his rivals to destroy *themselves,* if possible. We will not be so easily taken. We will not be so swift to oblige him."

Larkspur prostrated himself at her ebony feet, fingers reaching for—but not daring to touch—the silverfrost of her waterfall mane.

"Fear for your safety grips me all the same, Lady. I care not for myself. What would that avail? You are the only reason I am able to care about anything at all, for you rescued me. You alone."

"Come, now! Cease this foolishness. Rouse your courage and spirit of vengeance, for vengeance is a worthy thing to nourish, when it hungers as ours hungers. There is no time for reminiscence while we face a new, lurking crisis. Mark my words; the slave that's coming to him is the most vile and ruthless yet. He comes with the dark fruit of his handiwork, brandishing trophies."

"But we have seen that kind before, Lady. Why, even the current one has in his possession a host of—"

"Not like this one. And you know that this one's depravity will be magnified once he is empowered by his master for the execution of all imperatives."

"We are more than a match for his slaves, Lady! We have proved that again and again, you and I. The acolyte he has now does not dare face you, does not dare dip so much as a toe in the water! There are laws—you instituted some of them yourself—and we know the ramifications of violating them." Larkspur set his face in grim assurance. "He has as much to lose as we do."

"That is where you are wrong, Larkspur. We have everything to lose if the tide should turn against us. We may be a prize, but one gem lost among many is no catastrophe for the wealthy ... even for one so greedy as he. No, he is up to something innovative with this latest acquisition. Something we have not anticipated."

"What are you saying?"

"I am saying that He seeks a way to move, scuttling like a spider around the boundaries, to get at us. Just as I have found little ways around His assorted barriers. He is going to use this new slave, this coming abomination, as his spider."

"Then what shall we do?"

"We prepare ourselves. Failure to be watchful now may prove our ultimate undoing, but His new boldness might also be used against him, if errors come. Do not lose your faith in me, for even as I see the hours grow darker with endless midnight and our peril creeps closer, I tell you that the dawn of my Moment may be closer still!"

"I believe you, Mistress and Lady. I shall summon all of my own power on your behalf."

"Good. Hold fast, then, and do not quail or cower in the shade. I shall not desert you, no matter what happens."

Larkspur buried his forehead in the cool comfort of the soil and wept anew.

"I know you would not abandon me, not in all the dreams that have ever passed through the minds of the Worthy. Not in all the dreams that shall ever come to pass!"

"Then we shall take heart together, where and when we are able."

"Yes, Lady. And what, peradventure, is to become of the food in the wake of this new slave that approaches?"

She lifted an arm and with a graceful pass of her hand, half the stars were revealed once again in their phantasmagoric and pulsating sky. A smile of triumph crossed the lush plum-edges of her lips. Blue sparks erupted to dance yet again upon the wide and welcoming river.

"I have a feeling that the old slave will miscalculate and that this new slave may be inclined to toy unlawfully with his master's food, Larkspur. And therein may be found the means by which I can conquer them all."

"Let it be so!"

"We shall see. But until then, not a further word, goodly companion. Not even to your innermost thoughts. Not even in the remotest chamber of your heart. We prepare ourselves as best we can. For behold, the acolyte comes soon, and soon afterward the tempest!"

TO KNOW YOU

The van rolled back into the heart of Wistwood. Main Street showed signs of life; five or six people meandered around the cluster of sleepy structures. Brask's first glimpse of his fellow citizens. Horace was eager to play tour guide for at least a few minutes, before his chores, now that all arrangements had been finalized.

"That place over there on the left is Donovan's Mercantile. You can pop in, if you like, and get a few things to tide you over. Basic little shop, but interesting, in its way. Donovan's a collector of odd trinkets. Has them all over the store. You might get a kick out of seeing his do-dads. He loves to show them off, too, especially to newbies."

"Then that'll be high on my list, for sure."

"Yes, definitely stop in and introduce yourself." Horace glanced to the right and his eyes narrowed. He lowered his head with a scrunching of voluminous facial hair into the wool collar of his coat. "Well looky over there," he murmured, pointing a knobbed finger out the passenger-side window. "You see that woman coming out of Margie's Bar & Grill?"

"Yeah, I see her. Who could fail to see her?"

"That there is Miss—or should I say Mrs.—Neetha Grayle. My, but she is a fine piece of machinery, wouldn't you say?"

"Well, it's not my style to think of women as automatons, Horace, but she's something to see, I grant you that."

Brask watched as the buxom vision of bleached platinum hair and mismatched extensions, rhinestone-bedazzled denim jacket, black leather mini-skirt and six-inch Lucite heels stepped gingerly onto the wooden slats of the boardwalk in front of the bar. She paused to look at the strange white vehicle creeping up the street, inscrutable behind enormous blue-tinted sunglasses. Then she tottered off in the flamboyant shoes, navigating the weathered boards of the walkway with some difficulty. Balance appeared to be a particular challenge.

"She's had one hell of a boob job," noted Horace under his breath, still staring.

"Some ladies want them and they get them," said Brask. "I'm all for people flying their colors as they see fit."

"She flies 'em, alright. That Neetha."

Even Brask, whose heart was not inclined to judge the manner in which anyone—male, female, or differently gendered—chose to convey personal style, spared an extended glance at the awkwardly oversized breasts protruding from Neetha's chemise of crimson sateen. They were bursting from the flanks of the rhinestone denim jacket like nuclear warheads eager to inflict calamity. Neetha herself, a seemingly separate entity, maneuvered one precarious step onto the faded asphalt of the street and tottered to the driver's side of one of the three cars parked downtown. She leaned for a moment against a dusty but impressive cobalt Ferrari, fumbling with a set of keys drawn from a crocodile handbag.

"She looks like a nice lady," said Brask. Horace shot him a swift but sly sidelong glance.

"Not your cup of tea, eh? Well, that's nothing to be ashamed of. Most of the men around town like their women a bit more on the natural side, but Neetha is what you might describe as the paint that brightened-up this berg. At least for a few days. She and her husband have only been here a few days."

"Really? Newbies like me, then."

"Only they're renting a little vacation chalet. An A-frame over the hill. But Neetha's a nice enough gal, even if you can't see much that's real 'underNeetha' all that glue or whatever the hell else she's got stuck outside and inside of herself."

"Ha ha," cracked Brask dryly, with an added eye roll that he didn't mind displaying for Horace's benefit. He hated when men belittled women; his holy rolling sister being, of course, a completely separate case, and his case alone. "I'm sure she's a lot more than the sum of her parts might indicate. It'll be nice to meet her."

"You'd be surprised how accepting all the folks are around here, Brask, especially for a small town that ain't even incorporated, yet. Not even on the map, really."

"Believe me, I noticed that from the very beginning of this adventure."

"Sometimes places this cut-off from the world can be unforgiving when it comes to the way free-spirit types are treated," added Horace. "But not Wistwood. No sir. Neetha Grayle has gotten the same amount of love and respect as everybody else. I don't suppose it hurts her any to be glued to the hip of a genuine rock and roll star."

"A rock star, huh? Here in Wistwood?" Brask wanted to scoff at the idea, but thought better of it. "Well, I guess I wouldn't be surprised. This is California, after all, and Big Sur on top of that. Everybody knows the hills are full of VIPs from all kinds of industries, not a few of whom hail from the world of entertainment. They're like an invasive species, even up in Palo Alto."

"Is that so?"

"Sure. You must know that. They don't *all* congregate in LA. I mean, you've got your Silicon Valley big shots. They're everywhere up there. But movie people, too. They'll swoop in and buy either the most ostentatious homes possible or else they hoard property inland and live in chic seclusion, kinda like this. Anyway, I'm as curious as the next guy. Which rock star has Miss Neetha latched herself onto?"

"You ever heard of Lleyton Grayle?" said Horace as Brask put on the brakes and waited for Neetha to pull away from the curb. The Ferrari sped smooth-as-a-snake up the winding roadway that ascended a steep hillside for a quarter-mile, on the very edge of the downtown strand.

"Lleyton Grayle? You mean that old British outfit, whatever it was? He was the lead singer. Or the only singer. Damn. What was his hit? Or hits?

I think I know who you're talking about, but he was way before my time. Oh boy."

Brask wrinkled his nose, trying to agitate a recalcitrant brain cell or two, but it wasn't working. He glanced with a helpless mixture of gentle resentment at his phone on the little island between the front seats. "I used to be able to remember stuff like that on demand until I grew too dependent on that damned thing," he said with a jerk of his chin toward the device. The phone's battery had been dead and the screen black since first entering Wistwood with Horace riding shotgun. He had checked.

Horace stared at the phone, too, his eyes glinting with delight or perhaps some barely concealed, almost hungry bit of mischief.

"The Crucible," said Horace. "That was the name of Lleyton Grayle's biggest hit. He was a singer with a backing bunch. Big girl hair, all of them had it. Shiny trousers. No shirts."

"Yeah, that's right. I shoulda known that. So he and his girl are vacationing here, in Wistwood? And that Neetha is his girlfriend?"

"Yes. And she's his wife, actually."

"How far is the nearest tower, anyway, Horace?"

"The what?"

"The tower. Nearest cell tower. There's got to be a few along the Big Sur coast, even if they don't work for shit. *Especially* along this coast, I would think. Where's the closest one?"

"Why, it's exactly where it ought to be, I reckon," said Horace with another weary shrug. He tapped lightly with a gloved finger on the top of his cane. "Last anyone checked it was surely the same place it was when they left it."

"What's that supposed to—"

"Why look just there!" interrupted Horace, pointing to the left of the van as Brask parked at last along the curb. "It's the Reverend Jarecki, working hard on his chapel. Big restoration job he's got going on. Maybe even a *reformation*," added Horace, giving Brask a conspiratorial poke in the ribs with the tip of his cane.

"Hey there, Pastor Jarecki!" Horace leaned toward the driver's side window at such an acute angle Brask thought the old man was going to crawl across his lap. "Pastor J! In here! We've got a live one for the old Kimberton cabin over the hills. This is Brask Adams. He was nice enough to give me a ride back into town after signing on the dotted line."

Brask was momentarily surprised at first sight of the lanky, frazzled, and slightly sunburned man on the lawn across the street, standing before a rectangular structure of red brick being built upward from a cement foundation. It was a haphazard affair; parts of a wall were piled three feet high in some spots, or six feet and already listing precariously in others.

"So this is a preacher and his church, eh?"

"That's right," said Horace, waving amiably through the window.

Brask hadn't bothered to look closely at the place on their first pass through town, hidden as the project was near a crowded grove of oaks and almost entirely behind Donovan's Mercantile. It was already a disaster, this sanctuary; Brask could tell that much from one survey of his contractor's eyes. The guy clearly didn't know what the hell he was doing.

The priest or preacher, Reverend Jarecki, wore a grubby sweatshirt and jeans ripped at the knees as he struggled to push a wheelbarrow of freshly mixed cement toward a scattering of bricks. Sweating profusely, he abandoned his burden and ambled across the street to the van.

One sudden gust and that poor guy is gonna blow away down the street. He's Ichabod Crane as a frat brother!

Staring beneath a wiry shock of hair as black as coal from the deepest mine imaginable, Jarecki removed a work glove and offered a frail but calloused hand to Brask.

"Good to meet you. Welcome to Wistwood."

"Thanks. Good to meet you, too."

"How's the construction coming along, Reverend?" Horace still sprawled leftward, his face nearly resting against the steering wheel. Brask felt more than a little uncomfortable.

Small town ways. Better get used to 'em.

Reverend Jarecki shrugged, then gestured at the mess he'd made as if searching, disoriented and dismayed, for some far more pleasant dream that had escaped him upon the moment of waking. He blinked his big, hollow brown eyes and swiped the back of a hand under his nose, leaving a smudge of dirt and dust on his upper lip.

"Eh, it's not going so well," he finally muttered, shyer than almost any man Brask had ever seen. "Guess I'm not much of a builder."

"You'll get the hang of it, yet," said Horace. "Don't you worry. Have you tried prayer?"

"It'd probably take a miracle," lamented the cleric. "But I'm not too hopeful for one."

"Brask here was a contractor and construction worker for years, leastways until he became a famous writer. Maybe he could lend you a hand?"

"Hey, I'm not famous yet," cautioned Brask, nudging Horace gently with an elbow off his lap and back into an upright position on his own seat. "Only signed a book deal. The novel still has to sell when it comes out. No superstar guarantees. And, no offense, Horace, nor any to you, Reverend, but I don't build churches."

Bitter coolness drifted into Brask's mind. A familiar, stealthy cloud, sneaking on swift wings from unseen corners of the sky to block the comfort of sun on his skin, the light that wrapped a blanket around his better thoughts. He regretted allowing it entry, but when had he ever been able to thwart that intruder; faceless, forever cloaked in grey, determined to smother?

His mouth tasted sour. The verdict of a childhood, tried and found wanting, declared itself in echoes that rang and harrowed on the rise from depths he had long fought to seal. Layers of spiritual cement availed little. There it was. *There it was.* Another sudden visit. Present and accounted for. The incense. The sceptic, mothball stench of some old, velvet-cushioned confessional, reeking of shame and the pithy little sins of housewives, the idle fantasies of parochial students, bored into perpetual lust. Whispers. Bells mourning in the distance and in darkness. Fingertips burned from catching wax as it dripped from votive candles. Knuckles rapped for playing with the candles. Guilt. Always the fucking guilt.

For the world that was. For the world that was not. For the world that ever shall be. World without end. Amen.

He went pale as the preacher stood at the window, apparently lost for words. Staring in at them as if in the grip of some expectant trance. Brask's stomach churned at the thought of making further small talk. The burden of his sad, suffering mother's Catholic faith had been one thing. Far worse was his sister's half-assed, Jesus-Is-Coming-On-the-Clouds, Everybody-Get-Ready-for-Lift-Off brand of Bible-sucking insanity. But why was he feeling such revulsion now, at the mere appearance of this stranger who was doing him no harm, who was simply outdoors on a bright and pleasant afternoon, working hard and working alone?

This is none of my business. Stop letting people weird you out. Get away! Get away!

"I expect it'll turn out just wonderful," said Horace, breaking the spell of discomfort. "With a little more elbow grease, Reverend, you'll get those walls up. Don't get down on yourself. Confidence is key. Gonna be a nice little addition to the Wistwood landscape when you finish."

"Yeah, you're probably right. Anyhow, I'm going to start laying another layer of bricks," said Reverend Jarecki, as if addressing the wind. "Got to see how that pans out before I try anything else. Didn't have much luck yesterday, obviously. Anyone can see that from the mess. A whole day's work just tumbled to the ground overnight. Maybe it was the wind, though I didn't hear any. Maybe it's the way I mixed the cement. Who knows?"

"Church bells will be ringing in due course," said Horace.

Jarecki shrugged, embarrassed or exhausted or both. Brask couldn't tell.

"I'm back to work, gentlemen. Brask, was good to meet you. Hope you like it here. Hope you like the old Kimberton place. That's a nice little cabin. I would have snapped it up myself, if other accommodations hadn't already been provided. They were a nice couple, the Kimbertons. It's a shame we lost them."

"Lost them?"

"Well, now, we won't trouble you any further, Rev," Horace interjected with some insistence, sitting rigid and suddenly judicial in his bearing against the back of the seat. "Just paused to say 'hello' as we were driving in. Got lots of business to attend to, same as you."

The Reverend Jarecki trudged away.

"So what's the matter, Brask? Men of the cloth give you the willies?"

"Excuse me?"

"Oh, I didn't mean anything by that. Just noticed that you were a tad uncomfortable when we stopped to have a word with the good Reverend, that's all. You looked kinda like a little fella sitting in line, waiting his turn for the confessional when he knows he has to fess-up to a peek at a titty magazine. Or maybe he's pulled some little girl's hair in school. Or maybe he's been playing with hisself or—"

"Whoah! Hold on, there, Horace. I don't know where you're getting all that." Brask was mortified. It was like the old man had been reading his mind. "I was born Catholic, yeah. My mother was devout. And my sister is now a raging holy roller of some sort. Baptist. Nazarene, I forget. But I gave religion the heave-ho a long while back. I sure as hell hope I didn't sit here looking like some sort of snot-nosed kid in front of that guy. I barely said a word to the man as it is."

Horace raised a calming glove. "Now, you need not misinterpret me. It was just a hunch. A sense I had, is all. I notice things about people that they sometimes don't notice about themselves. No offense intended. And, for what it's worth, Catholic priests definitely give *me* the heebie jeebies." He let out a hoarse, strangled cackle. "Can't stand the sonsabitches, myself."

"But I thought you said this guy is a pastor. A minister."

"Oh, he is. *Now*. But he used to be a Catholic priest. Didn't I mention that? No? Well, he was a priest of the Roman persuasion, once. Smells and bells. Virgin spewing grace. The whole works. But I gather they either threw him out of the Church—made him swim the old Tiber—or he defrocked himself. Never did give anybody in town a clear explanation, though of course most of us don't want to pry about a man's personal business. Not sure about his reasons. Maybe he just wanted to have sex, eh?"

"I don't think being a priest has ever stopped many of them from that, if that's what they wanted."

"Ha! I expect you're right on that count!" Horace gave his own knee a playful slap. "But I like Jarecki a lot better as a Protestant or whatever the hell he calls himself now. Who cares about his history?"

Brask took a deep breath and tried to compose himself. He was bothered. The mere presence of the pastor had nearly creeped him through the roof of his already creepy van. But why? Even his sister never made him that unsettled. Still, the last thing he wanted was to fall into some trap, to appear prejudiced or antisocial concerning anyone's personal choice in Imaginary Friends From Above. Anything could be a litmus test, these days, and old Horace was clearly a much cagier creature than he had observed or suspected at the outset.

"I won't ever judge you on your beliefs or lack of them, Brask. But in my estimation, the sort of people who cling to infallible popes and infallible books made out of pieces of paper with little infallible ink-marks on them are generally stupid-ass folks, or painfully overeducated ones. I've met a few of those in my day, too. These fools quote a few lines straight from something that supposedly popped direct outta the mouth of the Almighty and it makes 'em feel superior. Makes em feel *special*. Well, it would make them feel that way, wouldn't it, if they believe such horseshit? It's ironic, though, because the ones who do that sort of thing know deep down they're all dumber than a bunch of goddamned sheep. Funny old world, ain't it?"

"That's putting it mildly, Horace, though I don't find myself laughing too much at it these days."

"Agreed. Now, if you'll excuse me, Brask, I've got a lot to get accomplished before this day is through, as I said, and you'll likely want to stop inside Donovan's for a few essentials, presuming you haven't got essentials already squirreled away in the back of this rig. I'm mighty pleased you signed on today."

As he opened the door and eased his ancient body out of the van, Horace smiled and brandished the manila envelope with the bloodstained lease agreement inside. "You're one of us, now. The other folks in Wistwood are going to love meeting you. Our very own famous author. Imagine that. Why, between you and that burned-out rock singer, I expect you'll put us right on the map."

TRANSFIXION ABUNDANT

Shep Daltry had not bothered to pack any of his worldly belongings, mundane or sacred. He would have no use for them. He knew this as well as he knew the world was coming to an end—that *his* world was coming to an end; the proper and most fitting kind of end.

He wouldn't be needing things like his uniform or his big-screen TV, which was an elderly behemoth of a model because he'd had to sell some of his better possessions and save money to buy the vat, the second freezer, another barrel, and some of the acids that had been required.

Clothing? He wouldn't need the unlaundered crap tossed haphazardly about the house. He wouldn't need the linens in the bathroom closet, or the toiletries in the medicine cabinet: no Aqua Velva skin-bracer; no Fleet suppositories for those less-cooperative days in which his bowels betrayed him and went obstinately off-script. He wouldn't need the prized photo of his graduation from the police academy, which waited like the last girl left without a partner at the prom, flung into a corner of the bedroom. Next to this was a garter he had saved from his wedding reception. The garter and its attached fishnet stocking were in a twisted heap against the paneling of the wall. To Shep, the garter looked like a slut, one who had been rightfully used and then kicked, senseless and obscene, to a wretched curbside. Why he had kept the damned thing, even as a memento upon which to focus relentless laser-like beams of hatred from his brain, was beyond him.

But what the hell did it matter, now? This was the end of everything.

He moved through the cluttered, meaningless rooms of the house, every one of them, and stared at all of the junk he would never see again, tabulating a spiteful inventory. A Go To Hell Because Who Needs Any of This Shit Anyway? kind of inventory.

"Who knows?" he said aloud to the filthy kitchen, thinking of his ex-wife. "Maybe the stupid bitch'll have the brass brassiere to broomstick her way back after I'm gone and snatch some of this garbage up."

He growled a bit at a lopsided painting of sailboats on a wall in the hallway. The sailboats were caught in a storm. Several crew members were tumbling, one after the other, into black and ravenous waves.

"Hell, maybe when she finds out about my victory, she'll come back and try to have herself a hot little garage sale! Make herself enough money to buy a whole closet full of clothes. Then she can wrap her ass up good and shake it down at her mother's two-bit goddamned country club over in Houston. Maybe catch herself a rich man dumb enough to try and stick his shriveled dick up the crack of her ass."

Shep laughed, the bark of a hyena reverberating throughout the house. Spittle flew from his mouth, flecking the crumpled vinyl cover of a Singer sewing machine. Then he went into the kitchen to yell at some old cereal boxes atop the refrigerator for a few minutes.

"I should've goddamned well killed her ass. Shoulda skinned her and turned her into a piece of carpet!"

He snorted at the ratty throw-rug in the nearby dining room.

"Shit," he grumbled after a few seconds of half-hearted scrutiny. "She wouldn't have even made a decent rug."

Stalking into the living room, Shep stood and listened in the midst of the dark and silent house, every window closed and locked, every curtain drawn tight. He towered above the furniture; sofa and chairs and end-tables seeming to cower in the shadows. He was sweating profusely again, arms akimbo, gloating in this last triumph, this finest accomplishment, over his own life. Over all life.

Yes, he knew it would have been a mistake to kill Wifey, though he had wanted to do so and had given the matter a great deal of thought. He had even planned at least half a dozen scenarios. Good ones. But killing her would have been a careless indulgence and far too much of a risk beyond the parameters he had set for himself, beyond the laws and rules and impeccable disciplines that had made his real work, his lasting work, so successful thus far. And it would have been a violation of his Orders, the strict fulfillment of which had brought him with such powerful certainty to this, his moment of Ascendancy, his hour of enthrallment before transition. Before transfixion.

She was gone. She had left him, but no matter how far away she had gotten, she was just a thing, now. An empty and useless article from the past, like the towels, the sewing machine, the framed grad portrait, the garter, the rug, the third-rate TV, the cereal boxes and the fridge full of nothing but empty bins and shelves, save for a carton of curdled milk, a six-pack of beer, and twelve quart-sized containers of rendered human body-fat.

Sinner lard.

The only kind suitable for stewing evildoers—*in their own juices!*—or for frying the occasional egg.

The Work was done.

The house sweltered at noon. Shep peeked out from behind a front window curtain, a great cobra rising to flare his hood and scan the world through a sliver of shadow. The neighborhood held its breath, the windowed eyes of all nearby houses un-watchful. Avoiding the obvious. Even clouds wanted no part of the sky above his territory. They were everywhere else, though.

This is no place for the living. Look away! Look away! The Summoned will depart our midst. Look away! Look away! For Time, Times, and half a Time.

This was damned good. Shep wanted no sounds beyond those of his own breath and his heartbeat. Blood rushing in a tidal roar through his brain. A chant. A symphony in each ear. He resumed moving from room to room. He didn't care that he was grimy, that he stunk. The sweat could stay behind, too. Sweat had never gotten him far in the fruitless work of the world, and what sweat he had expended upon his Masterwork would baptize it forever as a testimonial to success.

He pictured the faces of those who would sooner or later move through the house, probably even some of those who had once called themselves his friends.

Friends. He could see the idiots now, could practically smell their horror and disbelief. Their puke. He felt their astonishment as they learned—*oh, learning was too small a word for what they would experience*—as their minds were enlightened. Would they grasp their privilege? Would they appreciate that they would be given in broad, unflinching daylight the gift of being able to distinguish between Things That Mattered and Things That Did Not? Would they recognize work that amounted to nothing from Work that would go down in history?

No. They would not see the deepest differences. They would not see the vast chasm between bland, dust-covered items and the bleached, carved, and Resplendent Things waiting in freezers in the garage or slowly sizzling to their purest manifestations, to their essences, in the vats of acid lined-up in the cellar.

Shep would not take the name of Teacher. No, only One could claim it. Not he. But, oh, how majestic were the truths he would soon communicate by the example of his Most Righteous Anger, by the brilliance of secret deeds made manifest! This would be indisputable proof of his worthiness. This glory had been established because none had been able to resist or to interfere. None of the living had perceived him and plans were fulfilled. Soon the great truth would be shared with the world. The Venerable Task! The Seen and the Unseen would come to know that there is no safety, no protection from the Doom that awaits one and all, one and all.

No safety. No trust. Everything comes to nothing.

Now he would accept the reward long promised and well-earned, the crown of victory, the laurel at the end of the excruciating race, the New Job.

Spoil for the toil.

Yes. That was how his esteemed Patron described it in the labyrinthine pattern of employment ads, applications, emails, and to-do lists he had found, studied, answered, and feverishly completed over the months.

Shep spun around the murky living room for a last look. The treasures in the garage and down in the cellar had already been attended a final time and were quite secure; these leftovers would be found and worshipped and venerated and discussed and studied.

The work, the work, the Master Work

was safe. Its future was guaranteed. Now for the next step, the bold leap toward new employment with benefits and perks beyond imagining.

I will be swift!

He had arranged long in advance to have this day—of all amazing and incomparable days—away from his desk at headquarters, away from his beat. All was in order. No undue suspicions had been aroused, at least not enough for them to corner him in an office or come knocking on his door. The Sheriff had questions, apparently. Fuck that. Nothing untoward would occur until it was *time* for things untoward to rain down like hellfire upon those who least expected it.

He pounded up the stairs to his bedroom, huffing and grunting, taking the steps two at a time and nearly tripping in his haste. The ads. He would reread them, he would proof them, along with all of the subsequent correspondence, before carrying out the final instructions and making his way to the Interview. Double-checking was the only way to be on the safe side, to prevent last-minute mistakes and eliminate all potential impediments to the Transformation for which he had been so graciously scheduled.

He sat down at the computer-table in his bedroom, in front of the whirring and humming machine and its greasy screen. He woke the thing up. Sweat poured hot and then cold from his forehead as his eyes devoured the line of saved documents across the desktop. He opened each one and read silently to himself, starting with the blessed First Summons, the ad he had stumbled upon back in July under the category of "High Security Employment Opportunities." It had been meant for him—so clearly meant for him. Why, it had indicated as much:

Shepard Lee Daltry, this employment opportunity is meant for you and for you alone. Share this exciting prospect with no other person and, after reading the job description posted below, reply with a letter of intent by following the attendant link and await further correspondence and instruction.

There they were, all of the replies and encouragements that had come to him, guiding and preparing him for the best possible chance to land the long-term position, answering his questions succinctly and with impressive conviction. Here were the words that urged him to caution on this front, to ambition on another, advising prudence when necessary, helpful hints for avoiding the pitfalls …

...it is never easy for a man to change jobs in this world, Prospective Candidate Daltry. It is rather a serious endeavor deserving all focus and the involvement of all faculties. Not ever may a transition of such magnitude be taken lightly. Man is not made for change. Change is made for Man. It is up to Man, should he choose to subdue and tame the power of Change and bend it toward his own purpose. Follow all instructions carefully ...

Follow. Follow. Follow. The admonition had been constant, as had the heart-stirring affirmations, once he had proved himself to be the only worthy candidate

It is Our sincere belief that you, Shepard L. Daltry, are the only Man for this position. It is yours if you are willing to fill it and if you are ready to carry out the last few remaining instructions, which constitute a series of mere formalities that shall culminate in your new-hire Interview. Yet, beware, lest any detail escapes your attention and your admirable progress is impeded.

Shep began to cry. For joy. Tears mingled with the sweat. All of it spattered in great drops onto the computer keyboard.

What meaningless filth was the noise and nature of the world in which he had been languishing! This was an employer he could believe in. A company he could make shine brighter than ever it had. Perhaps even one day he might be judged worthy to take things over on his own.

The work. The work. The Master Work.

This was the bridge. Bones would form the bridge! And bloodshed beneath it like a sea.

And the bridge would endure long after he had crossed it.

The work! The work!

It was time. Time beyond Time.

Follow the final instructions to the letter, Shepard L. Daltry, failing in no directive and withholding no effort of will. Do exactly as the commandments indicate and arrive at the Interview as scheduled.

Shep's hands stopped trembling. His body stopped sweating. Tears no longer fell. He opened the document containing the final correspondence in the sequence of Employment Agreements and read it again, to be sure, though he had memorized it well.

"Yes, I see. I know it. I'll do it."

Indeed, he knew it. He was prepared. He had been prepared all his life.

Shep pushed the rolling chair away from the desk, stood, stripped until he was naked, and kicked his clothes away into a corner. Muscular arms dangling at his sides, he looked in dreamy expectation down at his cock, menacing and erect. His body tensed at the peak of his exaltation. By power of spirit alone he shot three arcing jets of semen across the desk and onto the computer screen. The thick fluid slid in rivulets down and over the Final Instructions.

The work! The work! The Master Work.

He took the hunting knife from its place beside the computer keyboard and put the blade across his throat, never taking his eyes from the words clouded but visible through his ejaculate.

Time for the Interview.

He said the one strange word he had been ordered to say at this moment, pronounceable in three syllables and quite beautiful, though he knew nothing of its true origin or antiquity, much less its meaning. After uttering The Word—the marvelous Word—he cut deep into his throat from the base of one ear to the other, without fear or hesitation. A crimson blast painted the wall, the desk, the computer, the carpet.

Shep transformed.

THE FINDING OF
THE GRAYLE

Lleyton Grayle already despised the town of Wistwood. It didn't even qualify as a "town," as far as he was concerned. In fact, he could not bear the thought of staying another day in the airy woodland sprawl, amid bustling squirrels and nattering magpies that seemed to mock everything he had ever stood for. Everything he aspired to enjoy in life.

He loathed the brain-murdering silence that rose from the very ground of the backwoods hamlet like a noxious, suffocating vapor.

He cringed at the thought of one more glistening sunrise over the hills.

His blood-pressure skyrocketed with every memory of his life in London, surrounded by mates well-chosen for their capacity to knock back whiskey with as much gusto as he. Mates inclined to chortle and agree with every slurring pub proclamation, eager to vouchsafe his ongoing status as king of a declining fiefdom.

Fuck Wistwood. Fuck this vacation. Of all the bad ideas to have at the rottenest time, this was the worst.

Lleyton shoved a couple of fingers between the collar of his turquoise buttoned Nehru shirt and his bloated neck, wanting to rip the garment off. Send buttons flying. But it was the only old shirt he still had, and a classic at that—a bit of trademark Grayle fashion left over from his days of glory on the stage, on album covers, across magazine pages. It was the shirt he wore on the day he and Neetha first drove into Wistwood.

Most everything else of value was gone, now, and there was no one to blame except the wretch he had been stupid enough to marry. Neetha. She was the instigator and essence of his downfall. The architect of ruin.

And Lleyton dearly wanted to kill her. With as much pain as might be possible for him to inflict in the process.

He had been thinking about it a lot, lately. Planning it. Wanting to do it here, in the middle of nowhere.

He had watched Neetha drive up the hill, returning from her trip to the idiotic general store, and probably from a quick pitstop at the bar & grill. Oh, she needed her little drink, that Neetha. That bloody succubus. He stared in his wheelchair from the downstairs balcony of their rented A-frame's master bedroom as she parked the Ferrari and got out. He wondered how it might feel in a physical way, as well as a mental way, if he could take one of the big round river stones perched on either end of the balcony's balustrade and just smash it onto her dried-out, platinum head. How would it sound? He'd have to be very accurate, but if sheer desire meant anything at all in the universe, there was a good chance it would be a memorable experience.

He sneered, watching her grapple with a grocery bag and wobble on her lucite heels. It was a bloody miracle she could do two or three things at once. In she came. Neetha.

Too stupid to ever glance crossways and catch sight of anything that might be hurled against her thick skull. Lleyton had no doubt about that. She was one of those useless people built and wired to look straight ahead and toward the ground, as if forever wandering through a dark tunnel in fear that her own legs would become entangled and tip her over. Too worried that a strand of overbaked hair might fall out of place amid its shellacked helmet. Terrified that she could suffer a broken fucking fingernail.

God, how he hated her.

Life was one big hazard-zone for Neetha the Moron, or, as he liked to call her, the "Whoron." For her, there was just one delight, a single, small opening in the black expanse of her stupidity, and that was forward motion. The thrill she got out of swinging her hips and thrusting her fake tits forward, clack clack clacking in the heels toward some shining object, like a moth too primitive to realize it was about to flutter its fat ass into a bonfire.

How had he been so stupid?

Jesus Christ, even listening to her fiddle with the jumble of house keys, as if opening the front door were some kind of intricate scientific process involving nuclear fusion, made him sick to his stomach. He didn't think he could stand to look at her again today. He'd have to lock her out of the bedroom. That was it. Had to be done. She reminded him of one of those swollen, colorful caterpillar worms that chewed on and on in gluttonous passes through a green leaf until it bumped accidentally into the next edible plant encountered, starting the whole mechanical process over again in whatever direction was required.

What had he ever seen in her? Why had he risked so much, losing half his fortune just as his career was beginning to tank, amid a bitter divorce to the first witch-wife? For what? The thrill of banging a brainless groupie who'd already lost her last brain cell to coke? The novelty of her well-oiled body sure as bloody hell wore-off as soon as the divorce agreement was signed.

It was all so unfair. His mother had warned him about women. Too bad she'd been one of them. At least that nuisance was moldering in a grave. This one was probably too dumb to kill. Stupid was like a bloody force-field around her.

Oh, but Neetha could use her last lingering brain cells in conniving fashion.

Neetha, the dimwitted Caterpillar of Gnawing Life-Destruction, had proved to be a savvy little schemer.

How and from whence she had produced the cunning to get him to marry her without a prenup was an absolute mystery to Lleyton. A smack in the gob. He had wracked his brain every day for the past fifteen years and every day he came up impoverished for answers. Maybe women like Neetha had been wired by eons of natural selection to achieve their goals once nature gave them the signal that a successful male was vulnerable for optimum parasitic predation.

Hell, Neetha and others like her probably never even had to think about it, to summon genuine cognitive skills or functions. It was probably a hormonal thing triggered by fuck pheromones. Yeah, that had to be it. They were insects. Once women like Neetha sensed an everlasting payday, the evolutionary gold-digging switch in their DNA flipped to the "on" position and they got what they wanted. Then, sated, they reverted back to the vacuous, blood-sucking leeches they'd always been, offering a lot less sex and a helluva lot more wheedling for shiny toys.

Fucking bloody amazing. No wonder the cold, cruel earth was said to be a Mother. No wonder!

How he wished he would have pulled Neetha's plug or yanked-out her battery or thrown some kind of monkey-wrench into whatever conglomeration of wheels and spinning gizmos made the woman's motor work. Instead, he had nose-dived: the chance for a more lucrative career-segue into producing was lost; his ability to buy and maintain the loyalty of powerful friends, friends capable of sustaining his marketability, dried up and blew away; the divorce settlement had eviscerated him. Oh, hell. The first Mrs. Lleyton Grayle—Gwendolyn, the venom-spitting spider—had been none too pleased to see him take-up with a retarded praying mantis like Neetha. She had punished him accordingly and, as things turned out, irreversibly, in the courts.

It was all so unfair.

These horrors had distracted Lleyton. He hadn't had time amid all the persecution to negotiate and secure a reasonable future in music publishing. Distribution and ownership rights to his back-catalogue were compromised, once the hits stopped coming and once record company execs stopped attending his parties. He had become a man at the mercy of unjust oppressors. Sure, it hadn't helped that a string of no-shows intermingled with a slew of drunken stage performances left him disreputable and, far worse for rock and roll commerce, completely uninsurable. But it was the women who had instigated all of it.

Who could deny the truth of it? He had been so mesmerized by Neetha's refurbished tits, implant-padded ass, and limitless capacity to suck and fuck for one magical year that he didn't even bother to notice that his longtime agent, Marty, had been robbing him blind at every turn and striking rights agreements for short-term peanuts payments that left Lleyton a hostage to his own work. Even if he had remained viable as a touring act or as a mugging coach potato on some late-night chat show lineup, he'd be forced to pay someone *else* money when he publicly performed songs that *he* had written!

God damn women and agents.

That was how Marty had repaid him. Even after he had generously let the man have a couple rolls in the sack with Neetha during one pharmaceutically lost and ill-advised weekend in San Tropez. Worse, after the sucker punch of the divorce to Gwendolyn, Lleyton had ballooned to two hundred fifty pounds. He suffered more panic attacks than usual. He drank three times as much. And his once-coveted heavy metal hair—the Grayle trademark and calling card—deserted him. Bald at fifty-five.

Oh, he had attempted to sit down and compose some new songs, ostensibly to perform in cabaret or acoustic settings; stadium and concert hall days were gone, baby, gone. He thought about pitching new material to A&R people and slowly rebuilding a reputation, but his hands trembled uncontrollably every time he picked up a guitar or passed his fingers over a piano keyboard. When his mind scrambled itself composing melodies and catchy lyrics, he would hit playback on his homemade demo recordings in breathless anticipation ... only to discover that his new songs made about as much sense as a two year-old painting nursery walls in its own shit and clapping gleefully with a sense of accomplishment.

Even Neetha had once wandered into his home studio like some ungainly, flightless bird long overdue for extinction while he had been playing some new material. She had stared at him the way an ostrich stares at a fencepost, complete-ly oblivious to rational thought. Turning her head in perplexed shifts and tilts, her beak drooping open due to her brain's lack of control, she had said, "Bloody hell, Lleyton. That sounds like a whole lotta garbage, if you ask me."

In the humiliation and emasculating agony of that moment, all the years of crowded arenas, gold records, flowing champagne, assembly lines of pussy, syco-phants, handlers, burgeoning bank accounts, and enough fine coke to conceal the top of an Alp—all of this magnificence had drained from his existence. A plug had been pulled at the bottom of the universe and everything worthwhile had spun forever into the outer darkness, where his mother probably floated, gorging on his agony.

That was when Lleyton decided to resist the frightful pull of the vortex as best as he could. There wasn't much left to work with, comparatively speak-ing. He still owned a rat-trap apartment building in Manchester and a few hundred acres of land in Colorado, bought on the advice of a business manager who had been as perpetually shit-faced as he had been in the years after his first two big-selling albums and tours. Lleyton had signed off on that deal and the land was still his, free and clear, but he had utterly forgotten about it until the moment his epiphany finally arrived. Then he had prayed audibly for the first time in his life that the purchase had not been some drug-induced hallucination.

It was not. Moreover, to his greater relief, he discovered that payment of the annual taxes on the property had been maintained over the years due to another established account he had forgotten all about, a side-scheme with his first record company, set up specifically for the purpose of paying those taxes. Set and forget it, that kind of shit.

Thank the bloody Baby Jesus.

All told, when Lleyton determined to take matters in hand, there was a quarter of a million in cash and the same in diversified stocks and securities, while the non-liquid assets—car collections and land—amounted to four million, at best, with no new money coming in for the foreseeable future, if ever. His expenditures were $20,000 a month, even at his most austere, ill, and sedentary. Neetha's acquisitions accounted for most of the ruin in that department, unquestionably. Every time she spied something shiny, her beak would clatter and caw.

Thus, he had taken many deep breaths and a fair but not totally stupefying amount of tranquilizers, quit drinking before noon, and spent six months dedicated to the sole task of saving what could be saved and getting his affairs in order before the gutter itself wagged a come-hither finger in his direction. Thank God he had seen some sort of light bulb flicker to life when he was at his lowest, although Lleyton believed even less in God than he did in the loyalty of managers and record company executives.

He had called what few meetings he still had enough clout to summon, had fired one round of bloodsucking lackeys and flacks, rehired a much more streamlined team, fired *them* when he deemed the outfit to be as untrustworthy as the previous lot, and then hunted feverishly for the kind of advisors he could count upon to refrain from dipping greedy paws into the cracked cookie-jar of his remaindered existence.

Somehow, he had managed to grab onto a perilous outcropping. More likely he had snagged somewhere, merely by chance. Once he figured out that he had reached the direst of crossroads, and that he wanted to at least avoid death and poverty, Lleyton desired a trajectory like the one travelled by men who survived into their old age. He wanted to "live to tell" about the wild times and the wicked times, the ominous plunges, and the detours into self-destruction under the pretense of heroic liberation.

He wanted to lean-in for secrecy's sake over drinks, to reveal in smirking whispers the tales of the other lives he'd trampled beneath the grinding wheels of his juggernaut. He ached to boast of the obscenities achieved, both public and oh-so-hidden from that part of the world that slept with a clear conscience and took in great draughts of air never touched by the stench of Want. He lusted to overpower and subdue the truly beautiful illusions of life as a dragon hoarding gold, leaving all others to choke and gasp on the outskirts, clutching for the one breath of genuine redemption that would never allow itself to be inhaled.

Fuck rock and roll and all its trappings if these should ever stand in his way. Fuck the stigma of being a jaundiced has-been, the goddamned punch line in so many jokes about lights that once burned brightly and now dangled in a state of burnout. Fuck the deals made wisely, the deals made in drunkenness, and the so-called friends that had passed through his life with all the substance and stability of holograms. Ghosts. The whole fucking bloody lot of them. Worse than fucking ghosts. At least ghosts were apt to hang around a bit, if only to keep things interesting and rattle the occasional chain to remind you that, yeah, they were still there. That you were worth haunting.

The only true horror that deigned to occupy his personal spookhouse was regrettably alive, well, and more frightful in her soul-sucking insipidity than any specter or incubus that could have crept up from the most woebegone cesspit of hell's bubbling gumbo of nightmare-denizens.

Neetha.

Of all the things Lleyton fought to salvage and bring into some kind of order, daily slick with the flopsweat of his frantic efforts to just chuck it all, Neetha was the one thing he could do nothing about.

Yet.

When all was said and done, Neetha remained the only burden that could not be gotten rid of, the only barnacle that refused to be pried from the helm when his vessel sailed its uncertain way into cleaner and calmer waters. She owned half of absolutely everything that was left. Her name was on all of it, from the bank accounts to the land, to the vehicles. His own drunken, drug-addled kindness had caused him to open the door of his once-resplendent kingdom to her in the first place. He had been a fool to rope such an albatross to his neck. Yes, she had tricked him, somehow, into going against the plaintive wails and admonitions of his lawyers, at the time, regarding the prenup. How had he ever been drunk or high enough to even hallucinate the notion that Neetha would be his eternal soulmate and doormat? That his life would continue as one glorious, ongoing orgy of sex, substances, and profligate spending? Lleyton had no answer, aside from his depravity.

And none of that was his fault. Not really.

Things were different, now. He had had the near-religious experience of all blinders being lifted and was able to finally see Neetha for what she was, to behold her in the completeness of her excrescence. The burden of that sudden, flooding vision had proved too much for his soul to bear; he quailed with rage and claustrophobic despair at the knowledge she had hooked her pestilential tentacles into every slice of pie he still had to his name.

So it came to be that Lleyton decided to make Neetha's personal life with him as miserable as he could make it, without giving her evidence too tangible for a messy divorce. Instead, he was hoping very much to drive her to an adulterous affair that could be captured for the courts by expert surveillance. Or else drive her insane. That tantalized him most of all. What a coup it would be to provoke some outrageous reaction by which she might be deemed incompetent and thus sequestered in a cheap mental ward where certain doctors, nurses, orderlies, or a combination of all three would keep his dear wife's veins full of the most potent sedatives known to medical science.

If that stuff didn't pan out, he would kill her.

His conscience did not halt at the prospect of seeing Neetha take a bullet to the head or suddenly wonder why the brakes to her Ferrari weren't working and the car had developed the ability to fly off a cliffside into the sea.

Already, he had tried passive-aggressive tactics, forthright humiliation, mockery, and even a bit of light hypnotism he had spent weeks working hard to master. Nothing bore the fruit of madness and he came to the conclusion that Neetha's Ferrari could be more successfully engaged and mesmerized than Neetha herself. The car, at least, could be driven somewhere, whereas she could not be moved in any significant way. After all of it, and to make matters worse than anything even *he* had ever been able to imagine, they had managed somehow to end up here, in Wistwood, a shithole of powerlessness to end them all.

Somehow. As if.

This wasn't going to work the way he wanted. Like everything else that was tinged with misfortune, Lleyton and Neetha's arrival and establishment of vacation rental space in Wistwood had been Neetha's fault. The woman simply could not stop ruining his life and he was now more ill-equipped to halt the chuckwagon of destruction than ever he was in the past.

He had suffered a stroke due to desperate thinking in the Spring. Now he was in the wheelchair.

We need a vacation to make you feel good again, honey. Some fresh air in the country. I'll take care of everything.

Lleyton sat on the balcony, staring into the misery of the day, despising the sunshine, the rolling hills, and all the fabulous trees. Every leaf quivering on its dainty twig. He could hear Neetha tacking around the kitchen in her freakish heels, making lunch, making plans, probably. Who knew?

His life was bound to her forever, but maybe there was a way to take her out, now that they were in the seclusion of Wistwood for a few weeks. The forest might have its advantages, remoteness some favors to grant. Otherwise, there was no changing his own imminent doom. No fighting it. No getting around the finality of it. It was written in stone.

And it was all her bloody fault.

ARIMATHEA

Her name wasn't really Neetha, though she had answered to Neetha for over twenty years. Her true name, the one given by her parents two days after being born, was Melissa, and Melissa-turned-Neetha loved Lleyton Grayle, former heavy metal chart-topper and current fallen idol, shadow of a wholly manufactured radiance forever dimmed. She loved Lleyton about as much as she now regretted the name "Neetha," which she considered to be one of the more unfortunate choices of her rebellious youth. It signified nothing, as she grew older, in terms of spiritual awakening. And Neetha was always looking for ways to awaken. On the contrary, for her, the name had come to imply by its sound and spelling some lesser status in the world, some weirdness and quality of being below more substantial realities.

Neetha nowhere never underneath teeth not needed Arimathea Neetha Grayle

She could scarcely remember why she had chosen the name, or why she had been so adamant about making the change legal, instead of simply adopting it for potential discard when time and better judgment worked their inevitable magics upon everyday existence. After her parents died, she considered changing her name back to "Melissa," but Lleyton had harangued her. She was his wife. That was the name she had when he met her. Changing the name would complicate their already convoluted financial relationship. She was already known to the rock public as Neetha, the beauty on the arm of Lleyton Grayle.

Neetha everywhere always above the heathrow needed Arimathea Neetha

Any switch too radical would undermine "proof of her devotion to his name and image as a celebrity," or so he said. She obeyed him because she had been afraid of him, once upon a time. He had insisted upon other things, as well. The painful breast augmentation, for instance. The uncomfortable outfits. The hair. Especially the hair. Now it was stressed and ruined, bleached beyond aridity to the dull color and consistency of straw scattered across a barnyard. The tugging, itchy extensions were even worse. These she had been obliged to incorporate into her "look" once the real hair started breaking off in clumps of abject surrender. Her mane—and its many non-native tendrils—was supposed to be platinum.

Lleyton loved platinum. Platinum was the color of million-selling albums. Platinum reminded him of better days, though she did not think her hair reminded him of anything special. When Neetha first met him, she boasted rich chestnut curls that shone with health and wholesomeness. All of that had been remade in the image of rock and roll sleaze. The same went for her beloved sundresses. These had been replaced by the trashy clothes he insisted she wear like obscene public relations uniforms for the glory of the music. He demanded this even after his meteoric but ephemeral place in the pantheon of pop divinities had been further reduced to the status of a trivia question on the occasional TV game show. Once, his name had been the answer to a clue in a tabloid crossword puzzle she was working. She had been so excited, she rushed into his home studio to tell him about it. He had slapped her. It took two days for her left ear to stop ringing.

Things were different, now. They were on a little vacation in Wistwood. A getaway. She had him right where she wanted him.

Neetha played as if everything on earth blew over her head in a breeze, but she missed little. She had watched him glowering at her from the balcony deck of their A-Frame vacation rental. Saw him give her the same look of desperate hatred, delusion, and childlike helplessness she had been seeing for at least fourteen of the fifteen years they had been officially married. It was the look that took hold ever since Lleyton's divorce was final and the magnitude of the settlement sunk in. It was the look that froze itself on his face once the drugs, the drinking, and the fizzling career finally assumed full and catastrophic control of his mind, inflicting the kind of irreversible damage that doctors and a few sensible friends, including her, had been warning Lleyton about forever.

Ever since, Lleyton's sort of damage had been unmistakable and debilitating in its fury. At a certain point, all warnings were too late. A mountain of second-chances—and even third and fourth chances—to stave-off ultimate disaster, crumbled away one day in the seismic indignation of Lleyton's arrogant self, as if all mountains were made of nothing but dust and a bit of ash.

Let him stare and make faces all he wants, from that wheelchair. Let him wish me dead and gone. I'll get him. I'll get his arse good.

Their marriage had been "over" for ages, but her love for him lingered, curiously, like one fragment remaining from the shattered jewel of a lost and radiant ornament, a slicing shard that once adorned the Truth behind all things worthwhile in the world. It was a small amount of love, perhaps, but enough to fill her, the way daylight floods into a room where the windows had been shuttered for years, banishing featureless phantoms of a life lived without any quickening of human spirit. She believed in that measly thread of love as a thing separate from Lleyton Grayle, believed in it as fiercely as any zealot had ever believed in a good or noble cause. It wasn't much, but it was the only thing she owned of soul value.

Bet he's thinking of a way to make me sign everything over. Some scheme. Some plan to leave me out in the snow and hire himself a little virgin nurse. Oh, I got news for that boy. I got news.

Neetha had tried more times than she could now count to rid herself of the burden of this thankless and genuinely dangerous love; reason alone told her from the time she met Lleyton and the abuse commenced that it was an ominous thing to let one's self love in such a manner. Ruin awaits those who cling in needful ways to mere fragments of gemstone, smashed and deprived of value. She was asking for trouble, asking daily and anew with each night, by surrendering body, soul, and spirit to a man who knew nothing of manhood. Too late for him. Too late for her.

ashes, ashes, we all fall down

She had been terrified, of course, when specialists informed her with clinical dispassion and rank coffee breath that, yes, naturally, or rather unnaturally, he had ruined his circulatory system, his liver, his heart, most of his mind, and would be an invalid for the rest of his days. Death was possibly preferable. Who could guess with precision when *that* might come? And Neetha knew better than many that stars dread obliteration more than most people. They are too accustomed to shine. She had simply wept a little and nodded and wondered in quiet chambers behind the storm-windows of her mangled heart if the curse of loving Lleyton Grayle would ever be broken at all, even if he died.

Why must he have this bloody hold on me? It makes no sense. I could divorce him with sufficient grounds a thousand times over. Who cares what his public might think? His public is gone!

Such were her fitful midnight contemplations; they came in waves that robbed her of sleep and the replenishment of senses and left her feeling as mad as a shithouse rat. That was The Thing her mother called her for sticking with a monumental wreck like Lleyton Grayle, money or no money.

God knew they came perilously close to losing everything. Lleyton might have stood a better chance of recapturing the imagination of his own generation and attracting subsequent ones if the hits had come a bit more frequently and on both sides of the Atlantic. He might have stood a better chance at longevity had attention-spans not become akin to endangered species traipsing through the deforested and weed-strangled jungles of the pop-culture consciousness. In the age of information supernovas and one technological Big Bang after another, Lleyton Grayle had been fated to experience his biggest success within a window of opportunity easily shattered. He had flailed and faded just before certain paradigmatic shifts and twists in the zeitgeist suggested the slimmest hopes for nostalgic endurance.

the boat, you missed it. your chance, you pissed it. your future, you kissed it bye bye bye

Thank God for stowed cash, the tenement in Manchester, and the acreage in Colorado. And she was the one who had cobbled all of that together, making arrangements in a race against the clock. Before she nearly lost her mind. Before Lleyton shat the bed in one final explosion of what she called "fiduciary incontinence."

Neetha had seen enough. More than one psychiatrist informed her that it was no crime to love someone and that her history of care-taking and troubleshooting indicated that, far from being crazy, she was quite a decent woman—a sucker for punishment with more than her share of chronic "fixer" issues, yes, but not mad or damaged in a permanent way. As for the things she had suffered, scars could be healed. Or minimized, with a bit of soul-paint.

I don't need any more bloody cosmetics, Doctor, outside or in. Look at me! He's already turned me into a circus sideshow and I let the bastard do it!

Trapped as she was in a body, a "look," and an often outwardly lurid lifestyle that Lleyton had contrived and grafted upon her person like some mad scientist in a never-ending fit of creative trial and error, she had no choice but to laugh. Laughing helped, when she wasn't in tears.

But Lleyton Grayle had never been a genius, not even a mad one. Neetha had acquiesced because she ached with love for the monster. And she had desired many of the extras—the money, fame, connections, and trappings of success—though she loved Lleyton for not a single one of those reasons or for the combination of them. They were perks, masking and easing the gruesome onset of a catastrophe in-development. Lleyton had been a lovable, giving guy, for about five years. Before his divorce. Then he got lost for good. Lost in the supercell of a storm that gathered strength and malignancy from the steady assimilation of other, outlying thunderbusters. These cloud formations gravitated toward the sinkhole of ruin that was Lleyton himself, the indisputable center of his own hostile and bleak horizon.

What else had she expected, once the winds really began to blow?

Even her girlfriends, before Lleyton sent them all scurrying away in pity with futile promises of retaliation on her behalf—no one had ever bothered to retaliate on her behalf; that *wasn't* rock and roll—even these pals told her how much they understood, as long as she took them to expensive lunches and invited them to parties. As long as resources allowed her to do so. Sure, most were blowing smoke up her ass. A few gave good advice.

"Neetha, babe, some women in this world have just got it bad their whole lives for one guy and one guy only, and Lleyton is your guy. Honey, he could've been a fucking plumber and you'd still have chased the moon down to get him. Men can get like that over women, too. Rarely, but it happens. Point is, he don't deserve you and you can't explain it, and none of us who love you can even get close to helping you solve it. But shit like this happens to a woman in life. Fuck yeah. Just think how sweet it is when it happens to people who *ought* to be together, babe. When a guy is worthy of that kind of love. Must be bloody something, when that happens. You think?"

Her old friend Regina had opened four bottles of wine between them, one afternoon in the Holland Park house, before they had to sell the Holland Park house. Those were shitty days, but at least she had a friend on her side, and a fun one, too.

"Ask any woman what's been around the block, luv. Hell, ask any woman *period*. When this happens to a girl it can be the greatest gift or the worst curse. You're going through a cursed phase. But that's where the hopeful part of it can come into play, babe. It might *just be a phase,* after all. Things could change. Everything depends upon how much you're willing to take, how long you're prepared to wait. I just don't want the sonofabitch to kill you or scar you for life, you know? I mean, I'd have tits like yours, maybe, if I could afford a pair, but the rest of this shit? That's not you. And those bruises sure as hell ain't you. You're in deep, luv. Deep and dangerous. But you're in it for love, and I get that. Even if I don't really get it. I mean it. You know what I mean?"

Regina Wickham might have meant what she said, but she certainly hadn't believed a word of what she said, at least in the case of Lleyton and Neetha. "Reggie," the wife of one of the roadies working for Lleyton's backing band, grasped nothing. She had overdosed and died two years later, caught-up in a coal-black world of drugs and self-immolation even worse than the one Lleyton called home. The irony was that her husband, Devon, had always been the one member of Lleyton's crew who remained clean as a whistle. Devon became a regular churchgoer after the act had "unofficially" broken-up amid the pyrotechnic distress of Lleyton's foolery. He had invested his earnings from the good years in a tidy little apartment building in Leeds, managing it with diligence and dignity to provide a stable life for Regina and their daughter. But Reggie had been unsuited to stability, for all of her philosophical inclinations. Perhaps because of them. Either way, she was dead and her advice still rang hollow.

Now, things had taken another weird turn. Invalid or not, Lleyton had something new up his sleeve. Why in the hell had they rented this place in Wistwood? Why drive to this dead end place she had never heard of. *That* had been a trip, with him snarling at her the entire way. Oh, at first she claimed it was a romantic surprise, a getaway intended to repair their relationship, but Neetha didn't buy her own line for a minute. Was she just trying to get him out of the city and jolt his thoughts away from whatever was simmering? And why were so many Americans hanging around here? It was like some sort of displaced cult. Some commune. People seemed nice enough, but she sure as hell stood out from the pack and the whole set-up gave her the creeps. And what mountains were these? Not the Berkshires. Pretty as a picture, though.

There was no way she'd survive the intended three weeks cooped up in the little A-frame with him. Enough was enough. She finally realized with a quaking sense of terror that it was time to think about putting Lleyton in a place where he could be cared for. Permanently. Their accountant would have to pull a rabbit out of a hat, but it was doable. And there'd still be a reasonable amount for her to live on. It was time to make her move. Maybe that's why they ended up here. To make the decision. But whose idea had it been to come? She hadn't touched a drug in ages.

Who made the decision and why the hell couldn't she remember?

She would figure something out, and she would set the wheels in motion tomorrow, right after meeting that old piece of crust, Horace, to talk about breaking the rental agreement. Lleyton, despite his revivified constitution, was not likely to be happy with her, but too bad. He was still out there, sitting in his spot on the balcony, blanket on his lap, plotting his own things. She knew it. Thank God she had brought a healthy supply of Thorazine along for the trip. Whatever drama was playing out in Lleyton's warped brain—and it couldn't be too exciting, given all the meds he was on—Neetha wasn't about to take a chance that his former proclivity for chaos might be let out for a little spin around the countryside.

Not now, not when she had finally decided to fight for the rest of her life.

PRECIPICE AT WHILES

"The new Destroyer is almost upon us," said She, glancing up through the weighted, leafy limbs of the orchard, each tree pregnant and aching with fruit. "The Gamesman has been acquired."

She searched the boiling red clouds of the sky and wiped her brow, alive like a hummingbird's breast with shimmering colors. The heat of both afternoon suns was oppressive, but gave her garden fragrant, explosive life in the heart of the rocky island. Her suns could interfere, for all of their power to banish shadows that fled in fitful, hissing whispers to seek refuge beneath the black, fertile soil. They brought their share of punishment, as well.

It was no impediment. She had created them to do just that. Suns were wont to do as much wherever they existed, wherever they were created. Praise and punishment in equal measure; sometimes, even, in the same caress of Light.

The Empress of TanTanTuoth sighed, brushing away the blood-sweat that beaded on her forehead, decorating her dignity with small, glistening gems of ruby and carnelian. She stared directly into one swirling orb of sun and then another, probing until the excruciating radiance burst in a riot of sparks from the creamy turquoise pools of her irises. These arrowed flames scattered on the breeze and began to writhe, darting in and out of a shattered glass cyclone that swept up and vanished among the branches bending toward her, drooping and so very weary, but eager to pay her the tribute she was due.

The Harvest was nigh.

Laden boughs boasted of their burdens, holding forth succulent fruit that could be plucked only by her fingers, or at her command, for such privileges were hers alone. She alone had coaxed them into being and had tended them for a Time, Times, and half a Time.

Blood would not be denied on this day. Now it streamed in thin tears long-withheld from the corners of her eyes. Each gleaming trail was spurred as much by sadness as by the pain endured while facing such stubborn solar glare. She had no other choice but to bleed on this day, for on this day only could a glimpse into the furious Fire Above reveal what she needed to know.

"As I feared, Larkspur, we have little time. He is almost upon us. He has found a way through, once again, despite my best efforts to fortify the hidden portals and make the labyrinth as tricky as possible."

"You did your best, My Empress."

"Yes. By night, I have raised mists and mazes. I have constructed deceptions, detours, illusions, and places of detainment. He has come close—very close—to being lost in his meandering forever, but he is wary and manages to evade every trap."

"What do we do now, Lady?"

She gritted her teeth until her skull sent fractured fingers of lightning, jagged and furious, to the very tips of her flowing, silverfrost hair. Every strand, every tress was consumed with the blaze into which she stared. She would not surrender.

"We have our talents," she murmured, penetrating depths and heights that threatened, ever arrogant and pitiless, to overwhelm her, to exact revenge for such brazen espionage and the audacity of her intrusions. He was lusting for her. But this was hardly the first time. She was not to be owned, easily or otherwise, by him or by her sanctuary or by any being she had encountered in a multitude of realms. The Seen and the Unseen exacted a price, indeed, for their multifold services, but she found the reward well worth the discomfort of offended elements. She knew their ways.

Was she not one of them, herself? Was she not among their number, after her own fashion?

"He has taken possession of his slave and enacted the transformation, Larkspur. We are about to be hit. Hard. You know how he must brag of his new acquisitions. Like others, this one is gifted with depravity and the hunger to follow. Oh, he'll be filled with power."

"Is there still time to stop him at the final crossing?" Larkspur reclined in the crook of a sinewy plum tree, gathering his own strength, but it was all becoming a bit much. Ages of such contretemps had dampened his enthusiasm. Soon he buried his head between his knees, propped against the trunk of the tree, and began to whine.

"You said you were getting weaker, and that is to be expected. But even in your weakness you are more than a match for these ridiculous overseers! Why must we be subjected to the indignities of the others, of his prey … his food? Send him spinning away, Lady, if this new slave manages to come near, for his nearness brings a most dismaying stench indeed."

"That it does, my friend."

Larkspur nibbled at the tips of his talons. *Think think think!*

"Perhaps there is a Portal of Wanderlust you have forgotten to place upon his pathway? An Obscuring Veil? Something of which you have grown forgetful in the art of weaving?"

"Oh, stay your whimpering," she said, withdrawing her upturned gazed at last from the solar discs, which seemed to smolder in a distant gesture of triumph. Wiping the blood from her eyes and smearing it across noble cheeks, as firm and fine of flesh as any midnight fruit in her orchard, she passed a hand and an arm draped in spider-lace across the sky. The gloating suns were forced to conceal their ineffectual umbrage behind a great contingent of swift and grey-marbled clouds.

She always managed to get the last word. Almost always.

Luminous but exhausted eyes struggled to adjust to the sudden shift to shadow in the shrine of the orchard. She moved, redolent with grace but as one blinded to take a place next to Larkspur in the cool and protective gloom of the trees. Boughs curled and twisted downward with menace, poised to strike any that might dare intrude upon this, the hour of the Mistress's doubt and discouragement.

"I have not forgotten any portal or weaving skill, Larkspur." She placed ringed fingers with comfort upon his spiny knee. Then she closed her eyes and laid her mane of hair, aglow with ice and grief, against the bark of the plum tree, allowing the winds that had prodded the cloud-cover to cool her face and fill her lungs.

"This is not even a matter of weakness. At least, I do not think it is. He is simply empowering this new slave more than he has done so with the others. Sending forth his will in a much greater show of force than ever. He is drawing this one in and warning him of my attempts to derail his journey. I daresay that an encounter with me shall be his baptism, whoever he is. Or was."

"Oh, but why?" cried Larkspur, trembling, his four muscular arms wrapped about his torso in the unsettling breeze. "Why this moment? Ah! I knew he would find a way to get to us again, even though he cannot do so himself. The new slave means to cross, doesn't he? I kept hoping it would never come to pass. That he would forget about us. I beg you, my Lady. Search your memory for a way to prevent this obscenity. I have come to be so happy here, even if I complain, and even it be for an eternity. Happy and lazy."

She reached to one of the lowest hanging boughs and pulled a fat and glorious plum from the tree, turning it this way and that in her hand. A sparkling purple jewel it was, even amid thickening shade.

"I cannot keep this one from crossing."

Her gentle assurance surprised Larkspur as much as it bothered him. He glowered at his Mistress.

"I have read the signs, Larkspur. I have tried my best to no avail. He will be upon us at dusk tomorrow."

Larkspur's blue flesh dimpled in the cold. The island world grew icier than he had ever known it to be, and he was a thing of times and worlds that had never known the touch or meaning of cold.

"Then we are wretched, indeed, Lady. Our Enemy will finish us."

She held the plum to her face and passed its smooth beauty across the midnight gleam of her cheek, savoring its delicate seduction for an instant beneath her nose, brushing it with a meager kiss between full and parted lips.

Power entered her and waxed within, even as the stars emerged to outrace the river, encircling the island refuge in strand after strand of webwork light.

"You worry too much for your own good, Larkspur. But," she added, clutching the plum between her breasts and warming it there, "being able to stop this slave once his feet have stepped upon the island ... well, that is a much different tale, indeed."

"A plan?" gasped Larkspur. "I thought we would have to take to the corridors and caverns below. Deep into darkness, beyond doom and forgetfulness."

"Please. That would not avail us," she said, fondling the immaculate fruit with her palm. "Mind you, I had always hoped to avoid this sort of confrontation and the method required to emerge triumphant, but we have no choice. Not now. I *will* be victorious. I must be."

Larkspur hopped down from the crook of the plum tree and rose tall on his cloven feet. He clapped his hands. Talons clicked in the gloom.

"This is splendid news!" he hissed. "Tell me—what marvel shall you perform? Reveal all, that I might not be paralyzed with shock at the sight of such wonders."

"Do not worry about paralysis, Larkspur. You won't witness any of it. If I am to be successful, I fear you are going to have die tomorrow."

"M-my *Lady?*"

"Yes, you will have to die. Painfully so," she said, rising to place the plum in one of Larkspur's trembling open hands. "But the good thing is that you'll only have to be dead for a day."

LATE COMES REGRET ...
EARLY COMES RELIEF

I t was accomplished.

The cabin would be Brask's fortress, his bastion against all attack and defeat. Within this enclosure he would overlook the entire world in all of its splendor, certain that splendor could be now be seen without guilt or deadening obstacles.

He had a new life.

No more qualifications. No more conditions to suck the spontaneity out of being human. No more scrutiny that withered a man into some scratchy, sun-bleached husk dependent upon the whim of the wind. Blow this way. No, that way.

Who the hell are you, anyway?

If only Jess could be here now, to see him at the pinnacle of redemption, dreams not merely realized but on fire with adventurous possibilities that would grow exponentially. She would have been the first to feel the thrill, from the top of her head to the tips of her toes, on his behalf. She would have recognized the change, the blossom of an emancipated spirit inside. She would have come back to him.

"Jess is probably not going to live out the month, Mr. Adams. I am so sorry to have to tell you this, but we have already discussed the matter with her, and she asked us to tell you. It would be difficult for her to handle telling you right now."

"What the hell are you saying? I thought things were improving. The last tests—"

"It's spread everywhere. A rare, particularly rapid metastasizing. We didn't expect it, either. But in her case, matters could always have turned quickly and irrevocably. You're going to have to prepare yourself. I know the two of you are no longer married, but we know you've been looking after her throughout this ordeal. It's made all the difference in the world that you kept her on your company's insurance plan even after the divorce. Your ongoing dedication will mean more than ever, now. Because it will not be long. Making her comfortable is our only goal, at this point. You're certain there is no other family member that ought to know about this?"

"No. She's alone in the world. Except for me. A few friends, but they stopped coming around when she first got sick."

"I see. I'm sorry to have asked that. She said the same, but sometimes extraordinary pain magnifies family estrangements, etc. If there were anyone else who needed to know, now would be the time. Hospice care is recommended. Your provider may cover some of that. You'll have to speak with them. But your ex-wife needs a safe, comfortable place to die as soon as possible."

She would have come back to him.

Jess's death nearly killed him, but he had always loved her enough to keep much from her. So much that had contributed unfairly to their divorce, he felt; things that might have changed her mind, had she known about them. Even now he was convinced that if he never took a single thing to his own grave except for the fact that he had made it through, it would be enough.

He had managed to take care of Jess to the moment of her last breath. Had kept his own hand from trembling until the moment she lifted her head that last time and, with all the agony and death flowing through her veins and swiftly into her heart, she had whispered a goodbye. He had watched as the light and the life and the love went out of her gentle blue eyes; an entire universe collapsing in upon itself, changing its decision to exist, newly born and seeing the pain that awaited in time and space, yet choosing annihilation. Sailing into the silence. Into the calm of Nothing.

She would have come back to him, if she could see how he had turned himself around.

Goodbye, Babe. I love you. Whatever comes next, you'll get through, just like you got through the troubles gone-by. I won't be there to break your heart anymore, though

I'd change places with you this instant. But you'll be happier where you're going. No more agony. Bye. See you later on the other side. On some side. Count on it. Just find me when the time comes, even if time hasn't got a thing to say about it. Look for me. Find me.

She would have come back to him.

Brask sighed and looked around the largely deserted stretch of Main Street. It was time to get some supplies and head back to the cabin. The Donovan Mercantile was still open. The lights in the place were on, at least. His phone had to be recharged tonight. There were bound to be at least a few texts and emails to answer. In all the excitement he'd forgotten to plug the damn thing in back at the cabin. It was another relief that the power was already on there. No hook-ups to negotiate. He got out of the Pontiac and stretched, arms entwined toward heaven, until his back cracked. Best feeling in the world, especially now. He strode the boardwalk above the tidy little avenue, tall and alive and still a bit dazed by the realization that he was a new, thoroughly official, and proud resident of this marvelous, life-saving place.

Brask Adams, author. Of Wistwood, California.

ALL GOOD THINGS MUST COME TO A BEGINNING

Horace approached the cloud that writhed amid the hidden hills above Wistwood. Today the cloud was a turbulent storm of green vapor, dark and mouldering with fertility or with death. Perhaps both. That had happened before. Rising in the sacred glade like the sail of a mighty ship cleaving the stream of the sky, its edges trembled and were shredded by a gale of its own creation. Expectation poisoned the afternoon air, but it was not Horace's expectation. He had been summoned, merely. And still the cloud spun, hissing with some unfamiliar hint of impatience, with a new agitation. A change was to be wrought, a rending of the vivid yet careworn fabric of that world within a world. Horace stood, silent and somehow noble. Hands steady and folded atop the cane before him. Rheumy eyes unblinking. Great white beard aflutter in the grasping wind that assessed and caressed. The message was simple, when it came at last to his mind.

You shall be unmade and cede the authority I have given unto you.

Horace was unmoved, save for the briefest twitch of an eyelid.

"I have served you long and well. I paid every due and every price you asked me to pay. With a full heart."

What of it?

"You know how many souls I've fought to present before you. You know the life I gave up to serve you, to be in your employ. You know how I've shepherded your Acquisitions from all manner of places, guiding them and preparing them. Getting them ready to be fed upon.

And?

"And you never said you were going to replace me, after all of this."

All things pass, even for the likes of you. All terms of service come to an end. Do you not recall the manner in which you replaced the one who preceded you?

"No. My memory isn't what it used to be. Not when it comes to the beginning of our association. I expect you have something to do with that. For your own purposes. But this is some of the best, tastiest food I've herded for you. Good eating, to the last. With more on the way. They keep on giving. I've kept the livestock happy. And now you would supplant me?"

You are old.

"What does that matter? You've always given me strength beyond that of twenty men half my age. Power to do things no person ever dreamed of doing. You said so yourself. Keep giving me strength! Make me young."

We have spoken of this before. I can work many wonders in my chosen realm while Time allows, but I cannot withstand what Time comes to claim.

"Well, that's a strange weakness. I always thought so."

You have only been thinking of it lately, because you sense what is imminent. In your youth you did not care about Time. You felt immortal, like all of your sad sort do in lively days, when flesh remains smooth and bones do not grind one upon the other. You laughed at the distant thought of coming death. It is not to be wondered at.

"So what happens to me after all this? You promised a lifetime of service to you in all your glory."

Then be content, for you have fulfilled this and have taken pleasure in your work—delights greater than the most ravenous of your species have enjoyed.

"But you said it would be forever."

Never have I spoken so. You are bold at the end, like every other. You witness my everlasting quality and mistake it for your own. You misled yourself. The terms of service were made clear to you from the start. Be content with your reward. Until the time of succession, you remain in my power.

"If you get rid of me, where will I go? What'll become of me?"

That, slave, is beyond my knowledge.

"I thought you knew everything."

I do not. Some matters are kept even from my sight, though perhaps not from my understanding. Be content with your reward and do not test my favor, while you continue to enjoy it, with insolence.

"What's waiting for me, then? Hell? The forever kind of hell?"

You have already been dwelling there. Satisfyingly so. If another one awaits, I cannot tell. I know only of this one. The one of my own construction.

"I won't go quietly. I won't make it easy."

As you wish. Your resistance is of no consequence to me. I shall make you do as I please. I always have.

The raging column of cloud vanished in a stinging reversal of one reality upon another, a trade between Time and Eternity, one existence falling in upon itself and returning as something else. Horace was thrown to the ground. The hills were quiet. The sun idled behind the tips of oak limbs.

After a few moments, he struggled to his feet and began to drag himself back to Wistwood. There were things to do.

CHUPACABRA

Brask opened the door to Donovan's Mercantile and heard a brief jangling above his head, like warped sleigh-bells at Christmas. But Donovan's was not at all what he had been expecting. The interior seemed thick with weariness, cowed by some heaviness of thought. It was a palpable lowering of dim corners and thankless years beyond count or consideration. Thick near the ceiling. Gathered in various crevices. Formless worries trying desperately to hide but piling one atop the other in the mad scurry to escape, hoping to remain unseen.

The place looked like one of the musty, dying hardware stores his father would drag him to as a child on agonizing Saturday "project days," mostly for idle chatter with some practically mummified clerk or owner. Donavan's boasted the same atmospheric indifference, as if some weighty regret had been left behind by one final customer, taking up residence on every messy shelf to become a sedentary presence all its own, as much a fixture as the creaking floorboards.

Behold the unneeded. There is much want, but naught that is wanted.

Brask stood in the doorway for a minute, taking all of this in with the strange but distinct sense that he had stirred something. Yes, something had moved. A weighty form. A small shift of awareness amid deep slumber, something fitful and reluctant to awaken amid the cluttered space and reaching silhouettes. These last extended from the cramped and crammed aisles like vines straining to touch him, to wrap around and draw him inward, to hide Brask until he, too, was left behind like a regret, as somnambulant as the approaching dusk.

Sleep. Come here! Curl up behind the decrepit refrigerator full of faded milk cartons, empty beer cans and bottles of black wine. Lay your ear against us. Listen to the dust whisper. Watch the drops of condensation fall inside our goddamned place and sleep. Rest your mind from worldly concerns. Join unwanted things. You are welcome! Swim to us through sadness. We are here, here in the deeper places.

"Hello?" Brask's voice was barely a croak.

Stay and rest. You have no business with a world that does not want you. None shall bother you here. Sleep as long as you wish. Let despair be your blanket. Let it cover you. Be troubled no longer by travail. Minds grow weary. Give in. This is the place to forget and be forgotten. Anguish is midnight in the chill, here below. Defeat is your burial. Come. Curl up. Cover your face with the pleasure of exhaustion and sleep, until you sleep as we do …

"Well, hello, there, Mister. Is there something I can help you with?"

Brask started and shook his head, surging out of deep water where he had been forced to hold his breath, submerged to the point of bursting both lungs or opening wide his mouth to drown. He gasped and began to lose balance in the middle of the oily, wooden-plank floor. What he had felt upon entering hit him hard; the odd pressure of the air, the depth of exhaustion, and the voice—*what voice?*—that pinned him in silence, trapped at the bottom of an icy pool. How could it be? He had stared up at the distant light of the moon through ripples in his vision, but not through water. No, not through water; it was sadness, and he had been drowning in it. He had wanted to.

"Say, Mister. You okay?"

The spell was broken and Brask fumbled for anything nearby to lean against, to steady himself, to anchor his core lest he should pass out. He was nearly seeing stars as it was.

What the fuck? Am I having a stroke?

"Mister, you maybe need to sit yourself down for a minute, I'd say."

"What?"

Who had spoken to him? The sensation of some enormous, hibernating presence in the vicinity was so strong that he envisioned turning to see a great, yawning grizzly point its maw in his direction from behind one of the shelves, roused to vengeful anger amid the stink of a cave.

Who has disturbed my sleep? Reveal yourself. Who has happened upon this sanctuary, where the days go unnumbered and we eat ourselves from within to remain alive in the black …

It was the faintest whisper, speeding forever away from him into space, fleeing like a comet, even as his proper senses rushed in. Buoyant waves churned apart the floodgates of his reason to fill the vacuum that nearly seized him. Then the fit vanished; the comet became an eel, and its tail slipped beyond the edge of perception.

No bear appeared to overwhelm him. No grizzly, at any rate.

"Mister, you better come on over here to the counter and sit down for a minute or two. You don't look so good."

"I … I'm okay," said Brask. "Just need some air, I think. Don't know what came over me. Damn. Some kinda head-rush. Been a longer day than I thought. I'll be fine."

"Well, so long as you're sure you can walk, you better come all the way in."

The pale man who had appeared behind the counter was tall, about Brask's height, but thick as a rain-barrel across a midsection sprouting shoulders and limbs beefy enough to shame a bull. His somewhat smallish head sported the razor fire-tongue of an old Mohawk punk-cut. The most astonishingly bright red beard Brask had ever seen hung in a great bushy bib from the brute's lower jaw, dangling almost possessively across pectoral muscles the size of watermelons.

"Jesus, it's like two pigs fighting underneath a blanket," muttered Brask without thinking as he stared at that chest. Mind reeling, he tried to get his bearings as the man approached and opened the front door just behind him, gentle as a kitten, each finger as plump and cumbersome as a bratwurst.

The bells rang awkwardly again and the inrush of mountain air brought instant salvation. Brask took a deep breath, swallowed hard, and stood a little straighter, sidling a bit to put a more comfortable distance between himself and the behemoth.

"That oughta air the place out for you, Mister. The store can get close, sometimes. Now what was that you were mumbling about pigs?"

Brask gripped the edge of a plexiglass ice cream cooler and tried not to laugh.

"Nothing, man. Nothing. I don't know what the hell came over me. I was hypoglycemic for about ten minutes when I was a kid but haven't had a spell like that in twenty-two years. Sorry if I startled you."

The gargantuan man scratched the top of his head with one sausage-sized digit and shrugged. "No law against having a blood sugar problem." At close range, his voice had the depth and authority of a bassoon. "My poor mama struggled with sugar her whole life, as a matter of fact. At least until it finally killed her."

He put sledgehammer hands on his hips and gave Brask a brutally obvious once-over.

"You're definitely new in town. Ain't seen you here before, so that means you're new."

"I'm as new as they get around here, I think."

Equilibrium regained, Brask made another swift, evasive survey of the store's interior and felt another shock.

The place had changed entirely from the flashing, lucid vision he had seen while hearing the voice, held beneath the mirror of water.

Gone were the shredded, moth-eaten curtains stained with grease and blood. Gone, too, were the mummified sludge-figures piled like charred lumps in the circle of chairs around a jagged and gaping hole in the middle of an empty floor. There were no longer any hornet's nests as large and as round as boulders pasted into the corners near the ceiling, protruding like mammoth, distended breasts and sliced open at the edges to reveal thousands of writhing larvae, blind and packed into chambers or falling with dull, moist thuds onto the floor. No hidden presence breathed in the shadows, slumbering. No foul planet before the awakening of the world, turning as if every breath were the rise and fall of a bitter and undesired creation. No voice, drowsy and with oblivion and umbrage at being disturbed passed its low, growling way through time to tangle ribbons of constricting darkness about him.

It was just a fucking country store.

A store like many he had seen in his travels, and smaller even than the one he had visited at the gas station in Big Sur. A Thomas Kinkade calendar hung from a thumbtack on the back wall, curling at the edges as it kept watch over the days. Beneath was a long counter that supported a cash register, a wire rack filled with an assortment of candy bars, another with a small selection of magazines, and a dusty revolving tree for sunglasses that looked cheap and several years out of style. To the side stood a cardboard cabinet advertising Winston cigarettes, but lacking any product.

The remaining space was lined with floor to ceiling shelves jammed with all manner of hardware, household supplies, canned goods, mouse traps, jelly jars, paper products, boxes of nails, canisters of baking soda, and God knew what other odds and ends. There was a Coca-Cola refrigerator for cold beverages in general, ticking and whirring next to Brask himself. Two relatively organized shelves running down the center of the store toward the rear counter were stacked with bread, boxes of baked goods, spaghetti sauce, pasta, bags of rice, bottles of aspirin, lip balm, toothpaste, potato chips, Oreo cookies, extra virgin olive oil, and Crisco cans. Directly behind Brask, cooling his clutching hands and slowing the sweat that had broken out across his forehead, was the ice cream freezer and apparent meat locker that ran the length of half the front wall.

Nothing but the simplest claptrap.

And here was Brask, barely recovered from some freakish fainting-spell, wobbling like a flustered child, muttering and babbling as if he were high on glue fumes in the presence of a red-bearded mammoth who looked capable of snapping him like a twig.

This is just great. Way to make that solid first impression, dude.

Brask evicted the disturbing images from his mind and offered a hand.

"Sorry if I gave you a start just then, man. Like I said, it's been a long day and I haven't had anything to eat since this morning. Dawn, in fact. Got a little dizzy, I guess. I'm Brask Adams. Just moved here today. Signed the lease."

"Congratulations and good to meet you, Brask. I'm Cal. Cal Donovan."

The face of the giant shaking Brask's hand betrayed no committed emotion or impression. Cal's eyes were unusually close together over the champagne-cork stub of his nose. Beady. *Wet little marbles.* Unreadable. He half-expected his own calloused hand to be crushed in the grip of the fellow's paw, but Cal Donovan's inclusion in the Manly Man's Firm Handshake Hall of Fame was far from certain. The hand clasping his own, though it seemed to be the size of a catcher's mitt, was damp. Diffident. Fingers drooped for a second in Brask's palm and then wilted.

"You sure you don't want a drink of water or something? You still look a little 'peaked' as my Mama used to say. God rest her."

"No, I'm good. Thanks again." Brask straightened his shoulders and fought to rescue what he could of his dignity. "Some supplies will do me fine, though. That's why I came in. Not to drop down dead on your ice cream cooler." His attempt at a little joke drew no reaction. As welcome as a tumbleweed. "Well, I need a bit of food to take back to the cabin overnight. Maybe a six-pack of Diet Coke. Or beer, actually. Yeah, who am I kidding? Beer."

"Grab what you like," said Cal, gesturing vaguely around his shop. "Nothing fancy, but the selection is decent."

Brask extracted a plastic shopping basket from the pile atop the counter. The handles were coated with dust and grime. He wiped his fingertips surreptitiously on the back of his jeans.

"So this is your place, huh? How long you been in business here in Wistwood?"

"Oh, for as long as I can remember. Not really, but it seems that way, sometimes." Cal arched a bushy red brow and reached out to wipe a panel of dust from the top of the cash register. "What about you? Horace mentioned he had a few interviews lined up to fill some of the recent vacancies. Didn't know he had actually made firm arrangements. But then I try not to pry too deep into Horace's affairs. So you're one of us, now."

"Signed on the dotted line," said Brask over his shoulder. He pulled a six-pack of Budweiser from the cooler and put it in the basket. Then he added another. "I rented a great cabin, back in the woods beyond those first few hills leading out of downtown."

"The Kimberton place?" murmured Cal, exposing a hint of pink tongue amid the wiry rug of beard and mustache. Wet marble eyes glinted for an instant. "I know it. Used to deliver groceries down to the Kimbertons when they first arrived and got caught-up in building all that furniture and remodeling that sweet little spot. Those two didn't even leave the house for the longest time. Very focused old couple, they were. Very devoted."

"And yet they just up and left almost everything."

Cal shrugged and drew fat fingers thoughtfully through the shiny tangle of red beard. "Folks get restless. They move on when the fancy strikes them. But their exodus paved the way for your arrival, so that's a good thing, eh? And it's always nice to see new blood in town."

"Thanks. I'm glad to be here." Brask added two cans of cheap stew and a loaf of bread to the basket. "It's exactly what I've been looking for ... for the longest time."

"People always have that reaction when they settle in Wistwood."

Brask put his shopping basket on the counter and reached for his wallet. "I can believe it. So stunning. Beautiful. That's why I was a bit surprised to learn that the Kimbertons left suddenly. Seems a perfect spot for older folks to retire, especially given all the renovation they did on their place, not even owning it and all. It looked to me like they meant to hunker down for the long term. Don't get me wrong, I'm glad they decided to seek greener pastures. Horace didn't say much, if anything, about where they went. I'd kind of like to find out so I can send them a little note saying how much I appreciate their handiwork. Tell them I'll take real good care of it now that I live there. Where *did* they go?"

"Haven't the foggiest," said Cal, ringing the items up on his register. "From what I hear, the both of them left without a word. Somewhat rude, if you ask me. But they're not the first folks to try and leave Wistwood thinking something better is gonna be just around the corner. I don't expect they'll be the last, either."

"But you don't know why they left?"

"Like I said, some people get restless wherever they settle down. Some aren't cut out to stay in one place, even when it's in their best interests to do so."

Brask added a bag of Pepperidge Farm cookies to his haul. "These, too, please. Thanks. So you must've known the Kimbertons pretty well if you're convinced it was in their best interests to stay." Brask's words were light and companionable, but something shaded, like a concealing caul, passed over Donovan's red face, dimming even the glimmer of his moist, Black Aggie eyes.

"I'm not the one around here who makes those kinds of judgments. You'll find out for yourself soon enough."

"Oh yeah? What's that mean?"

Cal's clouded gaze vanished as though a dazzling sun had risen over the mountaintop of his shoulders. He smiled and held bulging arms out wide, perhaps closing the question definitively, perhaps searching for a proper, more satisfying answer; Brask could not tell.

"I only meant that everybody tends to find things out for themselves, eventually. If they're observant enough. I'm sure the ole Kimbertons are having a ball—one helluva time—wherever they are."

"I hope so," said Brask, trying to figure out what sort of underlying message had passed between himself and this moose of a stranger. "So long as they don't come back and try to reclaim all that excellent stuff they built."

"Oh, they won't be back. You can count on that." Cal dusted the top of his register with a fingertip again. It was an idle, dissociative movement.

Brask felt once more the uneasy shifting of something much larger than Cal, turning with great effort in the shadows at the edge of his thought. Some deeper communication had taken place; it had the shape and feel of a challenge, maybe even a threat.

What could the owner of a local two-bit market have against me? Get a grip. You're in the woods. Deep. People take stock of newcomers and strangers differently than they do in the city. Deal.

"Oh, wait. You have any sandwich meat, Cal? Sliced stuff?"

"Middle cooler. To your left. Got some Oscar Mayer, turkey and bologna slices. Franks, too, if you want some of those. Again, nothing fancy at retail, but if you're after the real stuff, the kind that keeps hair growing on a man's chest and won't fill his veins full of all that processed shit, then I got a supply of my own down below, in the cellar. I field dress my own kill and everything. Deer, mostly. Some other things."

"No kidding."

Brask rummaged among the haphazardly dumped packages of lunchmeat in the cooler. The mental picture of Cal lumbering through the woods with a gun or crossbow in his hands was somehow particularly disturbing to him. A sudden wave of nausea crept upward from his gut. "I didn't think they'd allow a lot of game hunting in a place like Big Sur. Or so close to it. Isn't this whole Pacific Coast part of the National Parks system?"

"National parks?"

Brask decided upon sliced turkey and a pack of franks. Putting them on the counter, he gestured toward the coast.

"The park system. Most of this is protected land around Big Sur. And all down the coast, right? Marine sanctuary, too. But I guess you can always hunt on private property."

"You appear to know quite a lot about the environs, Brask. More than me."

"Really? I wouldn't say I know that much. Not more than a local, for sure. I'm from the Silicon Valley area."

Cal closed his tiny eyes and tapped an index finger slowly against his dashboard-sized forehead. "Sheesh!" he said, flicking spittle across the countertop and Brask's groceries. "Who's the one with the head spinning around, now? Don't mind me. I suppose I ought to get outta this store more often. The walls close-in real quick when you spend your whole day in the place. World gets *real* small. Guess that's one of the reasons I like to hunt when I get the chance." He gestured with his own flourish toward the outer realms. "National parks. Yeah. All around us. Very valuable things, our parks. When it comes to hunting, though, you're right about using private property, of course. Horace knows the owner of Wistwood real well, of course. The landlord. This is all private property. We're all allowed to hunt."

"You said you hunt deer and other things?" Brask took a paper bag from a pile on the counter and began to pack his own items. He wanted out of Cal Donovan's Mercantile.

"Yeah, deer. Way too many of them around this season, to tell you the truth. There's tons of rabbits, though they're barely worth the bother, for the amount of meat you get. Wild boar are easy to come by. I use crossbow for those. More fun. And I bet you won't believe me, but I shot a chupacabra just few weeks ago."

Cal was dead serious. Brask had to laugh in his face. "One of the goat-sucking things? That's quite a score, there, Cal."

Cal nodded. "I think so, too. And take a look at this piece. I picked this little beauty off last month." He reached over to a crooked shelf on the wall beside the Thomas Kinkade calendar and carefully, almost reverently, used both of his enormous hands to procure the hideous, grinning skull of some small, fanged creature that had presumably once inhabited the land of the living.

"That's not your chupacabra, is it?" Brask's face contorted in disgust. The thing smelled foul; he wondered if the scent had been the source of his nausea. But he hadn't smelled it until Cal brought it close, as if brandishing a delicate robin's nest.

"No! This here is the skull of a red fox," said Cal triumphantly. "I shot him on a Tuesday. He was coming up a little ridge, not too far from the Kimbertons' old pl—from *your* place, I mean. Maybe a mile up the hill opposite your driveway. There he was, framed in the sun, and there I was, hadn't caught squat all day. This little fella hadn't the first clue that I was anywhere near. Downwind, you see. Oh, not sly enough, Mr. Fox! Not sly enough. So I just pointed and—POP!—that arrow nearly split the damn thing in two pieces at the ribcage."

"You don't say."

"I guess it was a bit of overkill, but like I said, I was bored stiff out there and it was either shoot something or drop my pants and jerk off, if you know what I mean. And along came this opportunity. I skinned him right on the ridge. Left the pelt and the guts and bones behind for the buzzards."

"Of course. What's my total for all of this, if you don't mind?"

"Now, your basic fox stinks of musk something terrible, but I expect you know that already. Once I put the skull in some acid and cleaned the brains out and dried it and bleached it up, I figured it'd be perfect to put one of those little votive candles on top. So, I'm letting this piece air out down here in the store for another week or so. I aim to complete my collection by the end of this coming winter. Already have almost two dozen other trophies upstairs. Some have the candles in them. Others don't. I asked that preacher whose building his church next door if he could spare me a few votive candles, but he says he doesn't have any. I'm gonna have to order more. You wanna go upstairs and see my collection? I live up on the second floor. And in the cellar."

"Uh … no. No, maybe some other time, Cal. I've got to get things organized at my own place. Lots to do in the next few days."

Brask's face was frozen in a mask of stiff cordiality that barely concealed disgust.

What kind of fucking freak shoots a helpless fox so he can suck out its brains and shove a candle in its head? Why didn't I wait to get groceries? There's still a can of pork and beans in the van. Why didn't I just drive back into Big Sur, or even up to Carmel? I could have grabbed some more supplies from that hot little Kara at the gas station.

"Do you like to hunt, Brask?" Cal began to stroke the smooth bone of the fox's skull with his plump fingertips.

Brask couldn't believe it. "I hunted two or three times when I was a kid. A squirrel or two. My dad was a hunter, when he wasn't at the card tables or getting tanked. But I grew out of that phase. Quickly. Civilization rounds-up and processes enough animals to feed the masses from conveyor belts. I don't need to go after things trying to survive on their own in the wild."

Cal let out a whoop that seemed powered by the bellows of some magnificent internal furnace. "Squirrels? I can see why you grew out of it so fast!" Then he leaned over the counter, serious and concerned. "Didn't you ever get the urge to graduate to something bigger? *Anything* bigger? Neighborhood cats? Maybe a stray dog once in awhile? Go on, you can tell me. I won't breathe a word to anybody. I know what it's like to be a kid with a knife or a pump gun. Hell, I was a kid once, too, though you'd never know it to look at me now. I used to be quite a runt. Got kicked around a fair bit for being scrawny when I was a youth. Then I started eating whatever I killed and by the time I was twelve I started getting big, you know? Oh, it took a while and it took a lot of practice. Trial and error, all that stuff. But I learned. Some kill is better for putting on muscle than others. I figured it all out. Everyone figures it all out for themselves, eventually."

"I'm really ready to pay you," mumbled Brask, trying to avoid the Goliath stare emanating from the beady eyes. He pulled cash from his wallet, sickened.

"That'll be thirty-one dollars and forty-five cents. See, I was right about things when I was growing up," continued Cal, putting the last two items in the brown paper bag before taking the bills. "I tried different things, and look at me now. You ain't no big Sasquatch like me, Brask, but I can see you got a fair amount of muscle on your bones. I can see you stay in shape and look after yourself. You'd still make for a good hunter out there in the woods, I'll bet. We all need to be able to feed ourselves, if it ever comes to it in this world."

Brask took the change Cal handed him and shoved it in a back pocket. The air began to grow thick with impending visions again. The day—the tension and desperation and then the sudden floodgate reversal of those things—was getting to him. And this fucker was clearly not playing with a full deck. Brask didn't feel competent or confident when it came to saying another word. Cal was as wide-eyed as his minimal sockets would allow, almost awestruck, his pig-like ears pulled back tight on his scalp.

"You just keep the option open to go hunting again, Brask. I'd be glad to take you along if you get a hankering for it. In the meantime, welcome to Wistwood. It's been a real pleasure to meet you."

Brask smiled, a crooked line snaking across his jaw, and he thought of a fox, its coat as red as the beard of the man before him, framed against the sky on some idyllic ridge-top, flush with freedom and the pure uncomplicated awareness of simply being alive ... until it wasn't.

Not sly enough, Mr. Foxy. Not sly enough by a long way.

He gathered his grocery bag, nodded politely, and left without a word.

The deformed bells chimed with a swift violence, insulted, as the door slammed behind him.

WHILE THE DEW IS
STILL ON THE ROSES

Carlee Hawkins, enter the garden freely and of your own accord, that we may have a better look at you. The dawn is faint and greedy with its light. Shadows are strong and the grey sorrow of your own making still holds sway. Come closer and do not tremble. You shall find nothing here that you do not already know.

Carlee clutched her sweater around her shuddering torso in the grim daybreak but it was cold, cold within and cold without, rife with frost to the very edges of the murky sky that stretched in vain toward the east. There, a thin glimpse of sunlight shimmered; one golden thread piercing black horizon. She looked down at her feet.

The earth seemed parched, here, emaciated from a long, unending hunger for something alive, something purposeful. She had spent the night in terror of this moment, not even bothering to change her clothes, which were soaked in anxious sweat.

Her Interview had long been scheduled; she wanted only to get it over with, at last.

But why the smothering night where all else had been lively across sun-dappled hills? Why the frozen, unfriendly air surrounding this, the Manor House, where such welcome had been promised to her?

She knew only a little. She knew she would be given a choice, just as Ethan, her husband, had been given a choice. They all said that it would be simple. They all hoped she might choose wisely. The waiting, especially after Ethan chose and left town, had been akin to living on the edge of some infernal pool, a lake aflame with the same noxious resentment that had consumed her days and nights since his departure.

Turning in the dark, she heard a sound like the bowels of the earth groaning through miles and ages of time, a deep and ancient breathing that did not stop, that would never stop. Something would always be waiting in this place. Someone. Of that she was more certain than anything. Patience reigned here, an abiding expectation borne of midnight that could not end. There was nothing left to do. It was time to see for herself what sort of thing summoned and brooked no refusal. Time for the answer she feared and craved since they day she and Ethan first found themselves in Wistwood.

There was a rustling of leaves, laurel leaves, in a sudden gust above the gate in front of the Manor. The wind snaked its way with a soft sigh through branches that swayed, as if the coming dawn had exhaled pure gladness after an arduous climb around the breadth of the world, relieved to attain the destination of a new day at last. But something was holding the sunrise at bay, for the same golden thread kept simmering on the horizon, yet did not grow, defeated and obedient to the billowing layers of grey above. Unspeakable.

Did you not hear me bid you enter, Carlee? Do you wish you had never come?

The voice moved through her and she felt the last wings of her hope fly off toward the west, and to the famished regions of night receding and renewing themselves behind.

"I heard you. But I'm frightened."

Enter all the same.

She eyed the gate with its various spikes rising high and saw there a dove fluttering its wings gently, nesting between two of the upper posts. It was so pure, so delicate in its beauty, that her trembling ceased at once and the anguish that had clutched her heart in a vise for weeks was eradicated. The freedom was so profound and sudden that it was almost sexually satisfying, sweeter in its way than the first moments of blissful exhaustion after flesh had been offered and consumed. She thought of Ethan, and of the strange wind that grew strong all about her, setting her hair loose from the ponytail she wore until it flowed out and around her head in a nimbus, radiating like the petals of a sunflower in luxurious daylight. Banished was the danger and indifference of a Night that suffocated all.

You see how pleasant the garden can be for those willing to enter with glad heart and face nothing more troublesome than the truth?

The voice was full of seduction, muffled and distant now, as if coming in difficult bursts from something large that huddled, moving with slow but deliberate effort in the tall shadows behind the line of trees ahead. Carly felt her fingers move to the tips of her breasts, though she had not intended to move at all.

"The truth?" she repeated, drowsy in the burgeoning and strangely warm wind. For a moment she failed, the sunflower wilting against the harsh stones of the massive gate.

Yes. Nothing more than that.

She hesitated, tottering forward and then back upon a precipice. Clouds rushed overhead with the blurring ferocity of rapids that roared here and raged there. The columns of the ruined and crumbling portico ahead seemed to grow indistinct, as if she were looking at them through tears, and then, to her breathless astonishment, the vision shifted abruptly to a sun-drenched field of lavender. Each cluster of plants waved to form a vast sea of ripples. She breathed until her lungs ached and then exhaled the fragrance as purple vapor to match the army of immaculate blossoms, a shudder passing as one molten-tipped arrow through her most secret self.

This place is known to you.

The voice was pressing closer, a breeze moving above her skin and beneath it. The trees hiding the large and secretive thing were still on guard, off to the side, but they were not visible now to her eyes, only in her mind. The fields of lavender swayed and bowed gratefully beneath the platinum aura of a sudden star that extinguished the sky and revealed only the magnificent landscape below. Carlee staggered forward and swooned against the gateway, bending as she sobbed, tears pouring down her face to her chin, where they swelled in sparkling refractions of light.

And each tear that fell to earth became a serpent, small and shining, scaled as with gleaming onyx, and they slithered away from her into the secret places below the soil and between the endless rows and bushes of waving perfection.

She could not stay her sadness, and it seemed that an entire age of the world had come and gone as she wept, crying until the fields were full of snakes. They hissed above the rustling of the wind in the ocean of color and perfume. They flicked their tongues and fixed their eyes upon her as she sank to her knees, clutching the lamp-post that now rose high enough to skewer the sky and the unwilling star-courses beyond.

"It's a deception," she whispered after what might have been centuries of time. "The truth is always the most terrible thing to face, isn't it?"

For you, perhaps.

The voice had been waiting centuries, too, as patient as the asps that now moved by the millions among the plants, coiling and uncoiling, venom dripping from each maw and steaming above the rich soil.

"I didn't mean for any of this to happen. I never meant for things to end this way. Not for me. Not for Ethan."

We have dealt already with him. His choice has been made. Come. Remove your clothes and crawl naked into the field. We shall see for ourselves what you did and did not intend.

Carlee cringed, holding her hands over her ears, pressing, pushing the sounds and thoughts from her skull, as if they could be moved at all by force. They remained.

"I can't face it. I can't do it!"

The snakes rolled across the expanse to the very last, a living, moving layer of earth now writhing in the heart of each soaring blossom.

Crawl in your nakedness, woman, and make your choice. There is freedom in the Choosing, and the pain is oh so brief, though it be sharp enough in that instant to cleave a universe from its foundation. Crawl. Crawl toward the truth.

And then she heard, faint as the movement of a butterfly's wing upon summer air, unmistakably:

Crawl or face the consequences.

Carlee's hands shook and her fingers quivered like the legs of convulsing spiders scuttling across her blouse as she tried to undo the buttons.

"Who are you?" she whispered. "Who, goddamn it? Is this Hell? Answer me that, at least."

Hell? Not even in the same jurisdiction.

Carlee tore a button from her blouse and screaming threw it into the glorious field. The snakes grew agitated and began to twist as one body toward her. She howled and with all her will tore herself up and away, propelling her body from the courtyard and past the gate and then back toward the roadway. There, her reentry into the cold morning was a violent birth back into the world, pulled as she was from one sphere into another at its very edge.

Naked and covered in slime from head to foot, she fell in the dirt, breathless as a newborn taken from the womb. Gawping, she clawed at the gravel of the road and refused to look back. All was agony, for the fall had knocked the air from her lungs. Scrambling and gasping, she scratched stone and earth until her fingernails broke and splintered and bled. Then she staggered to her feet and ran, down and away from the awful place. From the truth.

Consequences it shall be, then.

The final hiss of the voice seared through her mind, and this sound echoed and reverberated in her skull, a shot ringing forever in a maze-addled cavern. She ran.

She ran until her body would obey her despair no longer.

GETTING TO KNOW YOU

B rask was not about to head directly back to the cabin with his grocery bag after the experience of meeting Cal Donovan. Two six-packs of beer wouldn't put a dent in the wall of weird discomfort that had been bricked-up around his psyche. He had to meet some normal people on his first night in Wistwood. People who might help get the spiritual stench of Donovan's Mercantile out of his brain. A double Bourbon would help, too.

The front steps of Margie's Bar & Grill creaked beneath Brask's worn and scraped-up work boots. The al fresco dining deck nearby was furnished with six round pedestal tables, each surrounded by tall wicker seats. These tables were now occupied by parties of people chatting quietly, picking at food plates, and sipping beer that foamed at the tops of frosty mugs. A few patrons stirred daintily around flared martini glasses with olives on skewers.

One woman, a windblown-looking soul behind huge sunglasses, her head covered in a chic kerchief emblazoned with hues the color of domed Mediterranean rooftops, sat alone and smiled at him as she toyed with the stem of her wineglass. Brask nodded, a bit bashful, but he was convinced that bashful was probably a prudent approach when entering communal territory as a completely unknown quantity.

Another person at one of the tables, a middle-aged gent in a straw hat and horn-rim glasses who looked a bit like Horace, only without the dramatic mustache and beard, raised his bottle of Stella Artois and tipped it in Brask's direction. He acknowledged the greeting with another terse nod and entered the charming little place through a patched-up screen door that squeaked as if it were in pain when he opened it. The yellow neon sign in the huge picture window blinked on and off, casting colored reflections in his eyes as he paused at the reception stand just inside. A piece of paper with a hand-written message in black marker was taped to the front of the stand:

**Seat yourself for drinks or food
but wait your turn and don't be rude.
If tables are not clean & set
be patient ... or the boot you'll get.**

Well, ain't that folksy.

Brask was hoping for a loose, perhaps even a bit bawdy, pub-style crowd. He prayed Margie, the presumed owner, wouldn't turn out to be one of the saccharine types sometimes found at the helm of bed and breakfast establishments. He had no interest in creatures of gingham and lace, eager to foist scones and self-righteous quips upon people because, in the Martha Stewart-obsessed corridors of their brains, that's what they imagined most people were dying to experience when visiting a rural establishment. Brask loathed Martha Stewart, and he hated quips more than her.

But the joint was not at all what he expected, surveying matters from the doorway. Horace had mentioned that Margie pretty much gutted the Victorian's entire downstairs to build a restaurant and bar, and he hadn't been kidding. Where there ought to have been sitting rooms and stately little corridors edged with polished wood and wainscoting, there was now an almost cavernous and lively space jammed with restaurant tables—mostly two-tops, but here and there a table for four. The whole area was dominated by an ornate maple-wood bar that stretched from wall to wall, broken only by a series of thick decorative columns and a service entrance to the back-bar and what was apparently the kitchen beyond.

The place was abuzz with chatter and activity: glassware clinked; chairs scuffled against shiny floors of dark cherry; water ran with bumping thuds in a big sink behind the bar. A pixie-faced waitress with a ponytail and a cardigan leaned in close to elucidate a couple's dinner order. Knives and forks scraped across thick white bistro plates. The food itself smelled terrific, whatever was on offer, and Brask's stomach mewed in approval. Response was demanded.

The restaurant or lounge or whatever it was was half-full; there were maybe fifteen people inside, not counting the full deck out front and the cute little fairy waitress that scurried between both portions of the establishment. There was also a stout older man, bald as Mr. Clean, clearing off a few tables, rattling glasses and plates carefully into a bus-pan. Those sitting at the tables were happily engaged with their meals and companions; groomed-looking folk dressed casually. No one inside even bothered to look up at Brask.

Well, what's it gonna be, man? Table or barstool? Can't stand here like a totem pole all night. Pick a spot and start drinking.

He opted for the bar.

A smiling, big-boned woman in a bulky green sweater and tight jeans greeted him as he sat on one of the stools. Her curly hair was as red as spun copper—*Jesus, she could be the twin sister of that crazy fucker at the store! S*he was behind the impressive bar, pouring draughts and expertly pulling glassware from the racks above. Brask's mouth began to water at the thought of a Scotch with a real beer for a chaser.

There were four other people perched on stools at the bar; Brask had chosen a somewhat vacant stretch in the middle. The buxom red-head with the outdated, feathered hairstyle smiled at him until her cheeks looked like moist apples balanced above the corners of her mouth. She grabbed a towel to wipe her hands, which had been dripping in sanitized rinse-water from the sink beneath.

"Hey there, stranger. Welcome to Tuesday night."

Her voice was rolling and cheerful, with an accent Brask could place only as a variant of some heavy New England drawl, all clips and ahhs.

"Don't worry," she continued. "We don't summon a marching band every time we get a new face in here." Putting her hands on ample hips, she sized-up Brask in neighborly fashion, eyes twinkling, each a tiny blue star. "I ought to be able to spot a new face, too, seeing as we get so few of them. But word gets around and I manage to catch a bit of it between filling beer mugs and mixing

Jack Daniels with just about anything else that's wet and sweet. You must be Brask Adams."

She stuck a hand, red and wrinkled from work and wash-water, over the salt and pepper shakers lined at the back edge of the bar, along with the ketchup bottle holding up the laminated menu card like a barrier between them. Brask accepted it gratefully. This woman's casual, wry warmth came across like a balmy breeze on an otherwise exhausting day.

"That's me. I guess Horace must've told you."

"Bingo. He dropped by a bit ago for his little nip of Tanqueray and told me the good news. I'm Margie, Brask. Welcome to Wistwood. You don't mind me calling you 'Brask,' do you?"

"No! No problem at all, Margie. Really nice to meet you, too."

"Yeah, well, we're awful glad to have you here. It's not much of a town for size but that means the addition of even one more soul counts for a lot. And congratulations on getting the Kimberton cabin! My God, isn't that a beautiful spot?"

Margie shook her wavy red hair in apparent awe of his new housing arrangements. The feathered panels on either side of her head rippled a bit to revealed the conservative gold-studded earrings just above the floppy collar of her sweater.

"I'm in love with it already," said Brask. "And thanks for the warm welcome. Horace had a lot of nice things to say about you, by the way, while he was showing me around early this afternoon."

"Ha! You'd best not believe a *word* of it. Not even the sweet stuff. *Especially* not the sweet stuff."

Brask began to feel a bit squirmy. This was all perfunctory small talk and he had grown to realize how much he despised chit-chat when he was essentially removed from society. But now that he'd been dealt back into the game it was time to freshen up the playing skills. He wondered what Horace had already told this woman about him. Not too much, hopefully. Still, there was no sense in worrying about it; that was all beyond his control, no matter what instinct did or did not tell him about the old man's self-declared trustworthiness. Besides, he rather liked this bumptious woman, immediately so.

"Now, enough with my chatter, eh? What can I get you, honey?"

An old Patsy Cline tune warbled its way through the sound system in the ceiling corners and around the great room at a lazy, pleasant volume.

"We got beer. We got full bar. We got food if your stomach's growling. Pretty good stuff, too, if I do say so myself. Jorge Alvarado is my guy in the back and he is a genius, doll. Total genius. Trained chef. Makes a mean quesadilla with grilled chicken and goat cheese. Three different kinds of pasta. Steaks. Chicken. Burgers. You name it, almost. Here, have a look, sweetie."

She grabbed the laminated menu from betwixt the ketchup bottle and the salt & pepper shakers and wiped a bit of grease off the edge before placing it primly in front of Brask. His eyes scanned the line-up of items without really seeing or reading a thing.

"You know, I'm definitely saving room for something to eat, but right this minute a Scotch, straight up, the best you have—with a beer back—would hit a certain spot that needs a good clobbering, if you catch my drift."

Margie laughed. Her hefty breasts moved like bowling balls in a sling beneath her sweater. This middle-aged woman was not his type, but Brask did not find the effect wholly unpleasant.

"We definitely have the ability to 'clobber' here, Brask. What'll you have for Scotch? Johnnie Walker is my well, but I do have a bottle of Chivas Regal and Springbank, too, if you fancy it. Twelve year old."

"Wow. I'll take the Spingbank. That's some good stuff. Bring it on."

"My my, you have some refined taste for such a youngster. Nice to see."

"Not that young. I'm twenty-eight."

Margie rolled her eyes playfully. "Uh huh. Enjoy it while it lasts."

"I will tonight, at least. This is something of a celebration for me, after all."

"It sure is, honey. Getting that fine old Kimberton nest. Gosh, it's all decked out and *perfect* for a writer. By the way, the bottled beer list is at the bottom of the menu, doll. Only three to choose from." She leaned against her side of the bar with the massive cushion of her breasts and then hiked a thumb at the taps behind her. "Sam Adams, Budweiser and Blue Moon is what I have on tap. No craft stuff, sorry, but it's cold as an Eskimo's ass on an ice-toilet in the Arctic. I guarantee that much."

"Oh, you can really guarantee that, huh?"

"Sure I can!" Margie stood back, saucy and batting her long fake eyelashes. "I was married to an Eskimo once. Lived with him on an ice floe until I got sick of fighting off the polar bears every night and had to divorce him. Nanook. That was his name. Nanook of the North."

Nawth. Brask had been right. This woman had to have hailed from Massachusetts or maybe Maine.

"Pale ale, please, as a back," he said with a laugh. "Sam Adams will do for me, Margie of the North."

"Coming right up." She poured the Springback, winked, and then fished for a cold mug as Brasked fiddled with the warped corner of a beverage coaster.

"So Horace told you I'm a writer. Obviously."

Margie looked over her shoulder and cracked a knowing smile as she topped off the draught.

"He did, babe. But don't you worry. That's pretty much all he told me. And *you* already know that he likes a daily belt of Tanqueray ... or three. I only spread one likable trait around about anybody in this place, and affection for Tanqueray seems a likable thing to me, as does being a writer, so there you have it."

"That's very considerate of you."

"Not at all. Here's your Scotch and your Sam, hon."

The first sip of Springback was abject heaven.

Sweet-burning ambrosia.

"And in case you harbor any doubts, Brask, I limit myself to single-item gossip with great discipline. I mean, come on. In this position I have to have *some* material to work with. But I use my powers for good, not evil. Besides, I had to practically pry that tidbit about you being a writer out of old Horace. Had to nearly grab a fishhook to land the information."

"I'm a big admirer of ladies who work hard to get what they want. This Springback is impeccable, by the way. Thanks for mentioning it. You want me to pay you now or run a tab or what?"

"Run a tab, if you like, babe. And don't go thinking that I'm incorrigibly nosy, either. I won't have you thinking that. Nope. I have a healthy curiosity about the basics, but all I did was ask Horace where you were from and what you did for a living. Scouts honor. I did not inquire about sensitive information that might get you in trouble with the federal government, I promise. Oh, wait, I also asked him if you were good looking, but he couldn't help me with that one. And now I get to be pleasantly surprised on my own. So. Do you forgive me for being the busybody barmaid?"

"Margie, you are forgiven and thoroughly absolved for all time and in all situations," pronounced Brask, appreciating the flirty creature behind the bar all the more. She reminded him of his mother, in happier times. The lighthearted sass. The homely comfort in her own skin. Margie, for her part, adopted a mockingly serious expression before ambling to the other end of the bar to tend a thirsty patron.

"Forgiveness is fine," she called back, "but don't start talking absolution. That'll make me think you're a priest and we already got one of those around here. Or an ex one, in case you didn't notice. I guess he's a Protestant now."

"Oh, I noticed the Reverend," said Brask, gulping a splendid, icy mouthful of the beer as she drifted off to serve someone else on his left. "Horace introduced us earlier. He's pretty well glued to that wheelbarrow."

"Ha! Him and that busted up old chapel of his. What an exercise in futility."

"You're making sport of the work of the righteous, there, Margie," said the man to whom she was now serving a sudsy mug of Blue Moon. He was two stools down from Brask. A black man, bald, horn-rim spectacles, maybe fifty, maybe sixty, if the look of world weariness and solemnity across his brow and on his clean-shaven face gave anything away. He wore a tweed sport jacket with his shoulders hunched over his beer, as if guarding it. It struck Brask that the guy was in some sort of physical pain and just barely containing it through a monumental act of will that left the rest of his body rigid. The man's legs, in tweed trousers to match the dapper jacket, appeared gripped around the legs of the barstool for dear life. Pain. Brask certainly didn't know why, but it seemed to emanate from the poor soul in an invisible cloud, though the sound of his voice was sonorous and almost as satisfying as the aged Scotch.

"Never pays to belittle the ways of the holy, Margie," the man added slyly, his voice a slow, pooling syrup. "Even if their ways are more than a little crazy to the educated mind." He laughed, then, low and resonant, like the sound of hummingbird wings motoring for an instant outside a window and then gone.

"I'm not looking to be paid anything, Walter Trumbull, except maybe for what you owe on your tab this week. Don't think I've forgotten about that special piece of paper. I haven't. Every beer is written down like a verse of scripture on that tab of yours. Like a stroke of the pen recording Gospel truth."

"See, there you go again." Walter shook his head ruefully. "You even have to bring the Good Book into it. Did you see how she did that?" He turned to Brask with a labored, almost tortured movement of his torso and gestured with a hand that was curled and curved inward like the ebony claw of some great predatory bird. Severe rheumatoid arthritis. Brask would have recognized it anywhere; his grandmother had suffered from the same disease. Well, that explained the stiffness in his posture and the vague expression of pain. *Poor sonofagun.*

"I'm not so sure I caught all of that last bit she said," offered Brask. "The Scotch I just downed was enough to take the hair off my chest and push it all the way up through my ears, I'm afraid."

The old fellow laughed, hummingbird wings again, only louder. Was there something wrong with his lungs, as well? He didn't *sound* in pain when speaking or laughing.

"You best stick to beer, then, my friend, because the older you get, you won't need any additional help growing hair out of your ears."

"Yeah, that's right," said Margie, placing a glass of chardonnay at the end of the bar for the ponytailed waitress who had hustled over with her tray. "Walt, here, has to take a weed whacker or whatever you call it to those ears of his at least once a week, so listen to an expert. Brask, meet Walter Trumbull, one of the founding fathers of Wistwood, I guess you could say. And a certified royal pain my ass, but I don't know what I'd do without him. Call me a masochist. Walt ... Brask Adams. Just moved to town today. Renting the Kimbertons' old cabin. And for the record," she declared at last, pink palms lifted and turned outward in a show of innocence, "I was *not* making fun of that wonderful priest preacher reverend who keeps dribbling cement and leaving his dirty footprints all along my alleyway."

Walt smiled at Brask, his big brown eyes as warm as the memory of being tucked, snug into bed, on a chilly night as a kid. The twisted and stricken hand held out was not so unsettling to clasp because of the ocean of goodness that seemed to swell, tranquil and deep beyond imagining, behind those eyes.

"Nice to meet you, Walt."

The crabbed fingers were warm and slightly damp to his brief but respectful touch of greeting. He had to make a mental effort not to wipe his own hand on the bar napkin next to his beer, though he felt an almost overwhelming impulse to do just that.

What the hell has come over you, man? The guy already caught you staring at his handicap. Get a grip on your head. You've been living in your truck for six months. Not in a frigging cave. These are people.

"Pleasure to make your acquaintance, Brask, and welcome to the neighborhood. We can do with some fresh new ideals and opinions in these parts, sure enough. I'm getting mighty tired of Margie's."

"Then you ought not to be sitting here front and center every night asking for my opinions," teased Margie, killing a housefly that had landed on her stainless steel counter with an expert snap of the bar towel. "Besides, it's a bartender's job to help her customers figure out opinions they don't even know they have."

Walt jabbed gleefully at his knee with the gnarled fingers. "You must've gone to some crazyass, newfangled mixologist's school, then, Margie, because in every other joint I been to in my life, it's the bartender's job to simply keep the glass full and listen!"

"How do you think I came up with all these opinions in the first place, Walt? Listening to the likes of you day after day, year after year. That's how. Besides, I didn't go to bartender's school. I'm self-taught, all the way."

"Yes," said Walt. "I can tell every time I order something more complicated than a draught beer that you are self-taught." He started to chuckle again, unleashing the wing-beats of buzzing laughter. Margie turned to Brask, pleading.

"Hey! New guy! Help a gal out, would ya? Take this joker off my hands before I lose it and ask the former-priest-now-preacher across the street how one goes about giving-up a life in liquor for the convent."

"Oh! You'd have to ring one hell of a bell to join the sisterhood," said Walt. "Maybe even three bells. Maybe a hundred, for all anyone knows."

"All you know plus fifty bucks still won't pay your tab for the week, smart mouth."

Margie shook her head at Walt, as if their verbal duel had been playing on and on for years in a cherished game. To Brask, it had the familiar echo of an old nursery rhyme that danced forever somewhere in the back of the mind; never forgotten and seldom encountered, but instantly recognized if one's ears happened to pick it up somewhere. This seemed another beguiling sign that he had stumbled upon a place, a world, that might prove itself entirely worthy of the designation "Home."

"Talk to Brask, there, Walt. I'm sure he's got a million things to say that'd entertain you far more than I. He's a big-time writer, you know."

"Is that so?" said Walt, making once again the awkward and anguished little move, the creaky shift with his torso. The gentle eyes grew round behind the spectacles.

"Well, I don't know how 'big-time' you'd be able to call me," demurred Brask, sliding a thumb self-consciously along the handle of his beer mug. "But I did just sign a pretty sweet deal with Fischer & Spade."

The opportunity to now tell people—*real people in a public setting, even if they were strangers!*—conjured a curious and sweeping mix of emotions. Brask felt accomplished and almost smug with excitement, but there was a sliver of embarrassment piercing the skin of his pride, too. He didn't know why. Signing the deal was the only thing in the world he had to brag about. It was now the only thing remotely interesting about him that didn't require a full retelling of childhood horror stories, the death of his beloved Jess, and other maudlin reflections on the pitfalls of life. Nobody ever really wanted to hear about such things, no matter how much they said they did, or pretended to listen with a fascination that was really only a mentally taxing show of politeness.

"Fischer & Spade, huh? You don't say. Can't say as I ever heard of them," admitted Walt, who did appear to be making a considerable effort to wrack the brain beneath his gloriously polished scalp. "They put out any of Zane Grey's books, by any chance?" he added, as if stumbling into some hopeful light. "God, I loved those Zane Grey books. You couldn't keep my nose out of a Zane Grey book when I was a kid."

"Um … not that I know of, Walt, but then again I'm not really sure who published the Zane Grey books. I mean, it could've been Fischer & Spade, I suppose. They're a pretty big, pretty old New York house, with offices in San Francisco, of course—that's what made things really sweet and easy for me, obviously."

"In San Francisco," muttered Walt, pulling the beer mug closer to his mouth atop the coaster, as if his poor hands were grappling hooks. He leaned in to sip until he came up with suds on his nose.

"Fischer & Spade have published some heavy hitters the last few decades. Great operation. Gosh, they've had at least a dozen New York Times bestsellers in the past year alone. Some prize-winning stuff. The *Hibernation* series. And Annabeth Marston won the Man Booker for *After the Volcano* a few years ago."

"After the *what?*" said Margie, squinting as she leaned on the bar between the two men.

"The 'volcano.' *After the Volcano* was the name of her book," said Brask. "Yeah. Pretty huge seller, too. Top Five on Amazon for months. Fischer & Spade is known for strong campaigns in support of their titles. They make a real commitment to developing the careers of new authors in their stable, so I couldn't be more pleased with the whole deal. Relieved, for sure. I guess that goes without saying when you've been a full-time building contractor and construction worker, but a part-time, struggling writer for ages."

The somewhat gaudily attired and accessorized woman Brask had seen earlier in the day, the rock star's wife, minced suddenly up to the bar in all her high-heeled and hair-extended glory.

"Would you refill my Pinot Grigio, Miss? Your waitress appears to be in the weeds."

"What the heck?" huffed Margie.

"No. No, it's no trouble," said Neetha Grayle. "We don't want to bother her. Looks like she's got enough on her mind already tonight. Just fill me up. Lleyton's fine. Nursing his iced tea. I think he's in an especially bad mood tonight. Just like your waitress. But I'm not complaining. I'm really not."

Margie took Neetha's glass and soon had a bottle of white wine procured and uncorked with the flair and speed of a magician.

"This one's on the house, Mrs. Grayle."

"Oh, call me Neetha. Please. I'd appreciate that."

"Okay. Sorry you had to come up and get it yourself, Neetha. I guess Carlee's a little spaced, tonight. She's had her first interview with the Landlord today and, well, she doesn't really doesn't know what to think about all of that."

"I'm sure I don't know either," said Neetha. "My Lleyton has some kind of 'interview' with this landlord, or whatever, and it's the day *after* tomorrow. What is all that about? Timeshare sales? We're just came here Friday for a quick vacation, and I'm not sure we're even going to stay until the weekend, at this point."

"Oh?" Margie offered Neetha a strange, exaggerated frown. "Well, I can't speak to the business that might go on between your husband and the owner, but I don't think you'll have to worry about much. They'll take good care of you up there, after you bring your husband to the interview."

"What's that mean?"

Margie tapped a palm to her forehead.

"Good grief, where are my manners? Neetha, you and your husband have been in the entertainment industry. Meet the newest member of our community. This right here is Brask Adams. Just signed his lease today. And he also signed a major publishing deal. He's in entertainment, too. Wouldn't you like to meet a famous author?"

Turning to Brask, she said, "This is Neetha Grayle. Her husband over there at that little corner table behind the fireplace is the famous rock singer, Lleyton Grayle. They're new here, like you. Visiting, I gather."

An old song by Breting Engel now began to flow, ethereal and anguished, over the restaurant's stereo system, the spectral voice conjuring phantom images of desolate roads leading away from the safety of life within a familiar Sunday, hinting at the loneliness of an exile imposed by equal parts street-fight and sea-change. Brask felt something pause within himself and looked up at the ceiling, momentarily stunned. The Engel record was one of his favorites. Another fantastic omen? Uncanny.

Neetha Grayle noticed Brask's momentary distraction but extended a delicate, bejeweled hand.

"Another man in the world of entertainment has found his way to this place?" she said, the exquisitely lacquered and manicured nails of her other hand clasping the glass of wine between the augmented breasts. "And one with a *current* contract, no less. My guy over there hasn't had one of those in a quarter-century, but at least he had me to hide some of his own damn money on him when things got out of hand."

"Wait … what?"

Brask jumped back on his train of thought and wheeled around to behold Neetha's beautiful but inexpressibly sad face. He shook her hand, as dainty and pleasant to the touch as poor Walt's had been knobby and unnerving.

"I didn't hear a word you said, Ma'am. So sorry. I'm lost at sea. Half this whole day, to be honest."

"That's okay. I don't expect anyone to be starstruck over my husband, anymore. I'm certainly not. It's nice to meet you. Congratulations on your book deal."

Brask glanced at the man seated in a wheelchair at the little two-top by the fireplace in Marge's dining room. Lleyton Grayle, rock star, was stuffing his face with French fries slathered in ketchup, his long hair draped like a shawl across the shoulders of his rhinestone-studded black shirt. He seemed otherwise unaware of his surroundings.

"I … uh, remember your husband's music. Great career. Songs from when I was … well, you know, I saw you earlier today when I was just coming into town for the first time with Horace. He was riding with me in my van. The creepy white one. You were leaving this place. Getting into a Ferrari. Real nice one."

"That sounds about right. I came in for a Bloody Mary. Two actually. And let me tell you, I needed them both," said Neetha, sipping Pinot Grigio. "I probably need one now. And don't worry about not knowing Lleyton or his music. You can't be more than thirty."

"Twenty-eight. I guess life's been hard on me."

"You wanna look at a face that screams 'hard life'? Look at this one." She pointed to her own face, bedazzled fingernails splayed as if underscoring the crescendo note of a tragic aria.

"I think you look great, Mrs. Grayle."

"Thanks, kid. And call me Neetha. I ain't your granny."

"Sure, Neetha. Look, as a former starving-artist, I don't want to meet your husband in the near future and look like a complete ignoramus. What's his story? I *have* heard of him. Remember some of his music. Sorta. I would've Googled for more info already, but my phone's been dead since I got here. I haven't had time to recharge it, what with the lease and that whole drama. Can't believe I made it a day without the damned phone, to tell you the truth. God, I hope you don't think I'm the rudest person you've ever come across."

"Oh, I don't think that at all. And don't feel bad about your internet connection. Nothing of ours has worked since we got here on Friday. Total unplugging! That old Horace knob said that one of the cellular towers is down or some such. It's been a real pain in the ass."

"What? I just talked to him about that today and he never mentioned a cell tower being down."

"Yeah? Probably forgot. He's old. Older than Lleyton. You want the book on Lleyton, Mr. Author? I'll give it to ya. Lleyton was a rock star. Past tense emphasized. And he's done everything—short of self-immolation—to extinguish his legacy since the early Nineties. Hell, sometimes I think he would've gone from has-been to legend if he'd *had* the good sense to immolate himself. You know, like the Buddhist monks did to protest all the shit they were going through back in the day? Whatever it was. Tibet? It's all a blur to me. I guess they still do it once in awhile. Who can say? But if Lleyton would've done it, he'd have made the news and made himself an icon, even if he didn't deserve it. God knows I've been tempted to douse him in gasoline over the years."

Neetha stole a wistful but wretched glance at her husband, who was still consuming French fries one by one, lining each fry with a spine of ketchup and slowly nibbling it down in systematic fashion, like a robot that had been programmed for that purpose alone.

"Lleyton had his string of hits before you were born, honey. And Lleyton's stuff was death metal, intended for a submarket, even though it was a market that spent big. His chart singles were tunes like *The Crucibles, Carve Her Up With My Devotion, Seize the Dragon, Grave Matters*—those were his biggest hits."

Somewhere a bell rang in Brask's pop-cultural storage shed.

"*Grave Matters?* He was the guy who sang *Grave Matters?* I have to admit, we loved that song as kids, when it turned up on a station … occasionally."

"Yeah. *Very* occasionally by that time." Neetha was getting tipsier by the minute, it seemed, but no one in the bar area was concerned except for Brask.

Brask looked once more at the slightly soft-boiled shell of a man astride the fireplace.

"I totally remember him and can see him in a cultural context, now."

"Sure ya do," said Neetha, dubious. She sighed. "At least Lleyton wrote all his own songs. I still have to give him credit for doing that. But you don't know what we had to spend to get the publishing rights back after he dicked a bunch of them away with some of his crazy deals." She held the wine glass toward the fireplace in toast of her mate. "And through it all, he came to believe that *I* am his worst enemy. Wouldn't ya just know it? Go on over and say 'hi,' if you feel like it. He won't care if you don't recognize him, luv. His brain has the consistency of cheesecloth, these days. It's all I can do not to drown him in his soup, sometimes. I dunno. I guess maybe I still love him. Maybe like I always have."

Someone's been hitting the sauce all day. What a performance! thought Brask.

In truth, Neetha seemed to possess an underlying, damaged quality of kindness he hadn't expected. She was also a tad smarter than he might have guessed, based upon one swift look at her in motion earlier. Wry, for sure. No wilting violet. But she wasn't shy about her issues, either.

What a spectrum of people to encounter in one afternoon, one evening. And Brask thought *he* would end up being the de facto oddball.

As for the former rock star and "pretty boy" gorging on Margie's crinkle-cut fries, Brask could summon something like a quicksilver snapshot in his brain, a late-night video of girls writhing around a cemetery or perhaps in a coffin. Hard to say. Maybe they had been writhing on top of Lleyton in a coffin. The images turned grainy. Death Metal had been as far off his sonic radar as polka music, back in the day.

"So enough about old skillet-brains over there," said Neetha. "What kind of stuff do you write? Tell us all about this book that's coming out."

"I was just about to ask that question, too," added Walt, running his claws along the edge of the bar and then drawing them hurriedly into the crook of his lap, self-conscious for the first time.

Margie was not to be left out, even if she was still fighting to get Carlee, her increasingly beleaguered waitress, on an even keel. "I wanna know all about this epic," she piped up from the little service station. Carlee tottered off into the dining room, a doomed balancing act uninterested in potential bestsellers and barely able to keep beer from slopping out of the glasses and onto her tray.

For Brask, the curiosity was but mildly unusual. "What is your book about?" was always the first, and inevitably the most discomfiting question people had asked upon learning he had finished a novel. Maybe sensitivities and curiosities took a different turn when you had the privilege of telling strangers you had not only completed a work but that it was about to be published. Human reactions never ceased to fascinate and perplex.

"Well, it's about a guy falling for the right girl at the wrong time, and what happens when you have to pay the price for choosing the wrong thing in life." He shrugged a little, not happy with his answer. Summing-up the essence of his work in an easy-to-grasp blurb was always a disappointing endeavor. He always thought the answer would just glide off his tongue, but thus far it had never done so.

The reception was mixed.

Margie pursed her lips with a half-smile. Walt gave a sort of abbreviated snort, whether in approval, derision, or bewilderment, it was not at all clear. Neetha exhibited a tiny shudder through her whole body, a vibration that seemed to end in the tremulous movement of her breasts and the tinkling of assorted bangle bracelets on her forearms.

"Oooh! That sounds like my kind of story," she purred. "And all the better told from a guy's point of view. You don't see that very often. What's the title?"

Brask sipped the newly refilled beer Margie had hastened to put in front of him and bowed his head, still bashful and hating the feeling.

"That's just it. I don't know the title, yet. I mean, I had what I thought was a good one, but the editor at Fischer & Spade didn't think it was marketable enough, and God knows everything has to be marketable, these days. Down to the last molecule."

"Well, what was your original idea for a title? I bet it was just great the way it was." Margie offered an encouraging jut of her round chin.

"Jet Stream."

"Huh?" grunted Walt. The women looked more respectfully puzzled.

"See? I guess that was the problem," explained Brask. "It's nothing to do with the core theme of the book and doesn't really explain to the potential reader anything pivotal or essential to the plot, which is why the editorial panel rejected my title. But 'Jet Stream' does refer to one key scene where my protagonist decides he's going to forego meeting his lover, his girlfriend in Italy, to propose marriage, and instead accepts a job assignment with the CIA—he's an agent—that'll put him in a lot of danger and—"

"Excuse me, people, I hate to interrupt a vibrant and fascinating conversation, but if I don't get the Perry couple's food out of the kitchen, they are going to hit the roof. They asked for those steaks medium-well, Margie, and I told them it takes a while, but it's been an hour! Jorge says there's some problem with the grill. Jesus! I'm just going to throw up all over their faces if they make one more snide little comment to me. I swear I will."

"Calm down, Carlee honey!"

"No, Margie. I've had it tonight. This whole freaking day. I will go back to that kitchen and I will personally take a runny shit on their steaks and tell them it's a marsala sauce—no extra charge because they had to wait. I cannot *deal* with this tonight! My nerves are strung tighter than a goddamn Stradivarius and I just …"

"Oh, Carlee, doll. Carlee, baby. Calm down, sweetie, or you're gonna have an aneurysm right here on my floor and nobody's gonna get their steaks. And for God's sake, girl, that's enough chatter about whipping up one of your shit-sauces. Jesus! We have a new fella in town and I frankly do not want him to get the wrong impression about my establishment, just because you're in one of your stressed-out moods. I know the interview was tough, but you'll get a second one. Horace already said so. Come and sit down on this stool for a few minutes and catch your breath. That's it. Pull yourself together. I'll go and talk to Jorge and learn what the hell is up with the food. Then I'll chat with the Perrys myself. Those assholes. Just sit tight."

Carlee clung to the stool like it was a wobbly pillar leaning outward from the roof of a skyscraper.

"I'm so sorry, Margie. I just don't have the stamina to deal with this stuff tonight, not with the way I fucked up at the Landlord's."

"There, there, now," said Neetha, putting an arm of comfort around the near-sobbing, about-to-lose-it waitress. "You just need to forget about that drinks-tray you cling to like a steering wheel. Compose yourself, is all. You want a little Xanax pill? I got plenty in my purse. Margie's gone right over to talk to those people and she'll tell them what's what. You won't have anything to worry about. Here, luv, dry your eyes with this tissue. Your little bit of mascara is running. You look like Cleopatra, or maybe one of her maids, on a crying-jag. That's a luv."

"Thank you, Ma'am." Carlee dabbed in dainty passes at her beady eyes with the Kleenex.

"It's Neetha. Neetha Grayle. I ain't your granny. And don't mention it, luv."

"I know who you are," said Carlee with a sniff. "You're married to the rock and roll fella over there. Margie pointed you out earlier."

"That's right. And this here is Brask … *somebody*. Sorry, Brask. He's the new guy in Wistwood and I assume he's single because I do not see a ring." Neetha added this last with a theatrical down-the-nose gesture at Brask's left hand. "Seems a caring and sensitive gentleman, too, which is probably why he's a published writer."

"Soon to be published," corrected Brask, bewildered by the turn such simple introductions had taken in so short a time. It was a good thing he was already buzzed from the Scotch and the beers. Strangers on the brink of nervous break-downs had never been quick to stir the surging tides of empathy in the depths of his 'sensitive' writer's heart. And what was he to make of this Carlee, this disinte-grating little waitress-woman with wrists as knobby as chicken bones poking out of her cardigan sleeves, threatening to vomit or shit on her customers? His first instinct was to pay his tab and bolt, rather than witness a complete meltdown. Such a tableau seemed imminent, but the sobs and sniffles subsided with each gentle pat Neetha administered to the hunched and harried soul's shoulders.

"I'm so, so sorry." Carlee began screwing her eyes shut tightly and flinging them wide open, over and over again, evidently trying to snatch her sanity back from the mental racetrack upon which it had made a one-hundred yard dash. She drew the top buttons of her sweater together, demure as a starlet trapped in her own drama, and nodded to the others, more than a little ashamed. She smiled at Neetha and Walt, but kept her eyes averted from Brask.

"I'm going to be okay," she mouthed silently.

"Feel better, kiddo?" Neetha's purple-shadowed eyelids drooped heavy with concern.

"Yes, I do. Please don't pay any more attention to my little freak-outs. It's just another one of many. Margie's been unbelievably supportive of me since Ethan … since he …"

"We know, little lady, we know," said Walt, extending a claw that was meant to be comforting and raking it across Carlee's knee.

"It's just … with everything that's happened and everything coming up, I'm afraid I was bound to lose it, if only a little. But I'm better now. Got my head back on straight, pretty sure. And I'm sorry to you, Mister," she said to Brask through one final sniffle. "Imagine someone new coming to town and the first thing he sees is silly me fall right to pieces. There'll be trouble as a result of this," Carlee added ominously, searching Walt's eyes first and then Neetha's.

Brask was more bewildered than ever. So was Neetha. *What kind of trouble? Who was this Ethan person and what had happened to him?*

They were both thinking much the same thing.

Carlee grew nervous again, though somehow in a different, frightened kind of way, and fished behind herself for the drinks tray she had placed on the bar. "I'd best get back over there and placate Mr. and Mrs. Perry. Smooth things over, you know?"

"No need for that now," said Margie, reappearing with a bright smile and a look of flushed triumph. "I got their steaks out and stood over those two bastards like a hawk until they each carved-in, took a bite, and swore that they were the best ribeyes they had ever tasted. What a pair! Jorge apologizes, honey. He said the grill's been acting up all day long, ever since that Reverend Jarecki started hanging out back with his wheelbarrow and tools. Jorge says he was tinkering with the outside fuse box, trying to find a way to charge one of those power drills or whatever. Who knows what that dumb cluck has done to my wiring? I've a good mind to tell him to go elsewhere for his water and energy."

"Then the Perrys aren't mad at me?" burbled Carlee.

Margie bustled to fill a few mugs and wineglasses and put them on the drinks tray.

"No. I told you. They're happy as two bugs in a rug, now that they've got their food. Two ugly old spider-mite bugs, if you ask me. But the folks sitting out on the porch and your two other four-tops might be inclined to get snippy if you don't deliver their drinks toot sweet. I took the orders for you while you were over here having your little moment. The Buds go to Hal and Rita Coombs. The two Chardonnays go to old Mrs. Plimpton, and the rest to the folks on the porch. I forgot exactly who gets what. Just ask when you get out there. They won't mind."

"Thanks, Margie, you really are an angel." Carlee eased the crammed tray off the top of the bar.

"Oh, I'm far from that, honey. You sure you can carry that tray? You got your shit together? I can do it for you if you want me to."

Carlee shook her head and slowly backed away to begin her tour of the dining room and front porch. Patsy Cline was singing again, more ghostly echoes from the speaker system above, some yodeling lament about a midnight walk.

"I can manage just fine," Carlee reassured her skeptical audience. She looked as if she might break like a matchstick under the weight of the crammed tray. "Just forget I had another crack-up, would you? And thanks again, guys. By the way, it was nice to meet you," she added hurriedly to Brask and Neetha, still hiding her gaze as she set sail like a listing ship leaving port, gliding precariously into the dining room with her cargo, using every ounce of vein-popping concentration to keep the tray in a horizontal position above the floor.

"I swear that girl is gonna drop the whole order all over the first customer she approaches and I'm going to have to fire her," muttered Margie. "Shit. I know she's got it a little rough right now, but who doesn't? Her adjustment to Wistwood has not been the most seamless transition I've seen in my day. I don't know. It's not up to us to determine how these damn things turn out."

"No, it is not," said Walt, going for another dive at the suds atop his beer mug. "We can't interfere in her affairs."

"What's her story?" said Brask, who had been baffled the whole time by the woman's unbalanced behavior and even more so by all that was said—and seemingly unsaid—by his new acquaintances.

"Yeah. What's the whole deal with that Ethan person she mentioned?" added Neetha. "That girl's not right in the head."

Margie began a perfunctory wiping job across the cabinets behind the bar.

"Oh, she's just like any of us who came here for a new start. That's pretty much the story for anybody who's decided to settle in Wistwood, to a greater or lesser extent, depending upon the person."

"Right again," said Walt, as if offering an 'Amen' to the Gospel acclamation of a captivating preacher. He struggled to pick up a napkin with his warped fingers. Neetha sipped her wine and said nothing, at first, staring up toward the place where Patsy Cline's voice seemed to be emanating.

"I'm not here for any new start," she said. "At least not a permanent one. Lleyton convinced me to get away for a couple weeks' vacation. At least I think he was the one who arranged it. Maybe it was me. But if *he* was thinking about some sort of new start, then I've got another one in mind for him. And he isn't going to like it. No offense to anyone who lives in this town," she was careful to add. "It's nice enough, and I like your bar and grill, Margie, but like I said, I don't think I'm going to last through the end of the week. I'm almost out of gas as it is and the phones don't work."

"Horace didn't give me too much as far as the history of this place," said Brask, perturbed once more by the mention of defunct phone service and now a lack of gas. He hadn't seen a station downtown. Still, what was the big deal? Big Sur was only half a mile away. "It's not really a town, I realize, but more of a mountain neighborhood made to look like a town. A hamlet, I guess some people might call it. Or that's what they'd have called it ages ago. Horace said I'd get a chance to have one of these personal interviews with the landlord at some point, too. Sounds kind of pleasant, if a bit feudal. But whatever. Gated communities in California have always seemed so damned antiseptic and uninspired, to me— even though builders and developers try hard to make people think otherwise.

For a relatively new development, or whatever it's supposed to be, this place has got some character."

"You're from California?" said Neetha.

"Yeah, Palo Alto, just up the road a few hours."

"What?"

"We're glad you're here, Brask," said Margie, now bent low, busily buffing the stainless steel refrigerator doors beneath the bar. "But I think everyone needs to let you be and give you a chance to settle. Enough jabbering about manor house interviews. How about another Springbank? I see that one's empty. How about one on the house? My house. A little extra welcome from me to you."

"Gosh, I'm not about to turn down a gesture like that. Pour freely."

"Atta fella."

At that instant, a stocky, handsome man emerged through the swinging door of the kitchen and brandished a steaming plate before the little gathering. Margie rose and cooed appreciatively before placing it in their midst on the bar. "Thanks, Jorge. Hey, look, guys—fried shrimp with cocktail and tartar sauce. I was a little hungry so I asked Jorge to whip-up enough for all of us. Have a nibble. Brask, this is our resident genius and chef, Jorge. Jorge, this is Brask. New guy in town. Signed on as of today."

Brask nodded his head and gestured. "Nice to meet you, man." They were too far away to shake hands and the chef did not approach.

"You, too. Good luck. By the way, everybody, the shrimp are fried in spiced corn-meal. Something new I'm trying out. Let me know what you think." Then he went back to the kitchen, wiping his large hands on the stained apron around his waist.

"Dig in, kids," said Margie behind the mound of shrimp. "Here's some rolled silverware for everybody. Brask, help yourself. It's on me and I know you've got to be hungry. Another Springbank coming up as well."

Normally Brask avoided fried food; it was a byproduct of the pervasive California lifestyle that had become early ingrained upon his being. But this heap looked and smelled too delicious to resist. Margie, moreover, was right; he was famished. Though he had managed to eat as healthy as he could even while living out of the van for a year, upholding previous standards had been far from easy. Soup-kitchen food tended toward the sensible, filling side, and he had hardly been in a position to be choosy. The memory sent a wave of shame through his system.

"Eat," Marge commanded, breaking the spell, and they all took their turn. The Springbrook was replaced and all seemed right with the world once more.

"So, Margie, what did you do when you turned this place from a bed and breakfast into a bar and grill, as far as getting a cook? Did you just put out an ad and along came Jorge?"

"Not exactly," said Margie, dabbing at a bit of cocktail sauce in the corner of her mouth. "At first I did all the cooking myself. I'm not too bad in the kitchen, when it comes to basic roadhouse fare, I guess."

"You were mighty good when you were doing it," agreed Walt, masticating his third massive shrimp.

"But when business started to pick up, there was no way I could get food out of the kitchen on time and tend bar, too, so I was on the lookout for some reliable help. One day, Horace introduced me to this nice young guy who'd just moved to town. Jorge's been here ever since. So has a steady line of customers."

"Jorge's a good man," said Walt, fryer grease moving down his lips and onto his chin like a slick pooling out the side of a tanker. "I never had a quesadilla so good as his. Of course, I had never eaten a quesadilla in my life before I ate his, but that's beside the point."

"Then Carlee came along. Jorge's been here about two years, now. Carlee and Ethan came a month ago. That's when I hired her. Needed a waitress as much as I needed a cook, by that time."

Brask couldn't help a brief chuckle. "Your waitress, Carlee, seems scared of her own shadow."

"Yeah, well, I agree with you on that." Margie said. "Carlee isn't very good at waiting tables and I don't expect she ever will be. But then again I don't have any plans to expand this place, and she can sorta handle the crowds we get. And I use the term 'crowds' very loosely. I'm here to pick up the slack if she gets in the weeds. Of course, that's about every night, but she's a sweet girl and everybody's kind of used to getting their food in quirky little installments by now. We make it work."

"And Ethan? Her husband or boyfriend who came here with her? What's he do?"

"Hopefully he's doing twenty to life somewhere, honey," said Margie with a frisky cluck of her tongue.

"I don't follow."

"Oh, none of us knows what he's actually doing. He left Carlee high and dry about a week after they came. Ran off with another woman, or so we've been told. Twenty to life is my idea of a fitting sentence for men who pull stunts like that. He's just gone. That's it. Dirty dog. That's the main reason Carlee's the big old mess we see before us now."

"What a shame," blurted Neetha, emerging from whatever private cloud of fun her brain had been lounging in. "She doesn't seem quite right in the head, but a man can do that to a lady. My guy may be a complete burnout, but at least he's still around. I guess there's something to be said for loyalty, even if a guy can't help it."

Margie and Neetha laughed knowingly, but Brask found himself feeling sorry for Carlee, as unlikeable as she had seemed to be, upon first meeting. It wasn't a pretty pass in this world to be deserted by a lover or a spouse, no matter what the circumstances. No, not one bit.

"You know, women can be awful, sometimes, too," intoned Walt, as if speculating upon the weather. He grabbed another shrimp, his curled fingers seeming tailored to hook and lift them off the plate to his mouth. "I know what it's like to be left in the lurch, is all I'm trying to say. I didn't get so much as a goodbye when my wife hit the road. No letter. Nothing but the bills. Still, I feel bad for Carlee, and you won't catch me making fun of her."

"NEETHA!" boomed a voice from behind them, a sudden, trumpeting moose-call that caused Walt to drop shrimp in his lap and Brask to slosh half a beer over the front of his shirt.

"Oh shit! I'm sorry, Brask. I'm sorry, Walt. It's just lunkhead Lleyton, at it again!" Neetha's manicured nails flew nervously through her hair.

"I know who it is, alright," said Walt, searching the area around his elbows for the lost shrimp. "You need to stuff a sock in your rock star's mouth."

"Margie, hand a me a towel so I can help Brask sop this up, would you?"

"NEETHA! Get the hell over here. It's time to go home!"

"I think you've been too long away from the table, honey," said Margie, frowning in Lleyton's direction. "Someone's getting antsy."

"Yeah, me," spat Neetha. "Antsy to roll his wheelchair off a cliff. Or knock him upside the head with a frying pan, only we haven't got one at the A-frame.

Neetha extended a hand to Brask. "It's been nice talking to you. I wish you all the luck in the world with the new place. You're probably going to fit right in here. We'll probably be leaving in the next couple of days if I can get Horace to refund our money, or Lleyton can get through whatever business he's got with the town squire. But we might come back in one more night, if I can get him to behave."

"Can't wait," said Brask, but with no hint of the sarcasm he felt. Neetha nodded her goodbyes and sashayed back to Lleyton's table, where her man drooled and fumed.

"That poor thing sure has her cross to bear," said Margie, handing Brask a rag for his shirt and a replacement beer in a new frosty mug.

"We all do," muttered Walt.

Brask shrugged. He knew about crosses. "I guess you never can tell with anybody, right? Nothing is what it seems to be, at least when you're on the outside looking in. People are really good at creating facades. Perfect little dioramas of the lives they want other people to think they're living. Or the lives they've actually fooled themselves into thinking they lead."

"Spoken like a proper writer," said Margie, impressed. "And I hear you loud and clear on that one." She put her hands on her hips again and eyed her mostly relaxed clientele like a proud mother hen. Neetha had already paid the discombobulated Carlee and wheeled Lleyton out of the dining room. Order seemed restored. "Everybody here has got a story fit for a novel or something else a fella like you might write. A screenplay or a Broadway show."

"More like off off off Broadway with this bunch," croaked Walt, visibly conflicted about whether he should be the one to go for the very last shrimp on the platter.

"That's right," said Margie, nudging the plate toward the old man and solving his ethical conundrum. "And that includes us, too. Why, I came to this place after the hospital I worked for for twenty years laid me off due to budget cuts.

Twenty damn years of self-sacrifice and dedication, taking care of those sweet little preemies and all the other babies in the neonatal ward at Sacred Heart in Detroit. I understand it was a privately funded hospital and things happen. Hell, Detroit was starting to swirl around the toilet bowl even then. We all knew something was coming, eventually, but that doesn't mean companies have to stop treating their longtime employees with respect and appreciation."

"I'm sorry to hear that happened to you, Margie."

"Thanks, Brask, but don't worry. I raised quite a bit of a stink about it. I am a woman who tends to speak her mind and stick up for herself. But that frigid bitch who was the executive director of the ward put the word out that I was a troublemaker. Blacklisted me. I couldn't get a comparable job to save my life in that town, after that." Margie shook her red, feather-styled bob ruefully. "No one can squash you like a bug the way hospital administrators can, when they start firing up their engines. I should've expected as much. So I said, 'to hell with it,' and took my savings and decided to make a big move. It was a risk, but it paid off. I found an ad for an old B&B in need of TLC on Craigslist and the rest is what they call relatively recent history."

"You seem happy now," said Brask as Margie fetched yet another beer for the restored Carlee, who was waiting at the end of the bar with her omnipresent tray. "You're doing well in a fantastic place all your own and you get to tend a bunch of babies all day and night."

"Yeah, I do." Margie shot him a sly look. "But I don't want you to think I'm bitter or anything because of what happened to me. Nobody's got more of a right to be, I expect, but I'm not. I'm way over those years."

"I came here after my wife left," said Walt, polishing off the last shrimp and swirling the tail around in a ramekin of tartar sauce. "Even before Margie got to town. Couldn't bear looking at the four walls of that apartment, thick with the smell of betrayal. Even the color of it. I had my military pension, so I filed bankruptcy and high-tailed it to Wistwood when I heard about it. Loved it from the moment I got here. Got me a nice little house up near the Manor Road. Life's good. I come down here, get a little drunk a couple nights a week. Eat all of Margie's fried shrimp and Jorge's quesadillas. This place is probably more home than an old crank like me deserves, truth be told."

"It's the same for all the folks sitting out there," agreed Margie, gesturing around the place with a flourish of her bar towel. "Carlee and that rat, Ethan, came here when they lost their family farm in Ohio. The Perrys, there, the couple that was giving Carlee such a hard time, with their matching bedazzled track-suits and their noses stuck up in the air like cats trying to sniff the wind, they sold their import-export company the minute Leroy got out of jail for running heroin. Got themselves a sweet spread about a mile north of your little place, Brask. Look at 'em—lily white and simpering at each other like they'd never seen a dark day to speak of. They tell me they feel they have 'recreated' themselves here in Wistwood. Several people have said the same thing to me, as a matter of fact. As for Neetha, who knows what'll happen to her?"

"She and the burnout are leaving," said Brask. "Sounds pretty clear-cut."

Margie raised her eyebrows but said nothing.

Carlee, meanwhile, had returned with a new order ticket. Margie excused herself, rattled glasses, pulled bottles, slammed cooler doors, stabbed maraschino cherries and, in a few minutes, sent the wiry, ponytailed server navigating through the dining room with an even bigger haul of drinks than she had carried before.

"See the Hendricks couple out on the deck?" Margie indicated the twosome in question with another flip of the bar towel. "They're the ones who love those godawful Manhattans. Total old fogey's drink—no offense, Walt—but *they* are a couple of rare birds. Only in their twenties and already retired when they got their place in Wistwood. We call them 'Mr. and Mrs. Retro' because they like everything to do with antiques and Art Deco and old-timey country club life. She's dressed pretty normally tonight from what I saw, but I've seen her pop in here decked out like a flapper, and it wasn't anywhere near Halloween, if you catch my drift."

"A bit eccentric, then, I take it," said Brask.

"Definitely. You'd think the two of them had just stepped right out of the Great Gatsby. Now *there's* a literary title for our new man of letters."

"I don't stand a prayer of entering *that* stratosphere." Brask crumpled his napkin atop the empty appetizer plate on the bar and went for his wallet. It was time to head back to the new digs and get ready for his first night in a proper bed of his own in over six months. He couldn't believe he would have a real chance to sleep with a wild breeze on his face coming through an open window, and hear a cricket chirp, or an owl call; anything so long as he knew he was roofed and safe at last. "I'll just be thrilled if my book gets reviewed in the New York Times and no one has to ask me for my advance back."

"When is this book of yours supposed to come out, anyhow?" said Walt with a confused grimace. "Maybe you told us already, but eating Margie's fried shrimp kills brain cells. Practically a well-known scientific fact. Beer is the only cure." He tapped a misshapen claw against his empty mug.

"I'm not one hundred percent sure, yet, Walt. It used to be you could count on at least a year passing between acceptance, contract, and publication, but the whole industry's changed radically in the past decade or so. Hell, the last five years have seen an upheaval. A panic, really. Agents can't look forward to their four-hour lunches in Chelsea, anymore. Editorial departments are drastically reduced. There's competition from the indie presses and online digital formats. It's impossible for me to keep up with that stuff and I don't know how they do it, but my publishing house is a good house, as I said. Old world meets new, best of both worlds, all that shit. At least that's what my agent tells me. I mean, there aren't even many bookstores around anymore, hardly. Everything is done online. I'm sure you both buy a fair amount of the things you want and need off the internet."

"I don't," said Walt.

"I haven't had much use for that since I moved to Wistwood, either," said Margie.

"Well, I'm supposed to meet Horace tomorrow and hash-out any remaining details or issues. Internet hook-ups and such. Electric is already on. I just wasn't up to a drive back to Palo Alto tonight, what with the cabin furnished so perfectly and all. I'm excited to get my first taste of what it's like to live in sylvan solitude."

"Not going to be too much of an inconvenience, living all the way out here, I hope," said Walt, nose back in his beer suds.

"Nah. I'll be called to make trips out and about when the time comes to market the book, and I've got friends in San Francisco and Silicon Valley I'd like to spend more time with, but mostly I'll be here … writing."

"That's a real good thing, Brask. Wistwood has a way of making a man happy to stay put and enjoy the scenery around him."

"I can believe that already. I only hope you don't expect me to patronize your outstanding little spot exclusively, Margie." Brask stretched and yawned, offering his most practiced wry smile.

"Oh, is that so?" Margie flashed a sardonic grin of her own. "You plan on setting up your own joint? Maybe a party-shack down at the cabin to provide me with a little friendly competition?"

"No, nothing that ambitious. I promise. I only meant that it's such a short drive to Big Sur and there are some nifty little spots along the coast that'd be fun to explore. That Nepenthe place looks like my kind of hang-out. During the day-time I can sit and stare at the ocean and drain a few margaritas or Bloody Marys on their deck. Also, there's a very attractive young lady working the cash register at a certain gas station in Big Sur. I'd like to bring her over here and introduce you, if I find myself fortunate enough to score a date. She wasn't familiar with Wistwood, but she's only been in Big Sur for a short time."

"Is that so?" said Margie, turning to watch Carlee take two plates of Jorge's dinner special from the noisy kitchen.

"Yeah. Her name's Kara. You may have even seen her there at the gas station when you go to fill up."

"Oh, we don't fill-up there," said Margie, idly selecting a wine glass from the rack above to polish and inspect in the muted light.

"You telling me you drive all the way into Carmel? I guess a lot of people around here probably do. It would make sense. Nearest supermarkets are there. I suppose I'll have to get used to that trip myself. Hopefully I can keep it down to only two or three times a month. The price of gas is insane and my van might give up the ghost just about any day, I expect."

"We don't go to any of those places you mentioned for gas or for groceries," said Walt, leaning forward and pondering his mug of beer as if he were expecting it to make some sort of comment. "And I don't think it's wise for you to get your heart set on such a thing, either, because you're not likely to be going *anywhere* for a spell."

"Walt, you are drunk and you have crossed a line," warned Margie. "There will be trouble over this. You know it."

"What is he talking about?" said Brask, chugging the last quarter of beer that remained in his own mug. He tossed his wallet on the bar. "My bill, please, Margie."

"Don't you pay any attention to him right yet, Brask. He doesn't know what he's talking about when he gets like this. Don't you worry about your bill, either. Everything's on the house tonight. My treat."

"Are you serious?"

"Dead serious. I do it for everybody. On their first day. You just make sure to get home safe and have a good night's rest. You've earned it."

ASUNDER

He came to the shore of the island while the twin suns were still dull yolks in a haze of scalded white sky.

And she was there, waiting for him.

He came, hungry and mad and panting with rage, aflame with the desire to obliterate, walking across the fast-moving waters of the river as if nothing but smooth stone lay beneath his bare feet. When his form touched the sand of the shoreline, it seemed as if the entire island and the wild river and the suns dozing dreary above trembled with fury, shaken by an intrusion that sliced something vital but unseen from the fabric of Time itself.

Something invaded, something more unwelcome than she herself—she who had found and crafted this place, fleeing from ruin, before the gift of memory had even entered the world of the living.

Heat lightning flashed an impatient sword in a sky she had rebuilt with a mere thought and a few well-chosen words. The multi-colored light flickered against the diamond sheen of her iridescent flesh and her eyes, now ivory and glowing, cast radiant beams about her body. These shimmered in an aura that enveloped her where she stood, expectant and resplendent, bathed in her own luminescent power.

This.

This was a display of strength intended to threaten and to warn he who dared trespass, to reveal the fulness of her true nature, even as the mystical light refracted back upon and then within her supple body, entering and reentering her like the energy of a star imploding, consuming itself by its own inner fire with mounting urgency.

This.

That her glory might shine all the more terrifying and unmistakable.

Her fingertips brushed gently against her thighs, still stained blue with the blood she had borrowed to win this confrontation, for win it she must. Her hair, as wild and roaring as a waterfall, blew out and around her noble features in a nimbus of writhing, bejeweled air, as if each tress undulated in a tempest of quicksilver wrath. Her gaze met that of her foe, betraying no fear and piercing the thing that had come before her with a contempt far more ancient than the body she now possessed.

When she laughed, brief and mocking, the sounds sprang as arrowheads, razor-sharp and dipped in poison from her lips. She breathed the invigorating scent of her own magnificence, the glowing rings that pierced the nipple of each breast rising and falling with righteous confidence, hurling jagged bolts of hissing, light-weirded energy at the Invader, at the One so bold as to seek the violation of her appointed domain.

And still onward he came, in negation of their mutual agreement, forged in the smoldering caverns of an ancient deceit and held binding through the everlasting trickery and vigilance of the deceived.

She had known this day would come, for it had come already to so many who had lived before her, in other realms where "before" and "after" were strangers to existence, banished as the treacherous exiles they never ceased to become upon infiltrating the Unwelcoming Lands.

Yet, greed finds a way, she mused, standing majestic as a storm-crowned mountain and as tiny as the first flutter of a newborn thought.

He was upon her.

It was she who spoke first—she had to, lest the Defiler deigned to take one more step upon her shore. There was courage in her voice, clean as the cloudless night of forever-Winter, but there, too, was a blood-red thread of pain, spooling around her words. For by the mere coming of his footsteps, her hallowed refuge was immaculate no longer and she would never be able to fully repair the violation or assuage a sorrow of such permanence.

"So you have come," she breathed, the maelstrom of light around her waxing more brilliant with each word. "A Lesser Prince arrives unannounced, inhabiting the body of a dead man. That is a new trick, indeed. Who would have guessed you might think of it?"

His voice repaid lightning with incomparable thunder.

"Do not be facetious, Traitor. You of all should know better than that. Moreover, do not pretend that I have arrived 'unannounced,' for it is quite clear that I was expected, at the very least. It is not every day that you put on such a display, here by this inconvenient river. I daresay you have robbed the poor stars of their every sparkle in order to conjure a scene of this magnitude. Impressive. I will give you that! But it is hardly the first time you have done this, Andrahsha, and it did not prevent me from meeting you face-to-face again, at last."

"No, it did not prevent you. And that is not your face," she responded. "What manner of unspeakable crimes did you commit to gain possession of such a sad excuse for spectral skin, I wonder?"

Now it was his turn to laugh, naked and taunting her with the enormous erection he allowed to surge upward, shuddering and hot, beneath the light of the watchful moon that emerged in the Unknowable Corner.

"I did not have to commit anything 'unspeakable,' as you call it." He reached down with a hairy forearm to wrap a fist around his tumescent weapon. The fist began to stroke, slowly, gleaming in the milky lunar bath. "So little direction is required with beasts like this one. They come up with all of their own ideas, these days. I suppose that is the price one pays for the way matters were established at the start of their evolution. You have heard me speak of it before. As their brains grow more complex, so do their little plots and problems. There are, of course, still a few basic things they can do as often and as well as ever they did. Behold."

"You are an abomination," she whispered, eyes flaming more fiercely than ever. "An execration—just as you have been told by Those with far more authority than I. Feel free to toy with the likes of Earth's offspring all you wish, but do not think you will so easily disgrace me."

"Kneel and put your prideful mouth on it, Witch. Taste my strength and I will reward you with ambrosia."

She spat flame in his direction, scorching the sand before his feet into shattered crystals of glass.

"Have I so offended you already?" He laughed in the face of her anger. "And only just arrived. Do not be taken aback by this demonstration. They have been entertaining themselves in this manner since they came down from the trees. The males like something large and sturdy to hold, since they no longer swing from the branches. It is comforting, if incessant, behavior."

She clenched her fists, cobalt bloodstains on black ice, and glared into the impassive face of the moon, the crimson orb of her own sky. She spoke her Word and summoned it to her cause, rousing it from dusty indifference. The nimbus of light around her body, lithe and poised for retribution, exploded outward in a rage of searing phantasms. The entire island shook as if in the grip of a cataclysm.

He was knocked over in the violence of the upheaval, thrown upon his back across the sand. The river rose up in sudden alarm and dashed against the smooth banks, confused and intimidated. She reined herself in with effort; the encounter was far from over and she could ill-afford to expend all of her strength. Not in one show of force. There were still things to learn from this impostor, this masquerading enemy, before she would know when and how to deliver the decisive blow.

Yet, deep in the vast corridors of her awareness, she knew that the outcome of any pivotal strike was by no means guaranteed. Cunning, such as she could summon, was still a weapon far more indispensable than her own raw magic. A lapse in concentration, a misguided spell, a failure to anticipate whatever else he might hurl her way—any of these could leave her vulnerable to enslavement, and from that wretched fate she had no means of escape, if he were to gain the upper hand.

She stepped closer to his purloined body, to the transfigured form of Shep Daltry; it was now a supine shadow upon the moonwashed sand as the river behind calmed and resumed its watery whispers. The sound of slow, patronizing clapping reached her ears, along with a choking fit of laughter. There was a throttling struggle for breath from the man-thing at her feet. On her island, it was entirely possible to knock the air from the lungs of an Acquisition—even one that had been fully possessed by a Power as formidable as the foe she now faced.

The clapping echoed in the silence of the beachside grove. Grating, stilted laughter made her unblemished countenance burn with disappointment. The first salvo had not been as damaging as she had hoped. Still, she threw up every shuttering wall in her mind to prevent any semblance of doubt or fear from being detected by her nemesis. The contest was not finished.

"Well done, with the tectonic shift, my Lady," sputtered the interloper, raising himself up, slow and wary. "Even so, I suspect that this admirable jolt constituted the best effort of which you were capable. Doubtless you had ambitious plans for such a shot across my prow, but it wasn't nearly good enough. Allow me to prove this."

With a harrowing snarl that echoed into the night-shrouded orchards beyond, He leapt up and upon her with the agility of a mighty cat, undeterred by the defensive bursts of light that streamed from every pore of her flesh and whipped around him in burning tongues of flame that singed and encircled them both as he grabbed her. He clutched her close to him, as if to extinguish every hint of radiance and then he flew with such force that she was carried far through the air, trapped in the constricting arms until he landed on top of her in the grass beneath the drooping boughs of a tree.

She fought anew, her mind lashing out wildly with fire and revulsion as he pinned her to the earth in her own holy place, gloating over the victory. She refused to cry out, even as his powerful legs moved brutally to spread her own apart in the fertile grove and she felt the swift hardening of the man-body's probing organ. He was seeking to pierce her, until all magic within was overtaken and destroyed. He wished to conquer her as surely as he had conquered the mortal soul that once occupied the human form of all its light and life.

So this is his plan. A rape. I should have expected something so vile.

But even as the fire within her was smothered by the coming assault and the writhing confrontation of their bodies on the ground, she knew that it was he, and not she, who had made the fatal miscalculation.

Her hair, glorious as any precious metal spun by the wheel of time across untold worlds and softened in the cool of moonlight, became caked with soil and leaves. It was then that she screamed, but hers was no cry of fear; it was a battle-cry, a wail of subversive declaration. The violence of his lust-craft had nearly found its target, pressing to cleave the source of her power in a flood that would drown all that she was, and all the world she had so painstakingly fashioned. He paused to revel in the endlessness of her scream, mistaking it as a plea for mercy. Covering her, smothering the light of her protector moon, he stared into her face, astonished.

"Anguish," he whispered, running a vile hand through her incandescent mane, splayed out in the mash of orchard soil around her head. Grabbing a fistful, he prepared to tear it from her scalp in triumph. "You offer me anguish, an incomparable delicacy at this, your last moment before the long and sleepless exile. Oh, how I have desired to taste your anguish, Andrahsha, through mazes of time that only the greatest among us are allowed to navigate, through forgotten mirrors beyond knowledge, where I have pursued you for ages. Through rock and fire and water and emptiness I have set my mind upon you, to take what is rightfully my own and most pleasing to my sight." He pressed against her; her world held its breath. "I will take what is most satisfying to the hunger over which I, and I alone, have been given dominion. And your anguish shall be the greatest prize captured in all the Shadowed Places of Worlds and Worlds Within."

He arched the muscled hips and buttocks of Shep Daltry's body to unleash the plunge that would uncreate her world, absorbing its light and purpose into the abyss of darkness that was himself.

But arrogance had been his undoing in the past; his delight in one final mockery had given her the chance she needed to conjure an escape. Behold! Already the gnarled limbs of the nearby trees in her orchard groaned their way to a more supple form of life, lowering themselves at her call like claws and tentacles in the stricken starshine. With a great heave, they snatched him violently away from her before his work of Obliteration had been achieved.

My fair ones! My orchard! My faithful and potent!

She scrambled to her feet from the dirt and debris beneath him as her minions tightened their coils and lifted the aggressor high. The thudding sound of ripe plums falling and bursting upon the ground could be heard throughout the island, each a new star exploding to life in her galaxy and empowering the spell. Slithering and creaking and rife with fury, the powerful limbs snaked about her oppressor's torso and sent their very narrowest tips to run rings around the mouth that had offered such brag and abuse to She Who commanded the Light of the Isle!

He glared at her from the unyielding clutches of the sinewy, slithering tree-limbs, suspended above the glade against a new backdrop of meteors blazing across her firmament. This was the flash of the aurora she had transferred from her own body to the vault of the universe; it mirrored her triumph and reflected it back in time and forward into infinity.

"Welcome to the Orchard of Heaven's Dream-Thief," she whispered, circling slowly beneath him as his eyes betrayed the same mixture of unending malice, rage, and haughty astonishment she had seen from him before, in other places and in other times.

"At least, this is one of my orchards," she added, gesturing to the army of watchful, menacing trees. In the ethereal haze of night descending they all seemed to have moved closer, to have gathered in an encroaching circle, each one lending its power and resolve to the next until their collective wrath accumulated in the constricting limbs. The Destroyer was trapped in their hallowed midst. Trapped, indeed.

"This is the grove over which I have been given dominion, and it has journeyed with me across the ages, and I have kept it hidden from you, even here," she said, her frail voice tiny and lost amid the murmur of cold wind that passed suddenly through the orchard. She was weakened, considerably, for she had gambled all, but now that she had him, there was no need for any further display of strength or show of bravery. No more need for any illusion of invincibility.

They each knew what the other could and could not do, now that the battle was effectively finished. There were some Laws that could not be evaded, after all. The only question that remained concerned the exact nature of his expulsion, the means of it. Delicate matters of this sort required great caution, but in this case improvisation was just as vital. Her orchard, stalwart as it was, could not restrain him until the dawn, even if the dawn was hers to control.

She wrapped her graceful black arms around herself and the tree limbs coiled tighter around the squirming, spectral body of Shep Daltry, particularly the network of branches that coiled around his mouth. It would not be wise to let him utter so much as a word. Not again.

"There are several ways in which I could dispose of you," she said, raking soil from her hair and moving deeper beneath the bower of a nearby tree. "Each of these ways is as effective as the next, and we both know that whatever I do will only rid my domain of this husk you've chosen to occupy in your insolence. I don't know how or where or from whom you stole this body and spirit, but I had seen it coming. I know why you did it and I possess enough imagination to envision the trail of disaster you left behind after all had been taken. And you dare to come here, showing off its parts."

His eyes glinted, fiendish and yet full of laughter, still. *As if you care for these wretched but useful beings any more than I do,* those eyes seemed to say, and the message was not mistaken or denied.

"No, I do not particularly care for them," she admitted. "But that is of no consequence, and you know as well that the ways in which we care or do not care for anything shall always be irreconcilable. Oh, this is the most clever ruse you have attempted since I have settled here, and the first time you have crossed the river with success. Alas, I cannot destroy you, not here and now as I'd like."

She stepped forward again into a panel of scarlet moonlight and glowered at him. He ceased to struggle, knowing it was useless.

"Yes, I saw you approach. It was necessary for me to call in a few favors from some of our more seldom-consulted associates. I was forced to do a number of … unpleasant things in order to accrue the strength to stop you this time. But, now that I know you're trying to ghostride your way around the Law, I'll be certain to prevent any future attempts. You'd be well-advised not to employ such methods henceforth. Now, however, it is time for you to leave, such as you are."

Gliding back for an instant into the shadows, she reached among the sprawl of tree-branches and pulled the head of Larkspur, her companion, down into the sheen of moon-glow. By its horns, she held aloft the lifeless and still-dripping skull, its clouded eyes bulging and jaw slack.

"This is, or was, my friend and servant here on the lonely isle. Someone I discovered lurking on the distant shore, long ago, desperate for shelter and hungry. So hungry. I gave him leave to cross over and he proved a most loyal helpmate since. Even unto his death, as you can see. His blood saturated the ground beneath the trees of this orchard, empowering the pinions that clutch you now. I introduce you not because I am proud of what I had to do—there was no other way to construct the spell—but to illustrate the fact that, while you and I are very much alike, our methods are different. And so shall be our destinies, I expect, if I can think of a plan to outwit you. One that will be as effective as your attempt against me on this night."

She lifted the skull higher.

"Larkspur gave his blood to me at need, without question or qualm. That dead-man you've crawled into," she added, nodding at the imprisoned figure of Shep Daltry, "that is something you took by wickedness and deceit. Something you summoned to yourself from the world of animals. I know your handiwork. I even expect you'll reconstitute your lusty fellow on the other side."

She gestured with a finger, beckoning another tree limb to lower itself, as fluid as a serpent uncoiling.

"We choose our chief companions for good reasons, you and I, and cannot bear to be parted from them for too long a time, once we become attached."

The limb she had coaxed down from the trunk of the tree dug a swift and deep hole in the pungent soil near her feet and then slithered back up to its place near the crown of leaves above. She dropped Larkspur's head into the hole and knelt to bury it with her own hands, muttering Words of Refreshment and Revival as the enemy watched her, baleful and impious. She patted the ground when finished, brushed the dirt from her hands and stood up to face him again.

"The soil on my island is fertile and potent. The waters of my river are rich with life-giving magic because I have made them so. In the time it takes for the sun to rise and set once more, Larkspur will grow up from this sacred ground and I will harvest him, alive and stronger than ever he was. It is he who does my bidding and tends to the parameters of my place, scouting for signs of trespass. He won't come back to me as something so unseemly as your throat-cut shell, either. I will pluck him from this spot as a living, breathing fruit of the island, and he shall be rewarded for his devotion. I daresay you will not have as much success with your dead-man, but your employees have never concerned me one way or another."

She laughed in the ominous sanctity of her island, her river, her orchard, her world.

"Now, get thee gone to places far more suited to a reprobate of your pedigree and splendor."

She glanced overhead, deep into the glistening aurora, and breathed deeply of its power, which was one and the same with her own. Then she exhaled and gave the command to the undulating coils of the trees, and to their host half-bent toward the orchard floor.

"Ye that hold him, uproot yourselves and carry him swift across the river, to the other bank. There destroy him and purge yourselves in flame!"

And the trees, with a deafening crack that reverberated unto the very edges of the moon, took themselves up into the night and obeyed.

A WELCOME OF BIRCH

"Mr. Slater? Mr. Horace Slater?"

"Miss Brody? It could only be you. Why, you're as pretty as a picture."

"Well, that's very nice of you to say. Please, call me Schuyler."

They shook hands before the stand of white birch trees. Leaves rattled in the thermal layers of an early Autumn heatwave. Indian Summer. Nothing new. The last few locusts of the season whined in the scrub or basked atop the majestic and broken archway, dry and dusty from an almost rainless season. The lantern atop the iron post crowned their acquaintance.

"Lovely to meet you, Schuyler."

"Same here. Gosh, I have to say I wasn't expecting you to be waiting for me by the roadside like this, right at the entrance. My word, look at that thing. This archway. Just like you described. I mean, I live only fifty miles away but I never knew there was such a ... *thing* as this around. What in the world kind of building used to be all the way out on a lost backroad like this one? By the way, I barely found this turnoff once I left the interstate." She gazed up again in wonder at the arch. It seemed to stare back, though not with wonder. "Gee, there must have been a huge structure attached if this is all that's left of it."

"Oh, this is just an architectural piece, an art piece, if you will. One that the owner took a liking to, once upon a time. Had it transported here, brick by brick, to mark the entry."

"The owner?"

"Of Wistwood, Schuyler."

"Wistwood has an owner? It doesn't even have a place on the map. Or in my GPS system."

She laughed. Horace did not.

"Every town has an owner of some sort, young lady. Someone or something that pulls all the various strings together and keeps it standing alive. Might be nothing more than the mere spirit of friendship that 'owns' a town."

"Hmm. Never did think of it quite that way, Mr. Slater."

"Uh-uh!" A gloved finger was wagged amiably before her nose. "Fair is fair. You must call me Horace."

"Of course. Horace. Well, one thing's for sure. If you hadn't met me out here, I might've taken one look at that arch, pretty as it is, and turned right around for home. Huh. Where are we? Is there really a little town back in that woods?"

"Most assuredly! A little unincorporated community, Schuyler. As I said during our phone chat. But a community well on its way. Yes, indeed. Well on its way. You'll notice the fine concrete paving of the drive into Wistwood. Brand new and smooth as silk."

A surface of wide white roadway snaked and vanished into the modest forest grove.

"Well, yes, it looks lovely. I'm just, frankly, a little surprised and a little shaken up. Did you see that dust-storm that passed through about five minutes ago? I had to stop the car. I mean, the sand was just stinging against the windows. Couldn't see a thing until it passed and then—poof! Here I was at this gate thing. And you're here, too. Here, like that lantern-post. It's not like we never have the occasional dust storm crop-up, but it was a little disconcerting. Unfamiliar area and all. My word, you must've been caught in it yourself. Are you okay?"

"Oh, I'm a hardy old gentleman. Dust devils don't slow me down. I even walked all the way out to the road to meet you. With the help of my trusty cane, of course. It's such a lovely day, after all."

"Well, that is so nice of you, Horace. To do that. Chivalry lives."

"Yes it does, young lady. And I am its face for the moment. Now, you are on time, which is much appreciated, and there's an antique shop on Main Street waiting for your perusal."

"I cannot wait to see it."

"Excellent. Your enthusiasm will not go unrewarded, I guarantee. Shall we?"

"Sure. Um ... you walked all this way to the road? Should I ..."

"I was hoping you'd give an old man a lift back into town. It's only a quarter mile, just beyond that line of elms, where the drive first begins to disappear."

There's no one else and nothing around here. Get back in your car and get away, girl! Don't let this old Santa Claus person into your car. Are you crazy?

"And I should tell you, Schuyler, that I do have two other interested parties coming to look at the shop in early evening, after they get off work. Most interested parties, like yourself. I want you to have enough time to take a good, leisurely look at the store and the apartment above and all the wonderful stock, but time constraints could interfere if we linger."

Time, Times, and half a Time.

Her world emptied of recognition. It no longer remembered what it was.

"Well, what are we waiting for, Horace? Come on around, hop in the old Mercedes, and lead the way. I aim to be the most interested party you ever meet."

Horace smiled. The birch trees were still, suddenly, still to the last sun-reddened leaf. Waiting. Knowing.

"Then, we're off!"

TO QUENCH A FIERY THIRST

Brask's first night in the cabin had been restless. When he got home he drank a six-pack of beer on the front steps, gazing at stars above the surrounding colosseum of oaks, just to put the finishing touch on a weird, wonderful, and disorienting day. The silence was more intoxicating than the drink. The bed felt great when he turned in, but he had tossed and turned for hours. Too much to drink? Sometimes that happened to him. Scattered dreams of Jess. The van plunging over some cliffside. An iron gate occupied by white doves.

Definitely too much to drink. And too much sensory stimulation at Margie's.

Caught by the dull, unflattering light of morning, he spent twenty minutes in the shower, scrubbing. Heaven reclaimed him. Fresh coffee and clean clothes hauled in from the van helped matters even more. He chuckled at some crows bickering in the driveway. Finally he charged his cell phone, though there was still no reception whatsoever. WiFi wasn't working, either. Horace would see to that. Then it took ten minutes for the damned van to start. He turned it off and toyed with the engine for half an hour.

By noon his head was aching and the quiet had started to give him the creeps.

You need a week or two to get used to this, man. No more interstate traffic-noise to lull you into catatonia.

Around three he thought about heading into Carmel up the coast just for an internet connection and some more substantial supplies. Then he thought better of it. If the van was acting up again, the last thing he needed was to get stranded somewhere on the Pacific Coast Highway. He drank the rest of the remaining six-pack.

At four he decided to risk a drive as far as Margie's Bar & Grill.

What the hell? It's only my second day in town. Acclimate slowly. And with some more hair of the dog. You deserve it. You've earned it.

This time the van turned over on the first attempt. *Sweet.*

Margie's place was already hopping when he got there. Not bad for a Wednesday afternoon. And there was the Ringmaster herself, taming the local lions with a cleaning rag slung over one shoulder, pouring beer for a skinny guy with slick, olive-colored skin who had sidled up to the bar. Scatterbrained Carlee was bouncing from table to table on the outdoor deck.

"Here you go, Theo," said Margie, sliding the sudsy pilsner across the polished oak. "You want me to put that on a tab?"

"Please, Margie," said the wan fellow, his hands trembling as he lifted the glass to his lips.

Margie gave Brask a friendly wink as he resumed his place on one of the stools. "Welcome back, handsome! Missed me that much already, huh? I'll be right with ya. Gotta grab some food from the kitchen. Hang on."

Brask watched the first man, Theo, sipping his beer gratefully. He had a boxer's face. Sharp and chipped and dominated by light brown eyes that were artless and unconcerned. The nose was hooked and lumpen. After a moment the guy wandered over to a small table next to a potted ficus plant. Brask tried not to make it obvious, but watched him sit down, bedraggled and somewhat depressed-looking in a grey suit crawling with wrinkles. The fabric clashed horribly with his sallow flesh. Theo slurped self-consciously at the top of the beer glass, his nose sunk in the foam, and seemed to shrink himself into the corner seat, as if he were beginning to fade into the wallpaper behind him, more than happy to vanish forever into that sharp angle where one wall meets another and one direction disappears into the next.

Another oddball local. This place attracts them. Welcome to the club.

Upon further, discreet inspection, Theo gave Brask the impression of a three-year old stuck in the body of a grown man who had seen and endured far too much in one lifetime. There was an air of unfamiliarity with his own space, with his own wiry physicality. The guy's frame was a reactionary network of little tics and twitches, elbows shifting, bony knees scraping one against each other, the corners of his mouth jerking from smile to frown, smile to frown. Brask could practically see the tow-headed kid that once was, poking up out of some threadbare adult suit he had found in the dark of a secret closet and tried-on for fun, only to find himself utterly lost in the creases and disappointed with the dress-up adventure.

What to do? What to do? This isn't nearly as much fun as I thought it would be.

"That's Theo Vasiliki," whispered Margie out of the corner of her mouth as she returned from the kitchen. Above, Patsy Cline launched into yet another clarion yo-del on the sound system. Brask was jolted from his drowsy, over-the-shoulder con-templation. "Looks a little bit dazed, doesn't he? Adrift at sea without a navigation system?" She leaned close. "Maybe he even looks a little punch drunk."

"I have to admit. He reminded me of a boxer when I first came in. A light-weight. Banty rooster. You know, one of the Golden Gloves types who's suffered way more TKOs than he's delivered in his day? Scrappy to the end, though."

Marge nodded admiringly. "See that?" she said with a sharp toss of her plump chin toward Walt, poised in his usual seat. "Wistwood's new, soon-to-be-famous author is a man of uncanny intuition. You've got a good eye for people, Brask. Must be a handy thing in your line of work."

"What? You mean that guy really *is* a boxer?"

"Close enough." Margie shrugged with one shoulder and set upon the cor-ner of her beer cooler with the omnipresent rag. "Theo was actually a carnival wrestler back in his home country. Romania. Or was it Hungary? Maybe Serbia. Damned if I can remember. Anyhow, that's how he made his living in the days when carnivals over there would let men buy chances to fight the sideshow freak or geek or whatever they called them. Theo was a lot stronger than he looks, to hear him tell it, and he made and saved enough money pinning the local pigeons to the mat until he could move to the States. Now he's got himself a little shop a couple of miles into the hills. One hell of a carpenter."

She tapped her reddened hand proudly on the bar.

"He put this bar in for me by himself and handled almost all the com-plicated renovations when I gutted the downstairs and turned the place into a restaurant. I think his years in the ring have left him a little slow on the uptake, if you know what I mean, but if you catch him sober with a saw and plane, his hands are as steady as time ticking away on the face of a clock."

"Someone like me would be hard pressed to tell," said Brask. "But I worked construction for years. Met a lot of guys who drank everything they made and managed amazing things the day after. Right now he looks like he's gonna twitch out of his skin any second."

"Oh, Theo just needs something to focus on with intensity. Like boards. Or that beer in his hand. That's what I think. He came to Wistwood when too many people started buying their cabinetry ready-made at chain stores and the economy out there collapsed for the twentieth time in ten years."

"Then I know exactly how Theo feels," muttered Brask. "Say, how about one of those Blue Moons before I start shaking too?"

"Coming up, doll. So how was your first night in the new place? Sleep like a baby or what?"

"Something like that. And thanks again, by the way, for the comped tab."

"No worries," said Margie, placing the mug front and center before Brask. "That was my pleasure. And first nights in a new town are never easy, but you did a great job getting acquainted in here yesterday. Everybody liked you."

"Nice to hear, though I'm not so sure about Mr. Donovan in the store across the street. I didn't mention it last night, but I went in there for a few supplies before coming in here. It was … an experience, to put it mildly. What's that guy's story, if you don't mind me asking? I can only imagine the kind of far-out scenario that brought him to this neck of the woods. Lucky for me I won't have to rely upon my 'uncanny intuition,' seeing as you've got the scoop on every single one of the locals, the new and the not-so-new."

"Ha! In Donovan's case, your guess would be as good as mine. He was here before the rest of us arrived, even before Walt, who was one of the first three or four people to settle in Wistwood. Ain't that right, Walt?"

"Right as rain, Margie. Right as rain. Donovan had that store already set up when I got here and it hasn't changed a whit since then, right down to the cobwebs and dead bugs in the windows. I think those came with the place, however he came about it himself."

"Wouldn't be surprised," said Margie, eyeing the store across the street, now closed, melding with the deepening afternoon shadows beyond the massive front window of her restaurant. "Donovan came with the territory, just like old Horace. Or something like him, anyway. He's a personal friend of the big man, Mr. P. The owner. The Landlord."

"Ah, so you know his name, too. Well, why shouldn't you? Horace told me yesterday. Palmarah. Sounds foreign. At first I thought Horace was speaking of a Mr. Paul Mara."

"Well, everyone around just calls him 'the Landlord.' Short and simple."

"And what do you know about him?"

"Not a whole lot, to tell you the truth. I've met him, of course. Socially. The ones that do know him well—Horace and Donovan, for example—are pretty tight-lipped about him, and about their own stories, with or without him. I mean, Horace is the nicest gent you'd ever want to meet, but I don't know a thing about his past. Learned awhile back that it was pointless to ask, so I don't even bother. As for Donovan, I can't admit to a whole lot of interest in that department, to be honest. I only know him well enough to say, 'Good morning' or 'Good night' if I see him opening up his shop across the way or closing it down. He never comes in here. Not even once. One thing about Donovan and that store of his, though: he always manages to come up with what folks need, one way or another."

"Yeah? Well, no offense to him or his store, but I like my selection a bit more diverse and a lot less dusty. Occasional trips to the Safeway up in Carmel won't be too much of a burden, once I get used to the new surroundings and once I get my van running reliably again. Hell, I expect I'll probably look forward to a big grocery run once a month. Don't want cabin fever to get the best of me, right?"

"Ah, you'll get used to old Donovan," said Margie, as if she hadn't heard a word about Carmel or potential cabin fever. "Everybody gets used to him, eventually."

"I'm not everybody," said Brask, tempering the ballsy assertion with a friendly wink of his own at Margie over the top of his beer mug. "But enough about him, especially if there's no incriminating biography to keep us on the edge of our seats. Let's see what you can manage to get out of me on my second night of revelry at the bar."

Margie laughed, looking more clownish than ever with her mane of impeccably immobile red hair, shellacked and feathered to within an inch of its life.

"You worry too much about what other people in this world think about you, Brask. I can see that clear as day."

Brask splayed his fingers philosophically in her direction. "Hey, I don't like being that way any more than the next guy, if I'm even that way at all. But I've learned that only the very rich or the very crazy can get away with not giving a shit about what others think. I consider it one of the more dismal facts of collective human existence, though I suppose there's a good reason things operate that way."

"Hear, hear!" croaked Walt, stabbing a mangled index finger righteously toward the glass-rack above his head.

"Perceptions are not an indispensable part of life, at least not here in Wistwood," added Margie. "Nobody around here lies awake at night, fretful about whether or not they're going to be liked or accepted or any of that garbage."

"People who come here are here because they really *belong* here, Brask," said Walt. "And if they really belong here, then the thoughts of others—good or bad—don't mean a damned thing in the end."

"He's right about that, you know." Margie tossed the rag from her shoulder into the stainless steel sink. A fountain of soapy water leapt up to soak the edge of her knitted sweater. "Damn. Look at that. What a klutz, huh? Anyhow, when it comes to the big guy, the Landlord, he's very generous with everyone who ends up being welcomed into his territory."

"His 'territory'?" Brask arched a brow. "What is he, a pit bull?"

"You know what I mean."

"I guess. So he really does own all of the land hereabouts?"

"He does. Now, we have what you might call 'life estates' for the property here, if we believe we've found our personal Shangri-Las and aim to pitch our tents for the long-term, but everything belongs to Mr. P. It's all his. And some parts of it are more *his* than other parts, which means that his private property is totally private. The hills around the Manor House—that isn't a place to go snooping around, by the way. Not without an invitation, which will be forthcoming, as you've been told. Not saying you're the type to snoop, Brask, but it never hurts to pass on useful information. And, let's face it, you've got so much fabulous room now, what with the acreage down by the Kimbertons' place. I mean, *your* place. Gosh, I'm gonna have to get used to saying that. The Adams place!"

Brask's eyes felt heavy. The room seemed warmer than last night. Maybe the heat from the little fireplace was getting to him, but he looked and saw only a smattering of bright coals pulsating beneath the grate. Patsy Cline had finished her echo-laden number from the murky heaven near the ceiling, shrouded in steam that had wafted out of the kitchen where dishes were being washed. He had the strange urge to put his head down on the bar and take a nap, and had to shake his head a few times to dispel the weary wave.

"Getting a little buzzed, Brask?"

"Not yet. At least I don't think so. Just beat. After yesterday's big adventure. Everything happened so quickly, which is good. Don't get me wrong. I think I need a few days to adjust, that's all. By the way, how's your waitress doing? She looks a little more upright this evening."

Marge fished around in the sink for her rag, immersed up to her elbow in sanitizer and suds.

"Carlee's not such a shambles tonight. She's feeling calmer now she knows she's going to get a do-over on her interview with the Big Guy. As you may recall from last night, her first one didn't go so well. But I think she'll be ready this time."

"Hold on. You've lost me again. Or maybe I missed something when Horace and I were hashing out the details of the lease. I know we were just starting to get into it last night before I left, but what, exactly, is the whole purpose of this interview thing?"

"Nothing for you to worry about yet, hon." Margie patted the stack of beverage coasters piled in front of Brask with swift but dismissive fingers. "An interview is just a chance to have a little sit-down with Mr. P up at his place. Gives him an opportunity to get to know everybody face-to-face. To rub elbows with people who've been lucky enough to find a spot in this wonderful community." She flung an arm outward, as if embracing the panorama of her own certainty. "An interview with Mr. P is considered an honor, around here."

"So he's eccentric, too," said Brask. "That's what I'm sensing."

"Most of your very powerful and important people *are* that way," affirmed Margie with Gospel conviction. Her eyes were as pale as ash on the surface of the moon, but yellowish streaks in her irises seemed to flicker and gleam in a glow from the track lighting over the bar. "He travels quite a bit, too. In fact, Mr. P only just got back into town again after—Gosh. How long has it been, Walt?— six or seven months away?"

Walt shrugged but offered nothing in the way of reply except for a muffled grunt.

"What's his background?" said Brask. "Big business of some kind, I presume. Old money? Anybody who owns so much choice real estate in this part of the country must've invented the damned wheel."

"He's always had a lot of irons in the fire, from what I gather," said Margie.

"That's nice and evasive. But don't worry. Even if he wants to size me up with some sort of interview, I don't expect to get into *his* business. I won't become his best buddy, or be invited over for drinks on a regular basis. If this is some sort of welcome wagon ritual the local squire puts on for newcomers, then far be it from me to swim against the tide. I'll be glad to meet him."

"Individuals of immense wealth and power are often reticent to addle the minds of others with the complexity of their affairs," Walt interjected, suddenly pensive, his head tilted with weary resignation against an arthritic palm. "The Landlord likes a more old-fashioned, one-on-one approach with residents of Wistwood. Likes to see what sort of personality you've got and, if you're up for it, show you a bit of his own."

"Like I said, I won't mind meeting him. Believe me, it'll be a pleasure to thank him personally. I really needed that cabin over the hill, let me tell you."

"We know," said Margie.

"What?"

"What I mean is, you have that kind of relieved look about you, Brask. I've seen it before. That's all. It's no judgment on you, honey, and I'll not ask you another thing, I promise. That's not my style. Is it, Walt?"

"No, Ma'am."

Brask frowned and ran a finger along the cool rim of his mug, contemplating. "I have a feeling people just tell you everything without having to be asked, Margie. And I mean that as a compliment. You're a sweetheart."

"Now that's what I call getting off on the right foot." Margie reached for Brask's empty mug. "You're going to have to pay for these tonight, though. A lady can only afford so much charity. But you did leave an egregious tip, I have to admit."

"I would have paid last night, if you'd let me. You don't know how much it means to me, to make a few friends so soon. To be treated with immediate kindness."

A whisper of hollow days coursed through Brask's spirit in that moment, laced with the delicate sting of eyes cast deliberately aside, swift and unwilling to acknowledge, seeing yet dismissive to the point of banishment, disintegration.

I'm alive! I exist! Flesh and blood, like you. Do not uncreate me. I will be clean tomorrow.

Overwhelming came the arid accumulation of judgments made by idle minds in passing cars as he stood in a roadside parking lot with others, waiting to get a sandwich and a cup of soup from the Salvation Army truck. Wheels sped by but the exhaled breath of disdain lingered, gathering and transforming indifference into dull arrows, one after another, each unleashed to fly. Fly and strike. Fly and strike. Unleashed to pierce, slow and grinding, between the shoulders.

I had the mark. No home. No place in the world of people. The mark. Eyes are arrows. Arrows must find their mark. I am extinguished.

"Everything okay, Brask-honey? You looked a little pale for a second, there."

"Yeah. I'm fine. I … just went off into a brain-fry. I was thinking. I meant what I said, though. It's something special to feel like I have friends again. Fast friends. Or new friends. Whatever."

"Darling, of course you do," said Margie. "You fit right in. I knew it from the moment I met you yesterday."

Brask was embarrassed, now. He hoped a gulp of the cold beer would erase the blush blossoming across his cheekbones.

"Thanks, Margie. Anyhow, cash on the bar is my policy from now on."

"Hear all that, Walt? Watch and learn. You could've gone far with me if you'd poured that kind of sugar in my bowl."

"Plain old vinegar worked well enough on you for my purposes," grumbled Walt.

"You only think it did."

"So, when will I get a chance to meet the Big Kahuna for my interview?" Brask finished the beer in two more passes. He would be sloshing his way back to the cabin, maybe on foot at this rate.

"Who knows, Honey? Whenever he can squeeze you in. You'll get an official invitation well in advance. Don't worry about that. Like I said, Carlee's scheduled for a second time next week. And transient rock idol Lleyton Grayle is going up to the manse in a couple of days, I gather. Provided Neetha doesn't drag him out of town. Trust me, Brask. From top to bottom, everybody will be absolutely taken with you, especially since you're going to be a famous writer and all."

Brask wagged a friendly finger. "You keep saying that, Margie, but I never mentioned fame as playing any role in my writing. It's not even a corollary of my work."

"But don't you *want* to become famous?" said Walt, as if the idea of not desiring fame were blasphemous. "Seems to me a writer who works hard to hone his craft and stick his neck out, put his work and his words out there on the chopping block, might want to be sure his stuff got read and appreciated by as many people as possible."

"Oh, I want all of that," Brask insisted. "But fame, at least as it crawls around today, is a different animal entirely. A rabid, revolting animal. Warped. Dangerous, even. Nah. That doesn't have to be part of the package, at least not for me. Shit. These days, fame is the venereal disease you catch and then ought to get rid of after making it, artistically speaking. After the whole climax that comes with being embraced by the public and your peers, after being given a chance."

"Don't know as I've ever heard it put quite that way before," said Margie. "But then again, I don't know squat about the publishing world and never sat down and really talked to anyone about it like this before, either, you know?"

"Yeah, well, I'm just pontificating, as usual. It's the beer. But trust me when I tell you that fame is nothing. I know I'm talking from the outside, but at least fame is not what it used to be, if it ever really was anything different from what it is today, and that's debatable. Jesus, everybody's famous now. Everybody! You all know that. I mean, you see it every day. Online. On TV." He looked around the bar for the requisite big screen. There wasn't one. Only Patsy Cline overhead and the low murmur of the dining customers entertaining themselves and each other could be heard below. Odd. He felt a cold finger, just a faint touch, brief and quivering at the base of his spine. "The sickness is all over the internet," he went on. "It's in every frigging cup of coffee you drink these days. Common. Vulgar. That's what fame is."

"You take this pretty seriously, don't you, son?" said Walt.

"Not at all. That's my point. When fame is being lavished upon or enjoyed by those without any merit beyond the mere fact that they are on some form of public display, then fame ceases to deserve general respect or awe. At least in my opinion. I think it's an anomaly, anyhow. I'll have another Blue Moon, please, Margie. Fame. Hell. It's a recent and relative societal dysfunction. An illusion. God, talk about how twisted our perceptions are and why we worry so much about what others think of us! I ought to write a book about the history of fame, the psychology of it all, and how it ended up being as destructive and as vile as a plague."

"Pah! You won't sell many books with that mindset," Walt chortled. "I don't recall ever hearing about Zane Grey bitching and moaning when it came to fame. Of course, I wouldn't be able to pick Zane Grey out of a line-up with my extra-strength lenses on, but I think you get my point. To my mind, you just read the words and know the name of the guy who wrote them, when it comes to books. And that's if the book is worth a read in the first place. We didn't care too much about faces, in my day, not when good stories were involved."

"Oh, it's all about faces now, I can assure you," sneered Brask, gulping his refilled beer. His buzz was returning faster than he had expected. He didn't want to get smashed, by any means, but he did want to float contentedly through conversation with these new pals and sleep without a hitch when he got back to the cabin. Driving wouldn't be a problem.

"You know what I always used to think?" said Margie.

"No, but I expect you're gonna tell us," Walt replied without missing a beat.

"I used to think—and it's a funny little thought, really—that the writers and so forth were the ones who really *had* to write books and movie scripts and TV shows and columns for newspapers and all that because they were too homely to make it in front of the camera or on the magazine pages."

"Are you implying that my tribe of aesthetic vagabonds and philosophical artisans is an inherently ugly tribe, Marge?"

"No, Brask. Not at all. It's just a thought I used to have. Besides, you prove that theory wrong yourself. Why, you could've played in any of those old James Dean movies. Yeah, that's it. You have that handsome rebel look the girls would go a bit wild over, back when I was one of the girls. Of course, James Dean was even a ways before my time. You're not quite as clean shaven as he was, of course. You've got that scruff. But the danger is there, alright."

"Much obliged, Margie. Ringer for James Dean. Imagine that. Looks like I'll be buying *you* a beer before the night is through, if you keep up with that kind of bull."

"No, I meant it. Don't you think he's got a hint of James Dean in his face, Walt?"

"Oh, don't ask me that shit, Margie. I couldn't tell James Dean from Jimmy Dickens." Walt waved his gnarled fingers in dismissal.

"Before you two get carried away, let me just reiterate that I'll be happy if my work is read and enjoyed by enough people to let me make a living at the thing I'm good at. Pardon the poor sentence structure, of course. I mean, I liked being a contractor, having my own outfit for awhile. Made good money. But the thing I love to do the most, and the thing I've always dreamed about doing, is writing. Since my wife passed away a few years ago, I've come to learn what's truly valuable in this world and what isn't. I've learned it in ways I never thought I'd have the objectivity to grasp when I was a bit younger."

"A sure sign of maturity," said Margie, thin lips pursed and carrot-topped head nodding in matronly approval. "And I'm sorry to hear about your wife. You're very young to go through a loss like that."

"Thanks, Margie. I didn't mean to get all morbid and preachy, sitting here tonight. Fact is, I used to kid myself thinking I even knew what it meant to be objective or subjective about the things that can happen to a person in life. But I learned the difference between the two, and I learned it the hard way. I'm glad I did, because one of the scariest things I learned is that some people never learn at all, even as hard as they get hit with the lessons."

"I'll drink to that," said Margie, and she did so, quickly pouring a shot of tequila for herself and downing it with a flourish. "And now I'm going to let you boys relax and contemplate the philosophical implications of what's been said. Or you can talk about the price of coffee. I have to get ready for the dinner rush."

Outside, the sun had set behind the western hills, bathing the forest treetops in a crimson sheen. People were streaming into the restaurant.

None of them knew what was coming.

The eastern sky, however, had its own ideas.

SCATTERSHOT

The glade among the hills behind the manor house was aboil with angry light despite the dusk. Shep Daltry was there, yet he was not. Not entirely.

"That was one hell of a first job," he said to the tempest of wrathful, swirling air. "If that's what the rest of my duties are going to be like, I may not be the man you've been looking for. Goddamn it, I don't even have a body anymore. What do you call this stuff I'm made out of?"

You might call it ectoplasm. But it has no name. It needs no name. And unfortunately for you, Servant, it is too late to resign from your duties.

"I figured as much."

Do not despair. All the promises made unto you shall be kept. Circumstances shall improve very soon and very much to your liking.

"What about her? Her of that island. The black and blue colored bitch. Seems she can put you to trouble. I don't fancy meeting her again."

Leave her to me. That is no longer your concern. Remember that you are a vessel.

"Yeah. You vesseled me right into her."

I was testing her reserves.

"Seems she's got a lot of them."

Not so many as she thinks. After all, I was able to get to her, with your unique assistance. That is something I have not been able to do for Time, Times, and half a Time.

"You said I would be a master of people, beyond my wildest dreams. She ain't no person."

Not a human person, but a person all the same.

"Well, I didn't sign up to be caught in the middle of a war between whatever you are and whatever she is."

You will do as I command and be amply rewarded. But forget her, at least for now. Inroads have been made and the first pleasure to be awarded for work well-done is before you.

"Pleasure? I can't feel *anything* anymore! I don't feel alive."

That is because you are not. But this will soon change, to a degree. The final portion of your orientation as a new employee awaits.

"Will I like it?"

Very.

"Well okay, then."

BOY MEETS SKY

The sound of the cataclysm struck like a thunderbolt that shook the entire building from its foundations to the rooftop, shattering the great front window and a few long-stem wineglasses in the rack above Margie's bar. The rest began to shiver like rattling bones.

"What in the hell was that?" yelled Brask, gripping the bar until his knuckles were white. His beer tipped over in front of him and swept the little pile of beverage coasters away in a flood toward the stainless steel sink that Margie herself had nearly fallen into. The tremor that followed the first deafening boom had sent her backward against the liquor display shelves. A bottle of Galliano fell like a neon missile to the rubber mats beneath her feet. Then she had reeled forward, banging her knees against the metal cabinetry.

"Jesus H. Christ!" she hissed, eyes blown wide and fearful.

Walt clung to the bar-post that had been holding him up for much of the night, curled and knobby fingers struggling to maintain their precarious purchase, his ass half off the stool.

Neetha and Lleyton, who had just been coming in the door, were thrown against the portal, with Neetha clutching a nearby shutter to regain her footing and Lleyton slumped in his wheelchair, moaning. The tray of glassware that had been flirting with disaster in Carlee's hands all evening finally smashed in a spectacular performance across the tiled stone of the front deck, bathing diners in a triangular outward spray of stinging glass and alcohol. Other customers froze in shock at their tables.

Brask covered his ears, heart racing, not quite able to believe the loudness of the strike. It was the angriest, most physically painful noise he had ever encountered in his life. Worse than the time his eardrums had ruptured when lightning struck just five feet away from him during a summer outing at Bear Lake as a boy.

"What I the hell was that?" he said again, incredulous. "Earthquake? I feel like my skull was hit with a sledgehammer."

"I have no idea," stammered Margie, pointing a pudgy ringed finger toward the front of the place. "Look at them all."

Most of the diners were now out of their seats, pushing past Neetha and the lowing Lleyton to get out the door or gathered near the remnants of the picture window. They were pointing at something outside and apparently down the street, out of view to those at the bar. Carlee clasped both hands over her mouth to stifle a scream of horror, staring at whatever the rest had seen. Jorge burst, wild-eyed and agog, from the kitchen as Margie gathered her wits and ran out from behind the bar. The elemental silence after the shock wave was deafening.

"Whatever it is, it's outside," hollered Margie, stomping toward the exit. "You people get out of my way and let me see what's going on."

Brask rose from his stool, dizzy from the jolt and an evening of beer. He paused to make sure Walt was safe on his stool before striding across the dining room after Margie.

"An earthquake, you think?"

"Didn't sound or feel like any earthquake I ever experienced," said Margie. "Besides, we don't get earthquakes here. It was like a damned asteroid hit or something. Out of my way, everybody!"

She pressed through the little crowd, Brask on her heels, and waddled out onto the street.

There, in the middle of the thoroughfare, where almost everyone in Margie's Bar & Grill and everyone who happened to be in downtown Wistwood for the evening had now assembled, was a sight that defied all the groping and fumbling of Brask's vivid imagination.

His own eyes flashed orange in the cool night before the sheer impossibility of what he saw. His nostrils twitched from the scent of acrid smoke billowing around the stunned onlookers in wild, whipping columns.

Two immense and twisted trees, charred and aflame, lay in the middle of Main Street, not thirty feet away from the bar. They lay as if hurled by some unseen Titan from Olympian heights. The stars waxed fierce in the sky above as the great trees, denuded of all leaves and smaller limbs, seemed to writhe like bodies beneath the twisting tongues of fire that engulfed and consumed them. The circle of perhaps twenty-five people, many of whom had been eating moments earlier in the restaurant, now stood at a safe distance, mesmerized. In their midst was Horace, silhouetted like a dark statue against the conflagration.

Brask's mouth moved to speak, but little emerged until he ran a steadying hand through his hair and wiped the sweat from his scalp.

"Trees? What the fuck is going on? Where ... where the hell did they come from?"

The outer line of the nearby forest was easily over a hundred yards away. Around the burning trunks were parked cars, buildings, and the cheerful paved-brick sidewalks that had been there all along.

"Margie, what in the hell is this?"

Margie stood silent beside him, her shoulders slumped forward, chin nodding toward her bosom, and her eyes half-lidded, as if she had just awakened from a long and pleasurable sleep or was about to fall into such a slumber. Her expression was not one of panic or confusion, but rather a gaze of grim consideration and query. It was a look duplicated, in fact, by every other face that stared at the impossible scene. Brask turned to behold the others, fixated as if they were in a trance, and then shook his head to dislodge the whole ludicrous tableau. Not possible. At last, he looked helplessly at the clear night sky, gesturing up and then quickly down with a palm.

"It ... was it ... an aircraft? Did these things fall from some sort of aircraft? What kind of plane drops trees in the middle of a downtown street at seven o'clock at night? I mean ... what the fuck? Does anybody have an idea?"

No one moved. They all kept staring in silence, with only the crackle and hollow roar of the flames filling the air. Even Walt had emerged from the bar, hobbling on his cane, to ponder the fiery missiles with a hypnotic expression plastered across his own face.

Brask gaped at the weird and hulking behemoths, more astonished and dismayed than ever to note that they had apparently been pulled up by their very roots, which now coiled and snaked away amid the inferno. After a few more seconds of trying to process what he was seeing, he looked away from Margie and the others toward the outskirts of the little crowd to behold Neetha, weeping in soft little fits, one arm around the shoulder of Carlee, the waitress, who was sobbing uncontrollably. Those two were the only other denizens of Wistwood who looked remotely sane, experiencing proper reactions. The rest remained as still as standing stones, as if they were all awaiting something, as if at any moment they expected the two trees to rise up of their own accord and dash back into the distant woodland from whence they presumably came, or perhaps fling themselves back up into the impossible abyss of space.

Brask steadied himself and took a few deep breaths. These burning monoliths could not have come from either forest or space, not in this condition. His synapses were firing well enough to make that conclusion. He pushed forward through the unresisting crowd, aghast, and placed his hand upon Horace's shoulder. As he did so, the flames on the ruined trees began to diminish in a sudden, slight wind that nevertheless burned upon their cheeks as it passed above the searing heat. Horace turned slowly to regard Brask, a curious and introspective look in his oily and black-marble eyes.

"Brask Adams." His raspy voice was a deadened monotone as it emerged from beneath the bountiful white mustache. "It's too bad you have to see a thing like this on your second night in town. Just plain unfortunate. That's a fact." He turned to stare again at the trunks, water and steam whistling like tears that had the power to scream from the bark of the blazing wood.

"Horace, what's the meaning of this? We were all in the bar eating and drinking when there was this unbelievable noise and then ... *this*. It's like they were ... they were dropped here. On fire! I've never heard or seen anything like it."

"They'll burn all night, if I know anything about such matters," said Horace in the same slow, laconic voice. "But the fire will be out come dawn and then we can see about cleaning up the mess, if there's one left to clean up."

"What? Horace, someone could have been killed. I just can't wrap my head around it. Where did they *come* from? I mean, isn't anyone going to call the fire department?"

"Ain't any fire department to call," said Horace. "They'll be burnt out by morning, like I said. Until that happens, this isn't anything for you to get yourself involved with."

Brask stared at the old man, incredulous. He started to form a curt reply until, at the edge of his vision, beyond the shudder and shimmer of firelight, he saw another young woman crying at the edge of the crowd, her face flickering in the fire-shadows, her tears glowing in amber rivers as they streamed down her cheeks. There was genuine fear and shock on that face, as there ought to have been, thought Brask, and quite unlike the others. Just as there was proper shock on Neetha's face, and on Carlee's, too. He stepped around the immovable pillar that was Horace and made his way to the woman. No one stopped him, but no one moved to let him pass, either. Still as standing stones.

"Excuse me. Miss? My name is Brask. Brask Adams. I just moved to Wistwood yesterday. I was in the restaurant. But I don't remember seeing you in there. Were you outside? Did you see what happened out here?"

The woman, perhaps light blonde or auburn-haired—he couldn't tell in the distorted hue of the firelight—looked up at him, terrified. Her face was that of a gamine, beautiful and intoxicatingly unblemished. Was that, too, a trick of the light? He watched as her full lips parted in soundless words. She blinked a few tears away, ran a delicate hand through her hair, and then offered the same trembling hand to Brask.

"Hey. Hi. I'm Schuyler Brody. I … I just got here today, too. This afternoon. I mean, I haven't moved in, yet, but I signed a lease agreement for the antique shop across the street, and the apartment above. I was inside with that guy," she pointed weakly, "with Horace, when this happened. Whatever *this* is."

"Do you want to go sit down somewhere?"

"No, I don't. I mean, I don't know what I want to do or ought to do right this minute."

"No worries. I feel about the same myself."

"I had just signed on the dotted line of my lease when all hell broke loose outside," continued Schuyler. "We both rushed into the street after we heard the crash or the thunder or whatever it was. I thought it was a bomb. I'm ... look, I'm sorry. I must seem a complete mess right now, but I'm a little freaked out. A little out of it."

"Hey, you are *not* alone," said Brask, not wanting to turn his back on the strange trees still wreathed with licking flames. "I'm not even sure I believe what I'm seeing."

"You know, I don't think I can drive back home right this minute. Not in the dark. My knees are shaking. What kind of crazy shit is this?"

"I don't know, but I think it would be wise for both of us to get off the street. Horace just told me there's no fire department in town, but that doesn't mean that we can't call one in from Big Sur, if no one else has gotten around to it, yet. I don't know why everybody's just standing, here, staring like fucking meerkats. But I think I need to sit down, and you probably do, too. You don't look so good."

"That's because I'm scared out of my wits. And I think I could use a drink."

She clutched a set of ornate, antique-looking keys. "This old guy, Horace, he said there's a bar next door. Maybe we could find it and get away from the Burning Street Trees that Fell from Space. You think?"

"Hell, yeah. The bar's called Margie's. It's right there. Margie herself is at the other side of this crowd, somewhere. Come on. I'll buy you a drink, if you like."

Schuyler held up her hand. It was bandaged. A pinpoint of blood had soaked through the gauze.

"God, are you okay? Did you get hurt?"

"What? No. It's nothing. I just cut my palm accidentally when I was signing the lease. The pen slipped and there was a little piece of metal filing sticking out. It's nothing."

Brask felt the hairs on his neck rise once again, but Schuyler was already sidling away from the flaming disaster and toward the bar.

"I'll lead the way to the alcohol if you won't, Brask. I need some. Badly."

TAKE WHAT YOU NEED BUT
NEED WHAT YOU TAKE

What was left of Shep Daltry—and there was not much to be seen, save by those with sight and strength enough to defy the camouflage of obscuring forces and other spheres of oblivion—drifted in a cloud of transmogrified puffs and curling tendrils of mist toward the clearing behind the Manor House of Time, Times and Half a Time. This essence coagulated behind the Sweet Place, and there it hovered, uncertain, as only a bit of aimless fog pushed across warm and dry earth could hover. What was left of Shep Daltry sensed that a bit more cohesion might be expected of him, especially in this spot, but all of the exertion of his disembodied and ethereal will could not draw the disparate strands together and enable him to take shape. He could not integrate as he felt a man of his stature ought, and he did not know how he had managed to find the strength to bring bits of himself to the glade at all, after what had happened on the island.

Horace was waiting for him, now, standing on a great slab of stone that was shot-through with a matrix of radiant quicksilver and slow-moving veins of bright red fire, pulsating like molten lava. It was the last stone in a long line that led away from and up toward the manor house itself, nestled between two solemn hills of grey rock.

"Is it night or is it day?" said Shep. At least he thought that this question had emanated from the lazy, floating mess of vapor that he had become.

"Doesn't matter," answered Horace, matter of factly. "Not in this place. No such thing as night and day near the manor."

He indicated the sky with his cane, which was as close overhead as a ceiling yet as distant as some archaic galaxy expelled at the beginning of creation. Colors exploded in phantasm-like bursts across the surface of this firmament.

Like minnows darting up to kiss the surface of a stream, thought Shep. And then:

"Why am I here like this, you worn-out old man?"

Horace merely shrugged.

"Do you mock me, old fella, or do I offend you?"

"Neither. I don't waste my time with the pretense of mockery and, if you don't mind me saying so, it is virtually impossible to take offense from a wispy archipelago of vapors that doesn't even have the wherewithal to coagulate into a decent fog."

"Pretense, huh? You're a smart mouth."

"Well, maybe I felt like wasting my time a little bit. Just this once."

But in truth, Horace was not offended. It was not within his range of abilities to feel such a thing. In another time and place long-forgotten, he might have possessed the necessary inclinations, but not now.

"You're here because you've been called," he said to what was left of Shep, "just like anybody who comes here gets called." He gestured to the shimmering boil of mist. "I see you didn't fare too well with Her of the Island. Barely a ghost of a ghost, now. That's what you've been reduced to. I expect even His Tranquility had to sweat a little to call you back up and gather the bits and pieces from wherever it was she blasted you. Not surprised you came, though, such as you are. His Tranquility is pretty capable when it comes to your sort."

What was left of Shep Daltry coiled and expanded in the gentle gleam of the minnow-stream sky.

"I remember ravens. Crows. Four of 'em, I think. And all the bodies. I was a collector. A master collector."

Horace shrugged again. "Yes, you were probably an adequate collector, and that must be what caught His eye. See, He's a collector, too. A much better and more important one than you or than I. Don't worry about having to remember that fact, though. He'll never let you forget it."

"Crows ... I saw the crows."

"Sure you did. He uses birds and other meager beasts to communicate his purpose, in some places, with some subjects. Seeing those crows was probably one sign of your calling. A herald of your special selection and privilege. He uses computers and billboards and movies and clouds and the patterns on a tablecloth. Anything he wants."

"I was there, on the island. I felt the water and the sand beneath my feet, but ... it was not me who stood before that ... that *woman,* the one with the stars in her hair and the diamonds on trees in her orchard."

"No, it wasn't exactly you. He was using you as a means of getting onto the island. It was something of an old trick he remembered and was attempting to employ to get his way, but Her of the island apparently saw the whole thing coming and she tricked him right back." Horace gave another shrug and laughed, low and coarse in the gloom. "It's happened before, with those two. I daresay it'll happen again."

"I want to make her pay for what she did to me."

"Oh ho! That's rich. Mighty rich, in fact. But you won't be having any further business with Her, not for a Time, Times, and Half a Time, the way I figure. And you ought be grateful for that. She can brush something like you away so easy ... well, she can brush you away like the waste of breath you currently are."

"What do you mean?"

"Oh, figure it out, boy! You were being Ridden. You were Occupied, when you saw Her of the island. Possessed. Owned. Empowered. But now it's time to forget these matters and turn your thoughts to other concerns. Travel some different avenues."

"What avenues are you talking about?"

"His Tranquility has another plan for you. That new job. It's a fairly steady one, too."

"I was blown to shit on the first job he gave me." The mists swirled and became, for an instant, a lively and gnashing vortex.

"Hey! Now that's the spirit a spirit ought to show when summoned for such an auspicious occasion," remarked Horace. "Don't worry your head too much—well, your ectoplasm—about the new job, though. It wouldn't do you any good to worry because you couldn't refuse the position now even if you wanted to.

"Oh? And how would you know that?"

"Because the job you're going to get is mine, and I should know about these things if anyone does."

"Why am I gonna get your job? Where are you going? What are you gonna do?"

"Oh, I expect I'll just be on my way, though I don't believe I'm in any position to ask questions. I've been told as much, as a matter of fact."

"What kind of work is this, really?"

"It's a young man's work. And there's always plenty of it, in all kinds of interesting locations, too. See, I've grown a little long in the tooth for this line, and that's something His Tranquility is not equipped to change, for reasons known only to him, of course. All you have to do now is make the switch and be ready to do his bidding. He'll fill you in on the details, just like he promised, before you got your ass handed to you in a paper sack by Her of the island. Anyhow, you can't refuse the position anymore, just as I said before, so we'd best get things underway without further ado. There's a lot to accomplish right away. This is a particularly busy time in Wistwood. I just came from downtown. There's fallout from your little encounter. The burning kind."

"You speak of a switch. How is this to be done, old man?"

"It'll be done in a way I think you'll find rather satisfying, if I guess correctly in your regard. But like it or not, it's the only way His Tranquility oversees this sort of transaction. You need a little corporeality, Mr. Daltry. A little—or a lot—of fattening-up in order to meet the demands ahead. A body is what you need, but in order to get one, you're going to have to feed off me."

The mists began to sway and dive with enlivened interest.

Yeah, I thought I was right about that part," croaked Horace. "I knew that would appeal to you. Well, I'd say that time is a-wasting, but, right here, it really isn't. Let's just get on with it, shall we?"

Horace grasped the head of his cane and twisted until the silver knob came off. From the hollow of the walking stick he drew a long blade that gleamed with pulsing reflections of the eldritch sky above. Sitting with some effort down upon the stone platform, he shook off his overcoat, and then laboriously removed his thick woolen sweater to reveal a sunken, gray-haired chest dominated by distended breasts and several tiers of spotted and drooping skin-folds.

Gripping the handle of the blade, he jammed it inward and, in one swift movement, drew it across his belly until the wet and purplish coils of his intestines began to spill out onto his lap in a torrent of blackish blood. He tottered for an instant but remained seated, cross-legged in the swelling pool. Beneath him, the silver matrix of the stone waxed like blinding starlight as the lava matrix boiled and surged. The mist that was Shep Daltry moved forward. By now Horace was panting. He coughed up a clot of blood that spurted out and up to stain his perfect white beard with crimson slime. But he still managed to lift an arm before he fell backward and beckoned the mist closer.

"Come," he said, voice rasping just above a whisper. "Enter through my belly first. Entrails is good eatin' for a ghost and I ... I've set a fine table for you." His eyelids began to flutter. "I asked His Tranquility if I could do it like the old Jap warriors, when they used to make 'em cut their bellies open during the war. It was the sweetest sight I ever saw in any world, in any lifetime. His Tranquility ... He ... He gave me this last honor, before I go to my reward."

Horace reached down and lifted a handful of his steaming innards up toward the mists, fingers splayed and dripping.

"Come and feast. Old flesh can still beget new."

He fell backward at last against the stone with a sickening thud and a spray of blood. The hovering mist overwhelmed him, then, and began to feed at the gaping wound, gaining strength rapidly and accruing form as it curled like smoke in and out of the sliced torso.

"Yes, feed on me," muttered Horace, his eyes staring blankly up at the miraculous sky. "And be vigilant for His Tranquility's every command. Take form, as he wishes, and do his bidding in this Time of Black Harvest."

A mouth, ghastly and fetid, had found the power to take shape and materialize amid the mist, rising from the nourishment of fading lifeblood. The head and shoulders followed, leaning over Horace to look at him, a quivering rope of intestine being gnawed and ground between teeth that were forming even as they chewed, rising into being behind the swirls of vapor.

"And why are you so quick to give your job to me, old man?" growled Shep, his mouth full of shit that had burst from a ripped section of the hot bowels.

"Cause this is how it's been done since before people was ever made, boy, and I ... I am only one in a long line of those who have served before me. Know that where I am now, you too are gonna be ... under the sky that knows no joy, in the shadow of the Lord of Wistwood."

"No, I won't be where you are now, old man. Never."

"You will, shit-eater. You will," choked Horace through a final vomit of blood. His eyes closed for the last time. "You have no choice, not when it's your destiny," he gasped. "Ordained ... before time. Before any Beginning."

Shep Daltry bent forward and sank his teeth into flesh, biting off the tip of one of Horace's distended breasts.

"Ordained by who?" hissed Daltry through a mouthful of gore.

"God," said Horace before something far beyond oblivion took him away at last.

"God ordained it all ..."

AFTERGLORY

B rask ended-up in bed at his cabin with Schuyler. He was as surprised as she
was about it, for the lead-up to their dalliance had been anything but romantic or even remotely tinged with the promise of a no-holds barred, bed-shaking
sexual encounter. Yet, this was exactly what the two experienced, shuddering and
electrified from the tops of their heads to the tips of their toes in the damp air of
the thickening night.

All signs had pointed to an evening of astonished, ongoing bewilderment.
Even the possibility of outright panic seemed more likely than sex following the
still-incomprehensible incident with the burning trees, hurled upon Main Street
in Wistwood like the discarded torch of some gargantua out of the Lovecraft nov-
els Brask had devoured as a kid. Thrown by something vast, something beyond
measure and comprehension. Something that jettisoned flaming things out of
nowhere from its domain in the impenetrable blackness of the Void.

Almost but not quite as unsettling had been the reactions of the people of
Wistwood, most of whom had regarded the freakish scene as if it were an irksome
puzzle to be studied and solved in silence. They had stood around the crackling
tree in their creepy collective trance, appearing to be no more sentient than cows
gathered about a country pasture to stare with bracing but idle bovine concern
at a crocodile that had somehow crawled into their midst. There had been a
tense, bothersome and underlying fear detectable in every countenance, a fear

that flickered like the firelight reflected on the skin of each solemn face, but not a word had been said beyond Horace's cryptic remarks.

Even after the flames began to subside and most of the crowd returned, heads bowed and muttering, to Margie's bar, answers were not forthcoming. Brask had bought the shaken Schuyler a few shots of tequila and a couple of beer chasers, but no one on either side of the bar was inclined to discuss the oddity. Margie shrugged and took up her tattered cleaning rag, averting her eyes from Brask and the new girl, mumbling something about Horace being in charge of clean-up duties around town. Old Walt had quickly paid his bill, bid them all a clipped good-night, and left, walking out in the rigid, stiff grip of rheumatoid agony. Carlee the waitress had not even been able to finish her shift; she and Neetha had been the only other ones in the entire vicinity to actually exhibit reasonable terror at the sight. Neetha had whisked Lleyton and his wheelchair away like a shot. Jorge and Theo had pitched-in to clean up the glass from the shattered window.

After that, Brask and Schuyler had tried to deflect their overwhelming sense of anxiety and helplessness with the comfort of small-talk, sharing information with which they were firmly acquainted and responding to questions their brains were quite comfortable accepting and computing.

A spell seemed to settle over the place, and into its arms they allowed themselves to fall. Within an hour, they could scarcely remember that burning trees had fallen into their world.

Brask, getting more inebriated by the moment, found it difficult not to steal an unabashed glance or two at the stunning newcomer. She was his type and there was no mistake about it. Sexy and pretty but unadorned by anything over-the-top. Confident in her womanhood, in her looks. Beautiful, but without the need to impose beauty.

The spell grew in power.

Even her hair was making him hard by the time he got around to finishing his final beer. He could smell her hair, clean and fresh, with the indescribably sweet scent of a woman who took good care of her body and soul. Brask's mind began to reel toward an almost agonizing desire. His sense of self-control was slipping into new and unfamiliar territory, a time when a man ought always to be alert and aware of his surroundings; mindful of the consequences that might come from stepping out of bounds with any stranger.

But he wanted to fuck her. He wanted to take her to the cabin, spread her creamy thighs wide in his bed, and bury his tongue inside her, pressing where it counted with the cleft of his chin until she grabbed him by the hair and ground his face harder into her, absorbing him, owning him. Then she would draw him to enter her, hard and smooth and thicker than any man she had known. His mouth would be a slave until she could taste herself on his tongue as they kissed, her legs encircling him. He would pound her, deep and steady as music until she quivered, every muscle squeezing around his mad cock and he let loose a raging flood of his own all the way up into her soul.

And the spell possessed them, working its potency beyond all rational thought and flesh.

The next morning, panting, stunned, Brask rolled gently from atop her and drew her close beneath his arm until the downy hair of his chest became the pillow to which she clung, fingers resting gently or playing in aimless passes along the muscled ridges of his abdomen. They lay that way for a long while. Silent. Were they sleeping? Was it all a dream? After such an encounter neither could be certain. Were those stars that Brask saw upon the shadowed swath of the ceiling or was the entire space open to a glittering night sky? He could not be certain of that, either. Presently, a clock could be heard ticking in his living room and the stark reality of what they had done finally settled down upon both of them. It billowed like a sheet cast by an unseen interloper to cover their nakedness, veiling the sense of awkward satisfaction that had consumed them and defined the very length and breadth of the night itself.

Schuyler made a sound like a little laugh and pulled playfully on Brask's chest hair.

"I think it is fair to say, Mr. Adams, knowing full well that I am about to lock, load, and shoot a lethal cliché—which you, as a writer, probably despise like a dyslexic critic with an axe to grind—but that was really damned good for me. How about you?"

Brask laughed and the sheet or veil of vague discontent vanished as swiftly as it had descended.

"Cliché or not, if you can use it alongside an analogy like that, then maybe I'm not the only one who ought to be dedicated to a career in writing."

"I'm a teacher, remember? They pay me to use words in certain ways, too," whispered Schuyler, twisting a shiny, manicured fingertip over and over in a circlet of Brask's hair. "Besides, I can think 'em up, but I'm not so sure I'd get as much of a charge out of writing them down as you do."

"Oh, you're a teacher alright." He drew her closer, savoring the warmth and feeling himself grow hard again. There was movement. Too much heat. He wasn't sure he wanted her to see it, yet. He did, but it might be wise to doze and just play a little. "You taught me that I ought to expect the most incredible sex whenever burning trees fall from the sky and land in the street."

"Oh, my God," gasped Schuyler, drawing hand to her mouth. "What in Christ was that whole episode about, anyway? I still haven't got a clue."

Brask shrugged against the pillow, sweat drying cold on his neck. "All I know is that it's officially the weirdest thing I've ever come across, in a lifetime of seeing weirdness. The tree and the reaction of the rest of the locals."

"No shit. Did you get a good look at Colonel Sanders's face?"

"Colonel what?"

"Sanders. You know. The fried chicken mogul of yore. KFC? I was actually referring to Horace. I think he's a dead ringer for the chicken king."

"Now that you mention it … but I don't see Colonel Sanders. I see more of a Richard Farnsworth thing going on with him."

"Who?"

"Just some old actor from a long time ago. A very good one. But if you insist upon Horace as Chicken Mogul, then I guess I can see Chicken Mogul, too."

"How gracious of you. Of course you can see that."

They laughed softly, pausing in the silence, listening to their own breath. Reveling in the satisfaction of their bodies.

"Do you think people have a tendency to engage in reckless behavior under stressful, traumatic conditions, or should most people be more careful?" asked Schuyler. "Even if the behavior feels unfuckingbelievably magnificent and natural, and the traumatized people have actually needed such behavior in their lives for months?"

Brask could feel the curve of her grin against his chest.

"Then the answer is yes, though I don't think many stressed-out people—even in the midst of heavy trauma—get to have it quite so good as we did. In fact, I refuse to believe that it's a common occurrence."

"You're sweet, ya know?" She kissed his nipple softly. His cock rolled heavy onto his thigh. "See, I only asked that because, well, I have been under an incredible amount of stress the past year, like I *think* I told you last night at the bar, freaky trees or no freaky trees, trying to figure out what the hell I want to do with my future. Dealing with those monsters at school, and the faculty, which doesn't help you for shit. Then, you know, getting this antique shop and just plunking down the money on pretty much an impulse. A good impulse, mind you. But an impulse all the same. And then … fucking trees! Flaming trees! Trees that came falling out of who the hell knows where, and I'm freaked out and it's late and I seriously need a stiff drink on top of everything else, and then you—"

"Me?" said Brask. His erection bobbed up lazily, a blunt shadow moving across his stomach. He wondered if she would reach for him.

"Yes, you, handsome and rational and sweet."

"Please continue, Teacher."

"Well, there's just so much emptiness all around, on every level. I'm so sick of it. Sick of recognizing it, not only in myself, but in other people. It was nice to see that's not the case with you. But maybe if I wasn't able to recognize the emptiness, to be revolted by it all, I wouldn't be in a position to want something different, would I?"

"No, maybe you wouldn't. It's the blessing and the curse of that whole ability to see too much," said Brask. "Two-edged sword. I've lived with that pretty much my whole life and I'm not so sure the insight has always been worth the agony."

"My Granny always said you have to have vision good enough to see what's missing in order to get a good look at what's truly in front of you, at what's really there. For good or for ill, better or worse. She was right about that, too. She was right about a lot of things."

"What did she have to say about men?"

"God! My Granny didn't have a whole lot to say about men. Granddaddy died when she was just a young mother, but at least he had the decency to die and leave her with a chain of little Texaco stations that took the edge off the whole survival rat-race. Not to say she didn't have hard times in that regard, but she rose to the challenge. You have to, when reality is the only thing there to greet you every morning on the other side of the bed."

"Pretty eloquent way to put it," drawled Brask. "I may steal that line for one of my future characters."

"Writer man. Go ahead. You'll be stealing it from my granny, because that's the way she put it. I'll never forget it." Schuyler shook her head in a moment of fond remembrance. "I never talked about men with my granny. Or with my own Mama, for that matter. I was raised to be a certain way and I stuck with that template, for the most part. It worked for me. Hell, it worked for a lot of girls in these parts. You must know how it is. Whatever the case, I wanted you to know the circumstances. I needed this. I needed it like a glass of water after an unplanned hike through the Sahara, but … I was a little bit not myself, if you catch my meaning. I mean, I realize it sounds so tired, but I want you to know that I don't normally, or even abnormally, do this sort of thing. Much less the kind of things I did while *doing* this kind of thing."

"So you're saying that this was pretty much a totally spontaneous act. That you were living on the edge. Taking risks. Throwing caution to the wind."

"Yeah. Uh … I got a little caught-up in the moment."

"And I can guarantee you that I have no diseases or other dastardly things, known or otherwise, swimming around in my body and blood. I had to take a full battery of exams for the insurance policy I bought into and—"

"Look, no need to explain, Brask. It's done and it was fabulous."

She smiled across his chest and he felt the warmth of her lips, the gentle tickle of breath from her nostrils cooling the last of the sweat on his skin. Then he felt her frown. A subtle tension entered her body. It was barely perceptible, but he felt it in her fingers and at the base of her neck where he had curled his arm against the cascade of her hair.

"Please tell me that I already told you I'm on the pill before we did this. I don't remember telling you. But I should have. Despite the lack of a sex life I protested way too much about, I'm covered in that department, so you don't have to worry about anything due to the fact you came inside me. Three times."

Brask's eyes widened in the dark. His erection softened immediately. An icy wind might have blown across his thighs beneath the blanket. He tried not to swallow hard, but it was a reflexive response to her words and she heard it and felt it, with the top of her head lodged cozily beneath his chin.

"Oh," Brask rasped. "I guess we both got a little caught-up in the moment, because I totally spaced on the fact that I was doing that. Or did that."

She drew her fingers across the muscles of his abdomen, slowly, as if caressing the strings of some unfamiliar instrument. It felt good to have a woman appreciate his body again.

"Just wanted you not to fret about it, and I thought it was important for me to reiterate."

"Whoah! Did I just hear somebody use the term 'reiterate' in bed? I could fall for a girl who reiterates regularly in these conditions. Better watch out."

He was trying to be playful to mask his own sudden concern about what was, from his standpoint, a thoroughly reckless and unprotected encounter, but the veil of awkwardness seemed to spread over the two of them, thickening to the consistency of a shroud.

"Uh huh. I am reiterating, smarty pants. Smarty no-pants, I mean."

Her hand brushed lower, lingering seductively against his cock. There was an immediate resurgence.

"I think we can both, in good conscience, chalk this up to a day and night of high stress, followed by euphoric relief at getting our rentals in this little oasis town and then being utterly mind-boggled by the sight of trees crashing down from the surface of some passing asteroid that obviously supports plant-life, because that is the only explanation I can come up with for that. Outside of a freak tornado or some sort of cyclonic cloudburst like the kind you hear about raining fish and frogs on people's heads out of nowhere on a perfectly clear night. Only nobody heard a tornado, so …"

"Point taken?"

"You tell me, Brask,"

"Yep. Taken," he said, almost praying that she would wrap her fingers around him again. The throbbing was painful. Exquisitely so.

"And seeing as you're the new guy in town, and I'm the new girl in town, and we're both free American adults who've done this while barely knowing each other, and are starting over for the improvement of our personal lives, I suggest we take things really slowly. Be as mature about this as possible. Because this, my friend, is one hell of a small town."

"That's for damned sure."

"It's even smaller than the smallest town in my county back home, and that's pretty damned small."

"Well, you know how it is out in the woods here, Schuyler. You get little pockets of elitism and redneckery side-by-side. Best of both twisted worlds. Total eccentricity. That's why most people seek out places like this. You must be as used to it as anybody. You mentioned you live only forty-five minutes away. Speaking of which, I don't remember where you said you were from, but I'm guessing it's not Carmel or Monterey, if you're talking about podunk towns. You must be inland, or south.

"Carmel and Monterey? Inland? What are you talking about?"

"Well, you'd have to live near—what's the place—Cambria or maybe Lucia? Believe me, I studied the maps of this region before I drove down here. Trying to find the Wistwood that could not be found."

She lifted her head for an instant and then nestled deeper against his shoulder, drawing his elbow and forearm closer around her in the chill of the morning.

"What are you going on about, Brask? I never heard of either of those places. And 'inland' from what? Lake Merrick? I live in Chesterville. Such a dump. But that's where I'll be heading first thing in the morning to start making arrangements and get a new life rolling at last. Thank God."

"Chesterville?" Brask murmured, running his fingers through her hair, basking with dreamy pleasure in the lingering smell of her sex and fragrant sweat. He thought of the map he had purchased at the gas station in Big Sur and subsequently poured-over while attempting to find Wistwood. "I don't recall seeing Chesterville on the maps I looked at. And who lives forty-five minutes away and hasn't heard of Cambria while teaching in the regional school district? Good thing you're not teaching geography. As it is, I may have to report you to the board, or quality control, if this is an example of American tax dollars at work. Then again, the state of California hasn't been exactly great at using tax money, these days."

"What's California got to do with anything?"

"I'd say the fact that you are living in it and employed by its Board of Education counts for something!" he said with a chuckle that dislodged her chin from its comfortable spot just above his ribcage.

"Seriously, Mark Twain. You've already played with my head enough in the past fifteen hours or so. Aren't you satisfied?"

"Very satisfied, but you're the one who asked me what California had to do with anything."

"And I'm still asking. What's California have to do with me or with Ohio?"

"Ohio?"

"Yeah. Ohio. This *is* where we live. This *is* where we just fucked each other's brains out and, apparently, it's where trees fall from the sky while lit-up like torches."

"You silly. Now who's trying to play with whose head? Come on, Schuyler. Where are you really from? Given the circumstances I think it's safe for you to tell me."

"I just told you. Chesterville. You must've heard of it. It's forty-five minutes away and not much to brag about, but I'm sure if you look again on that map of yours, you'll find it easily enough." She paused, deciding. "You know, you can even drive back with me this morning, if you don't have anything else to do. I could use some help. Only if you're up for it. But seriously, what gives with the California stuff. You trying to joke around?"

The veil that had enshrouded them, gossamer and damp with the remnants of their lust, turned cold and ominous, a black pirate-ship flag, suddenly torn and whipping in a gale. She sounded dead serious. Had he done something to piss her off?

What the fuck?

"Look, Schuyler, if you don't want to tell me where you currently live, that's okay. I get it. There's no need for a run around. I mean, I told you I was from Palo Alto, as far as I remember much of anything from the bar last night, which isn't all that much, come to think of it, but that's just me. I haven't been around too many people in awhile. I guess I'm quick to overshare. If you consider telling someone where you're from to be oversharing."

She struggled to sit up in bed, hair in her eyes, and propped herself on a wrist against the mattress.

"Yes, you told me at the bar that you were from Palo Alto, Brask, and maybe I should have done the logical thing and asked you when you decided to move out here to Ohio, but you were sitting there telling me that you just 'drove in yesterday' and rented your new place, so I figured I had enough of an answer."

"Schuyler. Hey, it's not funny, anymore. Come on. If I've done something to offend you, or said the wrong thing, somehow, please tell me. I'm a big boy. It's a lot better than trying to make me feel like some sort of idiot."

"You didn't say anything to offend me until just now, Brask. I don't know what you're getting at. I'm not playing any game."

"Then what's with this Ohio bullshit?"

Schuyler was thunderstruck. She gasped and looked around the dimly lit room, desperate to find some other focal point that might absorb and render harmless her growing agitation.

"Brask, we are in Ohio. I don't know what kind of game *you're* trying to pull with this Big Sur, California crap, but you're officially freaking me out, and that's not good. Not on top of everything else that's happened. Jesus, I have a good mind to drive back to Chesterville right now."

She pulled herself from Brask's lazy embrace and slipped quietly off the bed to look for her clothes.

"Oh, so you're going to drive back to good old Ohio this morning, huh?" Brask propped himself on his elbows and laughed, hoping to catch the edge of the joke, whatever it was. But Schuyler was not laughing. The morning sunlight outside the window was obscured by a drifting wisp of cloud and the room was suddenly overwhelmed with gloom.

"What are you doing, Schuyler?"

"Finding my clothes. I'm leaving."

Jesus H Christ, is she crazy?

A pang of terror rose from Brask's gut into his throat. He swallowed hard again, but it wasn't easy. His mouth felt as dry as some ancient piece of parchment.

Oh, my God, is he insane? thought Schuyler, feeling around the floor for her bra and panties.

Her fingers found her blouse and she snatched it up, fumbling with the fabric. She had to get something on. Fast. Her nakedness now felt damning. The mutual hunger they had shared now struck her soul as something dark and criminal. The sun emerged from behind the web of clouds and, pulling on her skirt, she groped the walls though the network of rooms into Brask's kitchen. *Thank God I followed him down here in my own car!*

Where had she put her shoes? Her purse? Her keys? Damn it! She thought about fumbling for the light switch, but was seized with horror at the thought of further illumination. He mustn't see her, not like this. She had no desire to see him.

"Schuyler?"

Her heart was beginning to pound, but when she spoke, she tried her best to sound as calm and quietly authoritative as she was with her most recalcitrant students back in Chesterville.

"Brask, I think right now it would be a good idea if we both just kind of get ourselves together and start thinking about all the important stuff we have to do today. It's been a lot of fun, but I have lost complete track of the time, and I have got to get on the road."

Schuyler found her blazer on the kitchen countertop and clutched it to her breasts as if it were a piece of armor, wondering wildly if there might be an old butter-knife or something else that could be used as a weapon in one of the nearby drawers.

Brask's head began to throb. Yeah, they'd had way too much to drink. There was no doubt about that. And some weird heaviness—something far beyond the grip of alcohol—had fallen over the bar, the town, the world, after the arrival of the trees.

The trees? The TREES?

A series of awkward movements followed. A stubbed toe. A string of muttered vulgarities. The sound of clothes being hurriedly donned, of long legs slicing, fast and furious, into denim. Grumbling. All of this took only a minute, but

Schuyler had found her purse and was already out the front door, trembling into the driveway.

Brask opened his mouth to call after her, but he wavered in the living room, his head swimming.

He never saw her in the world again.

ALL THE SLEEP SHE NEEDED

Lleyton Grayle rolled his wheelchair into Neetha's bedroom and listened for breathing. If he could only hear the sound of her miserable breath, the pathetic reminder that she was still alive, he knew he would be able to summon the rage required to wheel himself over and get one good slice across her throat before she knew what hit her. Before the Landlord was any the wiser. Lleyton had been replaying the moment over and over in his mind ever since he had made his choice. The time had come to kill the wretch.

He had to do it. He had to do it because, somehow, some way, Neetha would use her wiles to twist matters around and make sure that he, Lleyton, would never get to meet the Landlord at all. The thought of her getting any more credit or any further opportunity to destroy him—even here!—was too much to bear.

He was the one who had made it possible for them to survive the years, goddamn it! He was the one who came up with all the good ideas. The one who had managed to save both of their sorry asses from ultimate ruin. So what if it wasn't exactly what they had expected and she maybe had a reason or two to regret his decisions? There was no way he would let her destroy or sabotage what he had managed to put together. The Landlord would understand perfectly. Hadn't that been Horace's promise—that the Landlord would *always understand perfectly?*

The curtains billowed in a weak breeze as the sun rose over the hills behind the house. Lleyton and his wheelchair were lumpen shadows in the corner.

He placed the steak knife he had swiped from Margie's Bar & Grill atop his lap and took a deep breath, holding the air tight within his chest to listen. Just one, soft, whistling breath from Neetha's sleeping form was enough to make his brain explode with a blood-jagged lightning of resentment. It was time. Time to pay her back for all she had done to him and all she might have yet to do, if she had a chance.

"A piece of filth like her doesn't deserve to be alive," he whispered under his breath. "Doesn't deserve to make the choices others have earned the right to make."

He strained his arms and bent to his task, gray hair hanging down in straggling wisps on either side of his contorted face in the darkness. On the bed, Neetha's head stirred, her own hair a tangled mess, an octopus or some washed-up sea creature moving stupidly against the white pillow, he thought, sluggish as it drew-in air and looking ridiculously out of its habitat.

Lleyton fought to control his fury and managed to wheel without a sound to her bedside. His fingers groped for the knife's handle. He wanted to stab her over and over and over, but he couldn't start with that, as satisfying as it would be to hear her scream. No, he had to slice all the important things in her throat, first—arteries, esophagus, larynx—and then he could play a bit as she bled out and choked helplessly onto the pretty bedspread, soaking the white cotton sheets with red, unable to do anything but gurgle and gawp and flop around like the stupid animal that she was.

Her neck was covered-up by the duvet, but as he gripped the knife in one hand and reached over to gently tug the covers down with the other, the strain proved almost too much for his back. He worked, stifling a grunt of exertion until he thought every vein in his head would burst.

There, the neck was exposed at last!

His eyes widened in the dim interior. He would have to come down hard right below her ear and use all of his weight to drag the blade down and through the flesh. His torso shuddered with an almost hungry anticipation as he raised the serrated weapon and prepared to throw himself down and upon her, but the mounting excitement was too much for his compromised system to control and, instead, he let out a thin, shrill squeal of pleasure that woke Neetha instantly.

She screamed as her shadowed eyes flew open, comprehending everything as if she had been already dreaming of it, and flung herself across the bed in the other direction just as Lleyton landed, mouth drooling and lips moving in a terrible bellow of unmerited triumph as the knife plowed harmlessly into the vacant pillow. He went sprawling out of his tipped wheelchair in a clumsy crash, half of him on the bed and soon slipping to the floor beneath powerless legs that buckled and curled like pretzels beneath him.

"You dirty sonofabitch!" shrieked Neetha, flying toward a corner and knocking over a row of cosmetics. She bounced away from her mirrored make-up table and tried to gain her feet. "I knew you'd try to pull something one day, you crazy bastard!"

She began to sob, pressing her back up against the closed bedroom door and flicking on a light to make sure he had fallen out of the wheelchair. Lleyton growled and groaned in vexation as he clung to the side of the bed, unable to maintain any purchase. He clutched at the bedding, but it inched downward along with him. Neetha stared in a mixture of terror and disbelief at the knife gleaming among the folds of white. She put a hand up to her throat.

"You! Why, I oughta take that knife and go over there and cut your shrunken balls off and stuff 'em down your throat! You were gonna kill *me?* Jesus Christ. After all this shit, you were gonna kill me!"

"Get over here and chop my whole dick off, you worthless cow!" roared Lleyton, losing his battle with the linens and the sideboard of the bed. He landed with a thud on the floor. The wheelchair spun away from him even as his arm flailed weakly for the brake. "You've taken everything I ever had and threw it into the trash! Into the toilet! Into the sewer!" he yelled, angling into a fetal position near the wretched wheelchair. Overhead, the ceiling fan spun indifferently.

Knowing he was down, thwarted, Neetha gathered the hem of her nightgown and approached to glower at the sight of him through her tears.

"More of your crazy shit!" she spat. "And this is how it ends up all over again. I'm to blame for everything, when it was *me* who saved your useless, drugged-out, drunken ass. Me who made it possible for us to even have a life to hold onto after you'd pissed and smoked and fucked and gambled almost everything away. And then even that wasn't enough! You had to insist on a vacation here, in the middle of nowhere, so you could kill me!"

She gestured at the window and the looming hills rife with the first glimpses of morning mist beyond.

"You dumb, ungrateful, whoremastering waste of human skin. Thank Christ you're a clumsy slob and woke me up. You really thought I was just gonna lay there and let you cut me to pieces? What have you done to us, Lleyton?" she screamed. "I used to love you! But this is it. You are going away for a long time, pal, and they are never gonna let you out when I get through with you."

"Shut up!" Lleyton covered his ears with his hands and curled further in upon his sprawled and useless legs.

Neetha darted forward and kicked him hard in the gut with the heel of her bare foot as he began to laugh maniacally. She kicked him again, but forgot to use her heel in the thrall of her anger and felt one of her little toes snap. Howling in pain she reeled backward onto the floor, begging God, the Virgin Mary—anybody she had ever understood to possess a capacity for mercy—to get her out of her own mind.

That was when she felt the strong but comforting hand upon her shoulder from behind, lifting her gently from the heap she was in, speaking to her in tender but deep tones of consolation.

"Now, now, pretty lady. You don't need to go calling on those persons. Besides, you don't need their kinda help. Not here. Things ain't all that bad."

Neetha was picked up as if she were no more than a rag doll, stunned as she was slowly turned around to stare into the face of a man she had never seen before in her life, much less in Wistwood.

"Wh-who the hell are *you?*"she blubbered.

"Name's Shep Daltry, Ma'am. I'm the new Guy Friday in these parts and our esteemed Landlord, why, he got wind that there was something real troublesome going down over here at your place, so he sent me on the run."

"H-how?" Neetha's eyes were wild, looking from the cragged face of the stranger to the powerful hands that gripped her naked shoulders above the fallen straps of her nightgown.

"There's no need to worry your pretty head about the hows and the whys of it all, Ma'am. Wouldn't make any sense to you, anyway. Not yet." Shep glanced over Neetha's shoulder at the crumpled Lleyton, who stared breathless up from the floor.

"Looks like your husband had a bit of an accident over there. Doesn't look to me like he just fell out of the bed, neither."

"He … he tried to kill me in my sleep," said Neetha, the tears coming in rivers that sprouted tributaries of the mascara she had forgotten to remove the evening before.

"Hmmm," groaned Shep, drawing her closer in an almost brotherly hug. "Not a very nice thing to do, now, is it? But we all of us know he's been wanting to pull a stunt like that for a long time, eh? Way before you and him even came to town. And neither of you can remember whose idea it was to come here, do you? We know that, don't we, little darling lady?"

Neetha nodded, weeping into the harsh fabric of Shep's flannel shirt. "Yeah."

"But it was an especially bad idea for him to try such a thing now, when he's got an important interview with the Landlord tomorrow."

Shep held her away from him and lifted two huge, blunt thumbs to wipe away the tears and smeared make-up beneath her eyes.

"Now you listen to old Shep, honey. I'm gonna take good care of hubby over there, because I have a feeling the Landlord is gonna be none too happy when he finds out someone was so bold as to break his rules. In fact, he's already found out and, between you and me, the Big Chief has just about pretty much had it with ole Lleyton. He's practically whispering it in my ear right now, girl. He's got all the mileage he's gonna get out of your husband, so it's about time for him to move on to new adventures. You hear that, doll? You won't have to worry about a nasty steak-knife in the gullet while you're getting your beauty sleep no more. Ole Shep's gonna take care of everything. All according to plan. Right to plan."

Neetha stared up at the smiling, soulless face, dumbfounded. "What happened to … to the old guy, Horace, the one who set us up when we came here?"

"Retired," said Shep promptly. "With excellent references, I might add. Word is, he's moved on to a part time position in another field. I've got everything in Wistwood covered now."

"But what am I supposed to do now, after all of this?" croaked Neetha.

Shep took her face in both enormous hands and tilted it this way and that, inspecting it thoughtfully.

"First thing, Ma'am, I suggest you head out of the room and wait for me to clean up this little mess. It won't take but a minute and then you can come on back in, fix your hair, put on your goddamned make-up like a good little slut, get yourself dressed, and then, when you've had a chance to pull yourself together, you can get your ass on down to that bar and grill. They open at dawn, I believe. Have yourself a coffee. Hell, even have yourself a Bloody Mary. Just get your act together when I give you the signal, right? Then go about your day as if this little snafu never even happened. Because now *you* have a big appointment with the Landlord tomorrow. Got it?"

"Y-yes."

"That's a good girl. A real good girl." He patted her cheek twice. Hard. "See, the new boss is now in town, baby. In residence. And I have learned very quickly that the Landlord is a patient type, but he is running out of patience with people who deviate from protocol. So you don't wanna do that, do you?"

"No. No, I don't."

"Right. Now get on out of this room and make yourself busy for a bit. You can go to the toilet or run a fucking bubble-bath or burn some toast in the kitchen for all I care. Just get on out, shut the door behind you, and don't come back or anywhere near this room until I say so. And keep tomorrow's appointment well in mind, see?"

Neetha nodded, speechless in his iron grip.

"Get outta here." He set her free and she nearly flew out of the room, slamming the bedroom door in her wake. When her rapid footsteps could no longer be heard, Shep Daltry, cut-throat scar healed and smiling beneath his jaw, turned to the delirious form collapsed by the bed. He shook his head in wonder.

"You really thought you could get away with stealing His Tranquility's own property from him, rock and roll man?"

"I don't know you … I don't know you from shit," mumbled Lleyton from the midst of his ratty pile of gray hair. His face pressed hard against the wooden floorboards. "I don't know you from shit," he slurred again through a mouthful of dust.

"No. No, you don't," said Shep, moving closer, his shadow sweeping over Lleyton like a billowing cloak that spread across time and space, robbing all light from the room and the world, save for the sudden, crimson-red glow of his eyes. "But you're gonna know me, Lleyton Grayle, rock and roll man."

"You're gonna know me *real* good."

TO ERR MAY BE DIVINE

S hep strode across the enormous flagstone courtyard behind the manor. The sky was lower than ever, easily touched with a finger and disturbed, dancing with lights like minnows that flashed to the surface of the vaulted abyss, alive with ripples that shimmered and sped away. Beneath his feet, the quicksilver veins and pulsating lava matrix flowed like intermingling rivers that had no beginning or end beyond the flagstones. It was then he knew that the stone itself was alive in a way that he could never, ever hope to be again.

The old life wasn't worth a minute of this. Feel this goddamn power in me!

There was a small splotch of the old man's blood in a cragged corner, a spot he had missed during the feeding that had helped give him the new, much more useful, and interesting body. Every other trace of Horace's corpse—hair, skin, muscle, organs, bones—had been consumed entirely, first as mist, and then, when the teeth had finally materialized, by the frenzied gnawing.

My flesh is real food. My blood is real drink.

It was amazing, the things Shep could do now. He thought he had a bit of power in his former existence, but hadn't understood the meaning of power. Not until now.

He stooped and placed a hand over the last smudge of sticky blood and the stain was immediately absorbed into himself, leaving the stone as clean and slick as ice. Only a small drink, but he felt the surge of potency and dangerousness circulate through his own veins, a swift drug composed of razor-sharp molecules and stinging atoms. It was exhilarating. Looking up at last to the manor, he saw that it was shrouded in some kind of storm cloud. Lightning flickered gently in the boil of fog at the crown and then streaked down in jagged bursts to caress the crumbling columns. Shep had been summoned, but warned to keep his distance; he felt a hunger to approach, but held back. It was once difficult to obey, but no longer. The first thing he had learned upon meeting his new and perfect employer was that he had been destined from the first moment of conception in his mother's womb to obey.

"I'm here now, Your Tranquility."

The was no answer from the sprawling, malevolent edifice. The urge to move closer gripped him again. He longed to walk among the columns and explore their secrets, but that was a privilege to be enjoyed later on, or so he had been told.

"I took care of the rock and roll man, like you told me."

New lights like shooting stars streaked suddenly across the kaleidoscope mirror of sky and descended into the roiling miasma of storm clouding the columns.

"I saw to his wife, too, your Lordship. She's gonna do as told from now on. You can bet on it. She's the one you really wanted."

The silence grew heavier, watchful and considered from the manor. More bolts of lightning flashed, upward this time, as if the stone columns were communicating with the black cloud above. Then the Voice came, soft and certain.

A grave error has been made.

Shep cringed, in spite of his newfound bravado. "I'm sure I did everything you told me to do, just the way you said."

Not a mistake with those two. With another. The new arrival. Adams. Horace was the one who made the mistake, but I failed to notice it.

Shep raised a wiry brow. "You? Well, that doesn't even seem possible, if you'll forgive me for saying so."

Oh, it is possible, servant. Such things can happen in Time, Times, and Half a Time. When our energies are focused upon other, pressing matters. Distraction is a hazard, even for the most diligent. You will learn this. Also in Time."

"Can I ask what kind of mistake it was that was made?"

The tempest around the top of the manor swelled for an instant, gnashing with anger and a million little blasts of the strange lightning.

It is not for you to know, slave. Not yet. Know only that I have been made aware of it by one of my own. Another helpmate. It was an unintentional oversight, but one that could prove costly. Laws were unheeded.

This was interesting, thought Shep, though he didn't dare to think it too loudly. Still, he laughed, incredulous, at the billowing storm. "Someone higher up than you told you about it?"

We are all at the service of some Other. At least for now. Never forget that, though you shall always be in the service of another.

"I take it there's something you want me to do, then, Lord. You called me and I came."

Bow to me, face to the stone, and then rise and take hold of the one called Brask.

"But I haven't met him, yet, Your Tranquility."

A peal of thunder rolled out from the manor, blowing through its great bronze doors in an invisible, pyroclastic pulse of sound. It burned and bellowed and Shep was thrown onto his back. He was stunned that he could feel such intensity of pain with the new, improved body.

You had not met Grayle and his wife, either, yet you found them easily enough with my assistance. Rise up and do as you are bidden. Fly from my presence and I will introduce you to him at whiles. Do not question me further. I have no use for a slothful soul. You could be replaced, though not as easily as one might wish. Think not that my eye was only upon you when the time came to select a candidate. There are others who have been made suitable for the tasks at hand. Many others. I could call them from their worlds in an instant, if I choose.

"I don't want to find myself out of a job so soon after getting one, Lord." Shep scrambled onto his knees and bowed until his forehead was flat against the freezing silver matrix of the flagstone.

Then be off. I can ill afford another error, nor another loss as unpleasant as the one I sustained on the Dreadful Isle. Leave and see about the object of the hunt before

I summon a new slave to grind your bones to dust, just as you ground the bones of the slave who came before you. I shall give you speed.

The glimmering sky dimmed, the storm nesting atop the manse retreated and a vast darkness descended in a smothering velvet blanket. Shep Daltry vanished into its midst and was carried away.

RUN

When Brask stepped out of the van to have a look around, breath steaming in the early September sunshine, Main Street of downtown Wistwood was deserted except for Reverend Jarecki and his ever-present wheelbarrow, crossing idly. The neon "Breakfast" sign flashed soft pink, now, instead of yellow, in the fully replaced picture window at Margie's Bar and Grille. "Lunch, Dinner & Drinks" languished plain and lifeless underneath until noon, presumably. A furtive glance revealed no trace of activity at Schuyler's antique shop. Her Mercedes was nowhere to be seen. More astonishingly, there wasn't so much as a chunk of charcoal, smudge of soil, or singed leaf in evidence where the mammoth trees had lit-up the evening with fire and earth-shaking thunder the night before. Brask stood aghast at the now immaculate portion of road and pavement. Even the yellow line down the middle of Main seemed to have been scrubbed and repainted, gleaming with a ferocious perfection.

"You help with the clean-up, Reverend?" he called to the Jarecki, who was just about to heave his barrow up and over the curb and onto the chapel's lawn. The cleric didn't appear to notice him. Brask sauntered closer, jangling his keys in his palm.

"Hey. Good morning, Rev."

Jarecki stopped on the sidewalk and glared at him as if he had never laid eyes on Brask Adams.

"What happened to those crazy trees that hit the street last night?" Brask gestured like a nervous child to the stretch of roadway behind him. "That's quite a vanishing act, considering the mess, huh? You know, I was trying to think of logical explanations for that whole scene and I can't come up with anything. How about you?"

Jarecki was unmoved. "What trees are you talking about?"

"Excuse me?" Brask stopped short. He was certain he had seen the dullard cleric in the circle of onlookers entranced by last night's conflagration.

"I said, 'What trees are you talking about?' Brask Adams. Are you deaf?"

Brask felt the hair stand up on the back of his neck and on his forearms beneath the suede jacket. It wasn't the morning chill.

"You can lose the attitude with me, for starters, you Bible-sucking moron. And correct me if I'm wrong, but weren't you out here last night with the rest of us when it felt like the street had split in half and hell was sticking its nose up through the middle of it?"

"Hell doesn't need to stick its nose into the middle of anything," replied Jarecki, as if instructing a child in some tenet from a catechism. "Hell stays where it belongs and people tend to go looking for it on their own," he added, tightening his grip around the wheelbarrow handles. Brask took a step backward without even realizing it.

"Yeah, sure. Right. Whatever you say, pal." Brask met Jarecki's dead gaze with a glare as cold as he could summon. "Do you think in your vast knowledge of deep and meaningful things you might be able to tell me where I can find Horace? I need to get some things squared away with the services around here. And I need some answers."

"How should I know where he might be found?" said Jarecki with a shrug and a heave of the cement-filled wheelbarrow. "Can't you see I've got a chapel to build?"

Brask looked down and was horrified to see that the man's hands were bloodied and blistered. His clothes were caked with dust and streaked with dry blotches of cement and mud. Glancing over Jarecki's shoulder and across the manicured walkway through the line of birch trees on either side, he beheld the little chapel and his jaw dropped. The edifice at the end of the path, so meticulous in its rising construction the day before, was again a mismatched pile of rubble. Every red brick had been thrown in a heap to the ground. The foundation was cracked outward like streaking fingers of lightning from the front steps all the way to what had once been the rear wall.

"What in the … not again?" gasped Brask. "No one can be that bad at laying bricks. What happened?"

Jarecki stared, but once again it was as if he looked straight through Brask toward some distant and irresistible beacon.

"The chapel falls to the earth. I rebuild it. That is my task. Perhaps that is too difficult for you to understand."

"I don't know about that," said Brask, swallowing hard, "but I do know you might want to look into some professional assistance, of the construction and the psychiatric varieties, because you obviously need help in both departments."

Jarecki blinked languidly. "The chapel will always crumble. I will always rebuild it." Then he turned on his heels to push the loaded wheelbarrow onto the curb and up the winding walkway, hunched over as if he himself were on the verge of collapse.

Brask stared after him for a moment, dumbfounded.

"What in the hell kind of fucked-up people live in this place, anyway?" he whispered to himself. He felt as if someone had punched him suddenly in the gut. "What have I gotten myself into, here?"

Were you that desperate, idiot? Taking the first place you looked at? Yeah. You were that fucking desperate.

Lease or not, low rent and fabulous dream cabin notwithstanding, Wistwood was starting to look like it might have been a mistake made in the heat of his own instability. A frost-arrowed wind blew down the center of Main Street in the sunshine. Brask shoved his hands in his pockets and shivered. What had he been thinking? This had all happened way too fast.

And great, blazing trees appeared and disappeared for local entertainment in this berg.

Something's wrong with this place or else I've gone stark, raving mad.

Maybe Horace would let him out of the agreement. It had only been signed yesterday, after all. Hell, he didn't even have a working phone or an online connection, yet.

Then, looking around the piercing stillness of Main Street, he noticed the rest. Namely, that which could not be noticed.

No telephone poles. No electric lines. No transformers. No streetlights. Nothing.

Now that he thought of it, he hadn't noticed any utility poles or lines back at his cabin, either.

But the lights went on and off!

Even Donovan's store, darkened at this early hour behind the plastering of old-time cola ads and hardware clearance-sale posters in the windows, betrayed no connection with an electrical world from any visible point or portion of its exterior. To Brask's more horrified further inspection, the CLOSED—PLEASE CALL AGAIN sign hanging from the front door window seemed to mock his current thoughts with a low hiss of a whisper he could actually hear in his head.

CLOSED—PLEASE CALL AGAIN. AND AGAIN AND AGAIN AND AGAIN AND AGAIN AND AGAIN AND

What the hell does this town run on? Burning trees from space?

The neon lights in Margie's restaurant were flashing weakly. She had power. But from where? No lines connected to her building either. Brask stalked across the street and stuck his head inside the unlocked door.

No one was around. Not a soul was in sight to take advantage of the $7.99 Salmon Eggs Benedict and "Bottomless Mimosas" special advertised in florid writing on the chalkboard easel near the host's stand. Brask's stomach began to yowl at the thought of good food just as Margie herself, red hair as messy and as dense as a Brillo pad, emerged through the swinging kitchen door and lumbered into the bar area.

"Well, well. Wistwood's writer-man graces our humble establishment with yet another appearance," she said, drawing her omnipresent cleaning towel across the steel beer cooler as if making it dance like a ragged puppet in a ballet, holding it daintily between two fingers. "I bet you bounced right out of bed this morning, champ."

Brask felt his cheeks flush at the subtle tone of sarcasm in Margie's voice. The odd twinkle in her eyes seemed to outshine the gaudy rhinestone broach she had pinned to the lace front of her gingham dress.

"You come in for a little *more* hair of the dog, Brask? We got mimosas all day, if you want." Her eyes darted at the chalkboard and she winked. But it wasn't a friendly wink.

"No, thanks, Margie." Brask searched her open expression across the room for any clear sign that she knew what had happened between him and Schuyler, but apart from her cryptic remark she was unreadable. He didn't want to blurt anything out and give away what might already be known. Besides, he didn't really know this woman well enough to confide any more to her than he already had, under the influence of his own stress and her endless supply of alcohol.

What happened after we came back into the bar last night? I can't really remember a thing. I just think I do. How did Schuyler and I even end up in bed?

"I'm looking for Horace this morning, actually. Jarecki over there didn't have the first clue, but I'm guessing you might. Horace was supposed to get in touch with me about a bunch of things yesterday so I can get set up properly down at the cabin."

"Down at the cabin," Margie repeated in a slightly disturbing, almost sing-song fashion. "Well, sorry to disappoint you, hon, but when it comes to the whereabouts of Horace I am just as mired in the Dark Ages as the local former Papist."

"I see. Could you at least tell me where he lives, then? I'm sure you know that."

"Course I do. He's got a little cubbyhole of his own up at the estate. The manor house. But you won't be getting in there without an invitation. I can guarantee you that."

"I really need to talk to him about the wifi hook ups. I can try, can't I? Use your phone to call him, maybe? I still have his number somewhere in the van."

"Oh, you can *try* all you like, darling. I just thought I'd save you the trouble, is all."

"Yeah, well, never mind that. I'm going to drive into Big Sur, instead—maybe even into Carmel—and see to a few things before I meet up with him about finalizing this whole deal, anyway."

"You're gonna drive into where, honey?"

"Big Sur." Brask jerked his thumb over his shoulder to the West, steeling his voice as he searched those eyes so full of some unsettling, secret delight. "To be honest with you, I may very well change my mind about moving here at all, as it turns out. I think I may have been a bit hasty after seeing the place only two days ago. Not that Horace, or even you, for that matter, haven't extended every courtesy. I'm grateful. Sometimes a person just gets a different sense about things after the fact, you know? Maybe a person isn't such a good fit for a given place. That isn't necessarily a reflection on the people or the place, of course."

"Oh, of course not, doll. That kind of thing happens all the time. You know, they say it's particularly a woman's prerogative to change her mind, but in this era of what's good for the gander, I think the same thing can be said for the goose. Categorically speaking, mind you. But … um … you may have a technical problem with that fundamental right, my dear. After all, you signed the lease. You told me so yourself. Couldn't stop bragging about it, in fact."

Brask balked. "Yeah? So what? It was a two-bit paragraph of hen scratch practically written-up on one of your paper bar-napkins. And people have been known to blow-off far more complicated documents in far more complex housing situations."

Marge folded her bar towel neatly and pursed her lips. "Blow things off? Not *that* document, doll," she murmured. "And not if you bled on it."

Time froze for a bizarre instant. Brask's world began to spin. His head tipped back as if he were avoiding the strike of some invisible snake. The other digits on his left hand went unconsciously to the tip of his index finger, still covered with a band aid.

"What the hell did you just say to me?"

"You bled on it," replied Margie, flatly. "Nobody gets out of a blood lease in Wistwood, Brask. *Nobody.* You see, blood carries a lot, honey. Blood sees a lot. Covers a lot. Flows through a lot. The joy. The sorrow. The guilt. The jealousy. The soul. Everything. And when blood gets shed, it gets owned."

A sensation like a tickling finger dotted and tapped an icy path up Brask's spine. "How? I … I never told you I got blood on that lease."

He thought with a weird rise of panic to the moment he and Schuyler had laughed in the sex-drenched dark about the coincidence of their lease-signing lacerations.

"Oh, I think you did tell me, Brask. You said quite a lot at the bar your second night. A lot you probably don't remember. Maybe the Casting of the Trees got to you. Who knows? But don't be ashamed. It's not as if you and your little girlfriend are the first people to spill their guts to a bartender after a few belts of the good stuff. You won't be the last, either. I can promise you."

"You know something, Margie, between what happened last night and this nonsense about blood leases and whatever, I gotta say that this town and just about everybody in it has officially given me the creeps. Look, I wish you a lot of success and tons of good times here at the saloon, but if you see Horace, tell him I changed my mind and skipped town. He can toss the two or three things I left down at the cabin and keep the last month's rent money for his troubles. That's fine. I'll mail him the key as soon as I get settled somewhere else, if he wants, but I'm out of here. He won't be able to find me. He didn't even ask for references, as it was."

"My, but that's an awful lot of stuff for me to remember, Brask. Gee, you mind if I write that all down?" said Margie through a breath of soft and facetious laughter.

"Just tell him when you see him, Ma'am. I guarantee you're going to see him before I do. Goodbye."

Brask had to muster all of his self-control not to slam the door behind him, but he stomped out of the bar with as much swagger as he could summon. Neetha Grayle was outside, climbing the steps of the bar's front porch and the sight of her stopped Brask in his tracks. She was a walking disaster.

Dressed in a tattered pink tracksuit that was jarringly incongruous with the glamorous trophy-wife look she had sported before, Neetha wept and trembled, clutching the wooden railing near the entrance to Margie's, frozen with one foot on the pavement, as if the next step up might send her reeling.

"Neetha?"

She looked up, lipstick smeared unevenly across her collagen-inflamed lips, one eye sporting a luxurious set of false lashes while the other was void of all adornment, staring like a faint pencil sketch on the otherwise vivid roadmap of her face. The blouse beneath her tracksuit was ripped and her purple velcro sneakers seemed impossibly tiny even for her petite frame.

"What in the world happened to you?" said Brask.

Neetha put her hands to her face and doubled over in a sobbing fit.

"Oh, God. I was hoping nobody would see me out in public like this," she moaned. "I was just going to pop into Margie's and have a little Bloody Mary or something to calm my nerves."

Brask took a few steps down and put a tentative hand on her shoulder, thoroughly uncertain of what to say. Neetha pulled a little pink Kleenex from her pocket and blew her nose daintily behind her lacquered nails. "Is Margie's open, Brask?"

"Yeah, she's in there, but I can't vouch for her mood. Seems actually insane to me. At least today."

"Great. Just great," snapped Neetha. "There's way too much weird going around this morning, even for this lousy town."

"You too, huh?" Brask took a few steps back as the woman struggled to compose herself. "Believe me, I know how you feel. Where's Lleyton?"

Neetha waved the kleenex dismissively in the vague direction of her house over the nearby set of hills and burst into a newfound smattering of sobs.

"I just can't go into it, Brask. I can't. Last night's tree thing and this morning's bullshit really took it out of me, and I've been putting up with a helluva lot more than usual these days. That new freak told me I should just head down here and have myself a drink, but I don't know what the hell I'm doing, to tell you the truth. The ugly sonofabitch is up at the rental right now 'taking care' of Lleyton or whatever that might mean. As far as I'm concerned at this point, good riddance. I'm scared."

"What 'new freak' are you talking about, Neetha? Who do you mean?"

"That guy," she whimpered, splaying her magnificent fingertips in frustration. "That awful new man, whoever he is. I don't know him or where he's from. Hadn't seen him around here before. Says he's a new hire. Just showed up in the bedroom right in the middle of everything, and I guess it's a good thing he did or I wouldn't be here right now."

Brask shook his head. "Wait a second. Showed up in your bedroom? What the hell is going on up at your place?"

"I swear I can't talk about it, Brask. I think I'm in enough trouble as it is already. But I'll tell you one thing—I don't know how much more of this shit I can stand."

"Look, Neetha. You wanna take a ride with me?"

She peered up at him between her sniffles. "A ride?"

"Yeah, I'm heading into town. Into real town. Big Sur. Up to Carmel, if I need to. I'm gonna stop by the bank and make a few phone calls. Check email. Still no phone or online connection hooked up down at my place. Maybe the two of us can stop by the River Inn or Nepenthe for a couple of Bloody Marys and we can talk. Might do us both some good to get out of Dodge for an hour or so. I'll bring you back."

"Stop at the what? Go where?" Neetha stared at Brask through streaming tears, bewildered. "What are you talking about, honey?"

Brask wasn't about to tell her he planned to leave the place for keeps. But she was clearly bruised and in such a state he was happy to give her a ride out to contact proper authorities, if she wanted.

"Just trust me. You're in no condition to drive, upset the way you are, and I could use a drink myself. I just don't feel like getting one at Margie's this morning. Wait a minute, did you walk all the way over here?"

"Yeah." Neetha pointed pitifully down at her sneakers as Brask guided her across the street and toward the passenger door of his van. "I was too scared to go back in and get the keys to the Ferrari after I got outside. I nearly tripped about twenty times coming up one hill and down another. Thought I was gonna fall off into a ravine, once or twice."

"That's okay, Neetha. You just get in and we'll go for a little ride, you and I. I want to ask you some questions about Wistwood, anyhow. You got here a few days before I did. Maybe you can help me out and then I'll buy us both some hair of the dog once we get into Big Sur. It's not even fifteen minutes to town."

"But where is it you're going?" asked Neetha, bewildered. "Which road are you going to take? Not that winding one? You know about a safe road out?"

"The road to Big Sur, like I said." Brask hopped into the van and turned the keys in the ignition while Neetha fastened her seatbelt as if in a trance. The engine sputtered and then roared to life. "Of course it's a safe road."

Thank God this old clunker started on the first try.

"But where in the hell …?"

"Just take a deep breath, Neetha, and try to pull yourself together as best you can. You can tell me all about what happened on the way. Believe me, things will start to look a lot better when we're sucking down a few drinks overlooking the Pacific. I have to get my head together, too."

Neetha erupted in louder sobs than ever as Brask motored along the curve of Main Street and up the hill toward the snaking road that led out of Wistwood. When he made the first sharp turn to take the woodland stretch toward Crystal Creek Canyon and Big Sur, the size and density of the fog bank overwhelming the hitherto unseen sweep of forest was enough to push the breath from his lungs. He hit the brakes and sent the van into a brief but painful slide. Neetha's shoulders lurched forward against the old seatbelt harness and her head nearly hit the dashboard.

"Jesus, Brask!"

"Will you take a look at that fog," Brask said in wonder. "It was bad enough the day I came in here, but I've never seen a fog roll so thick, ever, and I've lived here in California all my life."

"What are you *talking* about? You said you just moved to Wistwood the other day," wailed Neetha, clearly frightened by the towering wall of iron gray cloud that roiled and curled, impassable, smothering the line of trees and straddling the forest road as if the great anvil cloud of a supercell storm had descended from the sky to guard its claim upon the earth.

"Is there something in the water in Wistwood that I don't know about? I'm talking about California, Neetha. I know you and Lleyton are English, but you must know this state well enough. Have you ever seen fog this thick? I mean, look! The sky overhead is blue, for Christ's sake."

"Good God, Brask!" Neetha held a taloned hand to her breast and exhaled in tiny, controlled bursts. "That fog has been over the woods outside Wistwood since we got here last Friday. And we are *not* in California."

Brask turned slowly, as if glancing at her out of a dream. She glared back at him, her mismatched eyes streaming tears, one river clear and the other streaked black.

"We're just outside of Lake Placid, New York. Lleyton and I were staying at our little place, there, getting it closed-up and ready for sale, when one of us—we can't remember who—decided to take a little vacation in the Adirondacks, to chill out before we flew back home to London. That's how we came to Wistwood. Met stupid Horace online. Made a reservation for the A-frame. What's with this California story?"

"Neetha, I don't know what's happened between you and Lleyton, and I get the sense that he is an abusive nightmare, and I'm genuinely sorry to hear that, but you are clearly overwrought and I am in no mood or position to—"

"Listen to me, Brask," begged Neetha. "Just turn around and head back into Wistwood right now. I don't think I want to go for a drive."

"No! You can get out and walk back in your little pink sneakers, if you want to, lady, but I can get through that fog if I drive slow with the beams adjusted and I intend to. It's just a bumpy country lane, anyhow. I'm going into Big Sur to start making arrangements to get away from any further crazy in my life. And, sad to say, that includes Wistwood. I made a big fucking mistake. Like I said, you can come along into town for a quick ride or you can walk back now."

Neetha went rigid with terror. "Please! I can't walk back on my own. Not with that fog out there. I'm scared. Don't make me get out. You don't know the kind of things that're out there."

"What do you mean?"

"Oh God. See, I tried to drive out once myself, the day after we got here. I needed my brand of cigarettes and the knob in the mercantile didn't carry any, so while Lleyton was napping I took the car out for a drive. I didn't wanna tell anybody cause I was afraid they'd think I was drunk or on drugs—"

"Shut up! Now you're starting to freak *me* out and I've had enough of that since last night. Jesus, this is nuts. Look, I'm sorry, Neetha. Can you just hang on until I get to town and at least hit an ATM and make a proper phone call? Then I'll drive you back or, hell, I'll even pay for a taxi, if that's what you'd like. This road is too narrow to turn around right here. This isn't your car. It's my hunk of shit. There's no shoulder and little ditches on either side. We'd tip over until we got to Crystal Creek Canyon."

He put the Pontiac into gear and headed toward the obscured stand of trees. The wall of mist became agitated; it rose like a swelling, dark mountain with a cavernous mouth. Waiting.

"No! Please. Don't drive into the mist. I'm begging you."

"Like I said, Neetha. I will call you a damn cab and pay for it myself as soon as we get to town. It's not even two miles, damn it."

"Cab? Two miles?" Neetha moaned desperately, covering her eyes with her hands as they began to roll forward. "I can't do this anymore. I … I just can't."

Brask was at his wits' end by the time they reached the edge of the fog bank and entered. The mist didn't seem so thick and intimidating from within as it had on the open roadway. But Neetha's whimpering only intensified.

"Look, luv, you have either got to calm down or I really am going to stop the van and kindly open the door and gently drag your ass out. And I don't want to do that to a nice lady. You hear me? The choice is yours. Damn! Why do I get involved in other people's shit? Your face is bruised and someone has beaten-up on you. I saw it on your face back at Margie's. We need to get you to town where you can think about some next move or call the cops or whatever. I'm not going to leave you alone."

Neetha sat up straight in the seat and swallowed hard, choking back a sob. She nodded and stuffed her mouth into the crook of an elbow, biting on the fabric of her track suit.

"That's better," said Brask. "Thank you. Try to take a few deep breaths when you get the chance. Relax. Everything is going to be okay and, if we have to, we'll get you to the local police department or a doctor or whatever you want or need. Okay? Just keep calm because I do need to keep an eye open in this pea-soup. I don't want to drive us off the road entirely. Look, I promise we'll be able to get where we're going and drive along just fine in the sun."

And so they did. For an hour in the interminable fog. That was when Brask began to panic.

"I don't understand it," he muttered, eyes straining over the steering wheel. The smoky gloom of the fog pressed around them like a mocking universe of ghosts. "This is the same road I took three fucking days ago. It has to be. There *were* no other roads. I didn't take any turns at all, much less a wrong turn. There were ... I watched carefully as Horace sat right where you're sitting. There were no off roads at all. We should've been on Crystal Creek Canyon road almost an hour ago."

Neetha had her arms wrapped around herself, as if freezing in the subdued light. When she spoke she was dazed.

"I warned you not to drive into the clouds. I told you you weren't in California. Now look at us. In big trouble, and you'd better believe it."

Brask felt a bit of hot sweat drip from his scalp down the back of his neck. He shivered. "Neetha, what in the hell do you know that I don't know? Out with it."

"You don't get any warning about trying to drive out of Wistwood when you go in, Brask." Her words were almost slurred. Brask wondered if she had been drinking heavily that morning before they met. It would explain a lot, but not about flaming trees, or Margie's blood diatribe, or the prison of the blind roadway.

"What's outside this town ... you just find out that it's all an illusion," she added.

"What's an illusion?" demanded Brask, slamming a fist against the wheel. "What kind of game are you people playing around here?"

Neetha's voice, as weak and distant as it had become, was suddenly chilling in Brask's ears. "Oh, it's no game," she said. "It's anything but a game. You're here because you're supposed to be here, one way or the other. At the bar the other night, I only talked about trying to leave our rental early to see if Margie or anybody else would warn me against it. But I'd already tried to head out on my own, like I said."

Brask's heartbeat was already pounding in his ears as his eyes darted back and forth at the tree limbs, all jutting like gnarled claws and twisted arms, reaching through the interminable mist, emerging from clotted layers of Nothingness. His throat constricted. The sensation of being somehow buried alive was almost too much to bear and getting worse because he could not tell where the feeling was coming from, exactly. The air within and without was moist and alive, almost electric with energy, but he felt he might drown at any moment.

A mounting impulse to leap from the moving van and run wildly into the snatching mist seized him; it was a desperate desire to enter some sense of vastness, of space beyond the crowding stranglehold of fear. He took a few deep breaths, closed his eyes for a moment and opted to roll down the window. The air that rushed in seemed enough to flood the van in a torrent, but it was cool and vaguely comforting. He gulped a few mouthfuls of it in an attempt to slow his pulse.

"I wish you wouldn't roll the window down like that," moaned Neetha. "Please put it back up."

"I have to fucking breathe, lady, if I'm going to get us out of this," he snarled and Neetha cowered in the seat as if he had slapped her.

"Wait a second," he gasped, eyes glinting and narrowing as he leaned forward to peer through the roiling sweep of vapor. "Look. There's a car up ahead. I saw a car through a quick break in the fog. I'm sure of it."

"Please, you don't want to stop for anything out here," Neetha whined. "God, don't do it."

"Shut up!"

It was a car. An old Mercedes. As he motored closer in the porridge of air, he recognized it as the vehicle belonging to Schuyler. The sight of the license plate, which he had never bothered to notice before, sent a jolt of terror through his brain.

Ohio.

The driver's side door was wide open and he could soon see that the car was half wedged in a small ditch, and half on the cragged roadway, tree limbs like fingers scraping just barely atop the roof.

"My God, it's Schuyler's. I remember looking at it last night before we … I know it's hers. What in the hell happened here?"

"Who's Schuyler?" Neetha eyed the ghostly car as if it were a dangerous beast lurking and waiting to pounce upon any victim foolish enough to pass by. "You're not gonna stop here, are you? Can't you just turn around, for Christ's sake? That's what I did when I was dumb enough to come out here. They might let us back if you'd just—"

"For the last time, Neetha, will you shut up so I can think? I have to get out and see what's happened. Schuyler's a … newcomer to town. Just like me. She got in late yesterday. I met her outside the bar when everybody was gathered around those crazy fucking trees. You didn't get a chance to meet her."

"It doesn't matter if I met her or not. If she came to Wistwood and couldn't get out, then she's probably in the same boat as the rest of us. Probably worse, from the looks of it."

Brask was tempted to launch into the shattered Neetha once more but looking at her he saw that she was nearing the point of some catastrophic breakdown. Her face beneath her now askew and hideous extensions was a canvas of smeared make-up, a contorted mask. She began to shake uncontrollably as Brask opened the door to get out.

"Don't! This will make things worse for us, Brask, and I think they're already bad beyond anything you could dream up."

He ignored her and walked in the ominous swirl of the fog to the Mercedes that Schuyler had inherited from her grandmother, shivering at both the amplified silence all around him and the chill that seemed to sink straight to the bone. Walking in this air was like passing through strands of cotton soaked in ice water. After only a few steps his lungs were wheezing and felt heavy with fluid. He lowered his head and peered into the front seat. The engine was off but her keys were still dangling in the ignition. Her purse had fallen onto the passenger's side floorboard. He scanned the surroundings of the woodland, what little he could make out of it through the heavy tumble and turn of cloud, straining to hear anything through the murk. Not even the sound of a tree limb snapping or a bird's cry or a leaf crackling on the forest floor could be detected. The whole landscape was dead, the car as blind and forbidding as the sentinel statue guarding an ancient and desecrated mausoleum at the edge of an abandoned cemetery.

"Where in the hell could she have gone, all the way out here?" he muttered, the words feeling like crystals of frost on his lips.

Going to Ohio. Going to Ohio. Only forty-five minutes away. Where was she?

Where was he?

It had to be a wrong turn taken; some stupid side-road he had failed to note on the first day in his nervousness and had now mistakenly followed in the confusion of the mist, not to mention the catatonic fit that had gripped Neetha. Who knew what she was yammering on about with her story of a threatening trip out of town. But what trouble was he in himself? He looked back at the van. Its white exterior was barely visible, but what he could see was being groped by a great puff of curling, vaporous claws that reached from the endless wall of gray. He was about to find his way back to it when a belligerent voice boomed in his ear from behind and nearly knocked the breath from his lungs in surprise.

"Who's out there now on my property? Don't move until I can get a look at you, trespasser! Trespasser!"

Brask whipped around, gripping the open door of the Mercedes and wishing in some vague chamber of his mind that he had a gun in his hand.

Wait! There's the tire iron behind the front seat in the Pontiac. Get it, you asshole, before some goddamn hillbilly hits you over the head with a shovel.

"Don't you move from that spot!" roared the voice from the fog and soon a lumpen shadow emerged, staggering into view. With every step of its approach Brask's eyes widened in terror.

It was an old man, bent at the waist, clad in denim jacket and camouflage pants, a green suede hunters cap upon his head. His face! His face was …

His face was half-eaten. Or missing.

The flesh on one side, from beneath the hat-brim and all the way to the jaw-line, was nothing but a shredded disaster of exposed muscle and yellowed bone, the rictus of hideous teeth working up and down, up and down as the thing approached. The other half was the grizzled maw of a wrinkled, unshaven horror. Red-ringed, milky blue eyes, one lidless and popping from the fleshless half-visage, regarded Brask with the hungry curiosity of a piranha. The teeth began to snap. The feet shuffled closer across the dirt road.

Brask was immobilized with terror, overwhelmed with a sensation he had never before experienced in his entire life; this was a helpless rush of the very soul seeming to drain from his body, a spinning of the consciousness, weak and feverish, before a plunge into bloodcurdling insanity.

A ululating scream from Neetha in the van jolted him out of his stupor. She, too, had seen the impossible visitor.

"You're the second one to come trespassing on my land today, boy," rasped the corpse-like abomination. "Do you know how much trouble you're in? My wife's mighty hungry today, too. Look what she did to my face! We already had to hand over the pretty little thing that came in this car, here. The Landlord wouldn't let her stay to breakfast, you see. Said she wasn't ready for eating. Not yet. Wanted her for himself. But you look like enough to fill the boiling pot. Same goes for that nice little dish you got in that big ugly tank you're driving."

The thing narrowed its one intact eye and cackled.

"Say! If it isn't the rock star's wife," it growled, the words as deformed and mutilated as the lips that were barely there to allow them any semblance of form and clarity. "Come out to see the poor exiles again, have you, Neetha Grayle? We know all about you. We were warned. Where's that no good husband of yours? It's about time his legs served some useful purpose again, and we get awful cravings out here in the Desolation. Mrs. Kimberton would love to lay those legs out on the long table and have at 'em. Get out of that van, Neetha, and you can *all* come to lunch. Forever and ever, and forever beyond that."

The thing lurched forward, arms outstretched, but its body was met by Brask's violent kick of the Mercedes's front door, the only thing that had been between him and the oncoming blasphemy. With a sickening thud the thing flew backward onto the road, crumpled and weeping suddenly in pain and disappointment. Brask lost control of his faculties for an agonizing instant and vomited in a violent spray onto the window of the car door as it swung back toward him. The obscenity whimpering six feet away curled into a grotesque fetal position and began to wail a litany of lamentations.

"Oh, it's awful what you done to a poor old man!" he cried. "Look at me, busted and broken on the earth. Who would hurt a man just struggling to feed his wife? She won't let up, I tell you! Day after day she eats the flesh from my bones, morning until midnight, and doesn't even stop with the marrow. She breaks me apart and gets at that, too. And come the dawn everything's grown back so she can starting biting and chewing at me all over again. You wouldn't believe the pain! It's time for someone else to share the burden, I say!" The thing kicked out petulantly and howled in frustration. "But no! Management won't allow me hardly any reprieve, ever. Oh … it hurts! It hurts, and I feel it all as she's doing it to me, every bite and every strip of flesh she peels off of me, and I can't get out! I can't get out!"

"What is this? What's happening to me?" screamed Brask, tearing at his hair with white-knuckled fingers. "What's being done to me? This isn't real! This isn't happening! It's a dream!"

The wretched form below ceased its moaning and turned a baleful gaze at Brask, blood and mockery oozing from the destruction of its mouth.

"What's being *done* to you? Why, what have *you* done to somebody else, boy? That's the question you should be asking yourself, out here with no hope in God or heaven, deep in the Canyon of Desolation. What have *you* done?"

"I expect he'll find out in due time, Harold. Everyone does, after all."

Another figure emerged from the mist, this one as harmless-looking and as comforting as the first had been incomprehensibly terrifying. It was an old woman, with hair as white and frizzy as dandelion tufts, pulled back tight from her smiling, round little face. Her gentle, delicate hands, covered in age-spots, rubbed together in the cold over a yellow polka-dot apron tied in homely fashion about her waist. Her bright green eyes gazed happily up at Brask, twinkling above rosy apple-cheeks. Her Birkenstock shoes tapped slowly on the hard dirt of the roadway.

"You must be Brask Adams," she said, mild and welcoming as the most doting grandmother. "Not to say that we were expecting you or anything, but a little bird told us that you are the nice young man now living in our cabin, down in Wistwood. I'm Ada Kimberton, and that, crawling on the ground like the spineless worm that he is, is my husband, Harold."

Brask staggered back against the car, his feet nearly falling out from underneath him. He sidled away as best he could, crab-like, gasping at the frame as the old woman approached, one soft but determined step at a time, her old, knobby fingers now clenching and unclenching.

"Tell me, Mr. Adams. Did you find the cabin up to your standards? Do you think it'll be better than living like a filthy bum in that beat-up old van of yours? I hope so, because we worked on the various improvements to that cabin, Harold and I, before we found it necessary to seek other accommodations."

Old Mrs. Kimberton smiled beatifically at Brask, and thick bits of gristle and gobbets of flesh could be seen protruding from between her set of brown and decaying teeth. Her breath filled the air and came as a stench of withering putrefaction, thick and oily enough to fill Brask's nostrils, mouth, and lungs until he began to heave in spasms, but there was nothing left to vomit. He fell and was soon crawling for the van on his hands and knees, gasping for air, scraping the gritty road until his fingers bled and his knees cracked in agony on the rocks and pebbles. Still, he could hear her coming toward him, soft wooden footfalls, one step closer, one step closer, and he felt his strength begin to fade, as it does when running from an unseen pursuer in the muddiness and mire of a breathless nightmare.

"This isn't happening!" he yelled. Neetha screamed and tried to scuttle under the jam-packed contents in the back of the van, but her desperate clawing only caused an avalanche that could not be resisted and she tumbled backward against the center console.

"This is most assuredly happening," said Mrs. Kimberton, another step closer, another step closer. "And if you hadn't been so wicked, Brask Adams, you might have been spared such happenings. But things are as they are, and, mark my words, if you don't end up on my table out here in the heart of Nothing, you'll end up on someone else's table. Maybe even your own. Such things have been known to happen, in places like this, because they really aren't places at all, and therefore *anything* can happen."

Brask roared with terror and the final, wild will to wrench the last bit of physical strength from his resisting body. He sprang forward in his crawl and was almost to the door of the van, his hand stretching toward it, straining for redemption, when he felt something step down hard on his fingers. He screamed in a deafening blast of anger and fear, certain that he would look up to behold the Kimberton woman, her grandmotherly sandal crushing his knuckles and her rancid mouth, slimy and poisonous, moving low to his face, ready to gnaw and to rip and to gorge. But it wasn't her shoe. It was the shoe of another, pinning the now-spent Brask to the road, breathless and paralyzed.

"You two get yourselves on out of here," Shep Daltry said to the Kimbertons. "Get on back to where you been put. These two runners don't have nothing to do with you. Go on, I said, back to the Empty, where no one can see y'all."

"We're lonely out here, all by ourselves," said Ada Kimberton, flatly. Her form faded slower than a waking dream, back into the fog until it was only a dull silhouette. Her husband, curled on the ground, vanished with her. "Lonely and hungry. All have needs. All can feel lonely," came her last, faint whisper.

"Lonely!" said Shep. "Well, I gather that's the general complaint in these parts, ain't it? But you both shoulda thought of that before you decided to live out here."

APOCALYPTICA

B rask awakened beneath the familiar sky, the one that flashed hypnotic kaleidoscopes of unearthly color and rippling bolts of light. He was naked and bound by his hands and feet, pulled across the cold flagstone of quicksilver veins and fiery threads. They were all around him.

Everyone from Wistwood, gathered in a circle as they had gathered the night before to contemplate the burning trees.

Margie, Donovan, Theo, Jorge, Walt, Jarecki, and all the others he had not met but had seen drinking or eating at the bar and grill. They surrounded him and stared down, expressionless and silent, as if peering from the looking-glass of a microscope and he were an amoeba on a slide, being analyzed by minds far greater and more consequential than his own.

No, it can't be real, he thought dreamily, looking from face to face beneath the unnatural, unhallowed sky. *They are empty vessels. Not me. I'm still alive. I'm still a person, but they ... they aren't.*

Shep Daltry pushed through the little circle and looked down upon him with a pitiful, crooked smile.

"Well, hey there, sport. It's about time you woke up and joined the party. We woulda got you up sooner but, well, the folks here in Wistwood are nice, considerate people, as you've seen, and you needed a bit of rest, anyhow. You wasn't looking so good back there in the ole foggy jungle."

Brask didn't even try to pull or struggle against whatever shackles were binding him. It felt like rope made out of razor-barbed threads.

"What do you want with me?"

He stared, unafraid and dazed into the lined, oily face of Shep, mesmerized by the military buzz-cut and bright red eyes glinting with menace beneath the furrowed brow.

"Oh, we'll get to that in due course, my brother. Soon enough. But first we thought a few pertinent revelations might be in order."

"Where am I?"

"Not too terribly far from the Estate, and a specific portion of the Estate that we like to call the Manor House. Dwelling place of the Landlord."

"Am I going to die? Am I already dead?" gasped Brask, suddenly sensing his nakedness. Fear coursed through his soul and body like a vengeful toxin. Shep only laughed a little.

"You ain't dead, buddy. No dead man could feel the kind of terror running through your sorry head right this minute. Not really." Shep looked down at Brask's stretched, muscular form and grinned. "Besides, they say the only one who ever got a rise out of a dead man was God the Holy freakin' Father, His high and mighty self, when up rose that crazy man back in Jew Land, or so they tell. I tend not to believe it. We all of us here believe in what we see. Now, would a no-account, everyday working fella like me be able to get a rise like this out of a dead man?"

He sneered and wrapped his fingers around Brask's cock, stroking it slowly. Brask writhed and struggled upon the pulsating, smooth stone until he thought his spine would snap, but to no avail.

"Get your goddamn hands off me, you filth!"

Spit flew from his mouth onto Shep's face, but Shep calmly wiped it off and used it. Then he stood up amid the circle and laughed.

"Will you look at that big thing, y'all?" said Shep, admiring his work. "Not quite a resurrection from the dead, but enough of a trick to prove to Ole Doubtful, here, that he is indeed alive and 'at attention' among us."

"Reverend Jarecki!" shouted Brask, his eyes rolling wildly toward the clergyman at the outer edge of the watchful array. "In the name of God, please help me!"

"Him?" said Shep Daltry. "I don't know what kind of help you want, there, Brasky-Boy, but I doubt the good reverend would do any less than that sweet little cowgirl you pumped full of the good stuff last night back at your cabin."

"Damn you all to hell!" screamed Brask, sweat pouring from his body and spilling onto the glistening, hissing stone as he twisted first one way and then the other. It was no use.

"A bit too late for that, Adams, but the sentiment is mighty appreciated, speaking for myself, of course."

"Help me!" hollered Brask, his voice echoing across the weird dell. Even the mirrored sky seemed to react to his cry with a rippling burst of new colors and emanations of energy. His howl might have been a pebble cast into the still water of a depraved heaven.

"There ain't nobody to help you now, Adams, least of all yourself, and do you know why? Because you don't *deserve* no help. That's why. You put yourself flat on your back atop this altar, sure as anything. You and nobody else."

"You lie!" yelled Brask, his voice now a dry husk scraping across some forgotten expanse of desert sand. "Horace!" he cried out in desperation as blood began to trickle from his nose. "Please, help me!"

Shep closed his eyes and shook his head. "Tch, tch, tch. No good on that count, either, bro. Horace'd be the first one to tell you the same thing, if he was here. That is to say, if I hadn't eaten him from head to foot and replaced him. Sorry about that. You kinda came to us right in the middle of what you might call a 'shift change,' and believe me, I know that can be sort of unsettling for folks that put a lot of stock in continuity and status quo and what-not. But things happen fast and furious and for a reason around here, especially when the Landlord is in residence, which ain't all that often, actually. See, most folks get to hang around a bit and enjoy the scenery in Wistwood before things come down to business, but what with the timing and all, you only get a couple of days, I'm afraid."

"Fuck you!"

"Aw, don't look so glum, chum. It doesn't have to turn out all bad for you. In fact, things could take a turn for the better, relatively speaking. I hear tell there could be a rather interesting offer for you on the table, if you were inclined to play your cards right."

"You're all devils and this is some kind of fucking acid trip, is that it? You bastards have drugged me. That's it, isn't it? Tell me. That's what you've done!"

Shep's head went back in mock offense. "Oh, what a cheap shot, Brasky. Blaming the devil and the bottle and the LSD or whatever the hell else people like to blame for their own mistakes, especially when they know deep down they got no one to blame except themselves."

"I don't know what you're talking about. Someone! Margie! Walt! Please! Help me."

"You do know what I'm talking about, Brask. You just have to be reminded, is all. Some people do when they get here. Memories get faint. Messy. But first, you need to be made aware of what's at stake if you don't start to accept things for what they really are. Old Donovan, here, can help. You know him from the mercantile, where I understand you got that bad case of the willies a couple days ago, am I right? Well, he's gonna give you a little glimpse in the What's What department. Take it away, O King of Local Commerce."

Donovan stepped forward and leaned in close to Brask. His face was upside-down as he stood beside the head of the stone, red beard brushing the top of Brask's head.

"You were right, you know, to get the creeps when you first walked in my place," he said. "That was pretty intuitive for a first-timer, in fact. That's why a few of us figured you had some potential. Real potential. Anyhow, it was probably my cellar you sensed, among other things. You'd be amazed at what I keep down there, at what I've been allowed to build and to govern. It's a whole different world. More than one, if you want to know the truth. But this is the one I want you to have a look at right now."

Donovan's lumberjack hand and forearm passed across the aurora of sky above Brask's eyes. The flickering lights faded and flashed until they coalesced into a new vision, an image from which Brask could not avert his gaze. There, in a windowless room with white-washed walls and a floor tiled with some obscene mosaic pattern that moved and teemed with figures alive on their own, was Neetha and the waitress, Carlee.

Carlee was doubled over, heaving in the throes of some seizure, as Neetha knelt before her, stripped of her wig and scalped alive, the grisly gleam of her yellow, bloodied skull contrasting with the purity of the immaculate walls. She was nude from the waist up. Her breasts had been torn open and the implants removed, the tatters of flesh hanging down in gory shreds. Carlee vomited in one great spasm and from her mouth came a thick, black serpent that undulated and coiled until its teeth latched onto Neetha's lower lip, wedged and wrenching ferociously. It pried her mouth open to wriggle inside and then slowly, chokingly, down her throat.

"No!" Brask slammed his face away to the side and closed his eyes to the horror, teetering on the edge of madness. Donovan waved a hand once more and the sky-vision faded.

"Oh, but yes," he countered. "That is only one of the sacred chambers in my cellar, in the labyrinth that I have been appointed to manage." The hulking, red-bearded horror was nearly breathless with pride. "That is where Neetha and Carlee reside even now."

"And that's exactly what's happening to them, and what's going to happen to them every day. Forever," interrupted Shep, leaning over to crowd the space above Brask. "And it's no more than what they deserve. See, Brask, every one of 'em had an opportunity to take a respectable position in town and hold onto it, for the good of the growing community."

"But they refused to do so," said Margie, stepping forward from the gallery, her fluffed hair framed against the flares of green lightning that streaked in fingers across the sky. "Carlee fled both of her interviews with the Landlord, who sees all and who arranges all. Neetha tried to drive out of town twice, like she did with you today. Like Carlee's poor Ethan did weeks ago, and like the Kimbertons tried to do before you came here and the Landlord returned from other affairs. Horace had to deal with those two, and you saw what became of them, out there in the Desolation. In the Canyons beyond."

"And things would've gone south for you real quick out yonder, Brask, if I hadn't stepped in," said Shep with a fraternal shake of his finger. "But you got somebody very, very important looking after you, writer boy. That's why you're here, in the heart of this loving intervention, so we can all help you see the error of your ways. So we can help you see that it was you, Brask, who deserved to come here in the first place, when you were called, and of your own free will, too."

"I didn't deserve any of this. I didn't ask for any of this," whispered Brask, his cheek against the eldritch stone, exhausted. The blood from his nose hissed in small bubbles on the matrix, along with his sweat.

"Yes, you did, Brask Adams. Just like everyone else, here," said Reverend Jarecki, stepping forward in his filthy work clothes, dried cement covering his hands. "This is the Fiefdom of the One Who Feeds Off Death in Envy, and He draws in those He chooses. And they come of their own volition. We all did."

"It's true, Brask," echoed Margie, her eyes as dead as the Void. "I was a pediatric nurse in that hospital I told you about the first night. It was the year 1998, in the way that the world reckons time, when I started smothering the babies. Just a few, at first, so as not to get caught or make things too terribly obvious. Then I learned to stagger my art, my smothering, so that no one would ever really know."

"Jesus God, what are you saying?"

"At night I would make sure no one was watching in that ward and then I would hold their little noses closed, ever so gently, and put my hand against their little chins until they turned blue and the new mothers had to be told. Yes, told, Brask. And if I was blessed, I could tell them myself and savor their tears. See, I was a barren woman in the world, and I coveted what other women could do, the life that they could engender. So I took away from them what I could not have, until suspicions were aroused, after a time. That's when I saw the ad for the bed and breakfast in Wistwood and knew I had to get out while the getting was good. It was in a town only fifty miles away. Who knew that I was being looked-for much more than I was looking for anything. But it came at the right time. They were onto me, Brask. Too close for comfort. But they had no proof, and I wanted to get well away before they came up with any."

"I was jealous of my brother," said Jorge, the cook at the grill, crowding like a vulture into the huddle. "My parents always loved him best and gave him anything he wanted, though he deserved nothing and pissed away what they did give to him. When my father died, he left Emanuelo everything and to me, he left nothing. So I waited until my brother was alone and I got him drunk one night and then pushed him from the window of his building, twelve-stories down into an alley while no one knew I was around. Still, his wife and children in Mexico suspected me, so I thought it best to leave town. It was by the grace of the Landlord that I saw the listing for a job here in Wistwood."

"I was once a Catholic priest and I resented the happiness of children" said Reverend Jarecki, "so I turned a blind eye to the actions of my bishop, who was and still is having certain of his favorites raped and then murdered. I did not care. I allowed him to extinguish their lives. I even helped him bury some bodies in places only he and I knew about. The bishop was going to murder me, too, to protect himself and his little hobby, and that's when I left the Church and became a Protestant preacher in shame. But mostly in order to hide. What else was I to do, after all? God-peddling was my only skill. Still, the bishop betrayed me and I was being sought. Thankfully, I received an unexpected letter from the management of Wistwood. Looking for someone to build a chapel in a little out of the way place.

"It was wise of me to accept a position wherein another powerful figure could protect me. When I learned that it was the Landlord who had rendered me the grace of this offer, I was hesitant, at first, but that is no sin. I soon saw that it was in my best interests to accept. Don't you think I was wise to do so, even though the chapel refuses to be built and I do not know when or if I shall ever speak of God to anyone that needs to hear about Him again."

"You're a monster," whispered Brask. "All monsters."

"My high school girl ditched me to ride off with some fool on a Harley Davidson," said Donovan. "I waited thirteen years to become friends with them and pretend that all was well and good, and then I did a little engine work on the Harley while they were out riding the rapids of the Grand Canyon on a raft. She died when they left to go home the next day, waving goodbye to me from the campsite like I was her best friend. Her man? He's paralyzed from the neck down and shits himself around the clock. Begs to die, only he can't tell anybody. All he can do is move his eyes for 'Yes' and 'No' and eat through a plastic tube and piss and shit out what he eats. That's his life. And I am happy to know it."

"Now, the Kimbertons, the former owners and restorers of your little place," said Shep. "They killed a neighbor just because he had a nicer driveway than they did back in Minnesota and he wouldn't kowtow to the zoning commission when the Kimbertons wanted to fiddle a bit with some land on his easement to make their driveway nice, too. They shot him. Harold and Ada saw a TV ad for experienced carpenters, so they drove the two hours it took to get from Duluth to Wistwood and signed-on to stay real quick, especially since they worried that the cops would find the body eventually and put two and two together.

"Their stay in town, here, however, did not have a happy ending. They've been exiled instead of embraced and employed, instead of contributing to the growth of an exciting new community that, I assure you, is going to wax stronger and flourish in the future. They also had an arrogant streak, those two. Even against the Landlord. Thought they could just make quick little visits out of town when they wanted. Got tired of being fed upon every month. So they were banished. To a place far worse than any jail back in the other world."

"I won't hear any more of this," said Brask, unable to sink his face into the stone. But Shep was far from finished.

"Lleyton Grayle broke the rules, too, after he was offered a nice place and a lifetime membership here. Why, I had to send him off to the Desolation just this morning, where you'd find him prowling around in that wheelchair in the fog, if you was to look. Looking for food. Scrounging. He'll probably run into Mrs. Kimberton. That won't be fun. Just ask her husband.

"But even I have to say it's a shame about Neetha running off with you like she did. See, she didn't really do anything. It was Lleyton who got his old lady into a jam without her technically being responsible. Oh, yes, that can happen, Brask. There is such a thing as culpability by marriage. Yes, there most certainly is. She didn't even know it when the rock star hubby whose ass she spent years trying to save paid a hit man to kill a record executive who wouldn't give him the time of day, anymore, but instead spent all his efforts on some other no-talent, long-hair singer. But, you see, it was Neetha who signed the bank draft as a down-payment for the hit, thinking it was a donation to Save the Children, and that hubby had started to turn over a new leaf at last. Envy. You see what I mean, Brask? It can poison everything, and anybody, and there's always got to be somebody to clean up the spill, if possible. That's what the Landlord does. And he gets rewarded accordingly. Everybody deserves payment. And that's what brings us to you, boy. Because you're just like everybody else here."

"What are you talking about, you damned devil?"

"Jealous to the core, Brask. That's what I'm talking about. But the Landlord is ... well, not exactly *merciful*. His work don't allow for that, but it does allow for common sense, or at least what passes for common sense among his kind. He's prepared to give you another go, despite your failed attempt to make a run for it. I suggest you take him up on the offer. It's a once-in-a-lifetime deal. While you've still got time for living at all."

Brask was twisting with rage and confusion. The shackles around his arms and ankles tore gashes into his flesh. His heart pounded until it seemed it would explode and end his life upon the stone that was itself alive and warm beneath his nakedness. When he finally found the strength to speak again, he was frothing at the mouth.

"Fuck all of you. I do *not* belong here, whatever sort of twisted hell this is supposed to be, whatever goddamned purgatory or Dante's fucking inferno you sick bastards have cooked up. I have never hurt anyone! My life has been back in my own hands because I fought and scraped and gutted-it-out after losing everything. My life has turned around. Do you hear me? I wrote a book and it's being published and the people who are publishing it are gonna come looking for me when I turn up missing and all of you—all of you in your sick little town of psychos—are gonna pay. God! Won't anybody help me?"

"No, Brask. You do not have a book that is going to be published," said Shep. "Not now. Not never. I have that on pretty reliable authority, too."

Brask stared wildly at him, his lips cracked and dry, his torso heaving with each painful breath.

"You're lying," he croaked. "Whoever you people are and whatever you're trying to do to me, you're lying."

"Not about this," said Reverend Jarecki.

"That's right," added Margie. "Fact is, Brask, your agent dropped you and your publisher cancelled publication after you stole that manuscript, lock, stock, and barrel from that poor, starving little writer fella who was homeless right around the same time you were homeless."

"Up San Jose way, don't you remember, Brask?" said Shep. "You befriended that guy and then you stole that guy's story, word for word. And when you won that contest with those Internet people and that publishing contract and the agent and the advance or whatever it is … well, that little homeless fella who could write rings around you, the one who you thought was nothing. The one who reminded you of your own reduced circumstances, whose work you pilfered out of sheer envy that someone so dirty and drugged-out could write better than you ever could. It ended badly for him. That fella walked into one of them internet cafes and he saw the online news about your winning entry, and he read an excerpt, and you know what he did then, Mr. Adams?"

"He went out and killed himself," said Walt. "He climbed up a tree, the same tree where you first found him sitting in the park, and he cried himself to death … with a little of help from the heroin. And he left a note. And they found it and you were properly disgraced, Brask, because you're a murderer."

"A murderer," said Reverend Jarecki.

"Murderer," said Donovan.

"Murderer," said Marge.

"Murderer," echoed all of the figures standing in the shadowy circle.

Shep Daltry threw his hands in the air. "Looks like a consensus, Brask."

"It … it can't be true!" Brask spread himself like a crucified man across the rock, even as every memory suddenly roared into his brain with the force of a tsunami.

"You wouldn't remember it, Brask, until right about now. See, the way the Lord and Master of this little operation handles his affairs, He walks to and fro about the world, keeping his eye open for likely candidates to take up residence in his town. Citizenship, if you will. But citizenship with benefits. Then he just tinkers a bit with certain recollections when he sees someone ideal and all the stars are aligned and circumstances are suitable. Only you would see the message about Wistwood, meant for you alone, on the TV or in the paper or on the internet or wherever. Even on a damned bulletin board, if it suited His Lord and Master. But you have to come of your own, absolute volition. That's a rule, you see. And only you would be in a state of mind so conducive to making a visit and maybe signing a lease agreement to get things started … with a pen like this one."

Shep drew the pen that Horace had brandished the day before from his pocket.

"I inherited this from my predecessor. It's very ancient, the material that this thing is made of. In fact, it wasn't always a ballpoint pen, from what I've learned thus far. It's been other things, in other times and other places. But it's always served His Tranquility's purposes. All you have to do is sign, or give assent, formally, and with a bit of unsolicited help from Blood Magic, you can't leave. Ever."

Margie smiled down at the victim, weakly struggling. "That Schuyler gal made the mistake of trying to run, too, Brask. I think you had a little something to do with that. And she got caught out there by somebody in the Waste, in the Desolation, before Shep, here, could intervene. We're not sure who got her. Might've been the Kimbertons. They get pretty hungry, as you saw. But her ending wasn't pretty, Brask, we're all fairly sure of that.

"Still, she deserved whatever she got, because you know what she did, that pretty schoolteacher? That gal you banged in your bed last night? She strangled her own grandma, and all because the old lady never had to work outside the home a day in her life, and Schuyler couldn't stand it. It was so miserable to look at that ancient woman there in her sick bed, day after day, just waiting to die, and griping about everything. And she'd never had to work a 'real' job. And it burned her granddaughter's ass to know it. Jealousy and envy, Brask. They kill, and somebody's got to be in charge of that specific brand of eternal rehabilitation."

Brask lay still upon the flagstone, beaten and ruined from within. He glanced up through tears at the sick ceiling of whatever world he had stumbled upon and knew he had forfeited his life.

"Do what you want with me," he whispered, a single tear slipping from the corner of an eye but not driven with enough repentance to make it past his cheekbone. "If this is Hell, then I deserve it for what I've done. But I didn't know about Louis, the guy in the park in San Jose. I swear he was my friend. I swear I didn't know he killed himself."

"Don't matter if you knew it or not," said Shep. "But don't look so down and out, pal. The Landlord is still gonna offer you a position. A powerful one, as a matter of fact. See, most of the folks here—Margie, Donovan, Walt, Jorge, Reverend J, and the rest—they serve a valuable purpose when they hand everything, and I do mean *everything*, over to His Tranquility. For example, they make excellent bartenders and store owners and drinkers and, well, *props*, for the town, if you will. You know? So it looks real viable when newcomers arrive. Puts folk at ease. Greases the wheel. That's important because, like I said, this is still a growing community, Brask. One of many, if you must know. But it needs to be staged. Like a house for sale. Do you know what that means?"

Brask nodded weakly. "Yeah, I know what 'staged' means."

"Good. Because Wistwood needs souls like you to make that happen. In addition, you might get to perform little tasks and sometimes even run errands off-premises for His Tranquility, every now and then. I think I can speak for everyone here, new as I am to the scene, when I say that these sorts of excursions can be highly enjoyable. Isn't that right, y'all?"

The gruesome assembly nodded as one.

"You don't even want to know what I did to land here," said Walt, "and what I get to do when I run errands once in awhile, because I've got special privileges."

"What do I have to do?" said Brask. "Show me the way."

Shep grinned and slapped one knee. "Now that, my good friends, is the attitude of a very reasonable man! Let's get him untied so he can be presentable for the Big Boss and the Big Moment, shall we? See, we have to have you naked on the holy stone, Brask, but the Landlord doesn't like the human form all that much. He prefers what's inside. What's eternal and invisible and more nutritious than flesh can ever be."

The pinions were undone, his clothes were brought, and Margie herself helped him to put them on with the gentle encouragement of a mother. It was only when he had bent to finish tying the last lace of his left boot, with all gathered around him, that Brask leapt, wild and maniacal, from the circle, knocking Shep to the ground with a massive blow to the chin, and then dashing away from the accursed place as fast as his legs and his fear could carry him, down the rolling hill away from the horrid and crumbling columns of the manor and toward the little town nestled below, screaming at the top of his lungs. Donovan growled and made a move to pursue him, but Shep held up a restraining hand.

"No. Let Mr. Writer Man run as fast as he can. See how far he gets. The Boss has to box a bit clever before he can take this one. I was hoping he'd come quietly and seal the deal of his own will, but we can't force him to an interview quite yet, unless it's by madness or suicide. Fact is, we may not need him after all, if he refuses until the end. Boss says we got something better, now. Something he doesn't know about."

"Why the hell can't you force him?" said Walt, moving to look over Shep's shoulder at the swiftly disappearing figure of Brask Adams down the hillside.

"That's none of your damned affair. Ya'll go back to your holes or rooms or coffins or who the fuck cares, for the time being. Leave matters to management. Go on, now. Back to your appointed places. There'll be new meat coming into town later today and, in the meantime, the Landlord and I can keep a good eye on Mr. Adams. You better believe we can."

HER OF THE ISLAND

B rask had thrown himself into a river, deep in the thickest dark of the unholy wood couched in the hills behind the manor house, behind the terror of Wistwood. Upon sight of the unexpected water he had not hesitated; without thought or cry he had plunged in his grief, stunned that no one in the dreadful cabal had followed him. He sank beneath the cold and embraced the assault of the current, swiftly losing what little had remained of his sanity. Let the roar of water and the shearing rocks bear him to a crystalline, rushing Void, a tomb into which he might annihilate his being before the ultimate terror of a broken mind. First he had swirled beneath the icy torrent that was eager to drown and thrash its sudden catch. Deeper than deep he spun, trapped in the conflicting grasp of an enemy he was pleased to satisfy, dragged from blindness into deafening thunder before gathering the courage to inhale, to breathe the Death he deserved.

So came to him the agony of suffocation, of certainty that All would finish, that Hell might take him at last upon completion of the deed.

Instinct alone drove him to thrash toward the surface as he drowned; there was no regret, only the raw impulse of flesh to survive. As his life—every forgotten triumph, every etched failure—flashed in silvery sheets of lightning across his consciousness, a fearsome hand of rescue latched onto his own and pulled him from Ruin. But it was not to the mere surface of the river that he was brought, choking and flailing. Not to the air of any world he knew or imagined was Brask Adams lifted beyond understanding and his own power to resist.

He was born, expelled from the relinquishing womb of guilt and destruction, then made to travel for ages he could not begin to understand, asleep and then soaring along the summit of unheralded mountains, weak and wondrous as a newborn, yet old, older than Time, Times, and Half a Time, bent with age and lost amid the remnants of a new forest, shattered by the weight of his own sorrow into shards of glass without number. Naked and breathless, he returned to a world of life, sprawled upon the sands of an iridescent beach. Staring up through mud, tears, and lungs full of river water, he beheld the strange, loving face of Louis, the homeless youth whose work he had stolen in San Jose, the one he had cheated and driven to suicide.

"Oh, God, Louis," he sputtered. "I'm so sorry. I deserve everything that's happened for what I did. I was so ... so damn desperate. Only you would know how desperate I was. Please. Please forgive me."

Then he was slapped, hard, on his left cheek. Water erupted from his lungs. His stomach vomited mud and small pebbles. Rolling in terror, he fought to take his first breaths.

"Louis?" said Larkspur. "Who is Louis?"

Brask raised his head as he felt air and life return to his flesh, his spirit, and propped himself onto his elbows as best he could, looking around. There was no sign of the baleful forest on the other side of the wild river that now shimmered beside him, its colors like fish scales reflecting a rainbow's light. There was no hint of hill country nearby or in the distance. On the other side of the river, only a vast expanse of flat, red desert fled away before him, as far as the eye could see, vanishing beneath a black blanket of stars that sparkled fiercely above.

"Oh, no ... where am I now? What the ... what the hell are you?"

"Come," said Larkspur. "Rise, when your strength will allow. I will show you greater things than what I am."

"Is this a dream?"

"It doesn't matter. Not in your case," said the blue-horned monstrosity, elegant but threatening. "If you prefer to think of it as a dream, then feel free to walk where you will, even into the warmth of the river. It is shallow and friendly to those who harbor no ill wishes. Cross the desert beyond, if that is your dream. Or follow me, as you have been instructed. She awaits you."

"She?"

"The one who has saved you, and who has saved herself. Follow me."

Andrahsha did not seem best pleased to see Brask Adams, naked, shivering, and drenched in the shade of her magnificent orchard. As for Brask, his eyes could not bear to behold the intensity of her radiance for more than a few seconds.

When he felt a sudden beckoning, wordless and rife with mercy, Brask was able to open his eyes, and this time he could see a woman, delicate and beautiful, serene beneath a canopy of trustful trees, her cornsilk hair forming an oval frame of grace about her face. He fell to his knees before her in the pungent soil and bowed his head.

"It is my fault," he wept. "I have failed everyone."

She touched him, after a moment, and he felt the might of tenderness upon his shoulder.

"No, it is not your fault. Not this predicament. A moment of this kind was bound to come. Rise up, let us go to the caverns and rest awhile, though it be brief, and we shall admire the stars as we await our journey. Larkspur, leave us and be well until I should return ... or be Lord of this orchard if I should not."

The impossible, noble creature she had called "Larkspur" bowed low and vanished into an expanding cloud of darkness that suddenly seethed out from the heart of the deep, fruitful forest nearby and took him. Soon after, they all vanished into its embrace.

Sleep seemed to overtake Brask again, like a burial beneath ages of rock and silence, beneath untold layers of the world, until the next thing he knew was that he was sitting by a fire that crackled cheerfully, back on the sugary sands of the beach, glittering in the moonlight like the breast of a hummingbird. He was still naked. She was sitting next to him, equally unclothed. They said nothing, but together admired the crooning flow of the river and the desperate antics of the stars. She hugged her bare feet close to herself and breathed the air of her domain as if each breath needed a specific remembrance of its own, a festival to mark its passing.

"What are you?" he dared to speak at last.

"A ruler of things. In this particular place. Or at the edge of the world that you know. There are many words you might use to describe me, but I would not recommend any one of them over another."

"You mean there really are … things like you? I never believed in any."

She shrugged gently in the glimmer of firelight. "Fortunately for us, and perhaps unfortunately for you, our existence has never depended upon your belief or disbelief."

"I was taught to believe in only one God."

"Were you? How helpful. That does not occur in every world, not by any means, but it does occur. One does encounter it. Moreover, the god of which you speak is said to be a much different … Person than the ones of which I speak. They are little gods, if you wish. Just as men, like you, are even littler."

"There is a One, then?"

"Most in a position to ponder such things deeply are convinced of that, though not I, nor anyone I have ever encountered, ever, in any place, has proof. We tend to think that One is merely watching, or perhaps asleep. Waiting. Who knows? Meanwhile, the little ones are quite active, indeed."

"How? Why?"

"That is the way the Greater Ones have ordained things. That is how power takes shape and moves through worlds, and worlds-within-worlds. Most of us know how it moves, and who moves most of it, but from whence it originated, none can tell. Not yet."

"What about the Landlord? The one on the other side, who tried to … take me?"

"Ah, that one. He is my other. You would perhaps call him my "husband," but that kind of designation is inadequate. Incomplete. Useful only for people in certain kinds of flesh."

Brask gazed around in the vastness. "Am I far away now, from Wistwood? I don't recognize this place."

"Nor should you, given your nature! You are far away from everything you would recognize. Even the stars are not the same, here. That being said, 'far' is a relative term in worlds like mine."

"If he is your husband, or like your husband, why do you allow him to do what he does to—"

"To the innocent? It is alright. You were going to say that."

"I am sorry. I know what I've done."

"As do I. I have kept watch. Over you more than many others. As for questions of 'why' and allowance, he does what is in his nature to do. It is His task to take vengeance upon and draw power from death wrought in envy. I have killed and destroyed in envy. That is why I am here."

"You mean that this is some kind of … trap? Like Wistwood was meant to be for me, for all of those people back there?"

"Yes. That is exactly what I mean. The only difference is that my nature and status afford me privileges and protections that you do not enjoy."

"Who did you kill in envy?"

"My offspring, as you would put it. Long ago. Oh, so long ago. Your earth, as you know it, was yet quite young."

"Why did you do it?"

"I was covetous of my child's power, so I killed and took it for myself."

"Just like I wanted Louis's manuscript, so I stole it when he was passed out in the park and passed it off as my own. And now he's dead. Dead. You are just like me."

She shook her head. "Only similar, for my other, the Landlord, has deceived you, and in doing so, he has brought about his own ruin. Or at least the ruin of that place he crafted, that web he spun to catch you."

"What do you mean? He isn't coming for me? I'm safe here?"

"No, he is not coming for you. Rather, *you* are going after him. And I shall accompany you."

"Back to Wistwood? Please, I'd rather die!"

"No, not back there. Elsewhere."

"I don't want to go after him at all!"

"You have no choice. You see, your crime and your willful response placed you at the mercy of Wistwood. Yet, just as extraordinarily, you have made it possible for me to finally catch him in a mistake and thus leave this realm I conjured to guard and protect myself. He and I are even now, because of you, and I can take my revenge. Because I saved you from death and gave you new life. A *real* second chance. Not the kind he and his foul helpmates were intent upon offering you."

"Lady, I don't understand."

"You stole something valuable, yes, but the crime did not end in death. Not yet. Your friend is alive, Brask Adams. Your friend Louis survived his attempt at self-destruction. In his haste to make transition between hired hands, my other failed to note this, and a great blasphemy was wrought. A law broken. Therefore, he has no real jurisdiction over you, according to the laws that even he must obey."

"H-how do you know me?"

"Because I touched you. That is all that was required. And I have other means of knowing. I have walked to and fro across your world for many centuries, though I am not from your world. In that time, I have learned much. What a curious animal you are. You and your kind. Since you've been able to reason and fall in lust with yourselves, you have often thought yourselves somehow above the workings of the dust and the wind and dirt and the water. You have set yourselves too far apart, when of these very elements you are composed. And still, in your hubris, you have oft come to declare that the very elements operate in deference to your fate, your destinies, your presumptions."

"We're stuck here alone, with no answers to the deeper questions. How do you expect us to be?"

"It is true that you and your kind are not alone in pride nor in vanity. I have witnessed at least as much arrogance in beings counted far greater than you, though no wiser. Do not despair at my reminder. At least some of your own have come to realize this truth, humility, while those mightier others carry on blindly and deceived. Console yourself with this: in this instance, you were caught in the midst of doings and conflicts and concerns far greater than yourself, yet in which you had a part to play. Even a crucial one, by chance. Count yourself fortunate. The result is hardly ever this beneficial for one like you. You have another chance, now. That is far, far more than many encounter, who happen to behold such superior conquests and affairs. Now, all that is left for you to do is to choose. Yes, I can even say that there is hope for redemption, as you would understand that idea. No promise, but a possibility."

"Will I have another chance if I stay here or … go back to the world?"

"That is not within my power to tell, nor within my interest. Your realm of existence is not common. Your kind of life. Your earth. Certain other beings in this universe and across many others have been and remain attracted to it for different reasons—some for reasons you would call benign, others still for purposes of sheer hunger or malevolence. Sometimes both. Be glad that yet *others* of greater stature pass by and pay you no heed at all. Oh, I could tell you of them, Brask, for I have seen them with my own vision, and surely nothing in your world—not thought, not memory, not past, not future—would ever have a chance to exist. And believe me when I say that they *have* noticed you and have deigned to move on without interference or curiosity. Pray this never changes, if you pray at all for your world or for its eventual transformation.

There was a sudden, frigid rush of wind over the island, one that did not seem capable of blowing across a distant and red desert. The leaves of every tree in the great orchard began to tremble. Their fire nearly went out.

"What was that?"

"Oh, just the first signs of the collapse of *his* little orchard. At least, that one. There are others. He tours them, as you would say."

"I still don't know what you want from me."

"Would you return to your own world, after all that you have endured, all that you have done? To your sister? To the disgrace that awaits you?"

"I should. I deserve it."

"And perhaps your child deserves to live without the fear of becoming a monster."

"My what?"

"Your child. The one you slept with in the webwork. Schuyler. The little murderess is pregnant. Now, do not gaze with such sudden wide eyes! You yourself knew this was possible. What you did not know—and still do not know—is that you coupled with her while under a spell, an enchantment wrought by my former partner. He did it after the trees were flown into your midst. That was my doing, by the way. My other has his reasons for implementing such a scheme. But know this much: he has taken her, this Schuyler, and her unborn child, and he will raise the child as his own, wherever he goes next. Unless he is stopped. You did not see her at the final little gathering, did you? Found only her empty vehicle in that rancid fog when you tried to escape?"

"My child?"

"Yes, Brask. To conceive a child in a place like Wistwood guarantees that the offspring will have very special qualities. My son will be interested to explore those qualities, to admire them as one in your world admires the crafting of a jewel by another … a jewel that can be purchased and worn as a sign of status."

"You think you can find him and defeat him?"

"I know that I can, now that the playing field has been leveled, as your kind would put it."

"But you coax me with mention of my child, while you set out to take revenge on your husband."

"A fair point. But our kind do not love as you do. In fact, we do not love at all."

"And what role would I play in this search? I'm just a man. Not even thirty. And not even a good man."

"But you *are* a new one, Brask Adams, and who knows yet what you might or might not be, given a chance in another world, or worlds?"

"Worlds?"

"Of course. He is not going to linger on this earth, not with me soon on the loose. And you will have plenty to do, as far as rescuing your child is concerned. That child is your own, after all. That cannot change. And you will have great influence over her."

"Her?"

"Oh. I slipped. Do pardon."

"A daughter. If that's true, then Schuyler will have influence, too. Greater than mine, especially if he's got her, as you say."

"Yes. Things could get interesting, depending upon how her interview transpires."

"Why are you willing to do this for me? To bring me along."

"I have my reasons. Some of them are quite selfish, to be honest."

"How can I trust you?"

She laughed until the stars in the sky of her own creation trembled silently, mirroring her joy with riots of color.

"Do as you will, Brask. I do not deceive. I may have murdered, once, but it was honest work in the doing. There is no time to explain the entire story. There may be, later."

"And we're going to leave this place?"

"Most certainly. We will have to do so!"

"How?"

"Leave that to me."

"What about that ... that thing that brought me out of the water?

"Larkspur? Oh, he will remain and be fine. He was only ever a passerby, like you, to some extent. One of many wanderers I have seen on the outskirts, from age to age. Not from your world, either, but a visitor. He once sensed my presence and pleaded for help. I obliged him and he became my willing servant. A companion. He did not even remember his name when I first met him, so I gave him the one he now possesses. It was one that I admired from your own earth. Fitting for him. What becomes of him after this is no longer my concern. He may survive and tend the orchard, as long as it stands. I will not unmake it. After all, I may have some need for it again. The Worlds and Worlds Beyond are very insecure. When I am gone, however, he may welcome companions of his own. Who knows? But he must choose carefully. As must you, and soon. The hunt is calling, and its voice is difficult to resist!"

THE FALL OF WISTWOOD

The disintegration began at the edge of the firmament, on the outskirts of what might be seen by anything possessed of vision. Not even the darkness was extinguished. No distance immersed between oblivion and the edge of starlight burned away from that existence into annihilation. One reality peeled away from another, skyward, and then into the hills; a curtain drawn from above or beneath? All was impossible to know or to tell. The manor house. The trees. The cabin. The unfinished chapel. The fog. The earth. The people. What remained was void, yet even in the end of a world, Void waited, ready and silent beyond all knowledge, for a new creation. It alone knew what It was.

And it waited.

JUST BEGINNING

"How am I going to live with this? Am I crazy? Have I gone mad? That's what's happened, right? I'm insane and this is what I deserve."

"No, you haven't gone mad, Brask. But you must decide now and we must leave. Windows open and windows close. I do not plan to tarry."

"What about the ones back there in Wistwood? What about Neetha and Carlee?"

She shook her head. "Too late for them. They gave themselves away in one sense or another. That's the part that was real. It is the doom of Death in Envy. But sometimes, He is satisfied with tricking people who haven't actually given in to it, people who are on the brink, just like you were at one point in your life. That's how he was able to deceive you, and lure you. Besides, they have all gone onward to their destinies, all unknown, at least to me. His lair has fallen. And we have work to do. I know a few in this world and in others who have the power to help me, to help us. To help your child. Those who have survived his snares—and there are a few; I'm now among their number—have a special power over his wiles and ways that they never lose, if they're careful."

"Then where are we off to?"

"Many places."

"Will we find her? My daughter?"

"Again, there is no promise, not in this world or in any other. Not in Time, Times, or half a Time. But we will try. Are you willing to witness things beyond your imagination?

"You mean *more* things?

"Yes. More things.

"Then, I'll trust you. And I thank you for this real chance. I'll worship you, if I must, Lady. I don't know what else I could possibly say. It wouldn't be enough. It wouldn't make sense."

"Then say nothing. We would be advised to make haste. The moon on my island reveals little and the stars—you see that little group in the east?—they are weak and reluctant. Apt to betray us in the thick of the night. They have no fear. And why should they? They hold sway."

"I'm ... I'm not perfect, Lady."

"You never had to be, Nebraska Adams. Not ever."

"Which way do we go?

"My way. Take my hand. Take it now. I will show you. And you shall hear in words that *you* can understand, although this incantation is older even than your own universe."

And thus she spoke:

No, you shall not deny me passage.
You shall open unto Me,
One who was born of your own flesh, and
who knows your every color.
One who was born of your own heart, and
who knows your every thought.
One who was born of your own magic, and
who knows your every mischief,
One who was born of your own essence,
and who shares your every breath.
For I am of the same weavework,
spun upon the same loom,
nurtured in the same soil,

infused with the same light.
No, you shall not deny My passage.
You will open unto Me, and make clear a path.
You shall open and let me pass
even as a womb opens
for a child that presses,
One with its Mother's Soul and Spirit,
awakened to its destiny.
You shall open unto Me,
that I may be born anew in my own Country.